Dear Vincent,

Thank you f
your interest in my
You keep reading and I
keep writing. Enjoy!

Timothy Love

Three Degrees
of
Separation

Timothy Lassiter

authorHOUSE™

1663 LIBERTY DRIVE, SUITE 200
BLOOMINGTON, INDIANA 47403
(800) 839-8640
WWW.AUTHORHOUSE.COM

First published by AuthorHouse 10/21/05

ISBN: 1-4208-7404-7 (sc)

Printed in the United States of America
Bloomington, Indiana

This book is printed on acid-free paper.

To all those who believed in me,
Your support made this possible
And I owe this all to you.

Chapter 1

This winter will never end. That was the first thought that came to Nicholas as he stood on the wooden deck of the New London Ferry administration building. From his vantage point, he could see out over the vacant pier where the ferry from Long Island would soon dock. Past the pier he could see to the mouth of the Thames River, past the New London Ledge lighthouse, and out into the Long Island Sound. The lighthouse was a strange sight; a square, red building standing alone at the mouth of the river, hovering above the water. Beyond that, the cold grey February sky met with the blue-grey waters of the Long Island Sound, making the horizon difficult to distinguish. A cold breeze whipped off the water and slammed into Nicholas's face, making him tuck his chin into his coat. He turned his back to the water and the wind, reached into his coat and fished out a pack of cigarettes. He flipped the top open and pulled out a red lighter and a single cigarette. Slowly, as if timing the flame between the blasts of wind, he lit the cigarette and placed it between his lips. Inhaling deeply, Nicholas watched as the red tip burned down an eighth of an inch, took the heavy smoke into his lungs, then exhaled.

He hated smoking. He hated the taste, hated the sick feeling that developed in the pit of his stomach after smoking an entire cigarette, and hated the after taste that seemed to last with him all day. He could not bring himself to exhale through his nose, terrified that the smell would make him physically ill. The only reason he smoked was because he needed something to do during times like these. Nicholas was a man that had to be doing something all of the time, he could never just stand still. He had been that way since he was a teenager in high school. Smoking gave his hands something to do when there was nothing for him to do but wait. He turned back to the Long Island Sound, searching for the ferry. Nicholas was half an hour early, and during the winter, the ferry was usually a half an hour late. However, this was his first big deal, and he was not going to let anything get in the way.

The deal, he thought to himself. Nicholas spent his life alone. It was the only way he worked. It wasn't that Nicholas was a loner; he had friends, a lot in fact. Nicholas was just the type of man who could not let anyone get close to him. He never felt as though he belonged anywhere. This mentality had made it very difficult for him to maintain relationships, which turned out for the better in his line of work. Nicholas was a drug trafficker, a man who made contacts everywhere he went, his job was to help the drug manufacturers get the product to the dealers, and help the dealers get the product out on the street with little police interference. Since his early twenties, while living in Norwich, Connecticut, Nicholas started with friends who were selling marijuana locally, then as their clientele grew in numbers, Nicholas helped them find people who were growing large quantities of marijuana to fill their clients orders. With every person Nicholas met, he ended up with five more contacts. Soon, he was working with cocaine and ecstasy dealers. His age was perfect in finding dealers in nightclubs and introducing them to manufacturers. In less than two years, Nicholas had a network in Connecticut, Rhode Island, Southeastern Massachusetts, and New York City. Nicholas was making tons of money, more than he knew what to do with, and since he never had to carry any drugs on him, he did not have to worry about run-ins in with the police. Nicholas's rolodex went from two-bit thug dealers on the streets, to influential businessmen and politicians. He considered himself a business man, and a very good one.

That was when the trouble began. A year ago, a small, local mafia wanna-be family began to muscle in on the drug trade. Robert Mullanno, with dreams of resurrecting the large mob networks of old, decided to take over cocaine and ecstasy dealing in Hartford. That meant getting rid of the current dealers, which led to a short period of bloody violence. Twelve horrific, gruesome murders took place in the span of two weeks. That was all it took, everyone knew who ordered the murder of the twelve drug dealers, and everyone knew that the Mullanno family was now in control of the Hartford drug racket. Before dealers were murdered, they were tortured for names. Nicholas knew that his name would have been given up more than once, and to make sure he didn't end up like the dealers, he presented himself to Robert Mullanno, and offered him a deal. What has been considered one of the most arrogant, ballsy moves ever made, Nicholas offered to help Mullanno by using his contacts to maintain the drug flow if Mullanno agreed not to interfere with the marijuana dealers already established. When Nicholas told his friends what he was going to do, most advised him against it, telling him to just pack up and move to a different city. However, Nicholas went ahead and presented his offer to Mullanno, insisting on a closed door meeting between the two men.

No one but Nicholas and Robert Mullanno knew what happened in that meeting, but most of Nicholas's friends did not expect him to leave the meeting alive. However, days later it was understood that Nicholas was working with Mullanno, and suddenly the Mullanno's drug interests were dealing millions all over the state of Connecticut. Thinking back, Nicholas could not help but smile to himself as he scanned the horizon, remembering how he had walked out of that meeting, Robert Mullanno's arm over Nicholas's shoulder, both men laughing. Many rumors quickly spread regarding the events of that meeting. Some thought that Nicholas had sold out, but once the details of the deal were made known, specifically where it came to the marijuana trade, Nicholas gained more respect than he had ever had before. In the drug underworld, Nicholas was trusted, and he was safe. However, Nicholas could never sit still, and he was never satisfied with the way things were. If things were good, he wanted to make them better. If he was making one million dollars in a year, he wanted to make five million the next year, and there was only one way to do that. Nicholas began using his contacts in other states, helping the Mullanno family take over the drug trade in Rhode Island first, then in Southeastern Massachusetts. There was only one place left to extend their hand, and that was New York City.

Nicholas knew that of all the deals he had made in his career, this was going to be the most difficult. The major drug trade in New York City was not controlled by any one group. In fact, different factions controlled different territories. Nicholas knew that to get them all to work with the Mullanno family, he first had to unite them in some way. That was the hardest part; each gang ran their streets differently than the next. The only way Nicholas could unite them was by having them all get their narcotics from the same distributor. Nicholas started by investing Mullanno and his own money into a young group from France. After they had the money, Nicholas helped them get the buildings they would need to manufacture the drugs. Mullanno used his old mafia contacts and was able to pull some strings and get the buildings. Now Nicholas had made it so Mullanno controlled half of the manufacturing of drugs in New York, but they were still missing out on the profits that came from selling the drugs. For that, Nicholas had to work with his contacts in the city to get the dealers to get their product from the French group. Now, after two years, the deal was almost complete. A dealer would be coming across on the Long Island Ferry with a bag containing ten million dollars. This dealer was to be a diplomat of sorts, sealing a deal that would make the Mullanno family billions of dollars. They would control both the manufacturing and dealing of cocaine, heroin, and ecstasy in New England. Nicholas had made this possible, and with this deal his future would be guaranteed. Nicholas held his smile, pleased with what he had accomplished. Then, like a distant traveler, Nicholas saw the white ferry appear from out of the monotonous grey, and he knew that this was going to be the best day of his career.

Chapter 2

The ferry grew in size as it approached, picking up speed as it left the waters of the Long Island Sound and entered the calmer waters of the Thames River. Nicholas made his way down from the deck of the administration building to the sidewalk. He passed the parked cars of the visitors who would be picking up friends and relatives departing the ferry on foot. He looked into the windshield of his own car, and nodded to a young man sitting in the passenger seat. Nicholas usually worked alone, it was the way he liked it. Nicholas was a man who expected perfection in those he worked with. He expected perfection out of himself, and that had made him a very hard man to work with on more than one occasion. Nicholas had wanted to meet the dealer alone, and bring him to Mullanno for the meeting. However, Robert Mullanno wanted his eldest son Anthony to accompany him to the pickup. Anthony Mullanno, as the heir apparent, was the next in line to take over the family business. It had been Robert Mullanno's dream to have the family business, this empire he built, be passed on from one generation to the next. However, Anthony Mullanno was a soft spoken child who, as far as Nicholas knew, had no interest in running the business. From what Nicholas understood, when Anthony graduated from high school, he had his heart set on going to college to become a teacher. However, Robert Mullanno had other plans. Robert Mullanno had forced his son to go to college at nights pursuing a business degree, while he spent his days learning the family business. Nicholas had been concerned that the dealer from New York would take one look at Anthony and lose all confidence, so Nicholas left Anthony with strict instructions not to speak unless spoken to.

As Nicholas stepped off the sidewalk and onto the large open driveway where cars boarded and disembarked from the ferry, he went over the plan in his mind for the thousandth time. The plan had been Nicholas's idea; he knew what to do and had considered every possible way this deal could go down. Nicholas had first been introduced to the man who would be bringing the money on his last visit to New York City. All the foot passengers were let off the ferry first, and Nicholas would look for a man in a black leather jacket carrying a large blue duffel bag. Robert Mullanno had insisted the money be brought in cash. This had caused the first wrinkle in getting the deal completed because no one wanted to carry that much cash around. However, at the last minute, with the threat of pulling out on the deal entirely, the money was put together and all points were agreed upon. Nicholas wondered to himself how big the bag would have to be to hold ten million dollars in cash. The largest amount of cash he had ever seen was fifty thousand dollars, and that was spread out over a dining room table. Nicholas would meet the man, who would set the bag down on his side and the two men would embrace first; ensuring the other man was not carrying a gun, then would shake hands and make their way to the car. From there, Nicholas would drive them to a restaurant Mullanno owned, where the money would be counted, and the deal completed. Nicholas heard a car door open, and then shut again.

"You know what you are supposed to do, right?" Nicholas asked without looking over his shoulder.

"I'm supposed to keep my mouth shut unless someone speaks to me," Anthony answered with a heavy sigh. Nicholas had gone over this with Anthony at least ten times since picking him up at his father's house this morning. Nicholas knew that Anthony did not want to be here, but he also knew that he did not want to upset his father, so he would do what he was told.

"The man will assume that you are a body guard or something," Nicholas mentioned. "He probably won't even talk to you. If he does…"

"I know, I know," Anthony interrupted. "Be polite but keep my answers short."

Nicholas smiled to himself as the young man answered. He wanted to laugh out loud but he knew he could not give Anthony the satisfaction.

The ferry was making a slow, wide turn as it started to approach the pier. Nicholas watched as the bow just missed the pier. The ship would be docked in less than five minutes, and as the crew was preparing for the cars to depart, the walk-on passengers would climb down the stairs to the dock. Nicholas scanned the railing and the deck two stories above the gaping mouth of the ferry where all the cars were parked. Excited passengers lined the railing looking for their family and friends as they waited for the ship to stop moving. Nicholas did not see the man he was here to meet, however, that did not bother him. The plan was set and he was sure that everything would go smoothly. After several minutes, the ferry came to rest to the right of the pier and huge mooring lines were thrown down onto the dock and the ship was secured. Slowly at first, then more rapidly, passengers hurriedly made their way down the stairway and off the ramp. One by one, Nicholas carefully watched every person, his eyes darting from one passenger to the next as he waited for the dealer to come down. He started to get nervous as the flow of passengers slowed, then stopped. Nicholas's mind was racing with the possibilities as he tried to anticipate what had happened. If the dealers were pulling out of the deal, there were other ways they could have gone about it. By not showing up and sending no word ahead, the dealers could be trying to insult Mullanno, or trying to alter the deal more in their favor. *Or it could be a trap*, Nicholas thought. His mind stopped suddenly, as if the magnitude of this one possibility were more than he could process.

A large ramp dropped from the ferry and the cars started to come off, guided by the crew. Nicholas stood there, watching the cars come off while his mind raced with questions. Just as he was thinking of turning back, something caught his attention. A large brown sedan had just rolled off of the ramp onto the pavement and the passenger in the car was waving in his direction, calling out. Nicholas could not hear the man, but something about him gave him pause. Suddenly, he recognized the passenger of the car as the dealer he was supposed to meet. Anger flooded him as he watched the car drive in a slow arch around other cars and then make its way towards the parking lot where they stood. Nicholas was furious, remembering all of the time he had spent going over the plan with the dealers. Immediately, he knew that this was a trap. He knew the dealers were up to something, and he was going to have to act quickly.

"Walk into the administration building like you don't know me," Nicholas said without looking back. "Call your father from inside and tell him that the dealers are setting us up."

"What are you going to do?" asked Anthony, unable to keep the sudden fear out of his voice.

"Don't talk to me!" Nicholas answered harshly. "Don't even look at me. These people are here to kill me and your father. We are being set up, and if we're lucky they won't know that you were here with me. Just walk into the building and do what I told you to do. Your father will know what to do from there."

Nicholas heard the young man mutter something, then heard footsteps and knew that Anthony was following his instructions. Nicholas and Robert Mullanno had gone over this possibility many times, and procedures were in place to protect them against this. However, Anthony was a liability that Nicholas didn't want to be responsible for. Now he had to figure out what he was going to do, and how he was going to come out of this deal alive. He knew that Anthony would make the call to his father the moment he got inside, and his father would not show up to the restaurant.

"Nicky boy," yelled the dealer, sticking his head out of the passenger side window as the car approached. Nicholas nodded in acknowledgement, trying to remain as calm as possible. Nicholas watched as the car pulled into a parking space across from his own vehicle.

"What the hell is going on?" Nicholas asked, as he crossed the parking lot. "I thought you were coming alone."

"No worries, man," the dealer answered. "My boss was just concerned about my carrying all that money alone. It looks a lot less suspicious this way, right?"

"There was a reason we made the arrangements the way we did," Nicholas stated. "I have to tell you, this is a little concerning to me."

"Hey, man," the dealer said. "It's not like we are going to jack you up. You can even check the money if you want to."

Nicholas smiled to himself, understanding the situation in which he had been thrust. If he agreed to check the money, he insulted the dealer and his boss. The trust that this deal had been built upon would be shattered. The dealer knew that Nicholas would not risk the deal by insulting anyone, even if he did suspect he was being set up."

"I don't need to check the bag," Nicholas answered, desperately searching for a way out of the situation. "This deal is good for every one; I can't imagine you not wanting in on this. So, you and your driver want to follow me up to Hartford."

"Are you alone?" the dealer asked. Nicholas knew where he was headed with that question; however, he refused to tell them about Anthony.

"Yep," Nicholas answered. "Just like I said I would be."

"Then why don't you drive up with us," the dealer said with a smile. "We'll bring you back here when we're done."

"I don't know," Nicholas answered, wracking his brain for options. The minute he got them to the restaurant they would kill him. If he went with them and tried to stall them, it would not take them long to figure out what was going on, and they would kill him. "I have to tell you that I don't like this. This makes me awfully uncomfortable."

"What, you don't trust us?" the dealer asked, probingly. "Look man, do you know how big a bag we had to get to carry ten million dollars. It's fucking huge."

"Look at it from my perspective," Nicholas said, stalling for time. "We set up these rules for everyone's protection. You showing up like this is a slap in the face. I'm thinking about my boss here, Mullanno is going to suspect something's up."

"Then why don't you call him now and tell him everything is alright," the dealer said. This was just the place Nicholas did not want to be, and his stalling had just given the dealer the upper hand. "Tell Mullanno that I came with a driver and that you are coming up with us and everything's cool."

This was it, and Nicholas knew it. His months of working the deal would go up in smoke right now. He was trapped, and there was nothing he could do about it. He sighed and looked down to the ground. He could not make that call to Mullanno. It would betray him and even if Nicholas was able to get out of this situation alive, Mullanno would track him down and kill him. Nicholas looked up at the dealer, who was smiling at him as if he knew something the other didn't. Nicholas knew the dealer had to know that he suspected what was to come. Just as he was about to answer, Nicholas saw a car turn into the parking lot, and he knew that his salvation had just arrived.

The police cruiser was obviously on a routine patrol, and it was headed right for them. Nicholas had to get their attention, and he had to get it when they were close enough to him to make a difference. Nicholas told the dealer to wait a minute and went to his car and reached in, grabbing his cellular phone. He then locked the car, and started walking up to the dealer and his driver, who was out of the car now. The driver was a bear of a man, standing over six feet tall and looked to be two hundred and fifty pounds of solid muscle. This was going to make things more difficult, but if Nicholas played his cards right, he could make it out alive. The police cruiser was just ten feet away when Nicholas walked up close to the dealer and shoved him, hard. The dealer had not expected this and went down to the ground fast, slamming his head against the concrete. The driver took two steps toward Nicholas, but before he could reach him, Nicholas had retrieved a Glock from a holster hidden between the layers of his coat. He pointed the weapon directly at the driver and suddenly he heard the sound of the police siren. Two officers jumped out of the cruiser at a remarkable speed and were pointing their sidearms at the three men.

"Put the gun down!" screamed one of the officers. Nicholas suddenly saw the dealer jumping up from the ground and realized he had a gun on him, too. Nicholas turned fast, pointing the gun at the dealer, giving the driver a split second to move. Nicholas assumed that at least one of the officers had their sites set on the burly driver. However, they were not able to react fast enough, and the driver retrieved two handguns from holsters on a shoulder harness. Suddenly, the situation had gone from bad to worse.

"I'm a police officer," Nicholas screamed. "Badge number 21911."

"Shut up," one of the officers screamed. "Everyone throw your weapons down and turn around, placing your hands on your head."

Nicholas knew immediately what he was dealing with. These were rookie cops, caught in a situation with three people with guns. The atmosphere was tense and Nicholas knew if something was not done quickly, someone was going to get shot. The officer's were still screaming at them, moving to more secure positions around the cruiser. Nicholas was now aimed at the driver, whose weapons were aimed at Nicholas and one of the police officers. Someone was going to do something stupid; it was just a matter of who broke down first. The desire to fire his weapon was becoming overwhelming.

All of a sudden, time seemed to slow down for Nicholas. The voices of the police officers, the drug dealer and his driver seemed to fade into the background. All Nicholas could hear was the pounding of his heartbeat, and the rushing of the blood past his temples. His senses were hypersensitive. He could feel the cold metal trigger of his weapon underneath his index finger. His finger was rubbing against it, fingering it softly; as if ready to pull the trigger. He heard, or felt, a presence in his mind telling him to pull the trigger back. Whatever it was, it was telling him to kill the dealer and his driver, it was begging him to do so. It was almost overwhelming, the desire to pump hot lead into these criminals. It took everything Nicholas had to shake off the feeling and concentrate on the situation at hand.

"Listen to me," Nicholas said, turning his head slightly to the police cruiser. "I'm going to back up to you, keeping my weapon aimed away from you. While keeping your weapon aimed at me, you will be able to reach into my back pocket and retrieve my badge."

"I told you to shut up!" the officer repeated. "Put your gun down before we drop all three of you."

The situation was impossible. The officers were not going to risk diverting any attention from the situation, and Nicholas couldn't blame them. Nicholas took a step forward, breaking his aim from the driver and he started to bend down, as if he were going to place his gun on the pavement. From where he stood, Nicholas was only two feet away from the driver, the only other person to have a weapon. He immediately knew the only way to defuse the situation, and he acted quickly. Nicholas let the gun drop out of his hand, and as he did he took a step forward, slamming his right shoulder into the driver's chest. At the same time, he grabbed the driver's outstretched arm and threw him over his shoulder, slamming the driver onto his back hard. The driver lost his wind suddenly, dropping both guns. Nicholas brushed the guns away with his foot quickly, looking up to gauge the response of the two police officers. Just as he did, he saw a nightstick coming at his face at lightning speed. Nicholas barely had time to turn away as the nightstick struck him on the left side of his face, knocking him to the ground. For a moment, Nicholas couldn't see anything but a blinding white light as the pain seared over his head. Then he felt a foot in his side, causing his stomach to seize, almost making him vomit. Suddenly he was on his stomach, his arms being pulled behind him. Still unable to see clearly, he yelled that he was a police officer again, just as he felt something smash into his head and darkness followed.

Chapter 3

Nicholas Grenier was jolted back into consciousness fifteen minutes later through the use of smelling salts by paramedics on the scene. It took a few minutes for the grogginess to wear off and for Nick to process what had happened. Police officers were all over the place, blocking off the entire parking lot outside the ferry administration building, questioning witnesses, and trying to understand what had happened at the scene. There seemed to be a lot of confusion and everyone involved had a different story. Once he had placed his thoughts back in order, Nick's first instinct was the beat the hell out of the patrol officers. However, there was more going on, and Nick had to find out where the deal stood. The deal was an undercover sting operation that had taken Nick two years to put into place. Authorities in three states were waiting for word from Nick to begin the largest drug bust in recent years. Nick grabbed the cold gel pack from the paramedic, slapped it against his aching head, and against recommendation, jumped up to find the dealer and the driver. Nick immediately found that was a mistake. A sickening feeling washed over him the moment he stood up, and he almost lost his footing. The paramedic grabbed him before he hit the ground, and Nick took a moment to steady himself.

Taking slow, deep breaths, Nick waited for the world to stop spinning around him, and then slowly made his way over to the patrol officers. Two other officers, weary of an altercation, quickly stepped in front of Nick, but he waved them off. Nick might have been pissed off, but he had larger issues right now, and he wasn't about to screw up this bust.

"Sergeant," the first officer began. "I'm really sorry. We didn't know who you were."

"And me trying to show you my badge didn't raise any flags?" Nick asked, angrily.

"We couldn't take any chances," the second officer. "Everyone had guns, what the hell were we supposed to do?"

"I just want to know which of you hit me with the nightstick," Nick spat. Neither officer answered, one of them looked to the ground quickly. "I think that answers my question. We are going to have a little talk about that later. Now what did you arrest them on?"

"Possession," the first officer answered quickly. "And carrying a concealed weapon. The serial numbers have been filed off of these guns, so there's that too. They had a couple ounces of cocaine in that bag."

"Was there any money in there?" Nick asked as he walked past them. The dealer and the driver were in the back of separate patrol cars now.

"There was a couple hundred dollars in there," the officer replied. Nick opened the back door and grabbed the dealer, yanking him out of the car.

"What the fuck man?" the dealer yelled. "This is abuse, I want my lawyer."

"Shut the fuck up," Nick ordered, slamming him against the car hard. "You haven't seen abuse yet. There is one deal, and it goes to the first person to start talking. If you don't talk, I'll get it out of your burly buddy."

"I ain't saying nothing," the dealer said, looking over to the patrol officers. "Do you see this, this is police brutality."

"What do you think officers?" Nick asked, looking over. "Is this brutality?"

"Is what brutality?" the officer answered, acting as though he had seen nothing.

"See that, asshole," Nick said, slamming the dealer against the car again. "No one here is on your side. And this questioning isn't going to stop until you start talking."

"Man, what the fuck do you want?" the dealer said, squirming under Nick's grip.

"I want to know who set Mullanno up," Nick said. "I want to know who gave you your orders."

"I don't know, man," the dealer said. Nick pulled him up again, getting ready to slam him against the car a third time. "Wait. Jackson told me that we weren't going through with it. He was going to hit the warehouse in New York after I confirmed that you and old man Mullanno were dead."

"See, that wasn't too hard, was it?" Nick asked, pulling the dealer up and then throwing him into the car. Nick slammed the door before the dealer had the chance to right himself. He pulled his cell phone out of his pocket and punched in the seven digits of the commander in charge of coordinating all the different busts.

"This is Grenier," Nick said into the phone. "Strike everywhere. You'll find Mullanno at his home. Jackson is getting ready to make a move on the warehouse in New York, so be ready for that. As for everyone else, proceed as planned."

Nick hung up the phone and slipped it into his pocket. He looked over the scene, his eyes resting on the administration building. Suddenly, he remembered Anthony Mullanno was inside. He didn't want Anthony questioned by the officers, so he slowly made his way up the steps of the wooden deck to the front door. He stepped inside and was immediately stopped by an officer. Flashing his badge, he stepped past the officer and found the investigating officer questioning an elderly lady about the earlier events.

"Excuse me," Nick interrupted, flashing his badge again. The wave of relief washed over the face of the old woman as the officer stopped talking and looked up. "Who hasn't been questioned yet?"

"Those three people over there," the officer answered, pointing to the corner. It came as no surprise to Nick that Anthony Mullanno was one of the three not questioned. He probably hung back every time the officer called a new person over. Nick thanked the officer and strolled over to the boy. Anthony looked him over for a moment, as if unsure of what to say.

"You're a cop?" Anthony asked. Nick nodded and said nothing, just holding the young man's stare. "And you were playing my dad all along."

"That's my job," Nick said. "I stop criminals, and your father decided to be a criminal. There were all sorts of other things he could do, but he chose this life. Getting busted comes with that sort of life."

"And you're going to arrest me?" Anthony asked. Nick looked at the young man for a moment, and then sighed.

"No," he answered. Anthony looked confused as if he had not heard him correctly.

"Why not?" asked the young man.

"Because you didn't ask for this life," Nick answered. "Your father made you work with him because of some deluded idea of being a big mafia don. You didn't want to work with him, and so far, you haven't done anything criminal."

"But I know things," Anthony said.

"Knowing things and acting on them are two different things," Nick said. "Did you ever wonder why I didn't want to bring you along with me?"

"I thought it was because you didn't like me," Anthony answered.

"This is what you're going to do," Nick said, handing Anthony his car keys. "You're going to take my car and get out of here. You'll take it up to the airport and leave it in long-term parking. Leave the keys in the glove compartment. Then you'll take a taxi to your place and you will stay there all night. Don't go near your father's place or you'll be picked up and I won't be able to help you. I'll pick the car up later, and it better be there."

"Why are you doing this?" Anthony asked. The young man was pale now and looked as if he were going to be sick.

"Because I think you're going to make a great teacher," Nick said with a smile. "Now get out of here, and don't ever forget what you saw here."

Nick turned and walked away, leaving the young man standing there alone. Nick flagged down an officer and told him Anthony was free to leave. He then exited the administration building, and stood on the deck, staring out over the water. His head began to ache again, and Nick tried to remember where he had left the ice pack. He had a vague recollection of leaving it on the hood of the patrol car before questioning the dealer. He knew it didn't really matter. His head was going to ache for awhile. That pain reminded him that he had one more thing to do before he left. Nick knew that he was expected at police headquarters in Hartford, and he knew that he could get a taxi to take him up there. Nick strolled off the deck and down the steps to the parking lot. Nick caught sight of one of the patrol officers from earlier in the day.

"Hey," Nick yelled. "Where is my gun?"

The officer reached into the patrol cruiser and pulled it out, holding it up for Nick to see. Nick walked over to him and took the gun, holstering it away at his back. The officer held out his hand as if making a peace offering. Nick looked at the outstretched hand, then up at the officer. With lightning speed, Nick slammed his fist into the officer's face, knocking him off balance and throwing him to the ground. Someone yelled something and suddenly two officers were running over to the patrol car.

"Apology accepted," Nick said, looking down at the officer. He turned then and walked away, searching for a cab.

Chapter 4

By the time Nick reached the police headquarters, the left side of his face had started to swell and he felt a continuous dull ache wash over his head like waves slamming into the shore. After five hours of filling out paperwork, getting updates about the operation in other states, and filing reports detailing everyone's involvement, the dull ache had become a sharp throbbing pain. Nick was having difficulty seeing through his left eye as the skin swelled. The overhead lights were only exacerbating his headache, so Nick decided to take some time out. After an exhaustive search for an ice pack, he settled on a bag of ice wrapped in a towel, and searched for an empty room where he could sit down without being bothered. The only quiet place Nick could find ended up being his boss's office. He had not seen his lieutenant since he arrived at the station, and Nick assumed he was out of the building. Nick closed the door, turned off the lights and eased his aching body into a chair directly in front of his boss's desk. Nick closed his eyes, placed the bag directly over his face, and reclined as far as he could without tipping over. Nick sat there, replaying the events of the last two years, making sure there was nothing that he had missed. He knew that he had not missed anything; his reports had been detailed and precise. Then he replayed the events of the morning. The more he concentrated, the harder it became to maintain his concentration. Nick had been running on adrenaline for so long, and now that things were starting to slow down, sleep was taking over his body. The more he fought it, the more tired he became until finally he felt himself slipping away.

It was just as he was settling into sleep, that Nick sensed he heard a sound, possibly the door opening. It was that sound that started to pull him back to consciousness. He could hear people talking just outside the door, and then the lights flashed on. Nick jumped forward in his chair, the ice pack starting to slide off of his face, catching the bag and towel just before it landed in his lap.

"And here is Mr. Grenier now," his lieutenant said, as he entered the room with another man. "Making himself at home in my office. Nick, I'm sure you know the governor."

Nick jumped out of his chair, reaching out to shake Governor Haisley's hand.

"Amazing work, Sergeant Grenier," the governor said, shaking Nick's hand vigorously. "We've needed a win like this and you certainly did deliver."

"Thank you, sir," Nick responded, just happy to have his hand back.

"Your lieutenant was just telling me that you have been deep undercover for over two years," the governor began. "That's got to be some kind of record."

"It is for this department," his lieutenant answered. "Nick's been away so long, I almost didn't remember what he looked like."

"I can imagine," the governor replied. The small talk was starting to remind Nick about his headache again, but he just stood and smiled. Haisley walked over and put his arm over Nick's shoulder. "I'm having a press conference. I wanted you to be present so I could show you off to the press; however, I'm told that for security purposes I can't. I want you to know that the state of Connecticut appreciates the extreme sacrifices you have had to endure to make this case. You will be promoted of course, and assigned anywhere you want."

"Thank you, sir," Nick stammered, genuinely amazed.

"Thank *you*, son," Haisley returned, obviously pleased with himself. "Do you have any idea where you will go from here?"

"I haven't really thought about it," Nick said. "I would like to go back undercover as soon as possible, though."

The governor looked at Nick for a moment, as if unsure of what he had just said, and then looked to Nick's lieutenant. Nick's boss shook his head slightly, and the governor smiled. Something unsaid but understood passed between the two men, and Nick suddenly felt foolish and out of the loop.

"Well," he started. "I've got to get ready for this press conference. Good luck, Nick"

Haisley shook hands all around and then departed, closing the door behind him. Nick turned and watched his boss walk around his desk and sit down. Nick leaned forward over the desk, looking at his boss intently.

"What the hell did I just miss?" Nick asked.

"What are you talking about?" the lieutenant asked back. This was not a conversation that he wanted to get into at this very moment. "You've just been promised a promotion by the governor. You're on your way up."

"I don't want to be on my way anywhere," Nick stated. "The promotion I'll take. I've earned that after two years, but I'm not going anywhere."

"Nick," his lieutenant began. "We have some time before we have to deal with that. We've got to put

Mullanno and the rest of these bastards away. Then we can worry about where to go from there."

"Why would I be worried?" Nick asked. "What aren't you telling me?"

"Nick, please," the lieutenant pleaded. "Let's deal with the present please."

"Are you taking me out of vice?" Nick asked. Nick couldn't stand not knowing what his boss was thinking. "Tell me what's going on."

"Alright," his boss yelled, exasperated. "Your work here in vice is over. You can't go back undercover after this; your cover has been blown."

Nick sat down suddenly, letting the words sink in. Nick knew that there was logic somewhere in his boss's thinking; though he was not processing the information fast enough to catch it.

"Think about it, Nick," his lieutenant started. "Even if we are able to keep your name out of the press, which will be impossible, once the trial begins your name will be in every paper in New England. Your picture will be on the television and there will be no way you can go undercover again. Instead, once we are sure that everyone involved has been arrested; we are going publicly promote you. You'll be a detective, and like the governor said, you can work anywhere you want. By the time this case goes to trial, you will be famous."

Nick looked down at the floor, finally understanding his lieutenant's logic. He couldn't believe that he had not thought of this before. Of course his career undercover was over, it was obvious. His lieutenant was right, and as the news processed, Nick was left without words.

"This isn't the end, Nick," his lieutenant said. "This is just the beginning for you. You obviously didn't catch on, but the governor loves you. You've just ensured him a second term in office."

"What if I don't want to be a detective?" Nick muttered. His lieutenant looked at him questioningly, and then sat down.

"Then it might be the end," his boss answered. "I hope it isn't, though. If there was anyone born and bred to be a cop, it's you. You are better at this than anyone I have ever known. It's in your blood."

"Yeah," Nick said absently. "A detective."

"And you'll be a damned good one," his boss added. "But before you get ahead of yourself, let's put Mullanno and his people away."

Nick nodded, unsure of whether or not he accepted what his lieutenant had been saying. He rose from the chair and grabbed the wet towel.

"Why don't you find a quiet place and get some rest," the lieutenant said. "I'll find you in case we need you for something."

There was a knock at the door, and both men were jarred from their thoughts. A young uniformed officer opened the door a crack and stuck his head in.

"Lieutenant," the young man said. "We have a problem. Robert Mullanno is in interrogation but he won't talk. The only thing he did say was that he would only talk to Sergeant Grenier."

"Tell him we don't need him to talk," the lieutenant barked. "We've got enough on him to send him away for thirty years, with or without his cooperation."

"Sir, you don't understand," the young man interrupted. "He won't say anything. He won't move, he won't talk, he's just sitting there. The only thing he's said is that he wants to talk to the sergeant."

"Well," the lieutenant said looking over to Nick. "Back to work."

Chapter 5

Nicholas Grenier stared through the one-way glass of the interrogation room, watching the two men inside. On the outside, Nick seemed calm and collected; however, inside his mind was racing. Nick was feeling so stupid for not seeing what would happen to his career by making this bust. All Nick had done for the last two years was work undercover, pulling this case together. This was all he knew. Now his life was flipped upside down, and he could not stop thinking about how this would change everything. Nick reminded himself that he had once had a plan of how he would climb through the police department, getting promotions until he was a lieutenant. However, since he moved to vice and started working undercover, that plan had changed. Nick had found his niche, he had found something he was good at, and he did not want to give it up. He hadn't thought about becoming a detective in a long time, in fact, he had not thought about anything to do with the police department in a long time. Nick realized immediately what that meant, and he knew that it was a good thing that he was getting out of undercover work. He knew that when you started to forget who you are, when you got too caught up in your undercover character, you were in too deep. He knew immediately that this was for the best; he just was having a hard time accepting it.

Nick watched Robert Mullanno as he sat at the large desk inside the interrogation room. He was surprised to see no hint of anger in Mullanno's face; he sat there with a stoic expression, conveying no anger or fear. Mullanno's emotionless state was in stark contrast to the man sitting on his right. A balding man in his early forties sat next to Robert Mullanno in his three-piece, navy blue pin striped suit. Nick guessed this man was Mullanno's lawyer, and he could tell by the impatient, angry look on the lawyer's face that he was not happy about being kept waiting. Nick looked from one man to the other. He could not imagine what Mullanno wanted him there for, unless it was to threaten some sort of revenge. Mullanno had never suspected Nick as being a police officer, and he certainly never suspected that he would be sitting in an interrogation room by the end of the day. As he collected his thoughts, Nick picked up a legal pad and a pen, clipping it to the yellow paper. Nick's lieutenant was standing next to him, and just as Nick reached for the door, he flipped a switch on the side wall, allowing him to hear any conversation inside. Nick turned the doorknob and pushed the door open, stepping inside. Both men looked up immediately, and Nick thought he could see a slight smile spread across Mullanno's face. He wasn't sure what it meant, but Mullanno did not look menacing at all.

"You wanted to see me?" Nick asked as he placed his pad on the table.

"How long do you plan on keeping us here?" the lawyer asked, ignoring Nick's question.

"Well, there is the matter of booking Mr. Mullanno," Nick said, looking down at his watch. "That's going to take a few more hours, as more people make deals. I'm sure we will be bringing more charges against him. Then there is the arraignment, which won't happen until tomorrow morning."

"This is outrageous," the lawyer stated. "I hope you understand that I plan to bring a lawsuit against the police department, the city, and you personally. I can't even begin to count how many of Mr. Mullanno's rights have been trampled in the process."

"Michael," Mullanno said softly, placing his hand on the lawyer's arm. "Why don't you step out and get a drink or something."

"What?" the lawyer asked, incredulously. "I'm staying right here. I want to know everything you are being charged with."

"Michael!" Mullanno said forcefully. Both Nick and the lawyer turned their attention to the older man, who sighed deeply and smiled. "Nicholas and I have some things to talk about, and I would like you to wait outside."

The lawyer opened his mouth to protest, but Mullanno shot a fierce look at the lawyer, and he immediately closed his mouth. He looked back and forth between both men, then collected his briefcase and rose.

"Anything he says is off the record," the lawyer said to Nick. Nick nodded and stared at Mullanno as the lawyer walked around him and he heard the door shut. Nick pulled out a chair directly across from Mullanno and sat down.

"Nicholas," Mullanno started. "If that is your real name."

"It is," Nick answered, nodding his head at the same time.

"So you are a police officer," Mullanno said softly, looking down at the table and shaking his head. "I had no idea. I like to think that I am a very careful man, and I didn't see this coming at all."

"I've been under for a long time," Nick explained. He felt as if he had to explain himself, as if he really cared what the older man thought. "No one suspected."

"I guess next you are going to tell me that you were just doing your job?" Mullanno asked, anticipating Nick's excuse.

"You once said to me that this was all business," Nick said, recalling the words. "You told me there was business and pleasure, and that mixing the two never worked. This was just business, nothing personal, nothing malicious."

"Where is my son?" Mullanno asked.

"He's at his home," Nick assured him. "I saw no reason to involve him."

Mullanno closed his eyes and bowed his head, his forehead almost touching the top of the table. He then lifted his head, a look of relief washing over his face.

"I appreciate that," Mullanno said. "You are a good man. I heard that we were set up."

"We were," Nick said. "They were coming to kill us."

"And you saved my son's life, as well as my own," Mullanno said.

"I did my job," Nick said. "Nothing more."

"It was all for the case?" Mullanno asked, smiling. He knew the answer to the question. Mullanno knew that if he had not suspected Nick of being undercover, it was because some part of Nick really wasn't. "I saw the way you handled yourself, the way you handled your *business*, how hard you pushed. You lost yourself."

"If I had lost myself," Nick began. "You wouldn't be sitting here under arrest."
Mullanno smiled a full broad smile.

"Touché," Mullanno said. "Please let the district attorney know that I will cooperate fully. I will tell them everything."

"Why?" Nick asked, suddenly shocked. He knew that Mullanno could use all sorts of legal maneuvers to keep from incriminating himself, and in the long run, all he would probably be charged with was a short list of petty crimes.

"It's business," Mullanno said, repeating the officer's words. "Besides, I have a family to protect. If I don't give them all the information they need, name all the names that we have worked with, then one of our, sorry my, competitors will try to kill them. No, I have to make sure that you arrest everyone involved and keep them in jail for a long time."

"Your life," Nick started. "It won't be worth anything. Everyone will be trying to shut you up."

"Then I will have to depend on the police to protect me," Mullanno answered. "Just like you did today."

Nick said nothing, just hung his head down, looking at the table.

"It's alright, Nicholas," Mullanno said, as if sensing the other's concern. "You did your job, and you went beyond by protecting me and my son. I have always understood the life I lead, and I know the consequences of my actions. Now, please call my lawyer back in, we have some things to discuss."

"Robert," Nick started.

"Nicholas," Mullanno interrupted. "Please get my lawyer. There is nothing left for us to talk about."

Nick fell silent, looking at the table as if searching for something else to say. After a pause, he reached for the yellow pad, picked it up and exited the room. Outside, the lawyer was leaning against the wall, waiting to be called back in. Nick pointed to him, and then walked over to the window where his lieutenant and the prosecutor were standing, a smile across the prosecutor's face.

"Excellent work, Nick," the prosecutor said. "If he gives up everything he knows, we could end up with hundreds of arrests. You have handed us a perfect case. The FBI is going to piss themselves when they see what they missed out on."

Nick ignored the prosecutor as he rambled on. Nick looked over at his lieutenant, who he could tell sensed Nick's uneasiness.

"You did your job, Nick," his lieutenant said. "Like Mullanno said, this is the consequence of his actions."

"I'm going on leave," Nick said. "Can you take care of that for me?"

His lieutenant just nodded, and then looked away. Nick turned away from the two men, and walked away from the case for good. Nick could not stop the feelings of betrayal that he felt responsible for. He understood that Mullanno had chosen this life, and Nick knew from the beginning that it would end like this. He knew that Mullanno was not the type of person to carry a grudge, to threaten Nick. Mullanno was the type of man to give himself away for the protection of his family. Nick had made this happen, had put Mullanno and his family in this position. Nick left the police station and hailed a cab. As the taxi pulled away from the curb heading off to the airport so Nick could find his car, he could sense the police station growing smaller in the distance as, at the same time, his desire to be a police officer waned the farther away he got. Nick had only one desire now, to take his badge and his gun and put them away forever.

Chapter 6

Jack stepped out onto the grassy field and took a deep breath in. As others pushed past him, hurrying to their place on the field, Jack took a moment to steady himself. He was almost exploding with anticipation. Finally, he was being aloud to play. He had always known that he was not the best player on his football team. He had always felt the feeling of disappointment that exuded from the coach everytime he tried to make a play. He also knew that he did not really understand the sport, at least, he did not understand the rules. However, he was too afraid to ask the coach at this point. Asking the rules now would only serve to make him look stupid, and it would make the coach angry. That he wanted to avoid most of all. He did not like it when the coach got angry. When the coach got angry, Jack knew that he would end up in a very bad place. As Jack breathed in he could smell the musky odor of sweat and plastic inside of the old football helmet. It made him feel as though he were like all the other boys out on the field, it made him feel accepted. Jack heard the coach yelling from the sideline for all of the players to get in formation, and his voice jarred Jack back into reality. Jack ran to the middle of the field where the young quarterback, an arrogant boy from school who though he was better than everyone else, recited the play the coach had given him as if he were making the decisions on the field. The young boys arrogance annoyed Jack, especially since he got more attention from the coach than Jack did. Sometimes, Jack wished he was a little bigger, the same size or larger than the quarterback. Sometimes Jack wished that he were a bully. However, now was not the time for those thoughts. The young quarterback relayed the play and spelled out where each player was going for the kids who were not as good as he was; Jack always felt as though those comments were directed at him.

The team moved into their positions on the field. The coach was on the sidelines screaming the same things he always screamed before a play. "Tighten it up. Line up with the man in front of you. Watch out for the blitz." Jack could not even remember what the blitz was, but he knew the boy in front of him. The boy was just about the same size as Jack and he knew that if he did not show any hesitation, did not let the other boy see a moments weakness, then Jack knew that he could knock the boy down and keep him from penetrating the line. Jack bent down into his stance, the enormous shoulder pads hanging so awkwardly on his thin, seven year old frame that he could barely get fingers to touch the grass. He was immediately uncomfortable as the shoulder pads pushed up into his helmet, causing the chin strap to pull tight across his face. However, Jack reminded himself that he was to show no weakness. He could beat this kid, this kid was not any better than he. Jack desperately wanted to prove to the coach that he could be a good player, and that thought alone was enough to make him endure any pain. Jack tensed his legs, the muscles tightening like springs just waiting for the right call to launch himself into the player inches in front of him. He heard the quarterback screaming the call, he could feel the teeth grooves of his mouthpiece as he bit down hard. He looked across at the boy in front of him, stared deep into the other boys eyes and even tried to snarl, though Jack was fairly certain that the intensity of it was cut off by the sheer size of the mouthpiece.

Suddenly, as if everything before now had been happening in slow motion, Jack heard the call that he had been waiting for and saw the entire line spring forward at lightning speed. Instinctively, Jack surged forward, smashing his helmet into the shoulder pads of the other player. Immediately, there was some resistance, then Jack felt the resistance start to give way as he realized that the other boy was not ready for the viciousness of Jack's attack. Using his arms like a blocking bar, Jack pushed and pushed against the other boy, making sure to keep his hands locked together so as not to get called for holding. Though he knew little about the sport of football, Jack did know how to avoid getting fouled. Unfortunately for Jack, he had learned the hard way, often making the coach very mad. However, now he knew that he was blocking properly, and saw the boy in front of him start to lose his footing. Suddenly, another boy from the opposite team came into view and it was at that moment that Jack remembered that this was a running play and the running back would be going to the left, in his direction. Jack knew that the new opponent meant to tackle his running back, and surged forward, blocking the defensive back's way. Jack was immediately knocked to the ground, as the other boy had both a height and weight advantage over the young man. However, Jack had given his running back just enough time to push ahead, gaining five yards.

The defensive back stepped right on Jack's chest as he made his way back to his own team's huddle, but Jack could not care less. He had helped make the play. Suddenly, he felt something pulling at the back of his shoulder pads and realized that he was being lifted up by someone else. Jack looked up immediately and found himself looking into the face of the running back. The running back, a kid who was in the same grade as Jack but in another class was suddenly surprised, not realizing that it had been Jack who had helped him out.

"Nice block, Jack," the running back said, brushing some grass and dirt off of Jack's shoulder.

"Thanks," the young boy answered, unable to come up with any words. He realized in that moment that this had quite possibly been the greatest play he had ever made in his short pee wee football career. Jack hoped that his father had seen him, hoped that his father had been one of the father's out there yelling for their boys. Jack saw the quarterback making his way to the sideline to get the new play from the coach, and headed that way too.

"Did you see that?" Jack yelled over to the sideline as he approached. "Did you see me on that play. I blocked two guys at once."

The coach just pushed Jack out of the way, grabbing the quarterback and relaying the next play. Jack was too excited to let that bother him though and stayed on the side of the field until the coach was finished with the quarterback.

"Did you see me?" Jack asked again, pressing. "I blocked those two kids, I did it."

"You didn't do anything, there spaz," the coach said. "Block like that all game long and maybe you will have something that I could get excited about. Until then, either get out on the field or take a seat on the bench."

Jack turned around, deflated, disappointed, alone. He walked back over to his team, hearing his coach screaming for him to hustle. He jogged over just as the quarterback was finishing with the play. Jack did not even hear the snap count before everyone was moving back into position. Jack turned to another player as they approached the line, asking the snap count. His teammate simply ignored him though, not wanting to give away the count. Jack went back into his stance and just hoped that he would not twitch until the ball was snapped. Jack looked up at his opposition and found that he was in more trouble that he knew. He first looked into the eyes of the lineman that he had blocked last play, and then directly behind him was the defensive back that he had stalled. Jack knew immediately what was going on. This was payback, and the two boys were set to inflict some pain. All Jack could do was brace himself, tilting his head off to the side in the hopes that he would deflect off of the lineman, decreasing the severity of the coming hit. The ball was snapped and without knowing the count ahead of time, Jack was a half a second too slow off of the line. He did not have the luxury of the knowing the moment the ball would be snapped and was too slow to avoid the onslaught. The lineman took him in a holding grab, just enough to keep him from getting loose and the defensive back came up so fast that he slammed into Jack's chest and knocked the wind out of him. The force of the impact was so great as to launch Jack off of his feet, the defensive back lifting him into the air just a few inches, then slamming his body back against the ground. The play went on, a pass was caught and ten yards were gained, but for the defensive back, revenge was had.

It took a few seconds for Jack to get back to his feet, but he did get back to his feet. His teammates were looking at him for a moment, wondering if he was alright or if the coach was going to have to carry him off of the field. Jack would not have that, though. He would not give the coach the satisfaction of being right about him. It was his hope that the coach saw him take the hit and get up, realizing that Jack was willing to take the pain of the game.

"Jack the jackass," he heard the coach call from the sidelines. "What the hell kind of blocking do you call that."

Jack felt as if everyone were staring at him. The only sound he could hear was the ranting, taunting of the coach. To the young boy, it was as if there was no other sound on the field that night. There was wetness in his eyes, and catching his breath became heavy and he felt as though he were going to cry. He wanted to cry, he was already humiliated by this man in whose eyes he could do nothing right. All Jack could do is remind himself that he would not give that man the satisfaction. He was going to make him proud one way or another. He was going to prove him wrong, and Jack knew just how. He had heard a term once, and it seemed to apply now. Fight fire with fire.

He listened intently to the play, especially focusing this time on the snap count. At this point, the young boy could really care less whether the play was going to be a passing or running play. There was only one thing he wanted and that was to inflict pain. He was going to hurt as many boys on the other team as he must to prove to the coach that he could play the game of football. Jack lined up against the other boy who was smiling and laughing at him now. The boy taunted him a little, but Jack tuned it out, just staring straight ahead as if not seeing the other boy at all. The snap was called and the ball surged backwards into the hands of the quarterback. Jack, however, knowing the count surged ahead just a split second early. Not enough to be noticed by the referee, but enough to get the upper hand on the other team. Noticing too late that Jack had moved, the defensive lineman braced for the block and tried to surge a little at the same time to gain the upper hand. Jack had anticipated this move, and simply brushed the lineman aside, before smashing the right side of his body against the other boy with all the strength he could muster. Jack heard the boy cry out in pain, but it was muffled out by the sounds of the other players. Immediately, Jack searched out his next target, the defensive back that had pounded him in the last play. Jack locked eyes on him, but suddenly saw another defensive lineman coming for him in his peripheral vision. Jack stopped short just a second, causing the momentum of the other player to pass him by. Jack took the opportunity to exact more revenge, grabbing the passing lineman roughly and pounding him into the dirt. Jack had used his hands there, and was certain that he would be called on a foul for holding. However, Jack did not care at this point, he lost in the gratification of inflicting pain. Now, nothing else mattered to him except for the defensive back. Jack ran forward a few steps and slammed his head and shoulders into the defensive back's side, where the padding was the lightest. Jack was certain he heard something crack, and watched in satisfaction as the other boy landed on his back, his feet pointing up in the air. Hearing the whistle, Jack stepped back and made his way back over to where his own team was gathering. They all stared at him, amazed and confused, and most of all, scared. Jack heard the coach calling him over to the sidelines. It seemed to Jack that every player on both teams were staring at him.

"What in the fuck was that?" the coach asked. "What were you trying to do, kill them?"

"I was trying my best, Dad," Jack said, momentarily unable to explain his actions.

"Don't call me that," the coach said. "Don't call me that when you embarrass me by your playing. I almost liked it better when you were running around in circles like an idiot."

The coach slapped Jack hard on the back of the head and told him to sit on the sidelines. Jack knew that he would not get to have another chance to play the rest of the game. He hated the fact that his father was the coach of the team, hated the fact that he could never please the man, and most of all hated the fact that all he wanted was his father's approval. Even though he knew that he would never get it, he could not stop trying. He sat down alone, embarrassed, and mad. It had felt so rewarding inflicting pain, especially as one against many. They were afraid of him now, and he knew that the boys from the other team would not forget that play. However, the pleasure subsided and all Jack was left with was the knowledge that he was not good enough in his own father's eyes. Jack looked down at the grass underneath his feet and closed his eyes, wishing he would open them far, far away from there.

Jack did open his eyes, and like many other times of recalling memories from the past, this time he was far, far away from there. Now he was sitting in his car, watching people stand in line, waiting to get inside the nightclub he was parked in front of, waiting. Jack, however, was not waiting. Jack was grown now, and knew who he was. He was a predator, and they were his prey.

Chapter 7

I am the Nemesis. That was the thought that went through the young man's head as he stepped past the enormous man that served as the bouncer for the new nightclub Insomnia. As he passed the bouncer, he slipped a one hundred dollar bill into his hand, posing as though he were just shaking hands with an old friend. That one hundred dollars had just kept him from having to stand at the back of the line of men and women waiting to get into the new super-hip nightclub. The club, which had just opened in January, was perfectly situated outside Mystic, Connecticut. College students from the colleges in Connecticut and Rhode Island, as well as sailors from the bases in Groton and Newport, frequented the nightclub freeing them from having to make the drive to Boston or New York City. This was the perfect hunting ground for this predator. The Nemesis was a killer, or would be one soon. Tonight was to be his coming out party, and he would come out in full force. He had been planning this night for years, ever since he knew who he was. The time was now right for him to reveal himself, to make himself known to the world, and most of all, to the only person who needed his help. The Nemesis walked through the narrow walkway with its black walls into an open area with large cushioned chairs lining the walls with little round tables every five feet. Ahead of this lounging area was the bar, large glass lined panels with some blue colored fluid suspended between with a thick black marble counter. Behind the bar rested every type of liquor known to man, behind which contained more glass with a fountain on the other side, giving the impression that it was raining. The Nemesis had only heard of a few of the many types of alcohol he saw above the bar. He was not a drinker, especially not tonight.

The Nemesis was here for a woman. She would be the first, the one who would introduce him to the world. He knew who he was looking for, he knew what type of woman she was, and he was aware of the difficulties that were ahead of him. Though his social life, especially his experience with women was not very extensive, he knew that women were already on the defensive. Knowing that they would be approached by all sorts of men, most of whom were not the type they were looking for, being on the defensive would make it very difficult for The Nemesis to approach just any woman. However, he was not looking for just any woman. The Nemesis knew that he needed something that would catch a woman's attention, and after years of patience, he knew that he had it. The Nemesis had spent years working out in gyms, sculpting his body to look perfect. He was well built and wore clothes that accentuated his muscle tone, while not being too obvious. Almost every woman he walked past looked at him, many turning slightly to get a lasting look as he passed, convincing him that he would have no problem approaching women now. However, every woman he past was not the type of woman he was looking for. He knew exactly what he was looking for, and he would know her the moment he saw her.

The Nemesis walked passed many women that looked like models, their thin, tight bodies twisting and gyrating to the music. He had no use for these types of women. These were the ones that everyone noticed. They were the ones who were here every weekend, known by name by the bouncers, and would draw attention to him if he were to leave with them. Besides, they did not interest him. They were not looking for anything more than a good time; there was nothing stimulating beyond the physical. He was looking for a real woman, a woman who wanted to fall in love, a woman who believed that there was someone perfect for her. He was looking for the woman who, were he any other person, he could fall in love with. This was the only kind of woman good enough for him, good enough to be his first. He knew he would find her. She would be a college student or recent graduate. A good student or a good person who had been convinced to come out to the night club against her better judgment. Since the night club life was not her style, she would agree to go as a designated driver, using it as her excuse, though hoping in her heart that she would meet the man of her dreams. He would save her, and she would fall in love with him immediately.

The Nemesis walked around the bar and approached the black metal railing that looked down on the enormous dance floor. The lounging area was lit by black lights, causing everything white to glow in a purple-white radiance. As he looked down to the dance floor, he was relieved from the unnatural colors by laser lights that seemed to dance between and underneath the moving bodies. Men were smiling, sidling up close to women, the women laughing and pushing them away teasingly. The Nemesis looked for groups of women, dancing together by the edge of the dance floor. A tall, black railed counter lined the edges of the dance floor, holding hundreds of drinks and beer bottles. The Nemesis came to a group of women all standing together, laughing and pointing. They were trying to convince a pretty young woman to come out to the dance floor, but she shied away. He could tell immediately that this was the woman he was looking for. He made his way to one of the winding staircases that led down to the dance floor. He made his way down, never taking his eyes of the woman until he reached the bottom, and then slipped out of sight behind the staircase. A scantily clad waitress came by and asked him if he wanted a drink. He ordered a coke, and then waited until she was safely away before he moved again. He knew that the time it took her to get the order back to him would show him how well the staff was paying attention to individual details. The Nemesis moved to a spot on the edge of the dance floor, about twenty feet to the left of his prey. A man had approached her and was talking to her now. She gave him her attention for just a few moments, before turning away and looking for her friends. Seeing them moving to the middle of the dance floor, she waved and turned back to the man beside her. She nodded absently, looking at him as if she were looking through him, her attention obviously a million miles away. The man was trying to get her to respond, trying to hold her interest, but was failing miserably. The Nemesis found the whole thing mildly comical. *What an idiot,* he thought to himself. The woman nodded and laughed quickly, desperately looking for her friends, feeling more alone now then ever. That was when he noticed the move. The man passed his hand over her plastic cup when she turned away to the dance floor. The motion was barely noticeable, and would not have been noticed by anyone who had not been watching for it. The Nemesis knew immediately that the man had put something in her drink. This was the moment he had been waiting for. *Men were so predictable,* he thought to himself. *Especially desperate little toads like this one. They made it all too easy.* The Nemesis smiled as he pushed himself away from the counter, walking towards the woman. He was about to become her savior, in every way.

Chapter 8

Tracy Scott looked out over the dance floor, desperately trying to get the attention of her friends. There had been rules made, rules that they had made before going out. Rule one was they were all supposed to keep within eye contact of one another, a way to make sure that this very thing did not happen. This guy had been too dense to take the hint, and as much as she wanted to just tell him to get lost, she didn't have the courage. *Why did I even come here*, she asked herself. However, she knew the answer to that question. She was tired of spending weekends alone. The guy next to her had been trying to pick her up for the last ten minutes, though to her it felt like an eternity. She had been polite at first, listening to his conversation, and brushing off his advances. Unfortunately, he did not pick up on her subtle clues, and persisted on. She would look away, not pay attention and still he stood there, talking as though she cared. She almost felt like just going out on the dance floor to get away from him, though she knew that would just bring on more trouble. Some drunken guy would sidle up beside her and start dancing with her, as if that were what she was there for. She turned away from the guy to her right as he kept talking about the work he did in landscaping. She saw her three friends in the middle of the dance floor, grinding each other, laughing at the male attention they were getting. They weren't even thinking about their friend they left on the side lines. All of the sudden, she noticed the guy next to her move forward, as if losing his balance. She turned her attention back to him, to find him inching closer.

"You want to dance?" he asked, cocking his head to the side as if to point out where the dance floor was.

"I don't dance," Tracy told him, knowing that was not going to be enough answer to make him go away.

"Come on," the guy said. "There's nothing to it. All you have to do is move your hips and feet."

She knew he was right about that. For a woman, all she would have to do is move her hips provocatively and look confident and it would seem as if she were dancing. This thought just reminded Tracy of how much she hated places like these. This wasn't her scene, and yet if she had any hope of meeting anyone, she was starting to believe that she would have to do it in places like this. She reached for her drink as the guy kept trying to convince her to dance. She started to lift her drink just as a man came out of no where and put his hand over the top of her cup, pushing it back down to the table.

"Don't drink that," the man said with a conviction that startled her and yet made her obey immediately.

"Hey, what the hell do you think you're doing?" asked the boring guy.

"Shut up, loser," the man answered back, staring the other man down. Tracy was suddenly afraid that there was going to be an altercation between the two men. A couple of people standing near them stopped talking and watched, but for the most part, this event was going unnoticed.

"Listen asshole, the lady and I..." the boring talker started. The new man quickly reached into his left breast pocket and pulled out what looked to Tracy like a leather wallet. The man flipped it open and pushed it up into the Boring Talker's face. Suddenly, the man who had nothing better to do than to bother Tracy had nothing to say. The man who had stopped Tracy from taking her drink lifted it and poured it into the boring guy's drink.

"You want to take a sip?" the man asked.

"No," answered the boring guy, quite obviously afraid.

"Then why don't you get your ass out of here before I have you busted." The boring man looked horrible, placed his cup of beer down on the table and took off, pushing his way through the crowd.

"What the hell was that about?" Tracy asked, thankful the other man was gone, but feeling as though she missed something important.

"He slipped something into your drink," the man answered. He took the empty cup and the other man's cup and placed them on the tray of a waitress passing by. "Can you get us two new drinks?"

The man ordered a coke, and Tracy, unsure of what to do, ordered another Midori sour.

"I'm sorry," The Nemesis said, extending his right hand. "I didn't mean to startle you. My name is Jack."

"Tracy," she answered, still startled. "What the hell did he slip into my drink?"

"I don't know," The Nemesis answered. He looked as if he were about to continue when he paused a moment. "Just watch your drinks. Don't leave them unattended. There can be some real creeps around here."

The waitress returned and passed out the drinks, which The Nemesis paid for before she disappeared into the crowd.

"What are you, a cop or something?" Tracy asked impressed with this man who seemed so smooth and confident, and yet didn't seem to belong in this environment.

"Or something," The Nemesis answered, flashing a playful smile. There was a brief pause, where he seemed a little uncomfortable. It was just then that Tracy realized she was staring at him. There was something magnetic about him, and she realized she was waiting for him to jump in where the boring guy left off.

"Look, really, I'm sorry I startled you," he said. "I've been watching that guy all night. You were the first person he tried that with."

"You were watching him?" Tracy asked, raising an eyebrow.

"Yeah, I guess that doesn't sound too good," The Nemesis answered, his smile disarming her. "These places aren't really my scene. I'm just here with some buddies."

There was another brief awkward silence, where he seemed to look at her without checking her out. Tracy had never met a man who didn't immediately check out your body. He also seemed to say just the right things.

"Look," The Nemesis said, turning to leave. "I didn't mean to bother you. Just be careful."

"No," Tracy said, reaching out instinctively to stop him. She placed her hand on his right forearm without thinking, and then was startled when she felt the hard muscle underneath the black cotton blazer. He turned back, looking down at her hand as if amused. That was when Tracy realized that she had unconsciously tightened her grip. "I'm sorry. Look, let me at least buy you a drink. You are my hero after all."

He smiled and looked down at the floor, as if embarrassed.

"You'll hurt my feelings if you say no," Tracy said.

"Well, I don't want to do that," he answered. "But we both have drinks."

"Well, then you'll have to let me buy the next round," Tracy said, asserting herself. She liked this man. He was strong and soft at the same time. He knew when to be assertive, and yet he seemed to know when to soft with her. Tracy felt so at ease with him, there was none of the usual warning flags that popped up when she was talking with other men.

"I hadn't planned on being here that long," he admitted.

"Oh," Tracy said, sensing he was uncomfortable. Suddenly, she was searching for the right words to back her out of her offer without looking like she just got turned down.

"There's this coffee shop just across the street," he said. "We can go get some coffee if you want, it would be quieter."

Tracy was continuously amazed at how he kept saying the right things, and yet, Tracy wasn't the type of person to leave with a man she didn't know. However, there was something magnetic about this man, something that made her want to, have to be around him.

"Sure," she answered, shocking herself. This could be considered the craziest thing she had ever done. "I'm here with some friends, let me just tell them that I'm leaving."

"You'll be right across the street if they want to come find you later," he said, as if reassuring her. She realized instantly that he was making sure she, and her friends, were comfortable splitting up. He was considerate; but most of all, he was different. "I'll meet you at the door. Do you have a coat you want me to pick up?"

Tracy smiled as she reached into her pocket, retrieving the numbered ticket she had been given when she checked her coat.

"Thank you," she said, genuinely impressed. "I'll just be a minute."

"I'll meet you at the entrance," he assured her.

Tracy watched as he melted into the crowd, stunned that she had found a man that she could consider dating in a nightclub. Tracy felt her excitement build as she slipped between the twisting bodies on the dance floor. She found her three friends, still dancing, laughing and pushing guys away who had tried to dance with them. She pulled her friend Kim away from the others.

"I've met someone," Tracy said.

"Ooh, is he cute?" Kim asked playfully, laughing. Tracy could tell that her friend was a little drunk. Kim looked over Tracy's shoulder towards where they had been standing off the floor. "Where is he?"

"He's getting my coat," Tracy answered, an embarrassed smile spreading across her face. Her friend looked at her in disbelief.

"You little tramp," Kim said, laughing. "You're taking him home?"

"No," Tracy answered slapping Kim on the arm. "We're going across the street to the coffee shop."

"Oh take him home, you prude," Kim said, thrusting her pelvis into Tracy's leg. "Live a little for once."

"One thing at a time," Tracy said, laughing and pushing her friend away. "I'll call you on your cell if something changes. Are you going to be alright here?"

"Of course we'll be alright," Kim answered, a devilish smile across her face. She started swinging her hips side to side, backing away from Tracy slipping back into the crowd. The last thing Tracy saw before Kim disappeared into the crowd of dancing bodies was her mouth the words "Have Fun."

Tracy smiled, relieved that her best friend had no objections with her leaving. Kim had always been a free spirit; always more comfortable in this environment than Tracy had ever been. Then again, Tracy always thought Kim was better looking than she was. Finally, Tracy felt as though she were doing something a little reckless, and yet she felt comfortable enough with this man to leave. He didn't strike her as an idiot guy, or a psycho. She climbed the steps excitedly, filled with anticipation. She made her way past the bar, found Jack standing by the hall that led out of the building.

"Ready to go?" he asked, helping her into her coat. She looked at him, smiling.

"Absolutely."

Chapter 9

Tracy Scott sat across from her new friend, engrossed. Jack was the very embodiment of everything she had dreamt of in a man. She could not believe she was here, with him. He was smart, charming, polite, and funny. All the qualities in a man that everyone told her did not exist in one single person, now sat across from her in the booth. As they talked, she kept reminding herself that she almost didn't come out with her friends that evening. The chances of two people meeting like this made her believe it was fate. They talked for hours, discussing all sorts of different topics. The longer they spent talking, the more she felt herself falling for him. Though she was a firm believer in the idea that there was one person for everyone, she was never a believer in love at first sight; until now. She had never believed it was possible, and every now and again she had to pinch herself to make sure she was not dreaming. After a while, she stopped pinching. She was at the point where she did not care anymore, she was with *the* perfect man, and she would enjoy it for as long as it lasted.

The one quality that amazed Tracy the most was that Jack was a true listener. She had dated all sorts of men, most of who did not really listen to what she had to say. She had dated the men who had just wanted her for sex, and she had dated the men who were looking to save or change her. There had been over-emotional men, and under-emotional men, but none of them had been what she was looking for. She had never found a man that wasn't looking for something more, someone who was pretending to listen or care so he could get what he wanted. Now, sitting across from her, was a man that did not seem to have any ulterior motive. He listened to her, laughed with her, and questioned her. After a while, she started to realize that this night would come to an end, and she dreaded it. She wanted to stay with him, here in this moment. Soon, she noticed him look at his watch, and she knew what that meant.

"I was just thinking that your friends might be concerned with you being gone so long," Jack said, sensing her concern.

"I doubt they've even noticed I'm gone," Tracy answered, suddenly hoping that she had not sounded too desperate.

"I'm sure that's not true," he responded.

"Do you have to go?" Tracy asked, bracing herself for the worst.

"Not necessarily," Jack said with a smile. "However, they will be closing soon."

Tracy looked down at her wristwatch, realizing that it was after midnight.

"I don't want to leave," she said softly, looking down at her lap. She had put herself out there; she had made the first move. Suddenly, she felt his hand on her chin, gently lifting her face to meet his gaze.

"Neither do I," he replied. Jack hesitated a moment, looking down to his empty mug. "I want to ask you something, and yet at the same time, I don't"

Tracy knew immediately what he was trying to say. She had been thinking the same thing all night long.

"Would you mind driving me home?" she asked, smiling.

The drive home did not take long; Tracy lived only fifteen minutes away. Neither person said much on the way home, a heavy feeling of anticipation weighing on them both. Tracy knew that he was nervous, probably as nervous as she was. She was so afraid of saying something wrong, of having mistaken something he said. Tracy directed him to her apartment/condominium complex, and Jack parked the car in the parking area around the side of the building. He insisted that she let him walk her to her door, causing Tracy to doubt herself. Was the evening truly over? She wished she could just invite him in, but she didn't want him to think that she was that kind of woman. Suddenly, a night spent feeling totally comfortable, now left her standing on the precipice. They reached her door and she turned to face him.

"I," Jack hesitated a moment. "You are an amazing woman. I would like to..."

Tracy stopped him, pressing herself against him hard. Standing on the tips of her toes, she placed her lips on his, praying inside that he did not pull away. She felt his hand caress the back of her neck, and she knew then that there had been no misunderstanding. Instead of pushing away, he pushed into her, wrapping his other arm around her waist. After a moment, their lips separated. Jack looked deep into her eyes.

"I'm not this kind of person," he mumbled. "I don't want you to think I picked you up for this."

"I know what kind of person you are," she said, trying to ease his mind. "All I know is that I don't want you to leave tonight."

"Then I won't," he answered, pulling her closer, kissing her again.

When their bodies parted for a second time, Tracy rummaged quickly through her tiny black purse, searching for her keys. Then she fumbled with the lock, the anticipation getting the better of her. From behind, Jack placed his hand on her arm, sliding his soft hands down her arm, then wrapping his hand around hers, helping her guide the key into the lock. Tracy closed her eyes, leaned back and kissed the underside of his chin. Tracy was gone; the logic and reason centers of her brain had shut down. She just let her consciousness drift away with this man; her man, at least for tonight. The only thing she knew or cared about was the fact that she was going to make love to this man.

Pushing the door open, she pulled him inside, twisting her body around to face him but making sure not to break contact. She ran her hands up and down his chest, tracing an outline of every taught muscle. Running her hands around to his chest, she deftly reached out for the light switch, but he stopped her. Jack reached around and grabbed her hands, whispering the word "no" as his lips slid down her jaw line to her neck. Tracy slipped her hand down, pulling his shirt out. Realizing he still had his blazer on, she pushed it off his shoulders, letting it fall to the ground behind him. She then slowly unbuttoned his shirt, kissing his bare chest underneath. He slipped his hands underneath her shirt, pulling it up while sliding his hands all over her skin. His hands were deceptive though, teasing while not directly touching the most sensitive parts of her body. She raised her arms as he pulled her top up over her head. He stopped pulling suddenly, keeping her arms raised over her head, unable to move. She gasped, feeling his lips and tongue snake down to the nape of her neck, and then finally pulling up allowing her to pull her arms through. She pushed his shirt off, then ran the tips of her fingernails over his broad shoulders and around to the back of his arms and down to his hands. His hands stopped at her waist, hesitating a moment without breaking the rhythm. She smiled to herself, then placed her hands over his and guided him to her belt. He deftly flipped the belt open and slid his finger to the buttons on her pants, pulling them apart without missing a beat. Tracy was thankful that she had decided to wear the black lace bra and panties, the sexiest underwear she owned.

After finishing with the last button, he traced his way back to her waistline, running his fingers over the soft skin of her abdomen. She squirmed as he touched her sensitive skin, and then turned her around so her back was to him. She moaned as his hands slipped between her tight pants and her underwear, and then slowly pushed the pants down. She was surprised and delighted that he removed one article of clothing at a time, savoring every part of her. They had only started five minutes ago, and already this was the most sensual experience she had ever had. As her pants slipped down her buttocks, she could feel his excitement pressing into her. Tracy was lost in the sensations that were washing over her body, unsure of whether her eyes were open or closed. It did not matter, there were no lights on, and she felt as though her sense of touch was heightened by the experience. When he could push her pants no further, she felt him use the friction of their bodies to lower them until she could step out freely. Their bodies moved as one, both desperate not to break the connection. His warm hands gently flowed up her back, then over the back of her bra. Just as she thought he was going to unfasten it, he moved his hands higher, sliding his thumbs over the shoulder straps of her bra, up over her shoulders, and down to her breasts. He slowly followed the seam of the bra around the outside of her breasts, following the underwire to the soft underside. Her body flinched to his every touch, his fingers causing her to feel things she had never imagined. Without touching the most sensitive places, he was causing her skin to burn with a desire she had never known. She raised her arms, her back still to him, and wrapped them around the back of his neck, allowing his fingers to trace along the seam of her bra to the back. His left hand slid up her left arm, and with two fingers of his right hand, he unfastened her bra with just a touch, then pushed it apart and slid it off her body.

Jack slid his hands over her own, then guided them down over her own skin. Tracy felt as if every nerve ending in her body were on fire. She titled her head back, resting on his chest as he drew his fingers over her bare breasts, carefully avoiding her sensitive nipples, making her want him even more. He then traced a line from between her breasts down her abdomen, around her belly button and stopped at her panty line. He guided his hands around her waist to her back, cupping her buttocks. Instinctively, she pushed back against him, arching her back. She sighed with pleasure as she felt his grip on her tighten softly. She rocked back and forth, sliding against him. She heard a slight moan escape him, heightening her pleasure even more. She felt his fingers slip underneath her panties, then felt a tug as he pulled from behind, causing the thin fabric to rub against her sensitive skin. The sensation sent sparks of electric fire throughout her body. As he continued, the delicious sensation made her feel as though she were on fire with pleasure. Finally, driving her to a point of near madness, he hooked his finger into the lacy fabric of her panties and pulled them down.

Standing there, totally exposed, he turned her to face him. Maintaining contact, feeling her bare skin slide over the smooth skin of his chest, she pushed against him, spreading her hands up his chest and resting around the back of his neck. She felt a slight movement on his part, and suddenly his right arm was beside her legs. In one fluid movement, he lifted her into his arms and started walking. Tracy did not know how he could see in the darkness, and at the same time did not care. He moved smoothly, sure of himself. She felt him turn and finally stop, then lower her down until she felt the softness of the bed underneath her. As his arms slid out from under her, she rolled slightly, propping herself up on her hands and knees. She felt the bed dip, as he climbed on behind her. She pushed herself up, her bare back against his hairless chest. His hands smoothly guided up her abdomen, over her breasts and up to the nape of her neck.

"You are the one," he whispered in her left ear. Tracy sighed, unsure if she were asleep or awake, relaxed and tense at the same time. Then, as if torn from the most wonderful dream, she felt his hands tighten around her throat and knew instantly that something had gone terribly wrong.

Chapter 10

The Nemesis was at the height of his arousal. As his hand tightened around the young woman's neck, his breathing became erratic, his senses alert to every sound and movement that occurred. This moment was his ecstasy. This was the moment that he had fantasized about hundreds, even thousands of times since he first learned who he was. Now, as he reached the moment of no return, he felt more alive than ever before. His grip still tight around the woman's neck, he shoved her forward, slamming her face into the mattress. He reached around to the back of his waist, where, on the under side of his belt lay sheathed a specialized knife of his own design. The knife itself was very thin, its handle only a half an inch thick, but it's contoured grooved to maintain his grip. From there the metal of the handle tapered down to a blade no thicker than a razor blade, but sharp enough to cut neatly through bone or wood. The knife was one piece, made of surgical steel. The Nemesis drew the blade expertly from its sheath, and maneuvered himself so that his bent right leg pinned both of the woman's legs underneath. With surgical precision, he sliced the blade through her skin just above the ankle, cutting through the Achilles tendon and muscle. Now the woman's feet were useless. After repositioning himself, he swung the knife again at the underside of the knees, severing the muscles and rendering her legs useless. Then, with her temporarily incapacitated, he donned a pair of latex medical gloves, using his teeth to pull it tight over his hands.

Even with the mattress to muffle any sound, the woman let out a bloodcurdling scream. The Nemesis had expected this, and in one fluid movement, pulled the woman up by her hair with his left hand. With his right hand, he slipped the knife through her larynx, cutting through her windpipe and vocal cords but making sure to avoid her carotid artery and her jugular vein. The woman flailed with her arms, a gurgling noise coming from her throat. The Nemesis had to move quickly, before she drowned in her own blood. Having anticipated every move, The Nemesis pulled a plastic pen out of his back pocket. He quickly took the pieces of the pen apart, carefully replacing all but the pen tubing in his pocket. Taking a rag out of his front pocket, he wiped down the pen, making sure he removed any prior fingerprints and keeping the rag between his gloved hand and the pen, made a quick puncture below the initial cut and placed the pen tube between her skin, allowing her to breathe. Confident that he had done everything to prolong her life as long as possible, he went to work.

His work did not take as long as he had imagined, in fact, the time seemed to fly by. As for his victim, the time must have felt as though it did not pass at all. Twice during his painstaking work, she passed out. He knew that the pain and shock must have been overwhelming, and had been prepared for this. The first time, he revived her with smelling salts; however, having brought only two, he decided to let her remain unconscious until he was finished. If she was still alive and he was able to revive her, he would try to use the last smelling salt when he was done. She was a work of art; he didn't want her to miss out on it. When he completed his work, having been very careful, he attempted to revive her again. He watched her jerk back as she snapped back into consciousness, desperately attempting to move her head away from the smelling salts but not having the energy. She had lost a lot of blood by then. However, she remained conscious long enough for him to show her his work. There was no reaction visible on her face, no appreciation of his hard work. He could not even be certain that she could see his masterpiece.

"You really are a wonderful, beautiful woman," The Nemesis said. "If I were any other person."

There was a brief moment of hesitation. He knelt down on the bed beside her.

"You are my first, and I promise you that I will love you until the day I die," he whispered. The Nemesis rose and carefully scanned the room. Once satisfied that he left no physical evidence linking him to the crime, he left the bedroom and walked towards the front door. Once he found his blazer, he extracted a small pen light from a pocket and searched the living room for a telephone. He finally found the phone in a corner next to the couch, and picked up the receiver unit and dialed the number he had come to memorize over the last few days, making the most important phone call of his life.

Chapter 11

Zombie. That was the only word that Nick could think of to describe himself. For the last three weeks since he had walked out of the police headquarters in Hartford, Nick's life had seemed like one long, never ending day. His sleeping habits had become erratic, being unable to sleep for thirty six to forty eight hours at a time, then suddenly becoming tired and sleeping for eighteen to twenty hours straight. He wandered the halls of the large house left to him by his grandmother, searching for something to do, always coming up with nothing. Sometimes he would just stand in the doorways of different rooms, staring off in the distance, not thinking of anything and not wanting to. When he had first moved into the house two months after his grandmother died, he thought living in Salem, Connecticut would be nice. It was a quiet small town, not more than thirty minutes from any major town or city. Now, walking aimlessly through the halls, the house seemed like a stranger. He had never spent more than two days at a time in this house since going undercover three years ago. He had stayed in an apartment in Hartford to maintain his undercover identity. Nick told himself that he was looking for something to do as he searched every room, but inside he knew that he was really looking for himself. He was looking for a spark, some lifeline to his past, and possibly, some insight into who he really was.

When Nick had gone on leave three weeks ago, he had been disgusted. He was disgusted with himself; feelings of betrayal to Mullanno conflicting with ideals he had once coveted from doing his job. He was disgusted with his inability to see the obvious truth; that he would never work undercover again. It had taken more than a week for Nick to understand why that bothered him so much. Nick's plan for advancement through the police force had never ended with undercover work. There had always been more. However, Nick could not stop thinking about who he had been. He knew that his natural need to be the best at everything he did had caused him to work so hard in his undercover role; a role that soon took over his life. After a while, he stopped pretending to be Nicholas the connected facilitator and actually took on the role, so much so that it became who he actually thought he was. Once he was able to accept that simple truth, to accept that he had gone way too deep, he fell into a deep depression. He played and replayed the events of the last year and a half in his mind, looking for any way in which he might have broken the law. He wondered if he had become as bad as the people he was trying to bring to justice. In some way he needed to find something damning, he needed some reason to punish himself. A conflicted young man floated between consciousness and unconsciousness, guilt and innocence, in a limbo that he could not break himself from.

And in the middle of this tug of war loomed something far more terrifying to him. The more he tried to ignore it, and the harder he tried, the larger this problem seemed to get. Nick had replayed the events of that morning on the pier hundreds of times, but he could not get past the confrontation between himself, the dealers, and the patrol officers. Something had happened to him, an overwhelming desire to cause the madness that had almost engulfed them. Simply, when his gun was drawn and aimed at the dealer, he felt the intense desire to kill. He wanted to shoot the dealer, many times, leaving him dead before he hit the asphalt pavement. The first time Nick confronted this emotion, it horrified him. It took days before he was able to start thinking about it again. Once he had accepted that these feeling had occurred, he tried to pass it off on the situation. He tried to convince himself that these feelings had surfaced because his life was in danger. However, he knew this wasn't true. Nick had been in dangerous situations like these many times, and he had never been terrified for his life. He knew he had not been terrified at the time of the incident. This was something else, something outside his conflicted feelings of betrayal to his job and to his undercover identity. This was a different beast entirely, something with a life of its own.

Putting this aside, Nick had tried starting different projects in a half-hearted attempt to get his mind off of his problems. However, none of them had worked. The only thing that did help him forget his problems for a while was intense weight training, which he did every day for almost four hours a day. One night, while watching television, Nick came upon an informational commercial about a home gym. After several hours of internet research, he bought three different home gym systems, all delivered directly to his home, all of which he assembled and stored in the basement. One of the systems was a tension-rod workout system, giving him the ability to work out his legs, chest, arms, and abdomen. The second had been a free weight system, and the third had been a rowing machine which he used for an hour at a time. Nick would turn the music all the way up and focus on his workout, concentrating on his form and technique, but most of all, he concentrated on the pain. The burning pain he felt when he ended a set; the dull, irritating pain that was with him every move he made for the last two weeks had been a welcome diversion from his conflicted thoughts. It had become an escape for him, and already he was beginning to see some results.

The only thing that Nick truly missed was his interaction with other people. Nick drove down the street every other day, getting groceries from the local mini-mart. He talked to the people in the store, but was not able to get any real satisfaction from it. He did not feel the same way as he had when he was on the street, making contacts, doing his job. It was then that Nick came to realize that he missed being a cop. He hated his feelings, hated the fact that he did not know who he was anymore; but most of all, he hated being useless. Nick wanted to call his boss and tell him he was coming back, but at the same time he was not sure of how useful he would be until he got his emotions under control. This frustrating, emotional struggle kept him from making any final decisions about his life. He knew he was going to have to make a decision, and he was going to have to make one soon, before he went mad.

Nick lay on the couch, pondering these problems until late, hoping that sleep would overtake him and put him out of his misery at least for awhile. The only light in the room came from the glow of the muted television across the room giving off an eerie illumination to the room. Suddenly, the phone rang, and Nick was torn from his thoughts. Nick reached over to the coffee table, where the receiver of the cordless phone rested on its side. He squinted as he tried to make out the number on the small display screen. It was not one he recognized. Usually, he would not answer the phone if he did not recognize the number. He had made that mistake five times since he had gone on leave. Four of the times had been from local television stations, wanting an interview for the local evening news. The fifth had been from his boss, asking Nick if he knew when he was coming back. Since then, Nick had just let the answering machine take messages, and so far, he had not responded to any of them. However, none of them had been at two o'clock in the morning. No one usually called him at this hour unless something was wrong. He pressed the talk button and placed the phone up to his ear.

"Hello," Nick said into the phone.

"Hello," a male voice answered. "Is this Nicholas Grenier?"

"This is," Nick responded, not recognizing the voice. "Who is this?"

"A friend," the man answered. "Hopefully more than that. I'm sorry about the late call, but I knew you would be awake."

"You did, huh?" Nick replied, rolling his eyes. "How did you know that?"

"Because I know what you're going through," the man answered. Nick was shocked at how sure of himself the man sounded. He was ready to dismiss this as a crank call, but something in the man's voice stopped him from hanging up. "I've been where you are now. I understand what it's like not to know who you are or what you're doing in the world. I know what it's like to walk aimlessly around; searching for something that connects you to the life you've made for yourself."

"Who are you?" Nick asked again, shaken. He was sitting up now; the caller had peaked his interest.

"I want to help you, Nick," the man said. "I've had that feeling you have. I've been afraid of that horrible feeling that you can't bring yourself to reflect upon. I've felt it gnaw away at me, that overwhelming desire, an itch you are too afraid to scratch. I had to go through it alone. I had to learn who I was by myself, and I can tell you its very hard. I don't want you to have to go through what I had to go through. I can help you."

"I'm sorry," Nick stammered, unable to comprehend how this man could put into words the feelings he had. "You've got the wrong person."

"I understand, Nick," the man said quickly, but compassionately. "I was in denial at first, too. It's a normal reaction to the feelings you are having. I won't push you. I will contact you again in a few days. In the meantime, I've left you a little present."

"Oh, yeah," Nick said. "What's that?"

"You'll see soon enough," the man said. "Think of it as my way of helping you to get back on your feet. We'll talk again, Nick. Goodbye."

With that, Nick heard the click of the disconnection of the signal, and he pressed the end button and placed the phone back down on the coffee table. He sat there, staring at the phone, trying to make sense of the call. There was something genuine to the caller, something that made Nick not pass it off as a crank call from some nut. There was an intentness, a true desire that refreshed and terrified Nick at the same time. He replayed the conversation in his head a few times, hoping to pick up on some clue. The caller seemed very honest and genuine, and his understanding of Nick's feelings bordered on frightening. Nick didn't know whether this was a stalker, but he did believe the caller would make contact again. Nick eased himself back into a lying position on the couch, his sore muscles burning from the movement. Nick tried to force himself to go to sleep, tried to force himself to stop thinking about the call, but no matter how hard he tried, sleep never came.

Chapter 12

The next day, Nick was up early. The phone call earlier had awoken something in him. While he was still conflicted, he was also energized. He clipped the cordless receiver to his waistband as he moved around the house. He cleaned the house for the first time since he had gone on leave. He waited for a call, anticipating another call from the man who had left him with so many questions the night before. When Nick tried to do his weight training, he found he could not adequately concentrate on his work-out, and gave up on it half-way through. Whether it was the call or the realization that a decision had to be made, something had been sparked in Nick, and it was quickly over taking his mind. Nick dialed the number to the police headquarters several times, wanting to tell his boss that he wanted to come back to work. However, Nick always cut the call off before anyone picked up. Nick knew that there was more than one decision looming regarding his return to work. Nick would have to decide what unit he wanted to move to. Finally, Nick decided that if he was going to go through with his return going back to work, he would have to be more prepared than he was now. He would need to have made all the decisions, and Nick knew he was not at that point yet. *One thing at a time*, he told himself.

Nick decided to start small. He decided he was going to work on getting himself out of the house, talking to people on the street, and honing the skills that he had learned while working as a cop. Nick left his small town for the first time in three weeks. He drove to Waterford, Connecticut, about twenty minutes away. He walked through the mall, stopping in at almost every store, finding something that interested him and talking to the sales people. He watched them, listened to them, gauging body language. Nick had always thought that retail employees were the best test for honing the skills needed for questioning and interrogating witnesses. He could usually tell which sales people knew their product and what they were talking about, and which ones were lying to make the sale. There were those who would flirt and tell you anything you wanted to hear to get you to buy something, and then there were those who did not care at all and just wanted you to go away. After four hours, Nick left the mall feeling very confident about his skills, even though he spent nearly four hundred dollars on clothes, work out equipment and some movies.

Nick pulled out of the mall parking lot and got on the main road, heading back towards Salem. When he looked in his rearview mirror, he noticed something that caught his eye; a car that he had noticed when he had made his way to the mall earlier in the day. At first, Nick thought his mind was playing tricks on him, that he had been too intent on honing his police skills and now thought someone was following him. Nick decided to pull into the driveway of a fast food restaurant. Sure enough, the dark blue sedan flipped on its right turn signal, and followed Nick into the parking lot. Nick pulled into the drive-thru lane and waited patiently while the line slowly moved forward. The sedan did not follow him into the drive-thru line, and from where Nick was he could not see the other car. He placed a small order, and pulled out of the parking lot and into traffic. He did not see the car again the rest of the ride home. Nick dismissed the notion of being followed and did not think about it again, instead deciding to focus on the strange phone call he received the night before.

The next day while driving, he saw the sedan again. By now, Nick knew that this could not be coincidence, and the first thought to enter his mind was whether or not the person following him was related to the strange call he had received two night's before. Nick drove as though he did not notice the sedan, hoping not to make the driver suspicious. Nick pulled into the parking lot of an outdoor sporting goods store, and shut off his engine. Just as he suspected, the blue sedan pulled into the parking lot and parked in the very last row, so as to maintain observation. When the sedan pulled into the lot, Nick was able to catch the license plate and knew immediately it was a police vehicle. Nick observed two men in the car, and knew that this was not the person who called him on the telephone, but was left with a more important question. Why were the police tailing him? Nick got out of his car, locked the door and went into the sporting good store. The store was huge and Nick could spend a lot of time inside, so he assumed the driver, passenger, or both would follow him in. However, when he stepped through the automatic sliding doors, he turned to his side to retrieve a cart, and saw no movement from the men out of the corner of his eye. Unfortunately for Nick, the sporting good store had no windows, so he would not be able to watch the men get out of the car if they decided to come in. He was going to have to find a spot at which he would be inconspicuous and still be able to watch the door.

Nick walked around the store and finally found the perfect vantage point from which to watch the door. Having no place to go, he waited to see how long the surveillance unit would wait for him. Thirty minutes passed, then an hour. Nick had been approached by several sales people, asking if they could help him. He got the feeling they were starting to suspect him of being a shoplifter. Nick would have to do something soon. He decided to walk around the store, staying in a place where he could still see the door. While walking around, Nick picked up a woodsman's folding knife, finding a nice one with a serrated blade. A few minutes later, he noticed the two men walk in, desperately looking back and forth for him, making sure he hadn't been able to slip past them.

"See those two guys there?" Nick asked the cashier, discreetly pointing in their direction.

"You mean those two guys who look like they've never been in a sporting good store in their life?" the young man asked, smiling. The two officers were in dark suits and almost looked like FBI characters in a bad made for television movie.

"That's them," Nick said, smiling. "I'm a cop and I've been following them all day. I think they're onto me."

The young man eyed Nick suspiciously for a moment, and then looked back at the two men.

"You're a cop?" the young man asked, unsure. "Do you have a badge?"

"Not on me," Nick said, secretly cursing himself for turning it in before he went on leave. "I have my police union membership card if you want to see it."

The cashier nodded and Nick pulled out the card and the man looked at the picture, then back at Nick.

"OK, you're a cop," the cashier agreed.

"If those men see me in here, they'll know I'm onto them," Nick said casually. "Can you do something to keep them in here a few minutes?"

"I can make the security alarm go off when they walk through," the cashier offered. "It's loud and there is an electronic voice that tells everyone to stop. My manager will be on them in a heartbeat."

"That would be perfect," Nick said, shaking the cashier's hand.

"No one is going to get hurt are they?" the cashier asked, suddenly concerned. "Nobody's going to lose their job are they?"

"Those two are cops too," Nick explained. "They won't do anything except give your manager a hard time."

"That's fine with me," the cashier said, shrugging his shoulders. Nick thanked the young man again and walked out into the flow of customers that just checked out. Nick could see out of the corner of his eye that the two men following him had just spotted him and they doubled back and headed for the exit.

Nick knew he was going to get through the exit first and he looked back to the cashier, who was already following Nick. Nick quickly reached into his bag and took the knife out of its box. He walked through the door and as he stepped into the cold winter air, he looked over his shoulder and saw the two men coming on the exit fast, and behind them, he saw the cashier carrying a magnetic security tag. Suddenly a red light flashed and an alarm sounded. As Nick jogged across the parking lot, he looked back as he heard an older man screaming and saw everyone suddenly stop and the sliding doors closed. Nick ran to the unmarked cruiser and with the pocket knife, slashed the two tires on the passenger side. He then stuffed the plastic bag and the small, thin knife box into the tailpipe. He then stabbed the two tires on the driver's side and then walked nonchalantly back to his car. He knew it would take a few minutes for all the air to escape, and though he wanted to stop the surveillance, he did not want to hurt anyone. He reached his car just as customers started exiting again, and he saw the two men run out of the store. Nick opened his trunk of his own car, making it look as if her were putting something away. He saw the men run to their car. He knew they probably would not notice the tires yet, so he climbed into his car and started the engine. He watched as the two men ran back to their car and jumped in. Nick pulled his car out of the parking spot and wheeled around quickly, racing for the back row. Once he reached the back row, he stepped on the accelerator, speeding down the row until he reached the unmarked cruiser and slammed on the breaks, blocking the cruiser in. Nick jumped out of his car and walked briskly over to the driver's side door.

"Who the hell are you?" Nick asked forcefully. "And why the fuck are you following me?"

The driver started to open the door, but Nick slammed his leg into the door, closing it again. The driver sighed, rolled down the window, reached into his coat pocket and retrieved his badge, and handed it to Nick.

"New London police?" Nick read aloud, questioningly. "What the hell is this about?"

"The fuck if I know," the driver said. "We're just following orders."

"Well," Nick started. "You tell whoever is giving the orders that if they want me, they should talk to me; not follow me all over the place, observing my shopping habits."

Nick threw the badge back at the driver and walked away. He climbed back into his car, catching a glimpse of the flattening tires as he pulled away. He saw the cruiser pull out of the lane and start following, then slowed and stopped. Nick pulled out of the parking lot and headed home. When he arrived home, he immediately called his lieutenant, who was unaware of any surveillance regarding Nick.

"There was talk of a surveillance unit right after the Mullanno bust," his lieutenant informed. "We were concerned that there might be some retribution."

"Why wasn't I told about it?" Nick asked, angrily. He had been thinking about this surveillance for thirty minutes now, and coming up with no answers, he was beginning to get very upset.

"Because you would have done everything you could have done to evade them," his lieutenant answered. "Thus defeating the point."

"Is that what this is?" Nick asked, unconvinced.

"I don't know," his lieutenant answered. "Give me some time to make a few calls, I'll find out what's going on and get back to you. In the meantime, try not to disable any more police cruisers."

Nick laughed, thanked his lieutenant and hung up his phone. After putting the phone down, Nick stared out the living room windows for a time. It did not make sense to him that three weeks after the Mullanno bust the police force would continue to authorize the expense of two police officers tailing one of their own, especially in a case like this. Even if the police force did authorize it, Nick could not imagine that New London police officers would be assigned to such a duty. Nick felt that there was something else going on, but he could not imagine what it was. The only thing he could do was wait it out. However, the police now knew that Nick knew of the surveillance, now all he could do is wait and see if that changed anything.

Chapter 13

31, 33, 44, 45, 51, Powerball 31. Alan Camden had already tuned out by the third number, knowing that he did not have any of the numbers matching those just called out on the screen. The sixty five year old man turned his attention back to his now warm beer, lifting it to his lips and draining the contents in one gulp. He placed the empty bottle back down on the pitted and scarred wooden bar counter, glanced to his right and caught the attention of the bar keeper leaning in the corner so as to get the best view of the television. The bartender reached under the counter and brought a new, cold bottle of beer into view, then took a couple of steps and placed it in front of Camden, removing the empty bottle in the same movement. Camden picked up the Powerball lottery ticket he had purchased this morning and turned it over. He had been playing the lottery with the same numbers for over twenty years, never winning so much as a dollar, but never giving up hope on the six numbers he choose. Camden turned his attention back to the eleven o'clock news, catching the end of the sports segment. This was Alan Camden's routine. He bought a lottery ticket in the morning, spent all day watching television, then went out to the bar at eight in the evening and stayed until twelve, making sure not to drink any more than six beers; his limit. This was what he did everyday but Fridays and Saturdays, when he spent his evenings at the Foxwoods Casino, sinking a couple hundred dollars into the slot machines.

Camden slowly drank his last beer, watching the television until a commercial came on, then turned his attention to the other patrons of the bar. He was pleased to see that it was basically the same old crowd; Camden liked things that stayed the same. His life had been one of monotony, and it had been that way for thirty two years. It had been that way since his wife left him. She left one day while he was at work, leaving him a note that she was taking off and would not be back. It hadn't really bothered Camden; the marriage had been bad since they had come back from their honeymoon. He had married because of the convenience of not having to date anymore. When he married, it was not because he loved her, but because he thought it was what he was supposed to do. However, he soon learned differently, and realized that this woman wanted a man that he would never be. She married him because she saw some potential in him, something he had never seen in himself. He was never unfaithful, never abusive, just never a real husband. She left, taking their six month old son with her. Two months later, he received divorce papers post marked from California.

His wife had marked the sections he needed to sign, and had even included a self addressed envelope for his convenience. She did not ask for alimony or child support, nor did she want any shared custody. This last fact suited Camden just fine, he had never wanted a child, he never thought he could be a good father, not with the role model his own father had been.

Camden finished the last sips of his beer earlier than usual. He placed the bottle down, pushed it forward to indicate that he was finished, and then rose from the barstool. The old man reached into his back right pocket of his soiled jeans and fished out a worn, black, leather wallet. He placed the appropriate amount of money on the counter, making sure to include the ten percent tip, waved to the bartender who was not paying attention, and stumbled out of the bar. Stepping out onto the sidewalk, Camden was assaulted by a bitter cold blast of wind that sobered him quickly, but not enough. Camden tucked his chin to his chest and crossed the parking lot, finding his white 1983 pickup truck, climbed inside and slowly drove home. The drive home from the bar was the only excitement Camden allowed himself on a daily basis. After drinking daily for over thirty years, his body had gotten used to the six beers he consumed nightly, however, Camden was always deathly afraid of getting into an accident, so he drove slowly and concentrated hard on the road, hoping that any passing police cruiser would not notice. The drive home took ten minutes, and though it felt longer, Camden was soon pulling into his driveway. He shut the car down, slowly climbed out of the cab, and made his way to the side door of the house. The old man could not remember the last time he used the front door, the only time he ever went down that hall was if the girl scouts were at the front door, selling cookies. Camden slid his key into the lock, pushed the door open and went inside and closed the door behind him. Sleep was starting to take over as Camden made his way down the hall to the living room, the room Camden spent all of his time in. He found his lounge chair, fell into it and slipped right into the reclining mode and was asleep within a minute.

Alan Camden's routine usually included a call to the bathroom at about two in the morning, however, when he awoke an hour after falling into the lounge chair; it was not a part of his usual schedule. Something had called to him, pulling at him from his unconscious state. There was a cold breeze continuously washing over him, and even in his state of sleep, his body knew that something was wrong. Camden opened his eyes, and immediately noticed something else. The television that sat in the corner of the room was not on. Camden had not turned the television off in months; he usually kept it on, the white light and soft noise comforting him, keeping him company. Now, however, the room was pitch black. The first thought Camden had been that the power must have gone out, but as he turned to the electric clock on the end table to his right, he saw the time displayed accurately. He had not put a battery in the clock for years and now whenever the power went out the numbers flashed until he reset the clock. Camden sat up straight in his chair and fumbled around for the remote control. Finding it, his fingers slid over the bumps until he found the one for the power and pressed it. Suddenly, the room was filled with white light and the volume blared. Turning his head away, Camden quickly lowered the sound to a low level. It was then that he was reminded of the cold, as a soft breeze washed over him again, causing goose bumps to rise on his arms. He shivered and turned his attention down the hall. There were no lights on and light of the television did not extend down the hall. Still shaking, Camden rose from his chair with a groan and slowly shuffled down the hall.

Camden reached the kitchen and found the door gaping open, with only the screen door closed. He could not remember whether or not he closed the door, though he could not ever remember leaving it open before. He pushed the door shut; pulling back on the door handle to make sure it was secure. He then turned away and headed back down the hall, stopped for a moment when he passed the bathroom, then went inside and shut the door. Emerging a few minutes later, he felt the breeze again. Frustration now mounting, he walked back down to the kitchen and found the door open again. Deep inside, he knew something was wrong, very wrong. It was something more than the breeze pushing the door open. He had made sure it was securely closed, and though his suspicion was mounting, he was still too drunk to put any real energy into his now mounting concern. With the door open, he checked both handles, making sure that they were both locked. He then slammed the door hard; pulling back on it again to make sure it was closed. He then turned and walked back down the dark hallway to the dark living room, and eased himself back into his chair. He closed his eyes and let the weight of his intoxication pull him back into sleep. However, there was a nagging pang of suspicion. He sighed, turned slightly in his chair and tried to concentrate on sleep. He reminded himself that he was in a dark, quiet place, trying to will himself into sleep. It was just then that he realized he was wrong. It should not be quiet or dark. He opened his eyes and stared out into the darkness.

"Son of a bitch," Camden whispered. The television was off again. He found the remote right where he left it, pressed the button and the light filled the room again. He pressed the button a few more times, turning the television on and off several times, and then placed the remote back on the end table. Just as he eased himself back into the reclining position, he heard a rustling upstairs. It was the floor boards creaking, a sound he had not heard in years. A chill of fear now washed over his body as he realized that he was not alone in the house.

Chapter 14

The Nemesis had been planning this moment for as long as he could remember. He had thought about this long before he knew who he was, long before puberty, long before he had first experienced the satisfaction of death. There had long been a hole inside him, a void from which the gravity caused a pain that it took him a long time to understand. That pain gnawed at him, causing him to become angry. After a while, that anger surfaced whenever he saw happiness and love; unfortunately, he saw it all the time. He saw it in his neighbors, he saw it in his classmates at school, and he saw it in nature. Everything that everyone else saw as cute, he saw as something else. Soon he was angry all the time, and the more he tried to hide it, the angrier he became. His parents attributed this to the fact that he did not have many friends at school. His father had tried to get him into sports, but he quickly realized that the boy was not athletically inclined. His father took him camping, but the young boy did not take to it, not being able to understand the appeal. Finally, his father gave up trying to find out anything about the boy. That was what had bothered The Nemesis the most. His father had given up; and it would be many years before he found out why.

His father had one ray of hope when on his ninth birthday, the young boy that would become the Nemesis asked for a pellet gun. His father had become encouraged by this request, hoping that this would lead the quiet, brooding boy into what he saw as a more "manly" direction. On the morning of his birthday, the young boy went directly for the long, rectangular package, knowing in his heart exactly what it was. Pulling the brightly colored wrapping paper from the box, the boy smiled with delight when he saw the picture of the compressed-air powered pellet rifle. He tore into the box, extracting the rifle by the plastic stock. He caressed the brown plastic that was made to resemble wood, and then eased his hand over the metal barrel, then back down to the trigger. He pressed the trigger, heard the click inside and smiled. He interrupted his father who had started to explain the responsibilities that came with owning the gun, reciting all of the rules his parents had laid down by heart. His father smiled, realizing that he must have said the same words fifty times since the time the boy had first shown an interest in the rifle.

Over the next few weeks, the young man practiced his marksmanship religiously. Once he was sure of himself, he started hunting. First it was inanimate objects, shooting the leaves off of trees and trash he found left in the woods behind his home. Then one day, while laying flat on a large rock, he spotted a squirrel. He watched the creature for hours, fascinated. Finally, without thinking about it, he aimed his rifle at the small unsuspecting animal and fired. He saw blood and a patch of fur fly into the air, then saw the animal lying on its side. The animal twitched just once, and then remained still. It was at that moment that he felt something lift within him, and as he lay there still on the rock, he desperately searched his mind and his emotions to understand what had just happened. It was hours before he realized that what he had felt at that moment was satisfaction. The Nemesis spent the rest of the summer trying to recreate the feeling, until he could find no more squirrels or birds to shoot at. He had found a joy that came from just inflicting the pain. There was joy in the thought of it, and there was profound happiness and satisfaction in the actual killing of the animals; but it was fleeting. It was like a drug high that dissipated as soon as it manifested, and he wanted to find a way to prolong the feeling.

The Nemesis heard the slamming of the door, and was torn from his memories into the present. Silently, he slipped down the hall, out of sight of the kitchen, and into the living room. The room wreaked, the odor of urine, rotting trash, and the stench of body odor caused his stomach to heave. However, the Nemesis controlled himself, concentrating now on the task at hand. He could not afford the trips down memory lane, not at a time like this. This was the dream, and he had to see it to fruition. He found the television remote exactly where it always was, pressed the power button and melted into the sudden darkness of the room. He heard the old man making his way down the hall, then heard a door close and knew that his prey was in the bathroom. The Nemesis quickly made his way back down the hall, turned when he reached the stairs and waited for the old man to flush the toilet. When he heard the sound, he bounded the steps two at a time until he reached the top, hoping the noise from the toilet would mask any sound the old steps would make. Waiting at the top of the stairs, listening for the old man, he heard Camden make his way back down the hall. He heard the creak of his old chair, and the Nemesis stepped carefully, making his way to the master bedroom.

Unwittingly, he slipped back into his memory, picking up right where he had left off, as if hitting the play button on a movie. He remembered how he had desperately wanted to prolong the joy he had when he killed the animal. He soon learned that wounding the animal, watching its reaction, caused his joy to linger until the he finally put the animal out of its misery. However, it wasn't until he once lured an unsuspecting cat over to him that he realized how to make the happiness and joy he felt last. The young boy quickly realized that there was a moment when any creature realized that they were betrayed, whether it be emotionally or physically, any creature; a moment of total dread and complete understanding. It was that moment that caused the most joy in the boy. It was that moment that he strived for; he practiced over and over again, until all the animals in the neighborhood were afraid of him. It was as if they sensed the kind of person he was, and that fear excited him.

Back in the present, the Nemesis moved as slowly and carefully as possible, until he entered the master bedroom, just as he had many times before. The Nemesis reached into his pants pocket and retrieved a small Mag-lite with a red plastic lens over the top of it. A small spot of red shown on the floor as he turned the light on then raised it over the unused furniture in the room, until he found the object he was looking for. There was a small glass jar with a candle inside, a candle that had not been lit in many years. Smiling to himself, the Nemesis walked over and doused his light, replaced it in his pocket and fished out a lighter. He lit the candle and stepped back, and as he did, he felt the floor boards ease underneath his weight, then heard something downstairs and was certain that Camden knew someone was in the house. In that instant, The Nemesis knew that the moment he had been waiting for all of his life was almost here.

Chapter 15

Alan Camden ascended the stairs of his home, fear coursing through his body, flipping on every light switch he passed. Many of the lights had not been turned on in years, and two of the bulbs blew the moment the electricity surged through them. Before going upstairs, Camden searched the hall closet, finding and arming himself with an old wooden baseball bat. He slowly climbed the stairs, clenching the bat tightly in his hands and trying desperately to fight off the wave of nausea that almost rendered his legs useless. As Camden reached the top of the stairs, a feeling of déjà vu overwhelmed him and he was suddenly transported to the memory of his past, finding his home empty and his wife gone. He had come home from work on a Tuesday, a day that had been ordinary enough. Usually, he would find his wife either in the kitchen or playing with the baby in the living room. However, on this day the house was quiet when he arrived home, no sign of life anywhere downstairs. He remembered climbing the stairs, unsuspecting. As he reached the top of the stairs, he saw the glow of the candlelight from the bedroom, the scent of his wife's perfume. He remembered looking over at the bed when he walked in, thinking that perhaps she would be in it. However, she wasn't; only a letter addressed to him lying on her pillow. Now Camden was there again, climbing the steps, seeing the candlelight. He was almost certain he could smell her perfume.

He remembered finding the room empty. He remembered reading the letter; and after all these years of denial, he remembered word for word what it said. She was gone, and though she did not say where, he knew that he would never find her, even if he cared to look. She had blamed herself, telling him that she had married him hoping to change him, hoping that he would become the man she knew he could be. She told him how she had purposely not taken her birth control so that she would get pregnant; hoping that a baby would help to change his perspective, make him more family-oriented. She wrote about how sorry she was for trapping him, how she felt as though she were responsible for making them both unhappy. He read the letter over and over again, and every time he read it he knew it was a lie. He knew that it was he who was responsible; she had never lied to him. He had known from the beginning that she had wanted a family; he had known that she wanted to be happy. However, he had always been afraid of her. She was so much smarter than he, and she was so beautiful. She was so much better than he, and he was so afraid of losing her. That was what had caused him to act the way he did, and his worst fear had come true.

He had lost her. He remembered how he fell asleep holding the letter, weeping aloud. When he woke, he read the letter again, and this time he accepted it. He accepted the lie that she wrote, convinced himself it was her fault, and buried all of his true feelings.

In that moment standing at the top of the stairs, he saw himself both then and now. He was suddenly disgusted, repulsed at the man he had become. In losing her, he had lost himself. He had given up on himself, and settled down to become the pitiful, drunken, bitter old man that he now was. For so long he had thought of her as the darkness, a cancer that had grown and taken over his soul, taking away the will to live life. However, he now understood that she had really been the light. Had he tried just a little, he would have found that she was what inspired him to be a good man, a great man. Instead, he had squandered her, in every way one human can squander the greatest gift of his life. His fear was the cancer, his fear was the darkness.

Suddenly, he realized that he was standing at the top of the stairs, transfixed by the glow coming from the master bedroom. Staring at the doorway, he felt a burning in his chest and realized he was holding his breath. Without knowing it, his arms had gone limp as he dropped the bat on the floor. He forced himself to take a step forward, and then a second. Time had seemed to slow, and his memory of that past day was intertwined with the present. He found himself longing, hoping that she would be in the bed, praying that the last forty years had been a nightmare. However, as he stepped through the threshold, all of his hopes were dashed. He looked over at the bed, and there again was a letter addressed to him. He gasped aloud, tears surging from the depths. He had not slept in this room since his wife left. He had buried the memory of this day, unwilling to accept his role in her leaving. As he moved towards the bed, he felt as though he were moving in slow motion. He reached out for the letter, emotions he had not allowed himself to experience washing over him. He could no longer distinguish between reality and his memory. All he knew was that he was experiencing the worst moment of his life; again. He grasped the envelope in his hands and flipped up the flap, finding the envelope empty just like his life. He put it up to his face, tears streaming down, hoping to catch a whiff of perfume. It was at that moment that he sensed movement at the far end of the room, and as he looked up, he saw Death approaching and he smiled.

Chapter 16

Jack felt the school bus lurch to a stop and pulled his backpack towards him, dreading the next few seconds of his life. Twice a day he had to make the long walk passed the kids on the bus, it took ten seconds to walk from the seat he occupied to the front of the bus, he knew the time by heart. That was twenty seconds a day that Jack felt as if he were taking the final walk down death row. Every child on the bus stared at him as he would walk passed, some stared in curiosity, as if looking at some disfigured creature in a zoo. Others stared at him in fear and hatred. Jack had not been fortunate when it came to making friends; he was quiet and unassuming, but there were rumors about him, rumors that had plagued him since elementary school. Some rumors told of how he almost killed another boy while playing football, while other rumors were that he had just hospitalized the boy. While neither of the rumors were true, the incident had become a legend very quickly, spreading across the school like wild fire. And like a fire, it grew with every telling of the story until this latest ridiculous version became what was believed. There were other rumors, rumors that he liked to kill animals. Rumors that he shot and tortured small animals for his amusement. This one was more or less true, far more accurate than the story about the football game, and to some, far more frightening.

These rumors did not make it easy for him to make friends. He tried many times, joined teams and clubs to meet new people, but it did not take long for others to realize how different Jack was. It did not take long for them to make it clear to Jack that he was to stay away from them. He tried to explain to them that the rumors were just that, rumors but the other kids were more willing to believe the exotic lie than accept the more plausible truth. When Jack reached high school, he was terrified that these rumors would make him a target of bullies. However, he quickly found that the rumors had lent him such a mystique, that even the bullies were afraid to see if he was really as crazy as everyone made him out to be. The jocks and the bullies left him alone, and after a while, Jack stopped trying to quash the rumors. In the end, he just let the other kids think what they wanted to think; he knew that it would not change anything anyway. Now he was walking with his backpack over his shoulder towards the front of the bus, trying to act as though he did not notice the eyes staring through him. He skipped down the steps and onto the street, heard the bus doors slam shut and the diesel motor growl as the bus driver stepped on the gas and was gone down the street.

Jack sighed and started walking down the street towards his home. The walk home always felt as though it would never end. When he was in middle school there was a young girl who he rode the bus with, and walking to the bus stop never seemed to take so long when he had someone to talk to. However, she grew up to be pretty and popular, and in high school, riding the bus was a sign of your social and economic status, and she was not destined to ride the bus for long. He had not seen that girl in many years, he could not even remember her name. Jack sighed again and crossed over to the side of the street where his house sat. As he looked up ahead, he saw his father's pick-up parked out on the street. He immediately realized that there was something odd going on, his father never parked his truck out on the curb. The pick up was always parked in the driveway, right smack dab in the middle, as if he were showing it off to the neighborhood. Because his father parked it there, purposely so that no other car could park alongside, his mother was forced to park her little beat up compact car on the curb. Now, as Jack turned came around the bend, he saw both cars on the curb, and he knew that something was going on in the house. His father was never home so early, not in good weather when there was a little league baseball team to coach, or a pee wee football team to intimidate. Jack reached the door and opened it slowly, careful not to make any noise.

As he stepped inside, he immediately heard the raised voices and the barrage of insults coming from the back of the house. Jack quickly closed the door, quickly but cautiously. His mother was always terrified of the neighborhood becoming aware of their personal business, but Jack also did not want to let his parents know that he was home. He hated when they fought, but at the same time, he liked it. When his parents were fighting, they seemed to be more attentive and caring to him. Even his father would pay attention to him and talk to him as though he were an adult. It was as though they were so desperate for someone in the house to be on their side, that they would try to coerce him to one side or the other. Sadly, Jack realized that those times were the only times that he felt truly loved, it was the only time when he felt as though he were even wanted. Jack crept down the hallway to his room and slipped inside, easing the door closed but making sure not to close it all the way. He would listen intently to their fights, in some ways, hoping that one of them would be fighting in favor of him. However, that happened very rarely and when it did, it was usually his mother trying to get his father to pay more attention to him. However, as he listened, he realized that this fight was much worse, this was the fight to end all fights.

"What do you mean you're leaving," he heard his mother scream. "We're a family. You don't just walk out on your family."

"I've had enough of this family," his father answered. "If that's what you want to call it. I never planned on this, this wasn't what I signed up for. I'm not going to grow old with the two of you hanging off of me."

"I thought you wanted a family," she cried. Jack could hear her sucking in her breath hard as she tried to talk and cry at the same time.

"This isn't a family," his father shot back. "It's the two of you and then there's me. I can't live like that."

Jack was taken aback for a moment. He never thought that his father felt that way. If anything it was Jack who felt that he was the one left out of the family, that it was his mother and father and then it was him, the disappointment.

"What about Jack?" his mother asked, desperate for anything that might make her husband change his mind. This is where Jack focused all of his attention. He even held his breath in anticipation of the answer to come.

"What about him?" his father asked, storming down the hall. Jack pasted himself against the wall behind the door, holding his breath, praying that they would not realize he was home. "It's not like I'm his real father."

Suddenly, Jack stood there paralyzed, sure that he had misheard his father's answer. He quickly replayed the question and answer back in his head to make sure that he heard it right.

"You're the only father he's ever known," his mother answered.

"He's not my son," his father replied. "I mean look at him, he's useless. He's his father's son alright, it's no wonder you left him."

Without realizing it, Jack had removed himself from his position on the wall and started to exit his room. He watched as his mother blocked her husband's way in the hall, a last ditch effort to make him stay. He just grabbed her and threw her roughly to the ground. He stepped over her and she was quickly back on her feet, following him out the door. Apparently, they had been too focused on each other to notice Jack standing in the hallway, in shock. He heard them continue as they went outside, a distinct violation of his mother's neighborhood code of ethics. Jack continued to walk down the hall until he was standing in the living room, looking out through the bay windows onto the front yard. Now they were just screaming at each other, none of their words making any sense. His mother's end of the argument was quickly degenerating into a slur of obscenities and as his father climbed into his pick-up truck she grabbed a ceramic frog from the edge of the tiny garden on the lawn and heaved it at the truck. The ceramic ornament landed harmlessly in the bed of the truck and his father peeled out onto the street and disappeared around the bend. Jack watched as his mother collapsed on the lawn. She sat there crying, Jack standing in the living room watching, replaying the scene over and over in his mind. His mother tried to get up, but lacking the strength, started crawling on all fours. She looked up and saw Jack standing in the window. Their eyes locked for just a moment and then he turned away. Jack didn't see his mother collapse back onto the lawn, but was aware that she did not come back inside for hours. Jack went back into his room and closed the door. All he knew what that his life had been a lie. Nothing anyone had ever told him had ever been the truth. The young man wanted to vomit as he looked around the room and saw nothing but a lie. It was at that moment that Jack knew he was truly alone, and it was that moment that he swore that he would find out who he truly was.

Chapter 17

The Nemesis moved across the room quickly, hoping to startle the old man as he stood there overcome by emotion. However, the moment he detached himself from the shadows in the far corner of the room, Camden looked up, noting the sudden movement. The old man looked puzzled for just a moment, and the Nemesis knew that he must use this opportunity to his advantage. He yanked the knife out from behind him, raising it high above his head, wanting nothing more than to plunge it deep into the old man's chest. As he moved closer Camden smiled; a soft, almost caring smile. Something about it caught the Nemesis off guard, causing him to hesitate for just a moment. The two men caught each other's gaze; the Nemesis nearly stopped and stared at the man. He searched his mind quickly for any feelings or emotions, any reason for which he should not do what he came here to do. The Nemesis felt nothing, only the anticipation of what was to come, and with lightning reflexes, slashed the knife out at Camden's throat, severing muscle, arteries, and veins. The old man instinctively reached for his throat as warm spurts of blood gushed out of the wound. The old man pressed his right hand against his throat in a useless attempt to stop the bleeding. The Nemesis stabbed out again, this time pushing the blade through the old man's right hand and into the bloody wound. Camden fell to the floor as the killer stabbed him, causing the knife to yank free of the old man's flesh.

The Nemesis stepped back, watching his victim flail around on the floor. There was no sound other than the soft gurgling sound of Camden's attempts to breathe through the blood that was oozing down his windpipe. The killer took two steps backwards, transfixed by the image that lay before him. He had been planning this murder for so long, hoping that this one event would bring a kind of joy to him that nothing else ever had. However, now standing over the dying man, there was very little satisfaction at all. Something about the way the man had smiled at him had disarmed the Nemesis, causing him to think twice. He wondered what the old man had been thinking at that moment, but it didn't matter now. As he watched the last twitches of life wane from the old man, he was reminded of the larger picture. The Nemesis was here with a purpose. He had been fortunate that this particular murder would serve two purposes, but now that his victim was finally dead he was forced to focus on the task at hand.

The Nemesis now alone again, turned away from the dead body and walked back over to the dark corner. He reached down, lifting a black canvas backpack from the shadows where he had placed it when hiding from Camden. Stepping away from the corner, he placed the bag on the floor and opened it, retrieving first two latex gloves. Replacing his knife and donning his gloves, he then reached back into his bag and pulled from inside a piece of paper, a brown clipboard, and an old style fountain pen. Then, returning to the lifeless body, he kneeled down and dipped the fountain pen into the bloody wound, then placed the pen against the paper and began to write. The blood was thicker and more difficult to write with than he had imagined, causing him to take longer with the letter than he had expected. However, he concentrated on the letter, writing the words slowly, relaying the message that he had agonized over for so long. Once finished, he folded the paper and addressed it with the person's name and then placed it on the bed.

Walking back over to the backpack, he removed his gloves, pulling them off so they would not drip any blood. He retrieved a plastic bag from inside his backpack, and placed the gloves inside. He took the fountain pen and clipboard and slipped them carefully back into their place in the bag. He then slipped his hands into a fresh pair of gloves, closed the backpack, threw it over his shoulders, and walked out of the room. He moved quickly down the stairs, down the hall back toward the living room. Using only the light from the television, he searched the room for the phone, and once finding it, he dialed 911. An emergency operator answered immediately, and the killer relayed his message. He then hung up the phone and made his way out of the house, satisfied with his work. He knew that he would still get the euphoric high that he so needed. Even though he had not derived the satisfaction he usually got at the time of the murder, he knew that by replaying it in his mind, he would get the full pleasure he deserved. As he closed the kitchen door behind him, he stopped for a moment and listened. All was quiet outside; no one had seemed to take any notice. It was three thirty in the morning and everyone was probably asleep, however, he would take no chances. He disappeared back behind the house, heading back the way he had come. His car was a quarter of a mile down the road, and if he was careful he would make it back unseen. He moved quickly, the police would be here soon, and then everyone in the neighborhood would take notice of Alan Camden; deceased.

Chapter 18

Nick sat at the counter of his local diner, a large plate of scrambled eggs, bacon, sausage links, and hashbrowns sitting directly in front of him and the day's paper to his right. Nick read each article, pausing only for a bite of his breakfast, than diving back into the news. There was nothing terribly exciting; the national news was the same as it always was. The local economy was taking a dive, and there was a story about the murder in Groton two days earlier. The reporter seemed to focus on the fact that the police were not giving out any information regarding the case, alluding to his readers that the police had no leads or clues to follow. That was the only article Nick read twice. He hated rookie reporters, most of whom were looking for a conspiracy in every story they wrote. Nick folded his paper, pushed it away and focused on his plate full of food. He waved down a waitress, ordered another tall glass of orange juice and started gnawing on a strip of bacon. There were only two other patrons at the counter and there were three elderly couples sitting at booths and tables around the diner. As he ate, Nick pondered over the business the diner received, wondering how they were able to remain open in a small town like Salem. Nick heard the chime of the bell fastened to the top of the front door, and felt a cold breeze rushing in. A hush fell over the diner, as if all the customers held there breathe as they were assaulted by the sudden rush of icy cold air. Then the door swung shut with a heavy thud as the door slammed against the frame, and the patrons returned to their conversations.

The waitress approached, sliding the glass of orange juice in front of Nick, though she did not make eye contact with him. Her concentration was focused on the customer that just walked in. She asked the customer a question that Nick did not hear, and then turned and walked away.

"Is this seat taken?" asked a female voice directly behind Nick. Nick turned and looked at the stool beside him, then up at the woman.

"No," he answered, realizing that he did not know her. Most people in Salem did not talk to, let alone sit directly beside a person they did not know, not unless they had to. However, the new comer sat down in the stool directly to the right of him, dropped a folder on the counter and started to remove her gloves, placing them on top of the counter.

"Can I get a cup of coffee; black," the woman asked the waitress as she passed by.

Nick focused on his plate, trying to contain his annoyance by the interruption of the woman next to him. He felt slightly uncomfortable; having someone he did not know sitting so close to him when there were plenty of other seats around the counter. He felt the same way in movie theaters when there were plenty of open seats but someone came and sat down beside you, not observing the empty seat buffer zone rule, the unspoken rule known to everyone. Nick realized that he was starting to feel more and more uncomfortable, and looked over to see the woman staring at him. He smiled and turned away, picking up the paper and began reading an article he had already read.

"You're Nicholas Grenier, aren't you?" the woman asked.

Nick sighed and closed his eyes for a moment, then opened them and turned to the woman.

"That's right," he said, curtly.

"I saw you on television," she said. "You looked better on the T.V."

"Thanks," he answered, turning back to his paper. He was unsure of how to take the comment.

"That was a pretty shifty thing you did to my detectives, disabling their car and all," the woman said, still staring at him. "You popped all four tires."

125

"The city can bill me," Nick answered, turning away from his paper to look at the woman. "Why were they following me?"

"How long are you going to be on leave?" the woman asked, ignoring his question.

"Until I can find a reason to come back," Nick answered, frustrated by her unwillingness to answer him.

"What are you going to do in the meantime?" she asked.

"I'm going to try to finish my eggs," Nick answered, pointing to his plate. The woman smiled and turned away.

"Fair enough," she said, taking the steaming cup of coffee into her hands. She watched her coffee for a moment, watching the wisps of steam rise and dance around each other before they disappeared. "Have you heard about that murder in Groton a couple of nights ago?"

Nick turned and looked at her, shifting on his stool to look directly at her.

"Yeah, I read about it in the paper," Nick answered. "Are you part of the investigation?"

"You couldn't have gotten much information from the paper," the woman stated.

"Look, if you're not going to tell me what the hell you want, then why don't you leave me alone so I can finish my breakfast," Nick said, turning away from her and staring down at his plate.

"My name is Brenda Hollings," the woman said. "I'm the head of Investigative Unit in New London."

Nick turned back to the woman, scrutinizing her. He had heard the name Hollings before, but found it hard to believe that this woman next to him fit the person he heard about.

"You're Detective Hollings?" Nick asked, suspiciously. "The same Hollings that was responsible for cracking those murders in Greenwich a couple of years ago."

"It was seven years ago," Hollings answered. "And it's Lieutenant Hollings now."

"Damn," Nick muttered softly, unable to hide his admiration.

"I'm not what you expected?" she asked, amused.

"I don't know what I expected," he answered. "I just didn't know you were still with the police department."

"We don't get a lot of high profile cases in New London," she answered, pausing to sip her coffee.

"However, I was asked to take over the murder of that girl in Groton by the governor."

"Congratulations," Nick said sarcastically. "Then why are you here talking to me?"

"I'd like you to take a look at my case," she answered. "I'm interested in what you think."

"I may have been promoted to detective, but I'm not really one," Nick informed her. "I've never worked a homicide before."

"I know," Hollings answered. "But I'm not the one who wants you involved."
Nick looked up at Hollings, questioningly.

"Oh yeah," Nick said. "Then who does?"
Hollings removed her gloves from the top of the folder on the counter and slid it over to him; the folder came to rest against his plate.

"The killer," she answered, staring at him. Nick put his fork down and passed his hand over the folder, feeling it with his fingers. "Why don't you come and take a ride with me."

Chapter 19

Nick sat in the passenger seat of the unmarked cruiser as Hollings drove, swearing and weaving in and out of traffic. Route 85 into New London was a two lane road with no way to pass other drivers. Hollings turned on the strobe lights that were located next to the headlights. Nick tried to watch her driving for a few minutes, and then figured he'd rather not know when she came dangerously close to two vehicles from the other lane as she tried to pass a slower moving car. To take his mind off of the peril that lay ahead, he thumbed through the file that Hollings had slipped him in the diner. He first looked at the file name marked CAMDEN, ALAN; he thought for a moment, trying to page through his memory to see if the name should have stirred some familiar note from the past. However, he did not know anyone named Camden, and when he opened the file, crime scene photos slipped out. Nick caught the photos in his lap, turned them right side up and stared at them intently. Hollings glanced over to him periodically, as he studied each picture, committing each to memory.

"I thought you said it was a woman who was murdered," Nick stated.

"These are from a murder early this morning," Hollings answered. "We've been investigating it since four a.m. These are unofficial digital photos that I had put together for you to review."

"I assume you think it's the same killer as the other woman," Nick said.

"There are some similarities," Hollings answered, pulling hard on the wheel as she swerved past another car. "They see the lights, why don't these fuckers pull over."

Nick smiled for a moment, deciding not to mention the momentary lapse in etiquette. He held onto the handle over the door as his body was pushed into the passenger side door. The photos began to slip again and he tried to adjust his legs to keep from spilling them, but as he did, Hollings pulled back in the other direction, causing them to fall to the floor. Just as he bent to retrieve the pictures, he noticed a piece of paper in an evidence bag, and pulling up to his face.

"Is this written in blood?" Nick asked, afraid of the answer.

"We think so," Hollings answered. "We haven't had it tested or anything though."

Nick focused on the letter and began to read.

Detective Nicholas Grenier,

I am sorry that I was not able to adequately capture your attention with my last work of art, but I am sure by writing to you directly, I will be honored with your full attention from now on. Please don't blame yourself for this one; he was always on my list. I am sure you are very confused, having to focus on this while dealing with this difficult time in your life. All I can do is assure you that what I am doing is for your benefit. As you read this, there are some things I need you to understand. First, this is not a game. I am not crazy, and I am not trying to play a game of CAT and MOUSE with you. As you will come to understand, I am DEADLY serious. Second, I realize that I will be caught sooner or later. This thought does not scare me, as I know that everybody makes mistakes. I do want you to know that I don't intend to stop; I am doing what I was created to do. This is something that you will come to understand all too well in time. Finally, I am not your enemy. This probably does not make sense to you now, but it will as time goes on. I hope that you will take these points to heart and not make the mistake of disregarding these facts. I look forward to meeting you in person, and helping you to find yourself. As I have said before, I know what you are going through right now, and I hope that I can be some benefit to you.

Yours truly,
The Nemesis

Nick read the letter several times, first reading it for the message that The Nemesis was trying to relay, then checking it grammatically, and finally, memorizing the letter. Once he was finished with the note, he placed the plastic bag back into the folder, placed the crime scene photos on top of it, and closed the folder.

"This is why you involved me in this case?" Nick asked. As he read the letter the second time, he had no doubt that it came from the same person who called him a few nights before. If Nick was to believe what the Nemesis said, the death of the woman in Groton had been to get Nick's attention.

"The woman murdered in Groton was named Tracy Scott," Hollings began. "She was cut up many times, as if filleted like a fish. I don't have those pictures with me, but you can check them out later. One of the first things we did was run a check on her phone, checking incoming and outgoing calls."

Nick closed his eyes now, knowing what was coming next.

"We can't be absolutely sure of her time of death," Hollings continued. "We found a call to your home number, lasting about three minutes, either just before or just after she was killed."

"It was after," Nick responded, his eyes closed and his head down. "Can you pull over for a moment?"

Hollings said nothing, just eased the cruiser off the road. Everything now made sense to Nick; Hollings had put him under surveillance the moment they found the call to his home. Now with this note, they did not suspect him as the killer, but they still suspected him.

"You want to tell me what the hell is going on?" Hollings asked, shifting the cruiser into park.

"A couple of nights ago, I got this weird call," Nick started, thinking back to that night. "A man called me and said he understood what I was going through, and told me he had given me a gift. I immediately thought it was a crank call."

"What did he mean he knew what you were going through?" Hollings asked.

The detective hesitated a moment, wanting to make it clear to Hollings without expressing his true feelings.

"The man said I was feeling lost, like I did not know what to do with my life, and said he wanted to help me," Nick answered. "Like I said, I hung up thinking it was a crank call."

"Is there anything else?" Hollings asked.

"Nothing I can think of," Nick answered.

"Is he right about you?" Hollings asked, staring at him intently.

"Right about what?" Nick asked, acting as if he did not understand. However, he knew exactly what she was asking. She had been able to see right through her.

"Are you lost?" Hollings clarified, her eyebrows raised in anticipation.

"No," Nick answered with a smile. "We are entering Waterford on Route 85. If you take the second right down here, it will take you to the Interstate 95 on ramp."

Hollings stared at Nick for a moment, and then smiled. Nick was afraid she was going to push the issue. He did not really want to talk about any inner turmoil right now.

"So the gift he was talking about was Tracy Scott," Hollings said, more to herself than to her passenger.

"Or the murder of Tracy Scott," Nick interjected. Hollings looked up at him suddenly, as if jarred from her train of thought.

"Well, for whatever reason, this killer wants you involved," Hollings said, turning back to face the steering wheel. She shifted the car into drive and peeled onto the road.

"So where are we going now?" Nick asked, desperately holding onto the handle above the door.

"We're going to give him what he wants," Hollings muttered, weaving through traffic again.

Chapter 20

Lieutenant Hollings pulled the car over to the side of the road with a jolt, the passenger side front wheel going up over the curb, leaving the car at an awkward angle. As Nick climbed out of the car, he saw a group of neighbors standing on the far side of the street, huddled together for warmth, and whispering in hushed voices about what was going on across the street. Hollings slammed her car door and motioned for Nick to follow her. He crossed the street with her, watching as a young uniformed officer wrapped crime scene tape around the yard, blocking it off from intruders. Men and women entered and exited the house, some in uniform and others in plain clothes. Hollings and Nick ducked under the crime scene tape, and walked into the front yard to where a group of three men were standing together. As they approached, the three men fell silent and seemed to suck in the chests. Nick hung back as Hollings walked over to the three men, choosing instead to survey the area. There was something deeply depressing about the entire scene, and Nick wondered if it stemmed from knowing that a murder had taken place here. He wondered what the on-lookers were thinking as they braved the blistering cold to get the latest scoop and gossip about their neighbor.

On the other side of the crime scene tape, however, everything was different. There was a buzz about the house as everyone went about their individual jobs, like bees whose singular purpose served the whole. The crime scene was like a bubble of activity in this bleak cold and otherwise quiet neighborhood. Nick looked around for an ambulance or the medical examiners van, but saw neither. He was sure that the medical examiner had removed the body by now, but was pleased to see the Crime Scene Unit personnel still working. Nick thought that he would have felt out of place here, but something inside him felt comforted. There was a warm feeling inside that he could only attribute to working as a police officer again.

"Nick," Hollings called out from a few steps away. Nick turned and saw her standing with the three men, all looking at him. Nick walked over quickly. "I'd like you to meet my detectives."

Hollings introduced the three men as Mark Anderson, Peter Wilkins, and Andrew Mitchell. Anderson and Wilkins were both quite a bit older than Mitchell and Nick determined immediately that the older two men were the senior detectives in the unit. Mitchell looked a few years younger than Nick and seemed to him to be very wide-eyed and eager. Nick knew that he could not have been in the unit for very long. However, Mitchell shook Nick's hand vigorously and seemed genuinely pleased to meet him, where the older detectives seemed very suspicious of him. Nick could not be sure if they were suspicious of him because of his association with the killer, or because he was a new-comer, but he was definitely sensing some hostility.

"CSU is still working in there," Anderson started, obviously addressing Hollings. Nick could tell that Anderson was trying to keep him out, going so far as to turn his back to him as if to block him from the conversation. All Nick could do was shake his head and smile. "They are not going to let us in until they're done."

"And the body?" Hollings asked, sensing the attitudes of her detectives.

"They took the body out of here just after you left," Anderson answered. "That was a little over an hour ago."

"We are doing some preliminary interviews of the neighbors," Wilkins chimed in. "But it doesn't sound like anyone really knew the victim. We'll keep asking around, but I don't think we'll get much from them."

Hollings gave the three men some further instructions and then turned to talk to Nick, but he had already walked away. Nick could understand why the senior detectives did not want him butting in to their investigation, especially when the only reason he was here was because he was somehow connected to the killer. However, Nick did not want to fight with them, nor did he want to sit there asking questions and only getting a two word answer, giving him no real information. Nick decided instead to do his own little investigation, and walked over to the front door, where men and women were coming and going. Nick walked up to the front door and looked inside. He saw flashes coming from down the hall and from up the stairs, where pictures were being taken. Nick craned his head around, trying to get a general layout of the house. Directly to the right of the front door was the staircase leading upstairs, straight down the hall was what looked like the living room, and there were two doors on the right hand side of the hall, and one area on the left that looked as if it opened into the kitchen. From where he stood, Nick could barely make out another opening on the far side of the kitchen where he assumed the dining room was.

"Hey, what the hell are you doing?" yelled out a male voice from down the hall. Nick looked up quickly, realizing that the voice was talking to him.

"I'm a detective," Nick said to the angry man standing at the far end of the hall. "I was wondering how long it will be before we can come in."

"As long as it takes," the angry man answered, directly. Nick could tell that he was the head of this particular unit.

"I was wondering if I could just step in and get a sense of the scene," Nick said, probingly.

"Hell no," the man spat. "I'm not having any dumb-assed detectives traipsing through my crime scene, destroying all the evidence. You should have been here earlier."

Nick shrugged and muttered something under his breath, then turned and walked back down the steps to the sidewalk. Anderson and Wilkins were still talking to Hollings, but as Nick crossed into the grass, he was approached by Andrew Mitchell.

"Hey man," Mitchell started. "You're not going to make many friends by stepping on everyone's toes."

"With all due respect," Nick started. "I don't give a fuck about anyone's feelings. I don't even want to be here, but it doesn't seem like I have much of a choice. I just want to get some answers without having to go three rounds with anyone."

"Well, you won't get any help from those two," Mitchell informed him, pointing back to Anderson and Wilkins. "They've been in this unit for seven years and they don't like new people, especially you."

"I gathered," Nick answered. "But I'm still going to have to get information. Maybe you can help me?"

"I'd be glad to," Mitchell answered. "They aren't much warmer to me than they were to you. I think it's a territorial issue."

"You don't think it's a racial thing?" Nick asked, trying to get an understanding of the other men, and also trying to get a good sense Mitchell.

"I don't think so," answered Mitchell without hesitation. "I'm not the only black guy in the department, and then there's Hollings. They love her."

"I bet," Nick laughed. "Well, what can you tell me about this murder?"

"Not much," Mitchell answered. "This investigation is really in its infancy. The victim is Alan Camden, a sixty-something year old man. He was killed upstairs in the master bedroom, his throat cut. There's blood everywhere, and it looks like he just bled out. There were some candles burning when the cops arrived."

"Who called it in? Nick asked.

"The call seems to have come from this house," Mitchell answered. "Though the cops arrived within five minutes, and there was a substantial amount of blood on the floor. It looks like Camden was already dead when the call was made."

"Which means it was the killer who called it in," Nick muttered under his breath.

"Yeah, but why would the killer call it in?" Mitchell asked. "Wouldn't he want to get as much time as possible before anyone knew he was dead? This guy might not have been found for days, and by then any possible witnesses might not remember anything."

"Because he wants us to know what he's done," Nick said, staring off into the distance. "This killer is proud of his work, and wants us to know he's killed as soon as possible. This isn't a regular murder."

"What do you mean?" Mitchell asked, but Nick waved his question off. Something was going through Nick's mind, something telling him what he was staring at was important.

Nick walked around the side of the house to where the car was parked in the driveway. He then looked up at the side door, which looked as if it led into the kitchen. On the sidewalk in front of the door was a small patch of mud in the form of a heel footprint. Nick knelt in front of the print and looked back and forth into the grass of the front and back yard.

"Has CSU run the evidence out here?" Nick asked.

"No," Mitchell answered. "They focused on the murder scene. This footprint could have been left by anyone."

"No," Nick corrected him. "It was made by the killer. Do you live in a house or an apartment?"

"An apartment," Mitchell answered suspiciously.

"When you were a kid, did you have a side door into the house from the garage?" Nick asked.

"Yeah," the younger detective answered.

"And I'll bet you used that door every time you left and came home," Nick said.

"Yeah," Mitchell responded. "But that print could still be Camden's."

"Do you see any mud around here?" Nick asked, pointing along the sidewalk and around the driveway.

"No, but..." Mitchell started. Nick motioned for him to kneel down and then pointed out over the grass of the backyard.

"Do you see those patches of disturbed grass?" Nick asked. "Those small areas that look darker than the grass around it, do you see how they're spaced..."

"They're footsteps," Mitchell gasped, cutting Nick off. "Holy shit."

"Yep," Nick answered. "They're footsteps."

"The killer came in from the woods," Mitchell said excitedly, following the patches from the woods to the sidewalk. "He picked up this dirt stuff from the woods and tracked it here."

"He probably wiped his feet on the mat here," Nick surmised, motioning to the worn doormat that lay in front of the door. "That's why there were no footprints inside."

"Damn," Mitchell exclaimed. "I thought you'd never worked a homicide before."

"I haven't," Nick answered. "Go get a CSU photographer. Have him take a picture of the footprint from directly overhead. Then have him get pictures of the sidewalk, the doormat and this door. Then have him get down on his knees and get pictures of the footsteps in the grass."

"What are you going to do?" Mitchell asked, heading back to the house.

"I'm going to see where these footsteps lead," Nick answered.

Chapter 21

The Nemesis stood under the burning hot stream of water flowing out of the shower, hot steam rising up all around him, shrouding the bathroom. The hot water burned into his skin, causing him to wince at first, then relax as his body became accustomed to the extreme temperature. He let the water run over his body, feeling the frustration, exhaustion, and excitement wash away. The Nemesis tilted his head back allowing the water to wash over his hair and face. *This night was a disaster*, he thought to himself. He stood upright and opened his eyes, peering through the thick blanket of steam that now filled the room like a dense fog. He then hung his head down and backed into the hot spray, as if stepping into a cloak of water that removed him from the world. The Nemesis had felt a deep frustration since leaving Camden's home. The murder of the old man had not been all what it could have been, and was certainly not what it should have been. There had been such joy and satisfaction in The Nemesis's dreams of the death of Camden; a vindication and emotional fulfillment that he had not experienced during the actual murder. He first realized his frustration when he was making the long drive back to his home, and the longer it took for him to get home, the more frustrated he became.

When The Nemesis had finally reached his home, he saw the soft subtle change of color off to the east, indicating the rise of the new morning sun in the next few hours. He stripped off his clothing the moment he closed the front door and stepped onto the thick plastic trash bag he had laid on the floor before going out the previous night. Once completely naked, he stepped off the bag and made his way to the bathroom, where he climbed into the shower to find some peace. However, now standing there reliving the crime over and over, he realized that there would be no peace, not this morning, not tomorrow; not unless he killed again. This was the first time that The Nemesis had not been able to derive any enjoyment from killing. He had always thought of himself as a hungry predator, someone who only killed when he needed it. However, lately the need to kill had come more often, the intervals between kills becoming shorter. Though this was only the second person he had ever killed, his brutal killing of animals had eased his need to end life for a long time. However, like an animal that tastes human flesh, only killing people would do now. *The frustration after killing Camden had been a fluke*, he told himself. He had derived much satisfaction after the death of Tracy Scott. Even now, he could still feel that excitement, the thrill of watching her die. There had been none of that with Camden; he had built up this particular murder in his mind so much that the real thing could not come close to meeting his expectations. He knew that he would have to let this one go, there was nothing he could do about it now. The understanding that The Nemesis had hoped Camden would have in his last moments of life did not come, and in that moment, standing under the torrent of near scalding water, The Nemesis came to terms with last night, knowing the only satisfaction he would carry out of it was that Camden was dead.

Even as The Nemesis stood there, after coming to terms with the disappointment of last night, he still had the lingering need to kill again. It was like an itch that if not scratched, it would just get more and more annoying until he did something about it. His heart raced as he thought of killing again, so soon after Camden's murder. As he lathered himself under a bar of soap, his mind was in conflict with his emotions. He knew that he should not attempt another murder yet, especially without the proper preparation. However, the need was rising, bubbling up like a pot about to boil. Even though the police were not on to him, it did not mean that he was safe. In every murder, there were always mistakes; it was inevitable. Being careful, planning, allowed The Nemesis to limit such mistakes, leaving only infinitesimal clues to be found by the Crime Scene unit, if found at all. Going out on a killing tonight was a rash and foolish idea, though very exciting. *It can't hurt to look*, The Nemesis told himself; a devilish smile spreading across his face. With that, he turned in the shower and grabbed the faucet nozzle, turning it sharply to the cold side. The water temperature changed instantly, and The Nemesis almost fell to his knees as the frigid water knocked the wind out of him. After quickly washing the soap off, he turned the shower off and stepped out into the bathroom.

With the water off, the house was unusually quiet making him aware suddenly of how empty the place was. He wrapped himself in a towel, opened the bathroom door and walked down the hall, pausing in the living room briefly to turn on the television. He then padded down to his room, where he dressed quickly. In his everyday life, The Nemesis was a creature of habit, someone who was obsessed with order. It was this trait that made him good at his job. As he opened the accordion style closet door, he was filled with satisfaction as he looked at the row of suits, all wrapped in plastic from the cleaners, as if sterile. Inside their clear bags, he could see his button down shirt specifically chosen for each suit, the slacks and jacket. The only thing not inside was the belt, which was hung on the hangar over the plastic. The Nemesis allowed his fingers to pass down the row of suits, his mind placed at ease by the calming view in front of him. He returned his attention to the first suit, gingerly pulled it out of the closet and closed the door. He placed the hangar on a hook on the bedroom door, and then dressed the way he always had, as if donning a surgical glove. After dressing and inspecting himself in front of a full length mirror, The Nemesis walked back down the hall in the direction of the living room, but turned right instead of left and walked into his study. Pushing files off to the right as he sat down at his desk, he cleared a space and then turned his attention to the file drawer on the bottom right hand side of his desk. He pulled the drawer open where inside sat a fireproof safe with an electronic keypad on the top. His fingers flew over the keypad until he heard the dull click from inside the safe. The Nemesis turned the handle and lifted, pulling the top up and to the right, revealing the contents inside. There were a few papers standing upright next to a weathered, leather satchel like folder. The Nemesis lifted the leather folder out of the safe and placed it on the desk, flipping out the three folding sections to the papers inside. He turned each page over delicately, as if handling an antique treasure, until he reached the page he was looking for. He scanned the paper, reading over and over though he had it memorized after reading it only twice. He memorized all the details on the page, a mental image forming in his mind. There was a feeling to the notes he read, as if he were there when it was written. Once satisfied, he folded the leather case back up and returned it to the safe. As he closed the safe, he told himself that he would think about this next murder. He walked into the living room where he watched the news anchor describing another murder in Groton, Connecticut; his murder. There were few clues revealed to the press so early in the investigation, however, The Nemesis knew that if he followed the story, he would hear more.

Knowing that time was rapidly passing, The Nemesis donned latex gloves and walked back down the hall to the front door. There he stepped carefully around the plastic bag, placing all the clothes from last night inside, along with his shoes. He then took the edges of the bag, tied a knot in the plastic and placed it back in front of the door. After retrieving his overcoat and briefcase, he made a cursory examination of the house, then grabbed the bag and walked back outside. He carried the bag to the trunk of the car, which opened by another button on his key ring. He shoved the bag inside the previously empty trunk, and then slammed the lid closed and climbed into his car.

He left his home and drove to work, leaving at the same time he always did. He drove almost directly across the state to where he worked, and finally arrived in front of his office building just under three quarters of an hour later. He climbed out of his car, grabbed his briefcase and closed the door, pressing a button on his key ring that locked the car doors remotely. He stepped up to the glass door and stuck his key in the lock. Though locked, he could see the lights on inside and saw some of the staff walking around preparing for the day. He turned his key and pushed the door open, stepping through and locking it again on the other side. All movement stopped for a moment as all eyes were on him. A young woman rushed up to the front and flashed a happy smile.

"Good morning, Dr. Westcott," the young woman said. The Nemesis turned to her and smiled back.

"Good morning, Cheryl."

Chapter 22

Nicholas followed behind a Crime Scene investigator as he placed small yellow cones in the grass indicating the trail made by the killer. The temperature was rising slightly, and soon the slight frost on the grass would melt, making it harder to trace the steps of the killer. After all the cones were placed, photographs were taken and three young Crime Scene Investigators were combing through the grass on their hands and knees. Meanwhile, Nick and Mitchell made their way slowly through the woods behind Camden's house, searching for a trail left by the killer. The two detectives found some tracks leading to the neighborhood on the other side of the woods, but they found nothing to indicate who left them. Finally, they made their way back to the house where Hollings stood on the sidewalk, waving them over.

"CSI is done with the house," Hollings said. "We can go in now."

Nick entered the house through the front door, as investigators were still checking parts of the kitchen for evidence. There was a constant bustle around the small house as detectives, investigators and uniformed officers made their way in and out of the house. The first thing Nick noticed when he entered the house was a stale odor that hung in the air. After putting on latex gloves and donning protective plastic coverings over his shoes, Nick made his way down the hall, opening every door he passed. Nick then reached the end of the hallway and stepped into the living room, where Anderson and Wilkins were standing together. Nick looked over the room as he entered, allowing the scene and the sense of the house to take hold of him. He scanned a dull, worn recliner chair directly to the right of him. The chair sat straight across from the television. Out of the corner of his eye, Nick saw Anderson take a step further.

"The body was found upstairs," Anderson said. "He probably..."

Nick held up a hand, and then placed his index finger to his mouth, silencing the detective. A look of shocked annoyance washed over Anderson's face, as he stammered for a moment.

"Listen rookie," Anderson began after collecting himself again. "I'm just trying to..."

"Please," Nick said, interrupting him. "Do you mind?"

"Fuck you, hotshot," Anderson said, walking past him. Wilkins followed, brushing his shoulder into Nick's. Nick shook his head, smirking.

"Was that necessary?" Hollings asked. Nick did not answer. He took two more steps into the living room, and then turned, taking in every piece of furniture, every detail, noting anything out of place. There was a feel to the living room, and warm sensation washed over the detective. Nick closed his eyes and inhaled deeply, trying to put a word to the feeling he was getting from the scene. Suddenly, Nick opened his eyes, smiling. *Lived in*, he thought to himself, *the living room has a lived in feeling.*

After Nick had opened his eyes, he noticed something strange. He felt as if he were becoming removed from reality, it seemed as though the officers around him were slowing down, as a movie began to play out in front of his mind's eye. He could sense the people around him, he even knew that they were eyeing him suspiciously. However, in his mind, he could see an old man, living day in and day out, his life existing in the room. He watched as time in his vision moved in fast-forward, the old man eating, sleeping, waking, and watching television all in that worn chair. In fact, as he watched the show playing in his mind he noticed that the television was always on, day and night.

"Was the television on when the police got here?" Nick asked, looking around amongst Lt. Hollings and the members of the crime scene unit.

"Yeah," answered a male member of the unit, looking at Nick suspiciously. "How did you know that?"

"What?" Hollings asked, watching the detective.

"This room is the focal point of the house," Nick said, spreading his arms out, palms down as if absorbing something from the air. "He lived in this room. I'll bet you anything that he ate in here, slept on that recliner, basically just lived in this room."

"Then why is his dead body upstairs?" Hollings asked, sarcastically.

"Why don't we go figure that out," Nick said, as he turned and shuffled past her. Hollings followed Nick up the stairs and into the bedroom, where they found the taped off area in the shape of a body lying on the ground. There was an enormous puddle of blood on the carpet, soaking through. Nick stepped gingerly to the far side of the room to get a better view.

"Responding units said they found the candles burning in here," Hollings reminded him. "Why would the candles be burning if he did not come up here?"

"Candles are a feminine touch," Nick pointed out. Hollings gave him a look, and Nick smiled. "Most of the time."

"What's your point?" she asked.

"My point is, Camden probably didn't light those candles," Nick answered. "Don't you feel that sense of emptiness and sorrow in this place?"

"You can't arrest someone on a sense," Hollings stated.

"Yeah, but you're still a cop," Nick pointed out. "Cops get hunches. It's how they chase down their best leads. Look at this place. I don't think it's been cleaned in years. Look at the bed, made perfectly, and has probably been that way for some time. Look at the layer of dust on all the furniture."

"What are you getting at?" Hollings asked, exasperated.

"The killer drew Camden up here," Nick said. "Camden saw the light from the bedroom, came up here to investigate, and was ambushed by the killer."

"Which would lead one to believe that the killer's sole intent was the murder of Camden," Hollings stated.

"It would look that way," Nick said, taking in the scene again. Nick waited a few minutes, thinking about the murder of Camden and the photos he had seen. He thought about the letter from the killer and took the next logical step. "I think you need to consider the fact that this is a serial killer."

"What?" Hollings asked, shocked. "We have two deaths, that's it."

"You've read the letter, you know what it says," Nick said. "Hell you've seen both crime scenes. This might just be a 'hunch', but this killer is not going to quit. We need to make it harder for him, we need to put pressure on him so he makes a mistake."

"Nick," Hollings began. "You are new to homicide. You haven't even seen the other crime scene. I understand what the letter intimates, but we need a lot more than we have before we dub this a serial killing. Hell, the media will go crazy.

"Is there anything else for us to see here?" Nick asked, realizing the lieutenant was right, but unable to dismiss his frustration and disappointment. Hollings shook her head and stared at him, waiting for a response. "Then we should get back to the department."

With that, Nick turned and walked out of the room, leaving Hollings alone watching him walk away.

Chapter 23

Brenda Hollings drove back towards the police headquarters with Nick in the passenger seat, reading the entire file containing all of the information on the murder of Tracy Scott and the preliminary information regarding Alan Camden's murder. Hollings remained quiet as she drove, making sure she did not disturb Nick. Without telling him, she had begun to respect Nick, especially the way in which his mind worked. She had been surprised when he had found the footprints in the grass, even more so when her own detectives had not even started to investigate. Then when he was examining the scene, there was something going on inside of him that she did not understand. There was an immediate comprehension of the crime scene, of the events that may have transpired that elicited a sense of awe from her. She looked over at the detective from time to time, watching him as he devoured every piece of information in the file. Knowing how much further he had to go in the file, she decided not to interrupt his reading by taking him to the department and showing him around, and instead pulled into the parking lot of a local restaurant for lunch. After being seated and ordering, Hollings sat back, watching the detective.

As for Nick, he found all the information in the file mesmerizing. There was something about these murders that tugged at him, a confidence to the killer that hooked Nick on the case. He finished reading all the case notes, but did not close the file right away. He was aware of the fact that Hollings had graciously remained quiet while he read, not wanting to interrupt him while he read. With the haunting words from the killer's letter coming back to him, Nick tried to think of all the people he knew, had arrested, and had worked with at any time who might possibly be the killer. Unfortunately, the more he thought about it, the more certain he was that he had never met the killer before. There was something about the sound of his voice on the phone, his type of speech, and the way in which he expressed himself, both in the letter and on the telephone that convinced Nick of this fact. However, he could not explain the killer's understanding of Nick's current inner turmoil. He had not spoken to anyone of his feelings. Finally, Nick closed the file and pushed it away from him.

"So," Hollings began. "What are your thoughts?"

Nick took a deep breath in, thinking before he spoke.

"It would appear that the killer is highly educated," Nick started, deciding to focus first on the killer. "He seems to know his way around human anatomy from the way in which he incapacitated the first victim. I am very interested in this murder weapon. According to the notes made by the Medical Examiner, I would not be surprised if it wasn't hand-made by the killer."

Their food came, and Nick suspended his analysis to take a few bites of his bacon cheeseburger. He felt Hollings's eyes on him, and looked up at her, immediately reading her obvious disgust.

"How can you eat that thing?" Hollings asked, pointing to the hamburger in his hands, grease mixed with ketchup dripping out of the back. "You'll have a heart attack before you finish it."

"Then I'll die happy," Nick said with a devilish grin. He then looked right in her eye and took an enormous bite while smiling right at her.

"Why don't you stop eating for a second and tell me what else you think about this case," Hollings suggested. "That way I can keep from throwing up right in front of you."

Nick shrugged his shoulders and put the hamburger back down on the plate.

"This guy is also very confident," Nick said, swallowing his bite. "He picks up a girl at a nightclub, convinces her to take him back to her place, and then kills her and calls me. According to the notes taken during the interview with Scott's friend, the victim didn't seem to know this man personally, showing his confidence in the fact that he would pick up a victim that night. That coupled with this latest murder, killing Camden and then calling the police right after leads me to believe that he is not worried about getting caught. He may even know more about police procedure than we think."

"It concerns me that you mentioned serial killer earlier," Hollings said between forkfuls of salad. "Connecticut has not had or been a part of a serial case in a long time. I'm concerned about labeling this as a serial case."

"What are you afraid of?" Nick asked, popping some french fries into his mouth. "The media attention, the political heat, or the public fear and hysteria that will undoubtedly surface."

Hollings stared at Nick for a moment, shocked by the bluntness of the younger man. She smiled, thinking about her answer.

"D, all of the above," Hollings responded honestly. "Labeling this a serial case could jeopardize the investigation. We will have scrutiny from the police, the FBI, and the media, not to mention the political pressure. So far, the killer has not done anything to elicit overwhelming media attention. We've been lucky that so far this has only played as a minor story on the local news. However, the moment we mention the words 'serial case', everyone will be jumping in."

Nick sat back in his chair, going over her logic in his mind. So far, she had mentioned nothing about public opinion, focusing only on the media and political attention. However, he knew that she was right, having dealt with a high profile case not too long ago. Finally, Nick leaned forward again and returned to his lunch.

"Then we need to be very careful how proceed," Nick advised.

"What do you have in mind?" Hollings asked.

"First," Nick started. "We need to limit the number of people involved in the case. I know that seems as though it will slow down the investigation, but the fewer people in the know, the less the likelihood of leaks. Second, we need support from people higher up the chain. This story will break eventually, and the moment it does, we need the media to know that we have the full support of the police chief and the commissioner. Especially, if we decide to keep this quiet for now."

"You think there will be more murders," Hollings stated bluntly.

"I think we can count on it," Nick answered flatly. "This killer wants me involved, and whether he knows I am or not, he's not going to stop. What I don't understand yet, is his motive for killing."

"What was that back there," Hollings asked, reminded suddenly about Nick's behavior at the crime scene. "The way that you guessed about the events at the crime scene."

"I don't know," Nick shrugged. "There was just this feel to the place. It felt so lonely and depressing. I know we don't know too much about Camden's life, but I'm willing to bet that it's pretty much the same."

The waitress came over and placed the bill on the table, then walked away. Nick and Hollings grabbed for the bill at the same time, and after haggling over who would pay, they left the money on the table and exited the diner. It was only a five minute drive from the restaurant to the police department. As he entered and followed Hollings up the stairs to the Investigations Unit, Nick realized that the world inside a police department was very alien to him. After so many years working on the streets with criminals, both large and small, drug dealers and mob bosses; he never really felt comfortable inside a police station. Hollings made a right up the stairs and walked down the hall through a door stenciled Investigation Unit. Nick followed her into a large open bay squad room with six desks in the middle. There was a large office at the far end of the squad bay with a desk directly in front of the door, which Nick assumed to be Hollings's office. Off to the right of her office was a room that led into another office. Both had windows overlooking the squad bay. Off to the left of the lieutenant's office was a hallway leading down out of sight. Nick knew that the interrogation rooms were down that hall. All in all, it was a typical unit.

Nick looked around the room, only recognizing Anderson and Wilkins, who sat at their desks which faced each other, talking and laughing. There were desks with case files piled on them, reminding Nick of how much this unit must have to deal with. Most small cities that did not have a separate homicide department melded their robbery/homicide units together; though that did not come close to covering all the different types of cases they were responsible for. Being a detective was usually the direction most police officers usually wanted to go in on their way to the top; however, Nick felt no desire to work in a place like this.

"Mitchell is out canvassing Camden's neighborhood," Hollings said over her shoulder. "He's the new guy, so the shit work falls on him."

An attractive young woman approached Hollings and handed her a folder.

"This is all the copies you asked for lieutenant," the young woman said.

"Thank you, Anna," Hollings answered. She then turned and faced Nick. "Nick this is Anna Meaders, Anna this is Nick Grenier."

The two shook hands before Nick looked back to Hollings.

"Anna is going to be your secre..." Hollings paused for a moment after noticing a scornful look the young woman was giving her. "I'm sorry, your administrative assistant."

"Hold on here," Nick said, stunned. "I'm not here officially. I'm just helping out on your case, I'm not assigned here."

"I know," Hollings said, turning away and walking back to the back of the squad bay. "You'll be in the office next to mine. Anna will help you with anything you need."

"Now you're giving me an office?" Nick asked his frustration level rising.

"It's just to get you out of the way," Hollings assured him, though Nick did not believe her. "I don't have any desks available in the squad bay, and that would probably give you a sense of permanence that would make you uncomfortable."

"That doesn't make any sense," Nick said, trying to comprehend her logic.

"Welcome to the Investigations Unit," Hollings said with a smile, extending her hand. Nick took her hand in his and noticed out of the corner of his eye, Anderson and Wilkins stood watching them with a stricken look on their faces. Even in his confusion, Nick couldn't help but smile.

Chapter 24

Right now, I am Dr. Westcott. The Nemesis had to keep reminding himself of this all day long. Every moment of the day he wanted to be somewhere else, scouting for his next victim. When he was stuck in an examination room, listening to the endless list of symptoms of lonely people who wanted something to be wrong with them, he wanted to make them his next victim. However, he tried to remain as attentive as possible. Every chance he got, he went back to his office and watched the news, looking for any more information regarding either case. Some relief came during the noon news, when he saw tape shot earlier in the morning showing Detective Grenier actively participating in the investigation. If Camden's murder brought about nothing else, at least it had finally sealed Grenier's involvement. That was enough to extinguish his disappointment for the murder. However, it was not enough to alleviate the overwhelming desire to kill again. In fact, the feelings were becoming more and more difficult to ignore. There were times when he was in with a patient and he would zone out, daydreaming of his next victim. When he would come back to the present, it was often to an annoyed look on the patients face. The Nemesis would have to pretend he had been listening, pretend to be interested.

It was after his lunch that he decided that he would take the next step. Though foolhardy, he needed to kill. If he didn't find a victim tonight, the feeling would just grow and grow, and The Nemesis could not keep feigning his interest in anything else for more than a day. He would have to do as much planning as he could before taking his victim. Every time he had more than a moment's peace, his mind would wander. There was more than once when he had to stop himself from getting carried away. In fact, if it weren't for a rather large patient load in the afternoon, The Nemesis would have already had his secretary cancel the rest of his appointments and he would be on the street right now. The Nemesis reflected on these facts as he sat in his office between patients. His two thirty patient was late and that had given him a much needed moment for himself. He realized at one point in the day that perhaps letting his imagination run away with itself and giving his mind a chance to wander might keep him from continuing to lose his focus with his patients. As he sat there, he thought of the instructions inside the folder he had read that morning. That file had become like the bible for him. He knew that he would have been lost without it. The Nemesis's thoughts were jarred from the his fantasies when there was a sharp knock at the door.

"Dr. Westcott," his office manager started, poking her head through the door. "Can you sign these prescriptions for me?"

He ushered Cheryl in, reaching for the handful of prescriptions.

"How many more do we have today?" The Nemesis asked, trying not to let on that he was eager to leave.

"Four more," Cheryl answered. "That's if your two thirty shows. It doesn't look like it."

"If she doesn't come in, call her and make sure that everything is all right," The Nemesis instructed. "We'll give her a prescription if she needs it and try to get her to come in tomorrow."

The Nemesis read over every prescription to verify accuracy, and then signed them quickly in an illegible twist of the wrist. He then shuffled through the pieces of paper, making sure he did not miss any.

"Is everything alright?" Cheryl asked, looking at her employer. "You seem a little preoccupied today."

"I'm fine," The Nemesis answered, scrutinizing the woman closely. "Why, were there complaints?"

"Some of your patients felt as though you were not paying attention," Cheryl stated, trying to be diplomatic.

"I didn't get any sleep last night," he explained. "I just feel a little out of sorts is all."

Trying to end the conversation as quickly as possible, The Nemesis dismissed his office manager, asking not to be bothered until his next patient arrived. After she left, he closed his eyes and leaned back in his chair. Inside, he attempted to organize his thoughts, trying to cap the upwelling of excitement and anticipation about going out tonight. He thought of the writing in the file, knowing exactly where to hunt for his next victim. However, he knew to find the perfect victim he could not go back to Groton. It was too risky. He smiled as he plotted tonight's activities.

Before he knew it, his office manager was knocking on the door again to alert him that his next patient was here. The Nemesis finished the day giving all the attention he could muster by this time in the afternoon. When his day was finished he hurried out of the office without as much as a good bye to his employees. He was eager to get this murder out of his system. It would be the last one for the next couple of days. After this next murder, the media would be swarming all over the case. They might even find some connections, which would make it very hard on him. The Nemesis would have to die down for a while, which was why this particular murder had to be perfect. He would have to feed off of the thrill for some time. The more he thought about it, the more amazed he was by the complete accuracy of the contents of the leather case. According to the file, the victim led a double life. The victim was two-faced;

appearing one way in public and saying whatever he needed to maintain the persona that he had built for himself, but feeling differently in his heart. The Nemesis knew exactly the kind of victim he was looking for, and he knew exactly where to find him.

Chapter 25

Hollings left Nick with Anna Meaders and attended other business as Nick was shown to his new office. Nick followed Anna through her office to a door on the left that led into the office given to him by the lieutenant. Once both he and Anna were inside, he could not help but laugh to himself. The room was little bigger than a walk-in closet, and the way the desk and chairs were positioned in the room left very little room for anything else. Nick immediately rearranged the desk and two plastic covered sitting chairs to maximize room what little space there was. Anna took a list of anything he would need, and then stepped out into her office. Nick sat behind his empty desk, feeling ridiculous in the barren room. Through the glass that overlooked the bay, Nick could see the angry and disgusted looks on the faces of Andersen and Wilkins. Nick got the feeling that they had their eye on the office as the senior detectives in the unit, and he was sure they did not appreciate being upstaged. He was not going to get any cooperation out of those two, and he did not know how to make the situation any better. The only consolation he took came from knowing that he would not be around for very long.

As he stared out the window, Nick heard a knock on the door to his office and turned to see Hollings standing in the doorway. She looked around as if unimpressed and stepped inside.

"Well," she started. "Did Anna get you all set up?"

"Oh yeah," Nick answered sarcastically, spreading his hands over the empty desk. "I'm ready to fight crime."

"We'll get you a telephone and a computer in here," she said, ignoring his sarcasm.

"Don't bother," Nick started.

"I know, I know," Hollings said, rolling her eyes. "You're not going to be here very long."

Nick placed the case file on the desk, stood and walked around to where Hollings stood.

"I think some other people had their eyes on this office," Nick said, staring out the window at the other detectives.

Hollings looked out the window following Nick's gaze to see Andersen and Wilkins huddled together looking over at the office window. Once they noticed her looking in their direction, they turned suddenly and started ruffling through papers on the desk in front of them.

"Don't worry about them," Hollings said. "We need to think about this case. The ME's office has put a rush on the autopsies and they are working on them now."

"I'm interested in the first victim," Nick said, stepping back over to his desk and opening the file. "These murders were both very different in the way they were committed. It seems as though Alan Camden was ambushed. He had no contact with the killer beforehand; he was drawn up to the bedroom by the lit candles, and was killed almost immediately. However, that wasn't the case with Tracy Scott. According to the case notes, she left the club with him of her own free will, even took him to her home, where he killed her. The file said she was naked, her clothes strewn all over the apartment."

"Yeah, so?" Hollings said, looking at Nick intently.

"Well," Nick started. "Don't killers usually stick to one M.O.?"

"Not all the time," Hollings said. "But most of the time yes."

"How many multiple murder cases have you investigated?" Nick asked.

"Three or four," she answered with a sigh. "Why?"

"How many of those were serial cases?" Nick asked, pressing her.

"None," the lieutenant answered. "Most of them were crimes of passion or opportunity."

"That's what I thought," Nick said under his breath, speaking more to himself than to Hollings. He rummaged through the loose pages in the files until he found the one he was looking for. "It says that a Kimberly Harris found the victim early the next morning."

"Kim Harris was a friend," Hollings explained. "They went out to the club together with a few other friends. According to Kimberly Harris, Tracy left around midnight. Kimberly said she went over to check on Scott the next morning."

"I need to talk to Ms. Harris," Nick said. "And I need to see the crime scene; and I need you to come with me."

"Why?" Hollings asked.

"I'm going to need a female with me," Nick answered. "I think I'm going to have some very pointed questions and it would help if there was a woman present to help take the edge off."

"Sort of good cop, bad cop," Hollings said. "Probably not a bad idea. However, I can't come with you."

"I really don't think we should wait," Nick said, thinking over the situation. "There was only the space of one day in between the last two killings. We don't know how long the killer will wait before he strikes again."

"Why don't you take Anna," Hollings offered.

"Are you serious?" he asked. "She's not exactly a cop."

"You're not responding to a robbery in progress," Hollings said, rolling her eyes. "You're just interviewing a witness. There is no danger, and if you tell her what you want her to do, I think you will find her very useful."

Nick thought it over for a few seconds then acquiesced. He collected the case file and a yellow legal pad and called Anna into the office. He and Hollings talked with her about what they needed, and she was eager to help. Anna called Kim Harris and told her to meet them outside of Tracy Scott's apartment, and then followed Nick out to the parking lot where they found an unmarked sedan and headed out across the bridge to Groton.

Chapter 26

With Anna driving, a usual fifteen minute drive across the Gold Star Bridge and into downtown Groton took seven minutes. A white knuckled, thoroughly petrified Nick could do nothing but stare straight ahead and try to anticipate which semi truck would be the instrument of his death. With his left hand braced against the dashboard and his right hand clenched firmly around the handle just above the passenger side door, it took everything for him not to scream when Anna weaved in between cars leaving nothing but inches between car bumpers. As they reached the end of the bridge, Anna swerved the vehicle across two lanes of traffic to get off at the appropriate exit. Suddenly, the detective was plastered against the passenger side door as the car banked on the sharp curve of the exit at nearly sixty miles per hour. Nick was shocked that the car did not flip over at that speed. Anna drove in the direction of Tracy Scott's apartment building, making sure not to speed in the residential neighborhoods and around school zones. Anna turned the wheel sharply, entering the apartment parking lot, and then skidded to a stop in an empty parking space. It was only after several seconds after they parked that Nick realized that he had not been breathing. He took several deep breaths and then stumbled out of the car, thankful to be alive and at a complete stop. Anna jumped out of the car behind him, nearly skipped towards the building.

"How was that for driving?" she asked, tossing the keys up into the air. Nick snatched them out of the air before they fell back into her awaiting hands. "I've never been allowed to go in on an interrogation before."

"These are special circumstances," Nick stated, taking a minute to allow his heartbeat to return to a normal rhythm. "I want you there for emotional support. If I start questioning her hard, I want you to reassure her. You know, from a woman's perspective."

As they crossed the parking lot to the lobby of the apartment building, Nick could make out the figure of a woman pacing back and forth nervously around the interior of the lobby. He pointed her out to Anna, who just nodded in return. When they entered the lobby, Nick watched the eyes of the clerk at the front desk as he anxiously watched the young woman. Nick immediately assumed that the clerk was a doorman for the building, whose job it was to make sure that people who did not belong there stayed out. Nick flashed his badge at the young man, who now was very suspicious. However, Nick had no intention of bothering with the young man and approached the nervous young woman pacing in the rear of the lobby.

"Kim Harris?" Nick asked as they approached. The young woman nodded as she rose to her feet. "I'm Detective Nicholas Grenier and this is Anna Meaders. I need to ask you some questions about the Ms. Scott."

"I went over everything with the cops that morning," Kim stated. "He even wrote down my statement."

"Detective Grenier has come down from Hartford to consult on this case," Anna stated suddenly. Nick looked over at her, surprised by her sudden professionalism.

"Grenier," Harris repeated, looking sideways at him. "You were on television lately."

"Yeah," Nick answered, grimacing. "That's me. I'd like to talk to you about the night before you found your friend."

Nick had decided to start off slow and cool. He tried to keep his references to the victim as impersonal as possible to keep Harris from becoming overwhelmed by her emotions for as long as possible. He needed to get a clear picture of that night, of the events leading up to the murder. This was the only person who could give him any information about both the night before and the scene the next morning.

Nick noticed Kim hesitate for a moment.

"I know this is hard," Anna jumped in. "I can only imagine what you saw. But we'd really appreciate it if you could take us through the scene, and it might help to face it."

"I have nightmares," Harris stated softly.

"We'll be right there with you," Anna assured her. Nick smiled outwardly, but inside was concerned that she was leading the witness down an emotional road to the very place that Nick did not want her to be right now.

"Let's start with that night at the nightclub," Nick suggested quickly, trying to bring everyone back on track. "Tell me everything you remember about that night. Start at the beginning.

"We were going out," Kim started, looking down at the floor as she relived the events in her mind. "We had heard about the new nightclub and had wanted to go. Tracy was not one for going out to nightclubs. She was the most reserved in our little group of friends. She had been lonely for a long time and we were all worried that she was becoming more and more depressed."

"Why is that?" Nick asked.

"Tracy didn't like being alone," Harris answered. "She had this Norman Rockwell fantasy of how life should be. Over the last two years she had dated three men, all jerks, and I though she was starting to feel as though she would never meet anyone. She was a pretty girl and men always noticed her, she just didn't have any confidence in herself and always ended up dated the wrong type of guy."

"How was it she ended up going with you to the club?" Nick asked, listening so that he could form a mental picture of the night in his mind.

"I practically had to drag her kicking and screaming," Harris answered. "She felt really uncomfortable and I think she finally came just to get me to shut up."

"What can you tell me about the guy she left with?" Nick asked, beginning to understand the victim more and more.

"Nothing," answered Harris. "I never saw him, nor did any of our other friends. We went on the dance floor. Tracy wasn't ready to come out with us and so she stayed behind. Then about fifteen or twenty minutes later, she found me and told me that she met someone."

"Were you surprised?" Nick asked.

"Yes and no," Harris said with a slight shrug of her shoulders. "Horny guys are a dime a dozen in a nightclub. I was surprised that Tracy had met someone that interested her; you know with her Norman Rockwell standards."

"Maybe she just needed to be with someone," Nick suggested in a questioning manner. "Maybe to make her feel better about herself?"

"You mean like a one night stand?" Harris asked. "Tracy was not that kind of person. She had never had a one night stand in her life, and she certainly did not seem as though she were going to lower her standards for a day or two. No, whoever this guy was, she must have thought he was the real deal or else I can't imagine why she would have gone with him."

Kimberly Harris continued to narrate the events of that night. It was obvious to the detective that the young woman had not forgotten any of the details as she described the last conversation she had with the victim. Nick took note of the coffee shop information and listened as Harris described calling Tracy the next morning and getting no response. Finally, concerned that something might have happened, she went over to her friends house and her worst fears were realized. Nick had hoped Harris would be stable enough to go up to the apartment with him and was now seriously concerned that she would have a breakdown if she were to step foot into the apartment.

"I have to go upstairs," he told the young woman. "I have to see the crime scene. I'd like you there. I know that it's going to be hard, but I really need someone who saw it firsthand."

Again, he noticed Kimberly Harris hesitate.

"If it's too difficult, then I understand," Nick said, failing to contain the disappointment in his voice.

"I have nightmares," Harris said again. "I see her body on the bed, then there are times where it seems as though I am walking in slow motion, she's not in the bed though. I'm staring down at the blood soaked bed and she whispers into my ear. 'Why did you make me go.'"

Nick sat down next to the young woman and looked her straight in the eyes.

"This was not your fault," he said, staring at her until he was certain that she was paying attention. "The killer did everything he could to make himself attractive to your Ms. Scott. He made sure that you and your friends never saw him. He knew what he was doing, and he knew who he was looking for."

"I just feel like if I hadn't pushed Tracy to go, then she would not have been killed," Harris continued. Nick looked down at the floor and shook his head sympathetically. Unfortunately, he knew that there was no good answer for her, in fact, she could have been right.

"You heard the detective," Anna answered, noting the look on Nick's face. "There was no way anyone could have known there was going to be a killer there that night. You said you were having nightmares, well maybe this is your chance to face them. This is your way to help us catch this killer and stop him for good."

Suddenly, the young woman's demeanor seemed to change drastically. A light was present in her eyes that had not been there before. Nick knew that the thought of helping to stop the man that had filled her with grief and pain. The man that had taken her best friend away.

"Follow me," she said, rising from her place between them on the couch. There was nothing else for Nick and Anna to do but follow.

Chapter 27

Kimberly Harris stepped out of the elevator first and made her way to the door of her friend's apartment. However, her resolve seemed to waver for a moment as she saw the bright yellow police tape across the door. Nick quickly stepped in front of her and removed a key from his pocket, slicing through the police tape before inserting it into the door. He turned the lock in the knob and pushed the door open. Harris gasped as she looked into the apartment for the first time since the day of her friend's murder. Nick retrieved shoe coverings from his back pocket and handed two pairs to Anna then slipped his own over his shoes. Anna explained to Harris what he was doing and the necessity for it, but Harris did not seem to care. Her eyes were locked on the interior of the apartment as she nodded absently and fumbled with her own shoe covers. Nick stepped inside followed by Harris and finally Anna who closed the door behind her. Anna was talking, telling Harris that she could not touch anything or sit anywhere. Again, Harris nodded though Nick could not be certain that she was actually comprehending Anna's words. Nick walked around the room to get a sense of the place and the kind of person Tracy Scott was. There was a very antiseptic feel to the living room. The victim had been a very neat and orderly person, he could tell. Anna watched the detective, and Nick turned his attention to Kimberly as she reached out for a picture on a side table and stopped short.

"Kimberly," he said softly. However, his voice was the first thing to break the silence and the young woman literally jumped at the sound.

"I remember when this was taken," Harris said, smiling. "We went to New York City one weekend to do some shopping. We saved money for three months to have enough to do the shopping that we wanted to do."

"Tell me about the next morning," Nick said, bringing her back on focus. "How did you get into the apartment?"

"We both have extra keys to each other's apartments," she answered, turning her gaze back to him. "I called around nine the next morning. Tracy wasn't the kind of person to sleep in, her internal clock could not let her stay in bed past eight. There was no answer so I waited another hour. When I called again and there was no answer, I decided to come check on her. At the time, I didn't know that she had taken the guy home with her. I didn't even entertain the thought that she could have been at his house. Like I said, she wasn't the type of person to have a one night stand. I got here and didn't see anything that would have suggested that she had been..."

Nick nodded understanding the pain she must be going through to relive the events of that morning for him.

"I went back to the bedroom, talking along the way like an idiot," continued Harris. "I just expected her to be back there. Maybe she would have been in the shower, or couldn't hear me. I just walked into the room and it was like...like I had just stepped out of reality into a nightmare."

Kimberly was about to continue when she noticed Nick brush past her as if she were not really there. Usually, she would have made a comment, and she was about to now without thinking until she saw the look on his face. His skin had gone pale and his eyes were turned away. Harris thought that he had just gone into a trance. Anna called out his name, but Nick did not respond. The two women could hear him take a deep breath, then exhale.

"She brought him back here," Nick said, staring at something as though he were watching some invisible events that Anna and Kimberly could not see. "She brought him back from the coffee shop, it started the moment they reached the door."

Nick pointed back behind him, but did not turn. The two women turned instinctively to see where he was pointing, then turned away from the closed door to watch the detective.

"It was passionate," Nick said, turning his head to the side. Anna stepped forward and took Harris's free hand just as she raised the other to her mouth in shock. Nick looked down at a clock beside the picture that Harris had told them about. "It was about one in the morning when they got back here. They made their way back to the bedroom, disrobing along the way."

"How do you know that?" Harris asked, more demanding. "There were no clothes on the floor when I got here that morning."

Nick however, continued on as though he had not heard her. He walked out of the living room slowly, down the hall towards the bedroom.

"She was consumed by him," Nick said. "She trusted him completely. She felt as though she had never met a man who made her feel like this before. And then..."

The detective stopped. Both Anna and Kimberly had been hanging on every word and were now holding their breath in anticipation of what he was going to say next. Kimberly felt herself not wanting to hear more but feeling as though she had to. However, after a minute they realized that he was not going to say more. Anna knew that he was still seeing something, that something was still going on in his head. The detective gasped once or twice, even flinched at what he saw. Suddenly, Kimberly was calling his name but he would not respond. He wasn't breathing anymore and beads of sweat were forming on his brow. Finally, Kimberly grabbed his arm with her hand and dug her nails in. The detective snapped back and faced her.

"There was a rumor around the crime scene the next morning," Kimberly began, knowing what Nick had seen though not understanding it. "They said that she might have been raped."

"She wasn't raped," Nick said, smiling a knowing smile. "There was no sex whatsoever. It was quick."

Then the detective turned and walked away. Kimberly started crying with the release of guilt that she had been holding in for so long. Anna, unsure of what to do, stayed with the sobbing young woman before leading her out of the apartment. Once she had Kimberly stable and back on her way home, she went to find Nick and to find out what had just happened.

Chapter 28

By the time The Nemesis had reached downtown Hartford, the sun had long since set and night had enveloped the sky. The Nemesis had taken the interstate all the way through southern Connecticut then cut back up to Hartford by route 32. It was the long way around, driving with the traffic made him stick out less. It took two hours for him to reach Hartford, but when he did, he knew exactly where he was headed. There was a relatively new club called The Range in downtown Hartford that specifically catered to homosexual men. The nightclub had been ingeniously designed, the entrance and first floor designed like a gentlemen's bar. It was the only place in the city where people could still smoke inside by catering only to cigar and pipe smokers. Cigarettes were strictly forbidden, as if they were beneath the cigar smoking class. The first floor boasted a lounge, a dining area, an extensive cigar and pipe tobacco selection, and a bar. The bar and walls were set in a deep wood grain, while the leather lounge chairs were set along the walls and the middle of the lounging area.

The dining area was in fact a restaurant, elegantly decorated and boasting a four star chef. The owner, Peter Wendell, had made it rich as a business man here in the country's insurance capitol, and having hid his sexual preference for so long, wanted to create a respectable place for homosexual men to meet, conduct business, and enjoy themselves. After hiding his feelings from friends and family, he had finally had enough; and he was sure that there were others out there just like him. Peter had been right, and he found his club quickly became a popular place.

However, the second floor which was actually downstairs from the lounge, bar, and restaurant that sat on street level, was another story entirely. No matter how successful the bar/restaurant part was, he knew that an actual nightclub was where he could make the most money; and he felt it was his duty as a gay man to create a safe and fun environment where men could meet. Wendell decided to turn the basement into a nightclub, and spent nine months and almost one million dollars to create the most exclusive club in New England. After expanding and refurbishing the basement that had been used for storage in the past, he had an elaborate, fully stocked bar put in, as well as a lounging area with small tables and chairs. Finally, he had a portion of the floor dug out and put in a sunken dance floor. Wendell sent out specially designed invitations that were hand delivered. Then, only on the night of the grand opening, did Wendell give them the password that would gain them entrance to the nightclub portion. The exclusivity and elegance of the introductions gave the event an aire of mystique that only enhanced the anticipation and desire to get in. Unfortunately, after a few months, the password became common knowledge, but the club itself maintained its atmosphere and reputation as an exclusive nightclub.

The Nemesis had never been to the club before, but it had always been on his list as a possible site for his predatory nature. The Nemesis had heard about the nightclub from many of his patients, a few of which had actually been invited to the opening night ceremonies. He learned the password from a patient who had been eager to discuss his sexual preference. After learning about the nightclub, The Nemesis had done some extensive investigation into the floor plans of the building. Soon, he knew everything he needed to know about the club, and had been eager to use it as the scene of his next masterpiece. Now was the opportunity he had been waiting for. The police and Grenier in particular would be blown away by this murder. They wouldn't know what to think. He was so excited that he could hardly contain himself as he walked into the front entrance off of the street. The Nemesis had to remember to remain calm and to not draw attention to himself. While he knew how he wanted this event to happen, he had not planned in detail. Much of this night would require going with the flow. There was no set plan other than the fact that he was going to murder someone, and he was going to get away with it.

The Nemesis stepped inside, informed the well dressed man at the door that he was here for the club, and walked over to the bar where he waited for a few minutes, taking a mental picture of the layout for his escape. The air was laden with the pleasing aroma of pipe tobacco, and The Nemesis felt as if he were in an exclusive men's club in Manhattan. The bartender approached him from the other side of the bar.

"What can I get you?" asked the attractive young man.

"I'm heading downstairs in a minute," The Nemesis responded, shaking his head. The bartender just shrugged his shoulders and walked away, wiping down the polished wood bar with a white rag.

The Nemesis examined the actual layout of the bar area, the lounge, and the restaurant on the far end of the lounge. The entire upstairs was bustling but not overcrowded. The Nemesis felt it would not be too difficult to get out of the building, especially if the people upstairs were not aware of any events downstairs. Finally deciding on an exit strategy, The Nemesis pushed himself away from the bar, and made his way to the hallway that led to the secret entrance to the nightclub. Passing a men's and women's restroom, he continued until he reached the end of the hallway where a large man stood in front of a wooden paneled wall. The man looked straight ahead as if the The Nemesis were not there. The Nemesis stopped directly in front of the man, looking up at him and clearing his throat.

"I have a meeting with Priapus," The Nemesis said, reciting the password. The large man simply nodded and turned, pressing a small panel on the wall, unhinging a single large panel and sliding it away. The large man stepped off to the side and The Nemesis walked past, through the door and onto a metal platform that led to a metal staircase. The Nemesis made his way down the metal staircase to the main floor. The floor was bustling with activity, men gathered around the bar, seated casually amongst the cushioned couches along the walls and talking intimately around the small round tables. The Nemesis reached the metal railing the overlooked the dance floor, which was packed with young men dancing. The Nemesis watched, trying to put out an air of uncertainty, as though he was not accustomed to this type of environment. It did not take long for him to be approached by another man. A young man dressed in slacks, a button down shirt, and a sports jacket approached and cleared his throat, trying to get The Nemesis's attention.

"I don't think I've seen you here before," the younger man said.

"This is my first time," The Nemesis answered, looking away sheepishly. "In fact, this is my first time ever in a place like this."

"My name's David," the younger man said, offering his hand.

"Jack," The Nemesis answered, shaking David's hand.

"Nice to meet you, Jack," David said. "Can I by you a drink."

"Ah, yeah I guess," The Nemesis answered.

"Just so you know," David began. "I don't ask everyone if I can buy them a drink, and I don't plan on asking anyone else."

"Alright," The Nemesis said, smiling. "I'd love a drink."

"What'll you have?" asked David.

"Whatever you're having," answered The Nemesis. David smiled and walked away, turning back for just a moment after making it a couple of steps away to make sure that his new friend was watching him. The Nemesis made sure that it really seemed as if he were checking David out.

The Nemesis felt as though he were participating in the role of a lifetime. Not only was he having to act like someone who was interested in other people, he had to act as though he were a homosexual. The thing that amazed him most was the fact that his new friend was buying it. David just assumed that he was gay; there was no other reason why he would be here. After a few minutes, David returned with two martinis and directed The Nemesis to a small table off to the side of the bar. The two men engaged in small talk for a long while, and finally, when they both seemed to feel comfortable with each other, David asked his new friend if he wanted to dance. The Nemesis acted as though he were not sure for a few minutes, finally letting David convince him to go out to the dance floor. David rose, offering The Nemesis his hand. He took David's outstretched hand and rose, walking around the table and following him to the short set of stairs that led down to the dance floor.

David stopped right after coming down the steps, not wanting to make Jack feel uncomfortable should he not be ready to take such a large step all at once. David could tell it was his first time in a gay bar without even being told, the newness of this environment was written all over Jack's face. However, as David stopped off to the left side of the stairs, Jack pulled him further along into the crowd of men dancing together. David just smiled and followed until Jack stopped and they both started dancing. As they started dancing, Jack looked very uncomfortable, and as he started to move his body, David could see why. Jack did not know how to dance. However, after a few minutes, Jack changing his movements to mimic David's, he seemed as if he had been dancing all of his life. A slow song came on and Jack and David moved off to the side of the dance floor to watch the couples dance.

"You're doing pretty well," David said.

"Thanks," The Nemesis replied. "I just copied you."

"Well, it wasn't obvious," David lied.

The slow song ended and a faster song came on and the two men moved out into the dance floor again. This time, Jack took David deep into the throng of dancing men, until they were almost at the far end of the dance floor. By now, the floor was too crowded and it was difficult to move without bumping into someone else. A strobe light came on and suddenly everything looked like it was happening in slow motion.

"I really like you," David said, yelling over the music.

"I like you too," The Nemesis replied. "I think you are the one I was looking for."

David smiled for a moment, though it wavered as if he was unsure of what Jack meant by his statement. However, his uncertainty faded away with Jack's ear to ear smile. The space was becoming more and more crowded by the minute and The Nemesis knew there would not be a better time to strike. He reached around to the small blade he had stashed on the inside of his belt and whipped it out carefully, making sure that it was not seen by anyone. David was making a slow turn as he danced, and just as The Nemesis was out of his line of sight, he struck. The Nemesis moved up beside him so no one would see what was about to happen. Then he moved his hand to the inside of David's thigh and twisted the blade in his hand, completely severing the man's genitals before slicing through David's upper leg. It was at that moment that several other men bumped into them, and for a moment David was unsure what had just happened. When he was able to turn around fully, Jack was gone. There was deep, agonizing pain in his leg that was accompanied by a wet feeling freely flowing down his leg. David put his hand up against his leg, and then brought it up to his face. Under the near nonexistent lighting of the dance floor, the blood looked black on his hand. Suddenly, a feeling of light headedness washed over him and David fell to the floor.

The Nemesis had reached the metal stairs that led up from the dance floor by the time David knew what had happened. No one called out, there were no screams. The Nemesis moved intently towards the staircase that led up to the restaurant and bar, trying not to attract attention to himself. He knew that if he could get up the stairs before anyone called out, and then he was home free. The Nemesis made it to the staircase and quickly bounded up the steps, two at a time. He knocked on the panel door, which slid open. Two men were coming in just as The Nemesis was slipping out, and the big man at the door did not even seem to notice him leave. Just as The Nemesis had made it through the threshold, there was a scream down in the club, and the big man turned suddenly and ran down the stairs, pushing other men aside. The Nemesis walked slowly down the hall to the bar, and then headed out the door. By now, a commotion was starting, and The Nemesis was able to slip out with a few other people just as everyone in the bar's attention was turned towards the hallway.

Stepping out onto the street, The Nemesis took a deep breath of the cold night air and headed across the street to a payphone. Donning latex gloves, he picked up the phone and dialed the number to the New London Police Headquarters. An operator came on and asked him what directory he wanted.

"The Investigations Unit please," The Nemesis answered. "I need to speak with Detective Grenier."

Chapter 29

Nick and Anna drove back to the police headquarters in silence. Nick sat there going over the murder of Tracy Scott in his head, trying to understand the particulars of the case. He felt as though there was something that was eluding him. Something that he should have understood already. He thought long and hard, trying to understand what it was he was missing from the case. As for Anna, she was still in shock. When they were all in the apartment, Nick had acted like he was actually seeing Tracy Scott's murder. It was as though Nick had left them and stepped into his own little reality. He would look this way and that watching the events unfold, as if it was happening right there in front of him. Something about his break from reality bothered her, and now he was just sitting across from her, staring out through the windshield, thinking. Anna was not even certain whether or not he was seeing the road. As they left the apartment, Anna tried to get him to let her drive, but he just mumbled something and unlocked the car doors. As she sat there, watching him stare off into space, Anna felt as though she should tell Lt. Hollings about it. In about fifteen minutes, Nick pulled the unmarked car into the parking lot behind the police headquarters. Anna quickly jumped out of the car, telling Nick she would meet him upstairs.

Nick could tell there was something bothering her; however, he could not concern himself with that now. His thoughts drifted back to Tracy Scott. Here was an intelligent, attractive woman who did not spend all her time at nightclubs and bars. In fact, that type of environment was quite foreign to her. The nightlife was not at all her scene, and according to her best friend, she was not the type of woman who just went off with strangers, especially taking one to her home. The vital piece of information was sitting there right in front of him; he just could not make out what it was. Nick entered the police headquarters and made his way up the stairs to the Investigations Unit. He entered the squad bay and looked around. The bay was virtually empty, with only two officers from the night shift manning their desks. One was playing solitaire on his computer while the other officer was surfing the Internet. Nick looked back through the big windows of Hollings's office where Anna was talking to the lieutenant. Nick knew that they were talking about him, and he would usually be concerned. However, as this was the only case he would be investigating, he did not let himself become worried. They could let him go for all he cared; they needed him and he needed this case to be over so he could move on with his life. Nick made his way back to his new office. He sat down behind his desk and dropped the case file on the desk. He placed his feet on the desk and reclined the chair back as far as he could so that he was almost parallel with the ceiling. Nick closed his eyes and let his mind drift off.

Alan Camden had been killed by someone who had familiarized himself with Camden's routine. Camden was a creature of habit, religious about his lottery tickets, his drinking, and his gambling. This was a man who had become set in a certain type of lifestyle, the eternally pathetic, lonely bachelor. Camden had been set in the same routine for years, never upsetting the delicate balance that was his life, nor upsetting the lives of anyone around him. There was no one who Camden dealt with in his life who would have gained anything from his death. That left Nick with one thought; Camden's past. Something in Camden's past made him a target; and the more Nick thought about it, the more sense it made. The killer went to some trouble to make up an elaborate scene upstairs in the bedroom. The killer could have murdered Camden at any time while he was downstairs, sleeping on his recliner. The bedroom had some significance, and Nick needed to find out what that significance was.

There was a sharp knock at the door, and Nick opened his eyes suddenly and shot up out of his chair. Hollings stood in the doorway, an amused look spread across her face.

"Taking a break?" Hollings asked, entering the room.

"Not really," Nick answered. "I've been thinking about this case. Something just doesn't seem right about it."

"Nothing ever seems right about murder," Hollings commented, tossing some papers down in front of Nick. "Why don't you read these first and tell me what your assessment is."

Nick sat down and turned the papers around so he could read them. They were autopsy reports from the Medical Examiner's office.

"They're done already," Nick said, scanning the pages. Nick stopped periodically, memorizing different bits of information. "Cuts were surgical, carefully selected places. Murder weapon was a scalpel of some sort."

"Does that fit with your thoughts?" Hollings asked, easing into a chair directly in front of Nick.

"Not really," Nick admitted. "I find it hard to believe a doctor spends his time at a nightclub, not to mention picking up Tracy Scott. She is not exactly in a doctor's league."

"The ME states that the attacks were surgical in their precision," Hollings said. "Who else would know exactly what tendons and ligaments to cut so as to incapacitate and prolong the life of his victim?"

"Anyone who has a library card," Nick answered sarcastically. "It's strange though. I was starting to get the impression that our killer was in law enforcement somehow."

"Where'd you get that from?" Hollings asked, confused.

"It's the only thought that made any sense," Nick said. "Tracy Scott is not the type of person to bring just anyone home. It had to be someone she could trust. Whatever happened between them before they left the club, the killer left Tracy with an overwhelming feeling of trust and safety. However, this report seems to make it clear that the killer is either a surgeon or extremely proficient in anatomy."

"It's not a bad theory," Hollings admitted. "Don't discount it yet. By the way, what happened at Scott's apartment?"

"What do you mean?" Nick asked, eyeing Hollings suspiciously.

"Anna said you went into a trance," Hollings answered. "She described what happened at Camden's house. You seem to zone out and see things that aren't really there."

"I don't know," Nick answered. "It's just a feeling I get every now and then. I take what I know and what I get from the scene and I can put together what happened. I scared her didn't I?"

"You didn't scare her," Hollings answered. "I don't think she knew what to make of it, but you didn't scare her."

"Good," Nick said. "She did a great job dealing with Kim Harris. It was like she knew exactly what I needed her to do."

"She's good," Hollings said, indifferently. "By the way, Hartford is sending your stuff from vice down here. They said there were some boxes that had your name on them. Anna already authorized the transfer. Hopefully, it won't be so empty in here for long."

Suddenly, there was a knock on the door and a uniformed officer poked his head in through the doorway.

"There's a call for you detective," the officer said. "The guy on the line said it was urgent."

"Put it through," Nick said. The officer disappeared and a moment later a light on the phone began to flash. Nick lifted the receiver to his ear and pressed the button beside the flashing light.

"Grenier," Nick answered.

"Hello detective," said a man on the other end. Nick knew immediately who it was. "I'm so glad to see that the police are taking me seriously now."

"They were always taking you seriously," Nick said, assuringly. Nick snapped his fingers, getting Hollings's attention. She looked up at him annoyed for a moment until she saw the look on his face. Nick pressed the button marked SPEAKERPHONE, and The Nemesis's voice was amplified throughout the office.

"I got your letter," Nick said, trying to keep the killer on the line. "Though I can't understand why you are involving me in all of this."

"You will soon," The Nemesis answered. "I will make everything clear to you when you are ready. Now, I know that you are probably tired from an exhausting day, but I have another case for you."

"Don't tell me you've killed someone else," Nick said.

"Just like following directions," The Nemesis answered. "I have to admit that this one was ahead of schedule, but Camden left me so unsatisfied, so unfullfilled. This one was in Hartford, I'm sure that you'll be hearing about it any minute now. Well, I don't want to keep you."

There was a click on the line and Nick knew that The Nemesis had hung up. Nick pressed the button to end the call and looked up at Hollings.

"He's a serial killer," Nick said. Hollings said nothing for a moment, just staring at the phone. "You heard him. He struck again ahead of schedule. He is going to need to kill more and more frequently."

"What did he mean by just following directions?" Hollings asked. Just then, the uniformed officer popped his head in again.

"There has been a murder in Hartford," the officer stated. "It happened in a gay nightclub. We traced the call that just came in. It turns out that the nightclub is directly across the street from where the call originated.

Chapter 30

Nick drove from New London to Hartford while Hollings made the appropriate calls to allow them access to the crime scene. Since the crime occurred outside of the her jurisdiction, Hollings had to grease the wheels a little to get access to the scene, however, once the powers that be learned that it was most likely the same killer as in Groton, they were only to happy to get Hollings's insight. Nick drove with lights and sirens the entire ride, cutting the traffic time down by half. In twenty minutes Nick had reached the greater Hartford area and ten minutes after that they were weaving their way through traffic right outside of the nightclub. Hollings had to flash her badge at three different checkpoints to even get close to the club. The scene was a nightmare. Hollings counted seven different news vans at the intersections of the street, reporters standing in front of a police barricade doing live remotes. Besides the reporters, a crowd of curious onlookers had started to gather. The police had to resort to using police cruisers as well as the barricades to hold everyone back. Hollings leaned over to Nick as they crossed the street to the nightclub.

"Do you think the killer is among them?" she asked, pointing to the crowd.

"I doubt it," Nick answered, shaking his head. "There is too much of a chance of being identified by someone in the club. He's gone, long gone."

As they approached, a middle aged man pushed himself off of a police cruiser parked on the curb in front of the club. He walked over to them, offering his right hand.

"Nicholas Grenier," he started. "I've heard a lot about you. I'm Detective Andy Kraft. I was told to show you and your lieutenant around the scene. I'm told that this is the killer responsible for the two dead bodies in Groton."

"It looks that way," Hollings said, stepping up and shaking the detective's hand. "We're not here to take over your investigation. We're just here to observe."

Kraft shrugged his shoulders indifferently, and then shook Nick's hand.

"Take it if you want," Kraft responded. "I have enough open murder cases."

"Can you run down the sequence of events as you know them?" Nick asked, wanting to get the investigation moving. Kraft turned and headed over to the club with Hollings and Nick following.

"911 got a call at nine forty-eight," Kraft said. "The person on the phone stated that someone was injured on the dance floor and was losing blood. An ambulance responded, as did a patrol car, and found the guy dead on arrival. The guy bled out in the space of five minutes."

The three officers stepped inside the club and found it filled with men of all ages, most looking either terrified or angry. Uniformed officers stood before them with note pads, taking statements.

"What kind of club is this?" Hollings asked, looking around.

"It's a club that caters to homosexual men," Kraft answered. "Upstairs here is a bar, lounge, and restaurant. Downstairs is a nightclub. That's where the murder took place."

"Let me guess, no one saw anything?" Nick asked sarcastically.

"Crazy, huh," Kraft said. "Everybody says they saw the guy stagger back and then fall over. The dance floor was crowded and apparently everyone stepped away when the guy fell. According to witnesses, it took over a minute before anyone even approached the victim. That's when they realized that he was bleeding profusely, and yelled for an ambulance. By then, it was too late."

"That leaves three to five minutes for the killer to make his escape," Nick said softly.

"I don't think so," Kraft said. "The killer is here. We are going to print everyone and get DNA samples."

"You think the killer is one of these guys?" Nick asked.

"The place was packed," Kraft said. "There is no way the killer could have made it to the stairs by the time the victim fell. The bouncer is an ex-cop and said that no one suspicious past him. The killer is here, I guarantee it."

"Well," Nick started. "I hate to burst your bubble, but the killer called us from the phone across the street at..."
Nick looked over to Hollings who was flipping through a small spiral bound notepad.

"Nine fifty-one," Hollings answered.

"That would be three minutes after people inside placed the 911 call," Nick said. "I hate to say it, but the killer got away."

"Shit," Kraft said, stopping in mid stride. He looked around the lounge and bar area at the people that had been detained for statements and samples. "They could have told me that before we got into all this."

"You can use their prints for elimination purposes," Nick offered. He could understand why Kraft was so upset. Kraft had put all of his eggs in one basket by focusing on the people inside the club.

"That's a shit load of eliminating," Kraft responded, then sighed. "Follow me."

With that, Kraft turned and walked down the wooden panel lined hallway to the end, where a panel had been pushed aside and Nick could see down into the nightclub. All the lights had been turned on, and from where he stood, Nick had trouble seeing the great expanse as a club. Kraft went down the metal stairs, followed by Hollings and Nick. The three detectives walked around the bar to the railing that looked down on the dance floor. Three men with CSU jackets stood on the dance floor, two knelt over the body and another taking pictures of the scene.

"The victim had his genitals sliced off and his femoral artery slashed open," said one of the CSU people over the body. "He bled out in a matter of minutes."

"Does it look like the work of a practiced hand?" Nick asked, thinking back to the autopsy report he had read less than an hour ago."

"The practiced hand of what?" the tech asked. "A murderer?"

"No," Grenier sighed, trying not to let his sarcasm take over. "I mean does it look like the practiced hand of a doctor, a surgeon?"

"No," answered the tech. "This was a real hack job. Though whatever he used to do the job was sharp, damn sharp. He knew what he was doing, and I'll bet you that it only took one slice to do all the damage here."

"And nobody saw anything," Nick said to himself. "You said the bouncer was an ex-cop. He did not see anyone suspicious?"

"He says that the moment he became aware that something had happened, he sealed off the entrance making sure no one went downstairs or came up," Kraft said, reading from his notes.

"That doesn't help if the victim wasn't down there anymore," Nick responded. "Why didn't he seal off the lounge as well?"

"The owner let everyone go," Kraft said. "He says he wanted to maintain the privacy of everyone he could. Apparently there are some very influential people who come here."

"Like I give a shit," Nick answered. "That's called obstructing a murder investigation."

Nick stepped away from the group for a moment and looked around the club. He could not believe that the killer had been so lucky as to find another perfect victim. There had to have been some kind of plan, Nick knew there was no way this was done on the spur of the moment. Nick could not understand how the killer picked his victim. He could not see any link between Alan Camden and Tracy Scott, but he knew that there was one. The killer had told him as much. There was a plan of some sort. The Nemesis could not have committed three murders so perfectly without some planning. Nick stood staring at the bar, when he heard Kraft speak from behind him.

"We'll check all credit card receipts," Kraft said. "We might get lucky there."

"I doubt it," Nick said. "The only receipt you'll find is from your victim. This killer is too smart to leave any clues."

Kraft was about to comment when Hollings raised her hand, stopping him. She nodded over to Nick, and Kraft watched intently as Nick took a step forward. To Kraft, Nick looked as though he were staring out into space. However, Hollings had seen that look before, as well as had it described to her.

Anna had been very clear and the lieutenant knew enough to stay out of Nick's way and let this happen.

"He came here alone," Nick said. "He wanted to make it seem as if he did not pick the victim, he wanted the victim to think that he was in control."

"What the hell are you talking about?" Kraft asked, not following.

"The killer let the victim approach him," Nick said, as if not hearing the detective. "The killer drew the victim in by acting shy. He said that he had never been in a place like this before."

"How..." Kraft started, but Hollings stopped him.

"The victim offers to by him a drink," Nick said, walking over to the bar. "Of course the victim would offer, this is his home turf. He's more comfortable here. They didn't go to the dance floor right away. They talked, probably over here."
Nick walked over to the small tables.

"After they felt comfortable, they move on down to the dance floor," Nick continued. "The dance floor was packed and that was what the killer was counting on. The lights were dark and no one was paying attention to anyone else. His weapon was hidden, and he was able to strike fast and put it away without anyone seeing him. The killer knew exactly what he was doing."

Nick stepped back over to Hollings and Kraft. It was as though his mind had returned to his body. His color improved rapidly and it was when she saw him turn to face her that she realized that she had been holding her breath the entire time, and knowing that his trance was over, she exhaled.

"He acted the exact opposite way he acted with Tracy Scott," Nick said to Hollings. "This guy is good. The point of this murder was to kill a homosexual. There are a set of rules in play that we don't yet understand."

"Then how do we get ahead of this guy?" Hollings asked.

"I don't know," Nick answered. "What I do know is that these victims were particularly chosen. There is, in fact, some link between them. We just have to find out what that link is. Our killer knows anatomy, knows police procedure, and is following a specific set of rules in how he chooses his victims."

"So what do we do now?" Hollings asked, becoming frustrated. The more Nick talked, the more it sounded as if he respected the killer.

"We need to find this guy's next of kin," Nick said, staring down at the lifeless body on the dance floor.

"I've got a hunch. I'll bet you a month's pay that he's married with a family. Our victim is living a double life."

Chapter 31

It was odd for Nick to walk into the Hartford Police Headquarters feeling as though he were a stranger. He had only been away from the job a few weeks. However, standing here in the Homicide Unit with the lieutenant from another city, he could not help but feel as though he was betraying something or someone. He knew these people, they were not best friends, and he did not know many of their first names, but he still knew them. The worst part was that they knew him. They knew him well. They all knew the circumstances behind his promotion, and they knew why he left Hartford. Now, to see him standing here on assignment from another city, he was sure that many of them wanted to know why he did not stay in Hartford. The truth is, he did not know himself. He had been telling himself that he was involved in this case against his will. He told himself that his actions were being dictated by a psychopath; but deep down he knew that was not exactly true. His weeks away from the police had been like a quicksand. He had been sinking into depression and despair, slowly descending lower and lower, until he no longer had the power to fight it. The truth was, that without The Nemesis, Nick would still be sitting at home, doing nothing, depressed. The Nemesis had given him a reason to live, and that sobering fact almost made Nick want to vomit.

Somehow, Nick had done it again. After investigating the nightclub, Detective Kraft had recommended that they come back to headquarters and see what they could find out about the victim. Kraft seemed bothered by Nick; by the way he acted when reviewing the crime scene. Nick thought back to the nightclub, trying to remember what he might have said or done. However, when he thought back to these events, it was like trying to remember a dream. He knew that he had been talking; he knew that he had been walking around, but he could not remember what he had said or done, only images of death and pain. It was the same when he tried to remember being in Tracy Scott's apartment or being in Alan Camden's house. Kraft had written down all the information he had needed from the victim's wallet at the nightclub, and now that they were all in the police headquarters, Kraft left Hollings alone with Nick in an interrogation room while he got the information on the victim.

Nick sat at the table, wishing he were anywhere but here. Hollings watched as the door closed behind Kraft and then turned suddenly to Nick.

"You've really got to cut that shit out," she said, looking down at him. Nick looked up from the cup of coffee that he was cradling in his hands.

"What?" he asked, not comprehending.

"That shit you do when you zone out," she said. "You were talking like you were watching the murder take place. Like you were there remembering."

"Please," Nick scoffed. "I was going off of what Kraft told us. He said the place was packed. The victim was lying there on the dance floor. I just put two and two together."

"That's not the messed up part," Hollings said. "If that were all you did, I could explain that away. What about when you were talking about the killer, how he acted, where do you get that?"

"I don't know," Nick answered, not fully sure what Hollings was talking about. "Like what?"
Hollings walked around the table and sat down to the left of Nick.

"I'm talking about what you said about the victim having a double life," Hollings said. "If it turns out to be true, they are going to want to know how you knew that."
A spark of recognition burst in Nick's mind. He remembered standing by the railing looking down at the dead body. Suddenly, he remembered everything

about the nightclub, and most of all, he remembered something about the killer.

"The Nemesis is the epitome of the psychopathic killer," Nick said, looking into Hollings's eyes. "The most terrifying killer is the one that can inflict pain long after the victim is dead. That is what our killer thrives on, causing pain."

Nick jumped up from his chair, suddenly on a train of thought; he kept talking for fear that he would lose his momentum.

"When he killed Tracy Scott," Nick started. "He attacked her in a way that would make her unable to fight back, but would not kill her right away. He wanted to take his time. He wanted to feed off of her fear. Not only was there the physical pain he inflicted on her, but the emotional pain that he inflicted on her friend. He knew that someone would find her. One of her friends would come over, looking for her when she didn't answer her messages, and find her body like that. He knew Kim Harris would feel responsible for not being more attentive to her friend, causing this emotional grief."

"But you don't know that," Hollings said. "For all we know, he could just be killing the first people he comes across."

"No," Nick said convincingly. "There is no way that he could have drawn these three victims out the way that he did. He appealed to their emotions, and that was how he was able to kill them. There was a reason he killed Tracy Scott, Alan Camden, and this new victim. There is a reason for everything he does."

"Then why did he say that he had to move up his schedule this last time?" Hollings asked, reminding Nick of the telephone conversation he had with the killer earlier. "That does not sound like a person in control."

"It's obvious," Nick answered. "It's because he was not able to draw out the emotional pain after Camden's death. Camden was an old man who lived alone. I doubt if there is anyone who is going to mourn his death. That's why he needed another victim, and he picked this guy. Now tell me, what is more devastating than finding out your husband has been murdered?"

Hollings sighed as she rose from her seat and stared off at the two way mirror of the interrogation room.

"Finding out that my husband was a homosexual," she answered, starting to understand Nick's train of thought. "Finding out that my husband had a secret life and not being able to find out why."

Suddenly, there was a quick tap at the door and then they heard the doorknob turn. The door opened and Kraft stepped inside, eyeing them both suspiciously.

"Well," Kraft started. "I'm guessing that you are going to want to come with us."

"Come with you where?" Hollings asked.

"To inform the next of kin," Kraft answered. "Our victim's name is David Martinez, he works at one of the insurance groups here in the city, and he lives with his wife and three children in Glastonbury."

"Yeah," Nick said. "I think we should come with you."

Chapter 32

David Martinez lived with his family in a two story ranch style home in Glastonbury, Connecticut; just ten minutes from where he worked. Nick was overwhelmed by an ominous feeling as the unmarked police cruiser pulled to the side of the road in front of the Martinez home. This was a part of the case that Nick did not have much experience with; informing the family. It was now eleven thirty at night, and street looked deserted as the three officers exited the vehicle. There was a hush to the neighborhood as if even the houses themselves were holding their breath in preparation for what was to come. Nick knew this would not be like questioning Kim Harris, she had known about her friend's death and had time to absorb it. This was going to be entirely different. Tonight they would be telling a woman; a wife and a mother that her husband was dead, and they were going to tell her that he was found in a homosexual nightclub. Nick did not know how it was he knew that Martinez was married; given the opportunity to closely investigate the body he undoubtedly would have seen the pale marking on his left ring finger from where the band should have been. However, he had not had that chance, he knew very little about the victim. He did feel as though he knew something about the killer. This killer loved to inflict pain, and right now he was using Nick as his weapon. He was using Nick to inflict the emotional pain.

Nick and Hollings followed Detective Kraft up the sidewalk to the front steps. Before they had left the police headquarters, Kraft had called the Martinez house to make sure that someone was home and to alert Mrs. Martinez that they were coming over. Nick could only imagine the sheer hell the woman must have been putting herself through, not knowing why the police were coming. Kraft rang the doorbell, and before he could take his finger off of the button, the door opened. Standing before them was a thin, pale woman in early to mid thirties dressed in jeans and an oversized polo shirt, obviously her husbands. Kraft introduced himself and asked if they could come in. Mrs. Martinez opened the door fully and stepped out of the way, allowing the detectives room to pass. As Nick passed her, he could tell that she had been crying by the dried red stained skin under her eyes. However, now there was a pale, excited look to her face. Nick knew that she had been beside herself worrying about her husband. The three detectives entered the living room, where they found an older man and woman, the woman bearing a striking resemblance to Mrs. Martinez.

"This is Detective Grenier and Lt. Hollings from New London," Kraft said, not wanting to introduce them as homicide detectives.

"This is my mother and father," Mrs. Martinez answered. "Is David alright? Why are there detectives from New London here?"

"Lynn, sit down please," the woman's father said softly. Nick had a feeling that he suspected the worst, and was afraid of how his daughter would react when she heard the news. However, Lynn Martinez just ignored her fathers pleading and stared intently at Kraft.

This was the moment, that instant of sheer dread that seems to last an eternity before one makes a vital and life altering decision. Nick could not imagine what was going on in Kraft's mind, but Nick was thankful that he did not have to give the family the bad news. For that moment before Kraft spoke, it seemed as though Nick could hear every little sound in the house. It was as if everyone and everything was bracing itself for this moment.

"Mrs. Martinez," Kraft began. "I am so sorry to have to deliver this news. Your husband was murdered this evening."

Suddenly, the straw broke. All of this woman's fears were suddenly and instantly realized. The dam of tears broke and the woman began to wail. It was a sound that hurt Nick just to hear. Immediately, her father, who must have anticipated this, was on his feet, catching his daughter before her legs gave out beneath her. The older woman next to her clutched her hands to her chest and opened her mouth but was unable to utter a sound. It was the look of pure horror and pain. Hollings rushed forward and helped Lynn's father ease her to the couch. Minutes passed as her mother rushed to the bathroom and returned with a cold cloth, draping it over her forehead. Lynn's wailing continued, tears cascading down her face. Her father kept urging her to breath, trying to get her to relax. Kraft and Nick remained standing as Hollings sat beside the grieving woman. Finally, the Lynn began to catch her breath and the moaning subsided. Hollings stood up to make room for Lynn's mother, who moved in immediately beside her daughter.

"How did he die?" Lynn Martinez asked between gasps for breath.

"He was stabbed," Kraft answered, not wanting to compound her grief with the details. "He bled out quickly, before paramedics could get to him."

"Was this a mugging?" asked Lynn's father, his arms around her shoulders.

"No sir," Kraft answered. The detective paused for a moment, unsure of how to continue. Lynn noticed the detective's hesitation.

"What aren't you telling us?" she asked, pushing her father and her mother away from her. Nick heard Kraft sigh, then take in a deep breath.

"Where was your husband this evening?" Kraft asked her.

"He was at work," Lynn answered. "He said he had a big project to finish and that he might in his office late into the night."

Kraft hesitated again, and Nick took the opportunity to ask Martinez's wife a few questions.

"What does your husband do?" Nick asked. Kraft looked back at him, an expression of relief washing over his face.

"He is an insurance agent," she replied. "He insures small businesses."

"Did he tell you what this big project was?" Nick asked. Lynn was already shaking her head.

"No," she answered. "I tried to seem interested in his work, but I never found it very interesting. Please tell me what happened."

"Mrs. Martinez," Hollings started before Nick or Kraft could say anything. "I hate to make this worse, but your husband was murdered in The Range."

"The Range? The Range is a gay club," she said, without thinking. Suddenly, the light went on and she understood. Tears started to stream down her face again as she put her hands up to her mouth.

"Did you have any indication that your husband might have been a homosexual?" Kraft asked. Lynn met his gaze with a look of extreme anger.

"My husband was not gay!" she insisted, nearly shouting. Her grief was now making her angry, bitter. Nick could understand her reaction to this shocking news.

"Would your husband's work have caused him to go down there?" Nick asked quickly, trying to deflect the woman's anger. "Did he every have to conduct business there?"

"Not that I know of," she answered. "However, it's possible. That must have been what he was there for. I mean, we've been married for six years. I would have known if he was gay."

Kraft looked back at Nick over his shoulder, an expression of irritation across his face. Nick had given the woman hope when there was none. Martinez had been found on the dance floor; he had been dancing with another man. Nick had just delayed the inevitable. She would learn about her husband, and she would have to come to terms with it. Hollings pulled Nick aside and indicated that they should head out to the car. Nick followed her out of the house and down the steps to the sidewalk.

"What did you think you were doing there?" she asked, flatly.

"The woman had endured enough pain for one evening," Nick answered.

"That's not our fault," Hollings stated. "Nor is it our job to make her feel better. Our job is to catch the monster that did this to her husband, and by giving her hope you just made it harder for us to ask her those tough questions."

Suddenly, the door opened and Lynn's father stepped outside. He called out to the detectives and Hollings and Nick turned and watched him hurry down the steps to them.

"Detective Grenier," he started. "Thank you for what you did in there. She did not need to deal with any more pain tonight."

"You knew your son-in-law was homosexual?" Nick asked. Lynn's father looked down at the ground, nodding.

"I suspected before they got married," he answered. "He was so emotionally considerate, never sexually overbearing. A father's dream. However, after about two years, she was pushing for children and told my wife that he was not as sexual with her. He would get calls all the time from men he said were just friends, but I always had my doubts."

"Did you ever try to tell your daughter?" Hollings asked.

"There were a couple of times before they had kids," he answered. "She would become so upset that after a while I just dropped it. Then they had the kids and she seemed so happy."

"Do you think she knows?" Nick asked.

"Deep down," her father answered. "Deep down, she must have known. It will be difficult; humiliating for her in fact, but she will come to terms with it. Right now, she needs to deal with his death; she needs to be there for her children. Then she can come to grips with his sexuality."

"Thank you for your help," Nick said, offering his hand. "We are very sorry for your loss."

"Find the bastard who did this," her father pleaded, shaking Nick's hand. "Promise me you will make him pay."

"I will," Nick answered. "I will."

Chapter 33

Nick decided to go straight home rather than return to the police headquarters in New London. Nick had secreted a copy of the Medical Examiner's report so that he could read it over in detail. Hollings dropped him off at his home, telling him to be in first thing in the morning before scooting off into the night. Nick opened the door to his home and headed straight for the living room, where he collapsed on the couch. He had every intention of getting up and making some dinner, even though it was after eleven. However, the exhaustion of the day's events had finally caught up with him, and Nick found he only had the energy to turn over and turn on the evening news. He could not believe that only this morning he was sitting in his favorite place at the counter of his favorite diner, eating his morning meal. Seeing the crime scene at Camden's house seemed as though it had happened days ago. So much had happened in such a short space of time, and yet Nick knew that he had not felt as though he had accomplished so much in weeks. He felt alive again, renewed. Being a police officer was his life, it was what he was born to do; and now, even through his hesitation at being a homicide detective, it felt good to be back on the job.

The evening news had just begun, and immediately the screen flashed to a reporter already set up in front of The Range nightclub in Hartford. Nick listened carefully as the reporter explained the crime, and then rolled footage shot earlier in the evening. Nick found himself watching Hollings, Kraft, and himself on television, something he found to be thoroughly surreal. The reporters were not able to give the victims identity, but the reporter was making a correlation between this murder and the murder of Alan Camden and Tracy Scott. Nick knew this would happen; it would not take the media long to start making the connection, and then the pressure would be on. Sitting on his couch, watching the television, Nick was surprised to see how much time the local news was devoting to the story. Finally, after ten minutes, they switched to another story and Nick pressed the mute button on the remote control, leaned back and closed his eyes. Not a moment later, the phone rang.

"Nicholas," the female voice blared. Nick cringed automatically in response to his mother's voice. "Do you know I just saw you on television?"

"I've been on before," Nick answered. "This is nothing new."

"Yes, but they say you are investigating a murder," his mother responded. "The news said you have been seen at two murder scenes today. Have you transferred to the New London Police Department now?"

"Not really," Nick answered. "I'm just consulting. Look, there is not much I can really tell you about the investigation so far, and I have to be in early tomorrow."

Hoping that she would get the hint and let him go, however, never usually worked. It did not seem to work this time either, and Nick wanted to collapse as he sat there listening to his mother update him on family issues. Finally, after twenty minutes he was able to say good bye and hang up the phone. No sooner had he set the phone down, and then it rang again. With a sigh of frustration, he picked up the receiver and answered.

"Nick, sorry to call so late," Hollings said from the other end of the line. "Have you seen the news this evening?"

"I have," Nick answered. "We were both at the same crime scenes. I was only a matter of time before they put two and two together."

"I expected the same," Hollings responded. "However, I did not think they would lump Tracy Scott into it as well. Nick sixty seconds after the story aired I got a call from the governor's office. He's coming down tomorrow morning and wants to see both of us."

"And so it begins," Nick muttered.

"What's that?" Hollings asked.

"The political bullshit that is going to tie our hands left and right," Nick answered without missing a beat.

"This is about to get hairy," Hollings stated, agreeing with Nick's assessment.

"Listen," Nick began. "I've been thinking about this, and I think we need to limit the number of people we put on this case."

"Why is that?" Hollings asked, confused. She had been thinking the exact opposite, hoping that the more people involved; the sooner real leads would develop.

"The more people involved, the more leaks to the press," Nick explained. "There is a lot of information we are not going to want the media to get their hands on. And if they find out that the killer has involved me, then there is going to be hell to pay."

There was a brief moment of silence on the line. Nick could not even hear Hollings breathing. He knew that she was quickly running through the ramifications of what he had just said in her mind.

He also knew that she would come to the same conclusion he had, there was no other alternative.

"Damn," Hollings muttered softly. "I never thought about that. If the media finds out that the killer included you specifically, we will never hear the end of it."

"I know you don't want to limit the number of personnel assigned to this case," Nick began. "But there is no other way. You are going to have to make a decision tonight and make a statement to the squad tomorrow morning."

"This is going to make you less liked," Hollings informed him, thinking of how her detectives would react.

"That's alright," Nick answered, falling back to his previous line of thought. "I don't plan on being here very long."

After muttering a sarcastic comment, Hollings hung up the phone. Nick placed the cordless receiver back on the couch and pulled out the copies of the Medical Examiner's report that he had taken from the department earlier in the evening. Nick was trying to put together a background on the killer, but was having trouble. His first thoughts were that he was dealing with a police officer, or someone who works with the police. He knew that Tracy Scott would not have taken the killer home with her if she had not felt comfortable with him. Something he said or did caused her to feel very comfortable, and the first, most logical thing Nick could think of was a police officer. This thought had been reinforced at the Camden house, when the police found that it was the killer who called the police, alerting them to a possible crime scene. The killer would to have had to know the police response time and what patrol cars were out in the area. It seemed impossible to Nick to think that the killer had just been lucky. There were too many possibilities, and the killer did not seem to be a person who took reckless chances.

However, now, reviewing the Medical Examiner's report, Nick was beginning to revise his opinion of the killer. According to the reports, the killer was highly knowledgeable in anatomy and physiology. He was also very exacting with his cuts in his attacks, suggesting a surgeon. Nick sat staring at the reports, frustrated that he could not put these two theories together into a workable background for the killer. Nick knew that a person could do research on anatomy, just as well as he could do research on police procedures. It was the surgical precision of the killer that seemed firm with Nick. Surgical precision was learned from years of study and practice. The more Nick thought about it, the more certain he felt the killer was a doctor of some sort. While that narrowed down the field considerably, it did not bring him any closer to knowing where to look. Suddenly, the phone rang again, interrupting Nick from his thoughts.

"Hello," Nick said as he answered the phone.

"Good evening, Nicholas," said the all too familiar male voice on the other end of the line. "How was your first day at work?"

"Busy, thanks to you," Nick answered, a sudden fury beginning to rise from within. "Are you calling to tell me that you've killed someone else?"

"No, unfortunately," The Nemesis answered. "I think I've caused all the damage I can for one evening."

"What the hell do you have to say for yourself?" Nick asked, astonished by the man's lack of concern over what he had done. "It doesn't bother you at all that you have taken three lives in less than a week does it?"

"I don't care about those sheep," The Nemesis answered. "These were people who had not or were not going to accomplish anything meaningful with their lives. Take Camden for instance, what a useless bag of bones. In his life, he had accomplished nothing. His wife left him, he doesn't even know his child, has not done anything meaningful since his retirement. Trust me, what I gave him last night was a release from his dreadful life."

"Touching," Nick said, desperately trying to write down every word The Nemesis said. "So now you see yourself as an angel of mercy. You can't tell me that you were saving Tracy Scott or David Martinez. They had their whole life ahead of them."

"Tracy Scott was nothing more than a sappy, romantic dreamer," The Nemesis responded, a biting quality coming out in his tone. Nick suddenly realized that The Nemesis felt as though Nick were antagonizing him, and it was causing the killer to react. "She had these stupid teenage ideas of what love should be. I played her like an instrument and she fell for it because she was so desperate for attention. As for Martinez, he was the worst one of all. He lied to everyone, as well as himself. He would never have ever come clean with his wife and actually made a decision; gay or straight. Instead, he would have hidden in the shadows, trying to have his cake and eat it too, destroying everyone who loved him in the process. Now they don't have to worry about their petty problems. They have been released; not that it matters, I wasn't doing it for them. I was doing it for you."

"Yeah, well, I still don't understand that one," Nick answered, trying to keep the killer talking. "All I see is the pain that you've created."

"I think it's a waste of a life to have such a remarkable gift and not be able to share it with the world," The Nemesis started. "All of those people I killed, they were all wasting away, waiting for something to happen to them. Now they have it, their lives have been given to bring forth a miracle.

They have died to call attention to the greatest killer to ever live."

"So now you are the greatest killer that has ever lived?" Nick asked, surprised by the sudden rise in ego. So far, The Nemesis had portrayed himself as a teacher.

"You still don't understand, do you?" The Nemesis said with a sigh. "You see the murders after they happen with a clarity that the police can't understand. It's a feeling that is not taught, it's in your blood."

"How do you know about that?" Nick asked, losing his composure momentarily.

"The same thing happens to me," The Nemesis answered. "There is an understanding of murder, of taking life that other people don't have. It's a part of you, a part that you are only now getting a chance to see because of me. I'm your teacher; I want to help you see what you really are."

"What?" Nick asked absently. He felt as if the room were spinning, suddenly. The Nemesis seemed to know so much about what went on in his head that it made Nick disoriented.

"I'm not the greatest killer who ever lived, Nick," The Nemesis said softly. "You are."

Chapter 34

Nick slept fitfully throughout the night, waking every few hours. When he finally rose from bed at six in the morning, he felt drained, both physically and emotionally. His telephone call with The Nemesis had bothered him more than he was prepared to admit. After he had hung up the phone, he had decided to wait to tell Hollings about the conversation until the next morning. It was the final words the killer had spoken that haunted Nick throughout the night. The Nemesis wanted Nick to think that he was a killer inside because of the way he reacted to the crime scenes. However, Nick could not believe that. He was not a killer; this was just an insight that was going to help him find the killer. The killer relating himself to Nick just made him more and more furious. Unfortunately, Nick could find no peace from his thoughts, and realizing that he was not going to be able to push this from his mind by lying at home, he decided to get up. After showering and dressing quickly, Nick headed into the department, hoping that putting himself into the case would help take his mind off of what The Nemesis said, proving him wrong. In the car, Nick played the music so loud that it could be heard from outside the car when he came to a stop at a traffic light, causing other drivers to look over at him, giving him dirty looks. However, Nick did not care, the music helped to clear Nick's mind.

When Nick arrived at the department, there were only a few people in the Investigation Unit, the overhead lights still off. There were a few lights on from desk lamps as the last shift was watching the clock, ready to leave. Nick noticed the lights on in Hollings's office, and he knocked on the door and entered. He relayed to the lieutenant the conversation he had with The Nemesis, leaving out the last part. He did not feel that it was relevant, since Nick had convinced himself that it was just the killer trying to get into his head. Nick emphasized, instead, the comments the killer made about releasing his victims and talked about the depth of background knowledge the killer had on his victims. Hollings agreed with Nick that these were not random murders; somehow, the killer knew his victims well. As they were reviewing the new pieces of information regarding the killer, there was a sharp knock at the door. Hollings stood up suddenly, Nick jumping up instinctively as the Chief of Police entered, followed by Governor Haisley. Introductions were made, and after a moment of brief awkward hesitation, the governor spoke.

"I'm concerned about this rash of murders we've experienced," Haisley started. "The media says the two murders in Groton and the one last night in Hartford are related. Is this true?"

"We believe they are," Hollings answered. "The same killer has taken responsibility for all three. His knowledge of the crimes seems to suggest that he is telling the truth."

"Is this a serial killer we're dealing with?" Haisley asked.

"Yes," Nick answered quickly, cutting the lieutenant off from her answer. Hollings looked down sharply at Nick.

"I take it there is some disagreement on that?" the Chief of Police asked.

"No sir," Hollings answered. "As you know, law enforcement anywhere is usually reluctant to jump to labeling a case as a serial case. However, now with three murders in such a short period of time, combined with the psychology behind it, we believe that this is, in fact, a serial murderer."

"That's not something I want the media finding out," Haisley said. "I'm sure that you have taken measures to limit leaks from your office."

"We have, sir," Hollings said.

"I don't need to tell you how important it is to catch this killer quickly," Haisley said. "I'm a first term governor who campaigned on cutting the crime rate. We need to wrap this case up before the shit hits the fan. The sooner you catch this guy, the better we all look."

"Not to mention the lives we save," Nick interjected, sarcastically. For a moment, no one spoke. Hollings and the Chief stared first at Nick, then at the governor to gauge a response. Haisley just smiled, his gaze firmly held on the detective.

"I like you Grenier," Haisley said. "I always have. You're the type of cop who makes me look good. The Mullanno case made me look very good, and is going to be very helpful for me. I'm a politician; it's what I was born to do. When people make me look good, I like to take care of them. When they make me look bad, I *will* take care of them. Wrapping up a serial case quickly will make me look good, which in turn will be good for you. The longer it takes, the worse it will be, for everyone. I hope everyone understands."

There was no response, but Haisley knew that he was understood. He rose from his place on the couch that lined the far wall of the office and offered his hand. Both Hollings and Nick shook, somewhat less vigorously as before, and Haisley bid them good luck and left. Hollings walked around her office until she was behind her desk again, while Nick stood in his place, replaying the governor's words.

"He's a politician," Hollings said. "If this thing turns south, I'm sure that he will have no problem pinning the blame on us."

"He won't have that chance," Nick said. "I'd better get to work. I need to get some background on all the victims, see how the killer knew everything he knows."

"Speaking of which," Hollings said, looking up suddenly. "We are having trouble finding a next of kin for Alan Camden. While you're doing the background, see if you can find one."

"The Nemesis said he has a son," Nick said. "I'll see what I can find."

Nick left the lieutenant's office and stepped through the threshold into his own. As he entered Anna's office area, he saw her behind her desk, typing away.

"Good morning," Nick said, gauging to see if she were still weirded out by yesterday afternoon's events.

"Morning," she said, bubbly. "I saw you on television."

"It seems everyone did," Nick answered, stopping at her desk.

"Did you get any sleep from last night?" she asked, seemingly concerned.

"Not much," he admitted. "I'm going to need a lot of help today. I need to do background searches on all of the victims."

"No problem," Anna answered. Nick stepped up to the door that opened up into his office and pushed, expecting it to give way easily. However, after opening just over a foot, the door slammed against something heavy. The door stopped suddenly as Nick tried to step through, causing him to slam his body against the door.

"What the hell," Nick uttered, putting his weight against the door to get it open. As it opened slowly, Nick found boxes of files lying on the floor, on his desk and on the chairs and a worn, plastic cushioned couch that sat just under the windows that looked out onto the bay.

"They came last night," Anna explained. "These are all your case files, and anything labeled Grenier from Hartford."

"These can't all be case files," Nick said. "What is the rest of this shit?"

"I don't know," Anna answered. "They said it was all your stuff."

"This is going to take me forever to sort through," he said with a sigh.

"I wouldn't bother with it right now," Anna said, leaning out over her desk. "Your file cabinets aren't coming until tomorrow."

Nick was about to tell her not to bother, that he was not going to be there for long, then decided against it. Putting the file he was carrying down on the desk, he opened all the file boxes one at a time, taking a quick mental inventory of the contents inside. There were some boxes with personal items that he had forgotten to clear out of his area in Hartford. Others were filled with case files that Nick had not thought about in many years. He fingered through the files, smiling to himself. Finally, he came to the box on his desk and flipped the top off. As the top hit the desk, a great cloud of dust billowed up from inside the box. Waving his hand in front of his face to push away the dust, Nick coughed and stepped back instinctively. Nick turned his head to the side, taking a closer look at the box itself. His last name was stamped on the side, but the box looked older than the others. Stepping forward again, Nick reached inside the box and pulled out a thick file folder, covered in a leather case. Nick opened the leather folder, not recognizing it at all, and began reading. Immediately, Nick realized that the case was misfiled. He did not recognize any of the names or places. Nick flipped forward a few pages, then back looking for a name on the file. He was about to call out to Anna when he found the investigating detectives name. GRENIER,

T. was typed on a line and Nick knew instantly what had happened. Someone had found a file of his grandfather's and assumed it was Nick's old case.

Sitting down at his desk, Nick lifted the old box off of his desk and placed it on the floor. He then spread out the old case file in front of him and began reading. As he read, a knot of sickness formed in his stomach. He flipped to the next page, reading quickly, and then flipped it again. As he read, a wave of nausea swept over him. He felt feverish, suddenly finding it hard to breath. He heard Anna walk in, but was unable to look away from the words on the page.

"You can access everything you need from your computer there," she said, watching him read. "I can show you how to get all of your background information."

"Get Hollings," Nick said softly, barely audible. Anna stepped forward to see what he was reading on his desk.

"What's going on?" Anna asked, curiously. Nick looked up at her, and she was stopped suddenly by the pale look on his face.

"Get Hollings," Nick repeated. "Tell her to come here now."

Anna turned quickly and ran out of the office. Nick looked back down at the file on his desk, reading about a killer his grandfather pursued sixty years ago named The Nemesis.

Chapter 35

April 7, 1943
Hartford, Connecticut

Terrance Grenier stood at the very edge of the sidewalk, watching the three inexperienced uniformed officers as they shifted nervously around the dead body laying face down in the grass. Terrance inhaled sharply as the youngest of the officers bent down momentarily. As the officer's hand neared the dead body, Terrance got ready to release a torrent of obscenities, but the officer snapped his hand back to his side as if sensing the detective's disapproval. The officer straightened himself and looked back at Terrance, who stood there shaking his head disapprovingly. Everyone knew about Detective Terrance Grenier, and everyone was afraid of him. Grenier had been on the police force for ten years, starting out in New London. He had a remarkable record of solving cases, and everyone respected and feared him. Terrance was a man of few words. Most of his subordinates were usually grateful when he passed them by without a word. He only usually spoke when he was angry, and when he did speak, no one wanted to be around him. He had a reputation, and it was not a particularly good one. He was known to be abusive, both emotionally and physically. On many occasions when the police had a suspect and little to no proof, Detective Grenier would be introduced to the suspect and given five minutes alone, after which the suspect was more than willing to give a full confession. After many successes in New London County, the governor decided that Grenier's talents would be better served all over Connecticut. Most murders were not very elaborate, usually stemming from a robbery or a fight. Though there were a few cases every now and then that needed a special touch, and Grenier had that touch.

Grenier ordered the officers to cover the body with a sheet as he happened to notice more and more neighbors coming outside to see what was going on. *Sick bastards*, he thought to himself. People had an innate desire to witness horrors. He wanted to yell at the bystanders to get inside and mind their own business, but he stopped himself. He was going to have to canvas the neighborhood later on to see if anyone saw anything suspicious, and yelling at them would not inspire people to talk to him. Grenier watched as two uniformed officers took a tarp out of the trunk of a police cruiser and covered the frozen body of the young woman. One enterprising young officer was already drawing a sketch of the scene on the front lawn. Grenier had assumed the young man had already drawn the dead body of the victim, how it was laid out upon the frozen grass, because he did not say anything as the other officers covered her up. Detective Grenier immediately felt a sense of admiration for the young man, the only person other than himself who had kept his head around the gruesome scene. Grenier walked over to him and looked down over the officer's shoulder, admiring the sketch. The officer immediately deferred to the detective, stopping his work and standing at attention.

"Sir," the officer said, devoting all his attention to the detective. Terrence Grenier smiled to himself, continually pleased with the young man.

"What's your name?" Grenier asked.

"Michelson, sir," the young man replied. "Jeffrey Michelson."

"Well, Sergeant Michelson," the detective began, looking around the crime scene at the other officers standing around, waiting for someone to give them instructions. "You seem to be the only person here that doesn't need to be told what to do while we are waiting."

"I thought it would be best to get a sketch of the scene," Michelson answered, unsure of whether or not he needed to defend his actions. "Just in case something happens, you know, before the photographer gets here, we will know exactly what the scene looked like; where everything was."

"You don't need to explain yourself to me," Grenier assured the young officer. "I wish all of these half wits had your sense. Finish your sketch, leave nothing out. If anyone gives you a hard time, tell them you are under orders from me. When you are finished, come and see me, I'll have some other jobs for you."

Grenier turned his back on the officer and walked away, hearing Michelson thank him as the detective left him alone. Grenier yelled out to all the other officers standing along the sidewalk, talking amongst each other. He ordered them to stay off of the lawn and make sure that everyone else did the same. No one was to step on the grass without permission from Grenier or Michelson. This got several glares from some of the officers standing around, especially those with seniority. However, Grenier did not particularly care. While he waited, Terrence decided to walk up the street looking for clues or anything that might seem out of place. He was angry that he had to wait to talk with the people who found the body. All the information Detective Grenier had at this point was that a woman, the mother of the victim, had stepped outside and found her daughter lying dead in the grass. The woman ran into the house, screaming hysterically, and her husband called the doctor, who came over immediately. It had been the doctor who called the police after making a cursory check of the body. Since then, the doctor had not allowed the police to question the woman or her husband, and so Grenier and his men had been standing outside the house, waiting for the crime scene photographer and the fingerprint expert to come down and begin their part of the investigation. Detective Grenier found the waiting infuriating, and was secretly jealous that the young officer Michelson had a job to do and he didn't.

Grenier walked up the street, letting his eyes glance over the street, the sidewalk, the cars parked on the side of the road, and the houses on either side of the street. He scanned the road for any tire marks, looked for any clues that might have been left by the killer or killers. It was very difficult for him to know what he was looking for when he knew nothing about the case yet. Grenier reached the end of the street, looked up to the right at the intersecting road, then turned around and headed back down the street to the crime scene. He walked slowly, despite the cold, gathering his thoughts and putting them in the proper order. He thought to himself of the questions he had for the mother and father; placing in order different plans of the investigation, how he wanted the area canvassed. When Grenier was in sight of the crime scene, he found Michelson walking briskly up the street in his direction.

"Detective," Michelson called out as he approached. He reached the detective, realized that he was not going to stop walking and quickly fell into step with the superior officer. "The photographer and the fingerprint expert have arrived and were insistent on getting to work."

"Did you finish the sketch?" Grenier asked.

"I did, sir," Michelson answered, handing the drawing paper over to the detective. "I made a detailed search, making sure to note anything of interest, whether it seemed to pertain or not."

"Very good," Grenier said absently. It was not often that the detective had any kind thoughts, much less spoke any words of praise. Detective Grenier had always been the type of person who worked best alone. In fact, Grenier had always been the kind of person who lived his life alone. The detective always found it difficult to work with people he thought were less intelligent than he, and unfortunately, he ended up thinking that way about everyone. However, as he walked back to the crime scene with the young sergeant, he felt as though he may just have found someone who was competent, someone who he might be able to count on.

"That was quick thinking, drawing out a picture of the crime scene," Grenier said to the young man. "I think that I will need your help on this case. God knows I could use someone who is actually competent."

"I'll do anything you need," Michelson said eager to cooperate.

Grenier reached the lawn where the victim laid, her body now uncovered by the fingerprint expert, who was directing a younger man to collect something off of the body. Terrence approached the older man, who he knew to be the senior fingerprint expert, and extended his right hand.

"It took you long enough to get here, Bob," Grenier said sarcastically.

"You can kiss my ass, detective," the fingerprint expert fired back. "You're lucky I'm here at all. This cold reminds me how desperately I want to transfer."

"Yeah, yeah, yeah," Grenier scoffed. "Quit your bitching. I need you to dust every square inch you can. I need fingerprints. I'm hoping that we will be able to match prints to some we have on file."

"You'd be lucky if you did," Bob answered. Robert Ferrier had known Terrence Grenier for many years, and their friendship had become stronger since Ferrier had been transferred to the State Bureau of Investigation when it was established eight years earlier. Grenier was one of the few detectives who could see the importance of science in criminal investigation. "Even if the prints are on file, it will take a month for our guys to analyze and match them."

"One day there will be a machine that matches prints in minutes, and cases will be solved in hours or days," Grenier said, fantasizing about things he knew he would never see.

"Yeah well, for right now you're stuck with me," Bob said. "And as for your pretty little victim, I have to tell you that there isn't much here to dust. We'll collect everything we can, and we'll dust everything we can; I'm just not holding out much hope."

"I know," Grenier said. "All I can do is trust you to do the best you can."

Just at that moment, the doctor who had insisted the officers wait outside exited the front door and approached Grenier.

"Are you the officer in charge?" the doctor asked. Terrence looked the man up and down and nodded.

"I'm Detective Terrence Grenier," he answered. "We can't wait around all day for these folks to pull themselves together. I need to interview them so I can get this investigation rolling."

The doctor smiled knowingly at the detective, as if Grenier's abrasive attitude could not intimidate him. There was something in the doctor's manner that Grenier did not like, but he could not put his finger on what the feeling was. The doctor stepped aside and motioned towards the house.

"By all means detective," the doctor began. "Question away."

Chapter 36

The inside of the house looked like a recruiter's office. Grenier walked down the hallway with Sergeant Michelson following closely behind him. Grenier was caught off guard by the abundance of military recruiting posters that hung on the walls all around the house. Michelson brought Grenier's attention to two pictures of young men, no more than twenty, one in a naval uniform, and the other in an army uniform. He could tell immediately that these were boot camp photos. So many people in this area had children in the war, and many of them had lost children in the war. As the two officers came to the far end of the hall, they could see a smartly dressed middle aged woman holding a wrapped cloth against her head with a man somewhat older than her sitting to her right, fanning her with a newspaper. Grenier knew the woman to be the victim's mother, and he could only imagine the shock of seeing her daughter, frozen and dead in the middle of the front lawn. If anything, he was surprised that she was able to remain as calm as she was. However, the moment

Grenier and Michelson entered the living room, the woman's face contorted, her lower lip began to quiver and the floodgate broke as tears washed down her face. The older man stood, kissed his wife on the side of the head, and approached the detective.

"Jack Larson," the man said, offering his hand. The detective could see immediately that the man had been crying, damp red streaks stained his face. "My wife..."

"I'm Detective Grenier," Terrence interrupted, saving the man from having to explain further. He shook the man's hand. "This is Sergeant Michelson. I need your permission for him to take a look in your daughter's room."

"Of course," Larson said, shaking hands with the junior officer. He then turned and gestured down a small hallway to the first door on the left. "Go on in."

Michelson squeezed past the two men and made his way down the hall. Larson offered the detective a seat and a drink. Grenier was always amazed by the reactions of a victim's family during tragedy. Grenier politely refused, and then turned his attention to the grieving woman.

"I'm sorry to have to ask you these questions," Grenier began, trying to show some compassion. "I can't imagine what you are going through right now. However, I need your help to catch the person who did this to your daughter. When was the last time you saw your daughter?"

"Last night," she answered between sniffles. "She was going down to the submarine base. She, you know, the sailors."

Terrence held up a hand, nodding. He did not need her to go on, he knew why she had been there. Grieving the way she was, he knew that she did not need to be thinking about what her daughter had been engaged in.

"I saw the pictures of the boys on the wall," Grenier said, trying to take her away from the grief for a few minutes. "Are those your boys?"

"Yes," she said, nodding. She smiled briefly, obviously reminiscing about them. "One is in Europe, fighting the Germans. The other is in the pacific, on the U.S.S. Iowa."

"You must be very proud," Terrence said.

"Yes, we are," she agreed. "This is going to break their hearts. They were all so close."

"I'm going to find this guy," Grenier promised. "I can't bring her back, but I can deliver justice."
The woman just nodded, but Grenier knew by the look on her face that she did not believe it.

"When did you expect your daughter to be home?" the detective asked.

"Her father demands she be home by midnight," Mrs. Larson answered. "She was always home before then. There was an unspoken agreement between us. We did not ask about her nightlife, she followed our rules without question."

"So you found it odd when she was not home on time last night," Grenier hinted, trying to prod her to continue.

"Yes, and…" Mrs. Larson hesitated for a moment.

"What is it?" Terrence asked, interested.

"She had been acting differently the last few weeks," the grieving mother admitted. "She had been very moody, not listening to us. I guess I did not find it too strange that she was not home. She had never done it before, but I knew this was something we were going to deal with sooner or later."

"Tell me how you found her this morning," the detective said. Mrs. Larson caught her breath in a quick inhalation; her left hand clutched her chest as her right hand covered her mouth. It was as if she had forgotten the horror of the morning for an instant, only to have it surge to the forefront of her mind again. For a moment, Grenier was afraid her heart was going to give out.

"I had gone out to call the dog in," she answered. "Sometimes the dog stays out all night. It doesn't usually happen in the winter," explained the grief stricken mother. "But last night he did not come in when I called before going to bed. When I got up this morning, I expected to find him hanging around the front door."

She stopped briefly, took several deep breaths and opened her mouth as if to continue but no sound came out. Her lips began to quiver again, and Grenier expected her to begin to cry. However, she stayed in that moment, unable to speak, and then suddenly it came to her.

"The dog wasn't there," she said, her voice cracking as she recalled the events just hours ago. "I stepped out and saw the mass in the yard, and I could not tell what it was. Even as I approached and knew it was a dead body..."

Grenier put his hand out and placed it on the left hand of the woman in front of him. It was the first time he had shown such compassion for a person he was questioning, someone he was interrogating. He did not need her to recount the events any further; he had seen the gruesome scene of the body frozen in the grass, icicles of blood tapering down into the grass. He was not going to put this woman through anymore pain, he knew that she had more than enough pain to deal with. He also knew that she had nothing else to tell him that would help him in the case. Mrs. Larson may have been the victim's mother, but she did not know everything about the world in which her daughter lived. There were others who knew that world, and he had to find them.

"That's enough," Grenier said softly. "I'm sorry to have had to make you remember that. There is one last thing I need you to do for me. I need you to write down the names of all of your daughter's friends and anyone else she has been in contact with this week that you know of."

Mrs. Larson smiled and nodded, apparently relieved that she was finished with the interrogation. She gladly took the small piece of paper and the pen from the detective and bent over the side table and began to write. Detective Grenier rose from his seat across from her and walked back to where the hallway met the living room just as Sergeant Michelson came down the hall.

"There was nothing of interest in her room," he said, disheartened.

"There wouldn't be," the detective assured him. "This girl has another life, one that doesn't exist in this house. She would have been careful not to bring it home where her mother or father could find it."

"How do you know that?" Michelson asked.

"There was an unspoken agreement between the parents and the victim," Grenier said, recalling what the mother said. "I think it was more with the mother and out of respect for their rules."

"So where do we find out more?" Michelson asked eager to continue on in the investigation. Grenier smiled, pleased with the young man's enthusiasm.

"From her friends," Grenier answered. Jack Larson approached the two officers and handed the detective the piece of paper with names on it. Grenier thanked him and repeated his promise to catch the killer. Larson just nodded and turned back to attend to his wife. Grenier walked out with Michelson behind him. As they exited the house Grenier looked around and sighed. There was nothing more that could be done here until Robert Ferrier could analyze all the prints he dusted. The detective turned back and looked at Michelson.

"How eager are you to be involved in this case?" Grenier asked.

"I'm not eager to be involved," Michelson answered. "I'm eager to catch the killer. I saw the body, I drew a picture of her; how she was left on the grass, the stab wounds, the blood. This is sick, and unless I'm wrong, it's not going to stop."

"My thinking exactly," Grenier said, pleased with the young man's response. "Well, let's get to work."

Chapter 37

Terrence Grenier and Jeffrey Michelson questioned all the names on the list that Mrs. Larson had provided, but were unable to come up with any information. Every person they questioned told the same story. Over the last couple of months her demeanor had changed. Some said that she had become more vocal about the war; others said that she seemed to be withdrawn. Most of her friends admitted that they had not seen Virginia in some time, and those who had seen her over the last couple of months said that she was particularly emotional. As Michelson looked over the list, he came to the last name the victim's mother had written down. Beside the name was a notation indicating that this last person was Virginia's best friend. Grenier called in and was given the information for Abigail Fletcher, Virginia's best friend. Both Virginia and Abigail were supposed to work together at a local diner, and after reaching the Fletcher home and being informed that Abigail was at work, the two officers headed out to the diner. Both Grenier and Michelson knew the diner, as did most of the police force, as it was only two blocks away from the Hartford Police Department. Grenier used to spend a lot of time there, before he started gaining weight and was forced to shed some pounds. Michelson, however, was a regular and recognized Abigail the moment he saw her. Grenier and Michelson sat down at a booth in her section and waited for the waitress to come over.

"We need to get some information out of this one," Grenier said, looking around the nearly empty diner. It was now mid-afternoon and the lunch rush had passed and the dinner crowd still had a few hours. "We haven't gotten shit out of anyone so far. She's been emotional over the last couple of months. Come on now, every woman's emotional."

"Abigail Fletcher was Virginia's best friend according to Mrs. Larson," Michelson reminded the detective. "If there is any information to get, Fletcher should be the one to have it."

"You realize that we don't have one solid lead to go off of," Grenier said, thinking over all of the information they had been given so far. "Not one lead or clue to go off of."

"We need to find out what changed Virginia's attitude over the last couple of months," Michelson said, thinking aloud. "I did notice something strange though. All of Virginia's friends said that she had been different for a couple of months, however, her mother said that she had been different for only a couple of weeks."

"So what," Grenier asked, not following Michelson's line of thought.

Michelson was about to defend his position, one that did not have much substance to it when Abigail walked over and greeted them.

"What can I get for you officers?" she asked.

"I'm Detective Grenier," Terrence began, introducing himself. "We need to talk to you about your friend Virginia."

"Why, is she in trouble?" the young waitress asked, looking back and forth between the two men, confused.

"She's not in trouble," Michelson assured her, trying to delay telling the young woman that her friend was dead. "We just need some information. Her mother said that she has been acting differently lately, and some other friends that we've talked to said she has changed over the last couple of months."

"Why are you asking me these questions? So she's been acting differently, is that a crime?" Fletcher asked, suspiciously. After a few seconds, it seemed as though a light had gone off, and suddenly she became visibly shaken. "Is she missing? Did something happen to her?"

Before Michelson could calm the young woman, Grenier slammed his hands down flat on the table, causing Michelson and the waitress to jump.

"Your friend Virginia is dead," Grenier announced his voice totally devoid of compassion. "We are trying to find out who killed her, so why don't you start answering some questions."

Michelson watched the young woman's reaction as if in slow motion. There was a vacant look on the woman's face for just a moment, as the information just delivered began to sink in. Suddenly, as Abigail came to understand what she had just been told, her mouth opened as if to scream, but no sound came out. Michelson watched as the waitress tried to speak and breath, and could do neither. The sergeant saw the girl take a step back, and then two and knew that she was going to faint. Quickly, Michelson scooted himself out of the booth and was on his feet just in time to grab Abigail as she fell. The owner of the diner came around the counter in a flash and helped Michelson with the unconscious young woman, as did another waitress.

A few minutes later, after Abigail had regained consciousness, Michelson was left alone with Grenier as the other waitress took Abigail into the back to help her regain her composure. Michelson, furious at his superior's uncaring attitude turned to Grenier in a furious rage.

"What the hell was that about?" Michelson asked, enraged. "You could have shown a little compassion.

Now we'll be lucky if she can tell us anything tonight. She's probably in shock and won't be coherent for a while."

Grenier just stared at Michelson, and then smiled as the young man yelled.

"I saw how you were with the mother," Michelson continued. "I know you know how to be kind. Why the hell did you have to hit Fletcher with the information like that?"

"Because she knew something was wrong," Grenier said, looking down at a menu as if unconcerned with Michelson outburst. "And she wasn't going to help us out until she knew what was going on."

"Alright," Michelson began. "I can buy that. But there are better ways of delivering that kind of information on a person."

"We don't have time to wait," Grenier said. "We've got to find the guy who did this, and we've got to find him fast."

Just then, the owner who was also the chef came up to the table and slapped a greasy hand towel down, causing a loud *snap*. He was a huge, burly man who looked as though he spent as much time eating in his establishment as he did cooking.

"Yes my good man," Grenier began sarcastically, still gazing at the menu. "My friend and I will have a cheeseburger and french fries while we wait."

"I'm not here to take your order," the owner grumbled. "Abby says she is ready to talk to you now, and I want to hear it from you that you are not going to upset her again."

"You can be..." Michelson started, before he was interrupted by the detective.

"We are going to ask the young lady some questions about her friend," Grenier said, looking up at the big man for the first time. "She is going to answer our questions because she wants to help us solve the brutal murder of her best friend. Now that is about all the assurance you're going to get out of me. Now, if you'll attend to our burgers, we can get this questioning out of the way quickly."

For a few seconds, both the detective and the diner owner stared at each other, neither blinking. Michelson was just waiting for someone to move, certain that someone was about to throw a punch. However, the big man in the grease soaked apron just mumbled something and told the two officers to follow him to the back. Grenier simply nodded, as if in deference to the owner and the two officers rose from the booth and followed him to the back. Grenier and Michelson were led to a small room where Abigail and the other waitress sat at a small folding card table. There were coats hanging on nails in the wall, and all around the room were boxes labeled with ingredients. Abigail dabbed her eyes with a napkin, shuttered as she tried to inhale, showing how hard she had been crying. The other waitress patted her on the arm, then turned and exited the room, sliding past the two officers. The owner left them at the small room and headed into the kitchen. Grenier looked down at the young woman sitting at the small table, and then kneeled down so as to be on her level.

"I'm sorry that I had to be so harsh earlier," Grenier said, looking Abigail directly in the eyes. "But I needed to make it clear to you how serious this was, no beating around the bush."

"I know," Abigail answered. "I'm sorry about being difficult. It's just Virginia is, was, my best friend and if she was in trouble…"

Grenier held up his hand, nodding. He understood what the young woman was trying to do. If he had a best friend, he would try and protect him too.

"I understand," the detective said, interrupting her. "Now, we need you to tell us everything you can about Virginia, especially any changes that she has been going through lately."

Abigail nodded and looked down at the floor, as if collecting her thoughts. She took a deep breath in, and then spoke.

"Where do you want me to begin?" the young waitress asked.

"What do you know about where she was last night?" Michelson asked.

"She was at work," Abigail answered.

"She was here?" Michelson asked, surprised. This did not fit with the information Virginia's mother had given to Grenier.

"No," answered Abigail. "She hasn't worked here in a long time.

Terrence rose from where he was kneeling, and both men leaned against the wall as Abigail began her story. She told the police that Virginia had stopped working at the diner three months ago, and had applied to work at a munitions plant in Manchester. Virginia told her friend that she felt useless lately, and wanted to help out in the war effort. Abigail told the officers that Virginia had been having nightmares about her brothers being killed, and something inside her had driven her to take up supporting the war effort here at home.

"Her mother was under the impression that she was going down to the sub base to see the sailors," Grenier said.

"She didn't tell her mother about the new job," Abigail informed them. "She knew that would lead to a lot more questions, and most of them were questions that she wanted to avoid."

"Like what?" Michelson asked.

"Like how she was getting from Hartford to Manchester," Grenier said, starting to understand the situation. Abigail just nodded, knowing that the detective knew exactly what was going on behind the scenes. "She had a boyfriend?"

"Yes," Abigail said, looking down at the floor. "She met him at a charity event raising money for war bonds. He was a Marine stationed at Pearl Harbor. He was wounded in the attack."

"Virginia didn't want her parents finding out that she had a boyfriend," Grenier said.

"It was more than that," Abigail said. "They were going to get married. They had been together for a few months, and she said she was really in love with him."

"When were they supposed to get married?" Michelson asked.

"I don't think they had gotten that far," Abigail admitted. "To be honest, she just told me the other day. It seemed as though it were something she hadn't thought about very thoroughly."

Grenier smiled to himself, as if he knew what was going on without being told. Michelson handed the pad over to the young waitress and told her to write down the name of the boyfriend and his address. She wrote down the name, but stated she did not know the address. Grenier thanked the young woman for her information, after making sure that there was nothing else she could tell them that would aid in the investigation. As the two officers left the diner, the owner caught up with them and handed them each a paper bag. Michelson could not help but smile as he realized that inside the bags were the meals that Grenier had ordered.

"It's on the house," the owner growled. "Ginny was a good girl, and a hard worker. When you find the guy who did this, don't bother arresting him."

Grenier thanked the man and walked away. The officers reached their car and climbed inside. Michelson stared at the detective, waiting for him to say something. However, Grenier just reached inside his bag and pulled out a few french fries and popped them into his mouth.

"So, do you think it was the boyfriend?" Michelson asked.

"No, but I think we should go see him," Grenier answered, fixated on his french fries. "He had been spending the most time with her over the last couple of months and he can probably give us some information. He was her ride to and from work the last couple of months; he should know what happened last night."

Grenier rolled the top of the bag and tossed it into the back seat. He then started the car and put it into gear. The detective was aware that Michelson was still staring at him, waiting for something.

"That can't be it," Michelson said. "I can see it in your smile. I may have only been working with you for half a day, but I know that you know something you're not sharing."

"Think about it," Grenier said smiling, pleased that the young officer had been so quick to read the detective's mind. "She had been acting very differently over the last couple of weeks."

"Yeah?" asked Michelson, prodding. "Some said she had been acting differently for a couple of months, since she had become obsessed with supporting the war effort. So what?"

"Abigail said she seemed eager to get married," Grenier reminded him.

"I'm not following you," Michelson admitted as he attempted to put the clues together in his mind.

"She was acting strange for a few weeks, she was eager to get married," hinted the detective. After seeing the blank look on the young man's face, he knew he would have to spell it out for him. "I think she was pregnant."

Michelson sat stunned for a moment, as if the answer had been right in front of him and yet he failed to see it.

"So the boyfriend could be the killer?" Michelson asked. "He could have killed her because she was pregnant or because she wanted to get married.

"He could be," Grenier admitted, pulling the car out onto the road. "But I doubt it. However, I'll bet you he can help us find out who the killer is."

Chapter 38

New London Police Department
Present Day

Detective Nicholas Grenier stood in Lt. Hollings's office, recounting the information he had gathered from the old case file to Hollings, Anderson, Wilkins, and Mitchell. Hollings listened intently, never interrupting the detective until he was finished. Nick knew that she would listen to what he had to say, and was pleased to see Detective Mitchell taking notes. However, he knew what he was going to get out of Anderson and his partner, and he knew that he would have to make them understand; they were a part of this case too. The detective recounted everything he read and compared the old case to the one he had he was investigating now. As he looked around the room, Nick could tell who was buying into his idea and who wasn't. Hollings said nothing, just stared straight ahead taking all of the information in. Mitchell sat shaking his head over his notes, but there was a look on his face that told Nick that he believed in the possibility of a correlation between the cases. As for Anderson, he just stood there with a slight frown on his face, obviously not believing a word of what Nick had to say. The only person Nick wasn't sure of was Wilkins, who stood there with his head down, looking at the floor. The detective was not sure what was going through Wilkins's head. Once he was finished giving his information and opinion, Nick stopped, stood up straight and waited for someone else to speak. It did not take long.

"So what you're telling me is that you think this is a copycat," Hollings said after a brief moment.

"No, not exactly," Nick answered. "The Nemesis knows too much about this case to be someone who just got his information over the internet."

"You can't tell me you think some eighty year old man is out killing people after sixty years," Anderson said, scoffing at Nick.

"No," Nick answered, frustrated by the other detective's closed mindedness. "The Nemesis is obviously not the same killer my grandfather faced."

"So this has to be a copycat," Hollings said. "Even if this guy has some inside information, he is still duplicating a murder sixty years old."

"This guy is only a copycat in a manner of thinking," Nick answered.

"At least we know why The Nemesis has brought Nick into the case," Mitchell said. "He wants to make this case as close to the old one as possible."

"You can't really be buying this bullshit," Anderson said, stepping forward. "This is some sick fuck who read about some murders sixty some odd years ago, and decided to have some fun with the police. Notice how the first murder did not happen until after Mr. Grenier's face was plastered all over the television."

"What makes you think this is more than just a copycat murder?" Hollings asked, turning her attention back to Nick.

"Just a feeling right now," Nick answered. He had known that she was going to ask the question, and he hated having no better answer for her than that. "There are things in here that match the old case to a tee."

"This is a waste of time," Anderson said, interrupting. "We should be out following leads, not sitting here reading a case file on another killer who has nothing to do with this investigation."

"How far have you gotten in your reading?" Hollings asked.

"Not far," Nick admitted. "The case file is very difficult to read. There are the police reports which are fairly easy to understand, but then there are all these notes in the margin and I have to find out where they enter into the investigation. A lot of them seem to be my grandfather's personal feelings about the case. Right now I'm just finishing the investigation into the first murder, a Virginia Larson."

"Well then," Hollings began. "It seems to me that you had better get busy reading."

"You can't be serious," Anderson said in an outburst. "This is ridiculous."

Suddenly, everyone in the room stopped moving and a dead silence hung in the air. Everyone looked at Anderson and then back to Hollings to see her reaction to this blatant questioning of her orders.

"Anderson and Wilkins will continue to investigate the case with the leads we have presently," Hollings announced, her gaze fixed on Anderson. "Grenier and Mitchell will work on comparing the old case to this one. You will all coordinate through Nick, who will from there coordinate through me. Are there any questions?"

Everyone but Anderson answered her, just standing there staring right back at her. She dismissed everyone and the four men turned to leave. Just as the detectives were exiting the office, she told Anderson to remain behind. Closing the door behind them, the men headed to their perspective desks and waited, not wanting to start anything should there be any changes to their assignments. After a few minutes of sitting behind his desk, the old case file spread out in front of him, Anna came in excited.

"I heard Anderson is getting it from Hollings," she said with a sadistic smile on her face.

"He just spoke out of place," Nick said, unsure of why he was trying to defend Anderson. "That's all. He just let his emotions take him too far, it happens to all of us."

"Then why is he still in there?" Anna asked, smiling. She knew that Nick did not realize that the reprimand had continued after five minutes. Nick got up from his desk and walked out of his office, Anna following behind him.

As he entered the open space, Nick found everyone in the squad bay staring back towards Hollings's office, watching Anderson gesticulate wildly. Through the glass window looking into her office, Nick could see Hollings was still sitting at her desk, in the same position she had been in when the detectives left. Every so often, Anderson would point back through the window into the squad bay without actually looking back himself. Hollings just maintained the look of quiet superiority as she listened to her detective rant and rave.

"I'm sure you all have something to do," Hollings's secretary said, staring into the squad bay. She had the ability of looking at everyone and yet at the same time making everyone feel as though she were looking at each one of them in particular. "Like catching murderers. You don't need to be standing here watching something that is none of your business."

Everyone started to shuffle around, trying to make it seem as though they were getting back to work, and yet without taking their eyes off of the scene unfolding in the lieutenant's office. Suddenly, Anderson threw something down on her desk, then unclipped his holster from his belt and slammed it down hard. He then turned and left the office, brushing past everyone as if they were not there. Nick watched the detective leave the squad bay, then turned and walked into Hollings's office.

"Nick," Anna pleaded as he walked past her. "Leave it alone."

However, Nick was already in her office when he registered what she had said.

"What the hell was that all about?" Nick asked. Hollings looked up at the detective, an expression of mounting annoyance beginning to materialize across her face.

"Detective Anderson did not like the way I ran this department," she said. "There has been an ongoing conflict."

"So he's quit," Nick asked, shocked.

"He's been with the police department for a long time," answered Hollings. "He'll be transferred to another department."

"There has to be a way to work this out," Nick said. "This is about his dislike for me. There is no reason for this to end up like this."

"This isn't about you, Nick," Hollings said, but the detective was already off. He left the office and followed the path that Anderson had made just a few minutes earlier.

"Leave it alone, detective," Hollings shouted. There was something in her voice that almost stopped him cold. Something that told him she was serious. However, there was something inside himself that told him he was not hearing the full story, and he was not willing to let it go until he knew everything. Everyone followed him with their eyes as he headed out of the squad bay in search of Anderson.

Chapter 39

When Nick walked out of the squad room, he turned right instead of going downstairs. He knew exactly where Anderson had gone. To the right of the Investigations Unit was a large locker room. There was one on either side; right was for the men, left for the women. As he entered, and passed all the sinks and mirrors, he walked to the far end where the lockers were located, and where Anderson was cleaning out his locker. Suddenly, watching the man throw his personal items in a duffel bag, he realized that he did not know what to say. He realized all of a sudden that it had not been too long ago that he had been cleaning out his own locker after being told that he could no longer work in the narcotics unit. He watched for a few minutes as Anderson tossed more things into his bag, muttering to himself under his breath. Nick understood then that the detective had not heard him come into the locker room. Nick cleared his throat, making his presence known. Anderson whirled around and glared at the detective.

"What in the hell do you want?" Anderson asked not attempting to hide his hostility to the other man in the least. "Have you come to rub it in?"

"Rub what in?" Nick asked. "I was told that you quit."

"Yeah well, you're the big shot now," Anderson said, turning his attention back to the business of the locker.

"What the hell are you talking about?" Nick asked. "I'm not the big shot at all. I'm just here for this case, against my will I might add."

"Yeah right," scoffed Anderson, laughing to himself. "Do you know how long I have been waiting for the lead detective position?"

"Lead detective?" questioned Nick, more to himself than to the other man.

"I have been in the unit for over seven years," the detective continued. "I have worked my ass off and I have a great service record. Finally Masterson, the last lead detective, retires and I figure this is my time to be promoted. Then you come in, with no homicide experience whatsoever, and take over the position I worked for."

"Listen," Nick said, not following. "I'm not here to take over any position. I don't want to be here, but I really don't have a choice right now. All I want to do is clear this case, catch this killer, and then I plan on being out of everyone's way."

Anderson turned around and stared at the other detective for a moment. To Nick, it seemed as if Anderson were trying to decide whether to believe him or not.

"You are so full of shit," Anderson said. "You're telling me that even though you got the office and the secretary, you are just going to walk away after the case."

"I don't know what you're talking about regarding Anna and the office," Nick began. "I just want to solve this case."

"Yeah well, whether you mean that or not, you're not going anywhere," Anderson said, turning back and checking his locker one last time. "Hollings is like a heat seeker, and she's got you in her sights. You'll be staying one way or the other, and I can't be second best forever."

"So you're just going to quit?" Nick asked, still trying to understand Anderson's thinking. There was a lot going on inside the Investigations Unit that Nick now realized he did not understand.

"Hell no," Anderson said. "I've been on the job for eighteen years. I may not be as famous as the great Nicholas Grenier, but I still have some friends in high places. I'll transfer and finish my last couple years as I seriously contemplate where to spend my retirement."

Anderson zipped up his duffel bag and threw it over his shoulder. He turned to face Nick then, slamming the locker door shut and headed to the exit, brushing Nick's side in the process. The detective stormed right out the door just as his partner Wilkins walked in. Wilkins said something to Anderson, but he was ignored and in a minute, Anderson was gone. Nick looked down at the tile floor for a moment, trying to make sense of everything Anderson had said. Wilkins stood there for a moment, shaking his head back and forth, then looked up at Nick.

"It wasn't your fault," Wilkins said. "This was a long time coming."

"What does that mean?" Nick asked, surprised by the sudden thaw in Wilkins's attitude.

"Hollings and Anderson have never seen eye to eye," Wilkins explained. "When the last lead detective retired, Anderson thought that naturally put him in line for a promotion. However, after six months, Hollings still hadn't named the new lead detective. In fact, during that time, she had become more hands on about the cases. She had her reasons."

"What reasons?" Nick asked, beginning to see the big picture.

"I don't know," answered Wilkins with a shrug. Nick knew immediately that he had said everything he was going to. "Well, it looks as though you're in line for the lead detective position, and if you don't really want it, I would make that clear now."

"Thanks for the advice," Nick said, as he walked past the detective. Nick knew that Wilkins was right. He had always felt uncomfortable with the way he had been given everything since the moment he walked into the Investigations Unit. He had known that Hollings wanted him to stay, that much had been made obvious. However, he had no idea what Hollings had planned for him, and he certainly had no intention of forcing others out in the process. Wilkins was right; he needed to have a talk with Hollings, and now was the best time. Nick made his way back to the squad bay, and ignoring the protests of Hollings's secretary, he barged right in without knocking.

"I suppose it's your turn now?" Hollings asked with a hint of sarcasm in her voice.

"I need to know what is going on." Nick said, trying to make it clear to her that he was serious.

"Well," Hollings began with a sigh. "I guess I need to know what you're talking about."
Nick looked at her for a moment, and then sighed himself.

"You do understand that I am not staying after this case is finished, right?" Nick asked.

"So you keep telling me," Hollings answered, standing and turning to a file cabinet behind her desk and to the left.

"Why didn't you promote Anderson?" Nick asked.

"That's none of your business," Hollings answered, pulling a folder out of the filing cabinet and closing the drawer. "I don't have to explain myself to my detectives, especially one who isn't really working here."

Nick stopped himself, realizing that she was right. He would never have questioned his former boss like this. Hollings's reasons were her own. The lieutenant noticed the look on the detectives face and knew that even though he knew not to pursue it, he would never be satisfied until he understood.

"Anderson was never meant to be a homicide detective," Hollings said. "He's a great police officer, and he has a great service record, but he was never going to get promoted here. This isn't what he was meant to do. Now you on the other hand..."

"This case and that's it," Nick said, interrupting her.

"That's not going to keep me from trying," Hollings informed him. "Now, it occurs to me that if you keep reading this case and are able to compare the clues, you should be able to get ahead of The Nemesis."

"The same thought occurred to me," Nick admitted. "I'll need everyone's help though."

"Well then," Hollings began. "I guess you better get busy."

Chapter 40

April 7, 1943
Hartford, Connecticut

Terrence Grenier sat in the empty car, thinking about his interview with Thomas Bettford, Virginia Larson's boyfriend. Grenier was frustrated because he had wanted Bettford's answers to lead the detective to a viable suspect; however, they had led him nowhere. Michelson, sensing Grenier's building frustration, decided to head out and find a phone to check in with the department. Left alone in the car, the sky darkening with every second, Terrence wondered why this case seemed so much more difficult than any of the others. For him, murders were usually very easy to solve, most of them not being planned or well thought out. Virginia Larson's murder was different, though. She had been murdered in cold blood, her body had been left on the lawn for a reason, and the murder felt as though it had been planned. The more Terrence thought about the facts, the more nebulous the case became in his mind. He could not help but feel as though the murder was committed by someone who knew Virginia. She did not seem to Grenier like the type of person who would have just jumped into a car with a stranger, however, he knew that there was no way to know for sure.

Thomas Bettford had told the detective that he had dropped Virginia off at work after having an argument. He said that they had been arguing about her pregnancy. Grenier had assumed that Bettford wanted his girlfriend to terminate the pregnancy, but Bettford said it was the other way around. That did not seem to fit with Grenier's mental image of the victim, though he had to admit to himself that his mental image had changed many times. Bettford told the officers that he had then gone to check in on his ailing mother, and when he went back to pick her up, Virginia was not there. Bettford claimed he even went inside and talked to her co-workers, and found out that she had left thirty minutes earlier. Grenier questioned Bettford for almost an hour more, and once satisfied that he was not holding back any information, he left with Michelson in tow. Grenier read the notes that Michelson had taken, searching for anything that he might have missed, though knowing that there would be nothing. After a few minutes, he saw someone approaching the car out of the corner of his eye and turned slightly as Michelson opened the door and slid himself into the car.

"What's going on?" Grenier asked.

"The chief said that the autopsy of Virginia Larson will begin in an hour at Hartford hospital," Michelson answered. "He said the doctor wants you to be there, something about the way in which Larson was murdered."

"Have you ever been to an autopsy before?" Grenier asked, looking over at Michelson.

"No," answered the sergeant, shaking his head.

"Then this should be interesting," Grenier stated.

"What do you think about Bettford?" Michelson asked.

"I don't know," Grenier answered. "He did not give us very much to go on. There are a couple of people to question to verify his alibi, but other than that, I'm at a loss."

"Do you really think that he wanted her to keep the baby and she wanted to abort it?" Michelson asked. "It doesn't seem very realistic to me."

"I know," the detective agreed. "It should be easy enough to verify though, since she saw a doctor, once we find the doctor."

"He said it was very unusual for her not to be there for him to pick up after work," Michelson said, studying his notes that Grenier left on the seat. "If he was truly worried about her, why wouldn't he have talked to her parents?"

"Because they don't know about him," Grenier said. "He had no reason to believe anything bad had happened to her, and if he went over to talk to the parents, he would have to explain how he knew her. He must have just thought that she was still upset with him after the argument."

"Well," Michelson began. "What's next?"

"Next is the autopsy," Grenier answered, slipping the key into the ignition. "After that, we call it a day. I need to put this case into perspective."

The two police officers arrived at the Hartford hospital just over ten minutes later. Terrence led the way as they made their way to the stairway that led down to the hospital basement where the morgue was housed. Terrence always thought it was strange how every hospital he had ever been in kept their morgue in the basement, as if it was the gateway to the underworld. Once they reached the bottom floor, the two men stepped out of the elevator and Grenier almost ran down a doctor on his way into the elevator.

"I'm very sorry," the doctor said, squeezing past the two officers. "I've got to watch where I'm going."

Terrence looked back as his mind flashed with sudden recognition. He watched the doctor for a minute as they all waited for the elevator doors to close. There was something familiar about the man, and yet the detective could not place him.

"Have you come up with any leads so far, detective?" the doctor asked. He must have noticed Grenier's difficulty in recognizing him. "I'm Dr. Westcott, the Larson's family doctor."

"Of course, doctor," Grenier said, extending his hand and feeling quite foolish. "We are tracking down every possible lead. Don't worry, we'll catch this monster."

"I hope so," the doctor answered. "Virginia was such a good girl, it's just such a tragedy."

With that, the elevator doors closed and a chime sounded. The two men continued on down the hall. Terrence pushed his way through the swinging double doors and flashed his badge at the young man sitting behind a desk reading a newspaper. The young man did not even look up, just waved the two men right in. The detective led the way to a small office where a doctor sat behind a desk, pen in hand.

"Detective Grenier," he began, introducing himself. "This is Sergeant Michelson. We were told we were needed for the autopsy."

"Dr. Reynolds," the doctor answered, rising from his seat and extending his hand. "After my preliminary evaluation of the body, I thought it best that someone from the police be here to document my findings as we go. I don't want anything to be missed."

"What did you find?" Michelson asked.

"I've never seen anything like it before," Reynolds said, as if ignoring the sergeant's question. "The stab wounds are not actually stab wounds. They are specific cuts all over the body, as if done with a scalpel. I don't want to bias my evaluation, but there is something very specific about these wounds."

"Are you saying that a doctor did this?" Michelson asked incredulously.

"I'm not saying anything," the doctor answered, walking around his desk and then out into the open bay. "Not until I'm finished with the autopsy."

"Before we begin, tell me about the wounds you examined," Grenier said, following the doctor. He glanced over to Michelson and waved his hand as if scribbling a note, indicating that the sergeant should start writing notes.

"Well, whoever did this is very familiar with human anatomy," Reynolds said. "Every laceration seemed to be deliberate, as if the killer were trying to disable her and inflict maximum pain while keeping her alive as long as possible. I'll know for sure when I open her up."

"Well then," Grenier said with a sigh. "Let's get busy."

"I hope you can write fast," Reynolds remarked to Michelson. "Because there will be a lot to go over."

The procedure itself took five hours, with Dr. Reynolds taking painstaking detail of every wound. As Michelson wrote down every word the doctor said, Grenier stared, amazed. The detective had seen a few autopsies before, and was unaffected by the post-mortem surgery. However, he was surprised at how Michelson maintained his professionalism, even when he turned deathly pale during the first few minutes when the doctor cut open the body. After the doctor described every wound, how he thought it was inflicted and why, Terrence could come up with only one conclusion; the murderer was a doctor.

"I just can't believe it," Reynolds said as he washed his hands of blood. "Doctors take an oath to save lives, not to take them."

"Than tell me who else could have done this," the detective said. The doctor just shook his head, unable to provide a good answer.

Grenier and Michelson left with their notes a few minutes later. They said nothing to each other for a long while, however, they were both thinking about the same thing. Reynolds had not been able to come up with any other answer. They had to be right, a doctor had to be the killer.

Chapter 41

Grenier lay awake, staring at the ceiling. He had never been unable to sleep before, but tonight was different. There were a million thoughts going through his mind, all of them running through his brain at incredible speed, and he was only able to grab onto a few of them. A cold blooded, methodical killer and it looked as though he were a doctor. An educated man, committing a murder in this manner seemed impossible to the detective. There were so many questions, and he had no answers. *What do I know*, he asked himself, desperately trying to put his thoughts in order. *I know that the murderer is a doctor or someone who went to medical school. I know that the killer is sadistic, wanting to keep Virginia Larson alive as long as possible while hurting her.* He was having difficulty concentrating, the image of the girl lying face down in the cold grass. The red, tear stained face of her mother. Grenier had never been affected like this before. He needed to clear his mind; he needed purge all of the noise from his head. Terrence rose from where he lay on the bed and walked over to an old dresser, an elegantly carved piece of furniture made by his father. On the top sat a record player, a recording of Beethoven all ready to play. The detective loved Beethoven; he felt there was something so amazing and beautiful about the music. It was as if he had been able to take action, words, and emotions and translate it into music.

Terrence lay back down on the bed and closed his eyes, letting the music flow through his head. He let the music push away all the clutter in his mind and felt all the tension of the day wash away. He felt a mental numbness as he drifted into unconsciousness. He felt as though he were being pushed by a warm current, his cares were gone, his stress was gone, he could see clearly. He did not know whether it was part of his memory or a dream, but the image of the crime scene materialized in his mind, however, there was no stress or sense of urgency to what he was seeing. There was a cool detachment, as if he were not really there. He could see Virginia Larson face down, her torso bent so that her head and chest were towards the grass and her abdomen to her legs were turned up to her right side. *She was dumped*, was his first thought. The words were spoken in his mind, his voice, deep and booming. *She was killed somewhere else. She was transported here.* New thoughts entered his mind, ideas that he had not been able to consider before. In his head, he was able to recall information provided by Virginia's boyfriend and her friend Abigail. Suddenly, a timeline began to develop in his mind. The pieces began to come together and form a picture.

Someone had picked Virginia up from work, someone she knew. This idea was supported by the fact that she seemed to have gone with the killer voluntarily, and he knew where she lived. The detective knew when Larson got off of work, and he had an approximate idea of how long the killer tortured her from the autopsy. *There was blood in the grass*, the voice in his head boomed. It took a moment for him to understand why this was supposed to by important; then he figured it out. If Virginia was dead when she was dumped on her front lawn, then she would have had to have died only minutes before. If the killer did not perform his torture in the car, which Terrence was sure that he didn't, then he would have to have had a place nearby in which to perform the grizzly act. It was as if a light bulb had suddenly been switched on. He had a place to look now; he had something to go on. The detective switched the light on near the bed and checked his watch, which read five passed four in the morning. Slightly disappointed, he switched the light off and lay back down on the bed. The music had long since stopped playing, the needle having run right off the edge of the record. Satisfied, Terrence closed his eyes and fell asleep, this time without dreams of the murder scene.

The next time Terrence awoke, it was to the sound of the telephone in the outer room. It felt as though he had just fallen asleep, hours flying by as though they were just minutes. Though the sun had not yet risen above the horizon, there was enough light filtering in through the wooden vertical blinds that covered his windows. He rubbed the sleep out of his eyes and climbed off of the bed, stumbling out of his bedroom towards the main room. Grenier reached the phone and picked up the receiver.

"Grenier," he said into the phone.

"It's Jeffrey Michelson," the sergeant replied, identifying himself. "I hope you don't mind, I got your number from your chief."

"That all depends," Grenier answered, slightly annoyed. "What do you want?"

"I had a thought last night," Michelson said. "This all really shouldn't be so hard. We know the killer is a doctor or trained in medicine, and we know that Virginia Larson knew her killer or she would not have let him pick her up. That should narrow the field of suspects."

"I was thinking along the same lines," Grenier said, realizing he had not narrowed the field down in quite the same way, but he was pleased that the sergeant was thinking like a detective. "I'll meet you downtown."

Without waiting for Michelson's reply, Grenier hung up the phone and rubbed his eyes again, wiping away the occasional blurriness. The detective turned towards the bathroom when the phone began ringing again. A surge of anger burst inside him as he yanked the receiver off the cradle.

"What," he yelled into the phone.

"Well good morning sunshine," answered the familiar voice of his chief. "I hope that's not the way you greet everyone on the phone."

"Sorry chief," Grenier said, checking his anger. "I didn't get a lot of sleep last night."

"I heard you've recruited a beat cop as a partner," the chief said, goading the detective.

"I wouldn't exactly call him a partner," Grenier said, correcting his superior. "He's capable though, and he thinks like a homicide detective."

"Well that's quite a compliment coming from you," his chief said. "I think that's the nicest thing I've ever heard you say."

"I have to tell you, this case is bigger than we think," Grenier said, updating his boss. "I think we've got some real solid leads."

"Yeah, that's what I'm calling about," the chief said. "I need you to come in immediately."

"Why?" Terrence asked. "What's happened?"

"It seems the killer has left you a message," the chief answered. "A note was left with the desk officer.

Without thinking anything about it, he had the envelope forwarded up to your desk."

"What tipped you off that the letter is from the killer?" Grenier asked, as he began to get impatient.

"The fact that the writing on the envelope seemed to be written in blood made me curious," the chief said very matter-of-factly. "I had it opened and we all think it's from the killer."

"What does it say?" Grenier asked curiously.

"I'd rather not say until you get in," the chief said. "So hurry up and get in here. I want you fresh when you read it so we don't miss anything."

Grenier understood immediately why his chief would not tell him what the letter said. He did not want to bias the detective's opinion, his chief wanted Grenier to read it in his own way, get his own idea from it before they dissected its meaning. The one thing that Grenier did know was that his chief knew that this was more than just a murder. This was something else entirely, and deep down, the thought that this was just beginning actually scared the detective. He headed into the bathroom knowing that time was now of the essence.

Chapter 42

Detective Terrence Grenier took a quick shower and dressed, making sure not to put on any clothes that he had worn the previous day; a real challenge due to the clutter that existed in his bedroom. He took off immediately towards the police department, a five minute drive. The anticipation of the letter was really beginning to wear on him, Terrence wondering what was actually written in the letter and whether or not it was really written in blood. He could only hope that the blood was that of Virginia Larson and not of another victim. A multiple murderer seemed almost unimaginable to the detective. He had never experienced a multiple murder case, nor did he know of anyone who had killed multiple victims at different places and times. The thought that really seemed to shock Terrence was the fact that the killer did not seem at all worried about making it known that he was educated in medicine. It occurred to Grenier that a doctor would know of ways to make a murder look like anything else, and the fact that this killer wanted to make the murder as gruesome as possible made it clear to him that the killer was not concerned with hiding anything, especially nothing about his own training or knowledge.

When the detective entered the police department, the first thing he noticed was the fact that everyone became almost deathly silent, all eyes staring at him. The desk officer was the only one not looking at him, seemingly unable to make eye contact. Grenier knew immediately that this was the officer that received the envelope, and that he had probably received a thorough chewing out by his chief over the fact that he had no idea what the person who dropped it off was. In actuality, the detective felt sorry for the officer. There was no way the desk officer could have known that the envelope was from the killer, and with all of the duties he had to take care of during his shift, picking out one inconspicuous person who was doing nothing more than dropping off a letter was almost impossible. However, Grenier was sure that the officer would notice everyone who came up to that desk for as long as he was a police officer.

Terrence climbed the steps to the second floor and entered the open bay where most of the detectives were assigned desks. He walked back to his chief's office and knocked on the door. The chief opened the door and waved the detective in.

"Take a seat," the chief offered. "Your partner isn't here yet."

"He's not my partner," Terrence said, reiterating the fact.

"I think you're getting soft," the chief stated with a big grin spread across his face. Grenier was the meanest, most stubborn, chauvinistic man he had ever known. Grenier had been through three partners, and each one of them had requested reassignment within three months.

"I think that's the last thing you have to worry about," the detective fired back. "Where's this note?"

"On the desk," the chief answered, still smiling.

Terrence bent over the desk and lifted the note at the upper right corner. The note was written in red colored ink, thicker looking than regular ink. The detective wished now that the chief had not told him that he suspected it was written in blood. The writing technique looked like pictures he had seen of Asian writings in the National Geographic magazines. Grenier read the note to himself silently, and then read it aloud.

Dear Detective Grenier,

I am very pleased to have you investigating this case. I think it is fate that you and I are brought together like this. I have watched you for a very long time. You, a mean spirited, hateful man who has never cared for anyone against me, a person who cares more deeply than even I can stand. I am very excited to have you as my opponent. I promise that this case will never be boring, and if you are open minded, you might be able to stop me, though I doubt you will ever catch me. This is the first murder. There will be more; how many is all dependent on how good a detective you are. Good luck.

Sincerely,
Nemesis

"What do you think?" the chief asked, watching the detective's facial expressions carefully.

"I think this was written by the killer," Grenier answered, unsure of what he really thought about the note. He reread the letter over and over again, unsure of what terrified him more; the fact that he stated there would be more murders, or the fact that the killer seemed to know so much about him.

"What else do you think?" the chief asked after giving the detective a few extra minutes to re-examine the letter.

"I agree with you that it was written in blood," Grenier started. "I also think that it was written with the murder weapon."

"How did you come to that conclusion?" the chief asked, examining the paper again.

"If you hold it up, you can see slash marks where the letters were written," Grenier explained.

"The blade of the weapon would have to be very thin," the chief remarked. "It would have to be very sharp."

"Last night at the autopsy, the doctor said the same thing about the murder weapon used on Virginia Larson," Grenier stated. "In fact, because of the surgical precision of the wounds, we believe that the killer is a doctor, or someone trained in medicine."

"You can't be serious," the chief said, surprised. "How many murders have you seen committed by an educated person?"

"The person who wrote this note was an educated person," Terrence explained. "Whoever he is, he thinks he is better than us, he thinks he is better than me. He believes he is up against me personally, this is a direct challenge. Have you had this dusted for fingerprints?"

"Not yet," the chief answered. "I'll have someone come over right away."

"I know someone," the detective stated, thinking of his friend Robert Ferrier. Since his friend had dusted for the prints at the Larson crime scene, he figured it would be easier to find a match if the same person were involved.

"So the killer knows you, and you think it is a doctor," the chief said, putting together the information he had so far. "Sound like anyone you know?"

"No," Terrence answered. "But whoever he is, he also knew Virginia Larson."

"So what's the next move?" the chief asked, eager to see his detective bring this to a quick resolution.

Grenier put the paper back down on the desk. He turned to face his chief and just before he began to speak, he could see Sergeant Michelson coming up the stairs. He smiled and then turned his attention back to the chief's face.

"We find the right doctor," Grenier answered and stepped passed his superior and walked out of the office.

Chapter 43

New London Police Department
Present Day

Nick had been taking down notes as he read the old case files, trying to make sense of what had been written in the formal report and the personal notes his grandfather had jotted down in the margin and off to the sides of the reports. On many pages, he his grandfather had attached separate pieces of paper, leaving Nick unsure of whether or not these notes were added to the primary reports. He knew that it did not really matter; all he could do is read on and hope that these reports helped give him some insight to the killer he was dealing with now. So far, the only thing it had done was give him an insight into his grandfather, a man he had never really known. He had known that his grandfather was a police officer, and even knew that he had been a detective for a period of time. Nick had remembered his grandfather as being an angry man and a suspicious man, not so much with his family but always with other people.

Nick had assumed this came from years on the force, making him cynical and suspicious. Nick could see his grandfather's personality in the personal notes he kept on the case. His grandfather had clearly noted his concern about the case, about how different the case was from anything he had ever dealt with. It seemed as though his grandfather's Nemesis had made him a part of the case, feeling as though he were competing against the detective personally, just as the present day Nemesis did with Nick.

It was not until Nick came across the letter from the Nemesis left for his grandfather that the detective actually felt sick to his stomach. The similarities in the cases had now become too close to ignore. Nick read the letter over and over again; unable to believe how closely they matched each other. There was an idea creeping up in Nick's mind, something he could not fully understand yet, but it was becoming more and more clear the further on he read. Nick kept taking notes on his yellow legal pad. Tracy Scott was supposed to be the present day Virginia Larson. *What similarities did she have to Virginia Larson to make her a target?* Nick was beginning to question his initial assessment of the Nemesis, his Nemesis. Nick wrote down all the qualities that his grandfather had noticed about Virginia Larson, and tried to find out whether or not Tracy Scott had any of them in common. So far, he had come up with nothing. The only similarity they had was that they were both women. Outside of that, Nick could find nothing that connected them or would even make Scott stand out as a victim. Nick decided to leave the comparison for a moment and continue on with his grandfather's notes. Many of his personal notes read like journal entries. He wanted to read on, jump ahead and read about any future victims, but he knew that he had to find out what the comparison in the victims were so that he knew what to look for in potential victims.

The work was agonizingly slow. Every so often he would look up through the window that looked partially out on the squad bay. People were busy going about their business, working either on this case or on their own. Nick wondered what the general thinking about him was now that Anderson had left the department. Nick still had some questions he needed answered, some assurances from Hollings that she understood the nature of his involvement in this case. However, he did not have the time to argue with her right now, and he knew that was exactly how their conversation would end up. Nick needed to find some clue as to who The Nemesis was. His first clue came from the similarities in the type of murder committed in Virginia Larson and Tracy Scott. The wounds were inflicted with an almost surgical precision. As he read on, Nick found that his grandfather even suspected that the killer was a doctor or trained in the medical field. Nick had suspected the same from the wounds on Tracy Scott, how the killer tried to incapacitate her before killing her. He finally felt as though he was making some headway.

The detective went back to looking for more similarities between Tracy Scott and Virginia Larson; however, the more he looked the more differences he found. Larson had a boyfriend but according to Tracy Scott's friend, she did not. Larson was pregnant and yet there was no evidence that Scott was pregnant. Nick made a mental note to check the autopsy report on Tracy Scott again. Virginia Larson was becoming more extroverted, a person with a cause that seemed to stem from her brothers being away in World War II. On the other hand, Tracy Scott was an introvert, her first attempt to step out into the world getting her killed. *What was it that linked these girls? Was there anything that linked these girls?* These were questions that were beginning to gnaw away at the detective. The only link he was able to find was in the killer, a fact that Nick's mind continued to drift back to time and again. Both killers are doctors or somehow trained in the medical field. He read the letter from his grandfather's case file again. Both killers seemed to have a need for attention, a need to prove themselves. Both killers had chosen a particular detective with which to compete against. Nick had to wonder who the killer would have chosen had Nick gone into another profession. An eerie fact was how much both killers knew about the detectives, the personal information. Nick's grandfather had written something in his personal notes that now stood out prominently to the detective. The killer knew his competition, he knew Terrence Grenier well enough to know what kind of man he was. Nick's Nemesis seemed to have the same insight into his own life.

Nick looked back and forth between the case file, the old letter written in blood and the notes he was beginning to make, comparing the two cases.

There was something there that he felt he should be examining in more detail, that idea that had been gnawing away at him and yet he could not quite put his finger on. The old Nemesis knew Terrence Grenier, and the present day Nemesis knows Nick. Nick's Nemesis knew intimate details about the old case; Nick had always known that it was not a coincidence that he was brought into the case, and after reading the old case file, he knew why. The killer needed another Grenier. Thoughts began running through the detective's mind. *Both killers are doctors. Both killers know personal information about the lead detectives. My Nemesis knows intimate details regarding the old case.* Then, the little idea that had been growing in Nick's mind flashed, like a secret suddenly revealed. He felt stupid for not seeing it before.

"Oh shit," Nick exclaimed before he could catch himself. Instantly, he heard the creaking of metal in the next room and a moment later Anna popped her head in the door.

"Everything alright?" she asked, looking concerned. Nick leaned back in his chair and raised his hand to his forehead.

"I can't believe I didn't see it before," Nick said aloud, as if she were not there.

"See what?" she asked, curiously.

"Where is everyone?" Nick asked, ignoring her question. "Wilkins, Mitchell, and Lt. Hollings, are they still here?"

"Yeah," she answered. "Why?"

"Get them all to meet me in one of the interrogation rooms with all of their notes in five minutes," Nick said. "I want you there too. I think I've just found out something about the killer."

"What?" Anna asked her curiosity and frustration mounting with the fact that the detective would not answer her questions.

"You'll have to wait and see," Nick said with a smile, reaching across his desk and assembling all the paperwork he would need.

Chapter 44

Nicholas Grenier came to the interrogation room six minutes later, carrying several overflowing folders in his right hand and pulling a large, two-sided chalkboard on wheels behind him. Anna followed the detective, giving the rolling chalkboard a few shoves every now and then, when the wheels would hit a spot of uneven tile on the floor. Nick turned the knob and pushed the door open, dragging the chalkboard behind. Detectives Wilkins and Mitchell were sitting at the interrogation table while Hollings stood leaning against the olive colored wall. Nick pushed the rolling chalkboard until it was parallel with the far wall and then walked back to the table and started opening some of the files. He spread out the papers in front of him then leaned over the table looking at the detectives.

"I've been going through the old case file, searching for any similarities and searching for any clues that will lead us to the killer," Nick announced. "In the reports and notes left by the lead detective, he indicated that the wounds were inflicted with a surgical precision. While the wounds themselves are not in the same place, the wounds on Tracy Scott were also inflicted with surgical precision."

Nick looked around the room into the dull, blank expressions of the two detectives. Even Hollings seemed uninterested. Nick sighed and stood up straight.

"The murders sixty years ago seem to be committed by a doctor," Nick explained. "The murders that we are investigating also seem to be committed by a person with an extensive medical background."

"So the murderer is a doctor?" Wilkins asked, seemingly unimpressed. "Is that the big news?"

"No," Nick answered. "That's just the start. There are some similarities between the murders, or at least the murder of Tracy Scott and the first murder sixty years ago. Both were young women, and both were killed in the same manner."

"I have to agree with Wilkins," the lieutenant said. "This isn't mind blowing information."

Nick knew that they would react like this, and he had been saving the better evidence. However, the detectives seemed as if they were going to dismiss him all together. Nick smiled and reached into the old case file.

"Where is the first letter written by the killer?" Nick asked. Mitchell sat up straight suddenly and turned his attention to a manila folder in front of him. He opened the file and shuffled papers around until he pulled out the plastic bag with the letter inside. He read the letter aloud, watching everyone's expression, then extended his hand and Anna put a strip of tape against his finger. Nick then fixed the tape to the plastic bag and secured the bag to the chalkboard.

"Now, listen to this," Nick said as he pulled out the note from his grandfather's case. He read the note aloud, then slipped it into an evidence bag and stuck it to the chalkboard next to the new note. "I want you to bear in mind that these two notes were written sixty years apart."

"But they sound almost the same," Mitchell stated. He rose from his chair and walked over to the board to examine the old note.

"How many of you have ever heard about a serial killing involving someone calling himself The Nemesis before the last week?" Nick asked, coming around to his point. Everyone shook their heads indicating that they had not. "Who here remembers the last time Connecticut had a serial case?"

Silence filled the room as all eyes were on Grenier. Then, pushing herself off of the wall, Hollings spoke.

"There was a case in the late seventies, early eighties," she answered.

"And where is the killer now?" Nick asked.

"He's on death row," she answered back.

"Whoever is committing these murders knows about the old case sixty years ago," Nick explained. "And for all of my checking, I can't seem to find any mention of it in newspapers. The big thing was the WWII back then, and the police did a good job making three murders seem unconnected. As far as I can tell, the only place one can find any information on the old case would be these records, and they were in archives."

"Are you saying that the murderer is a cop?" Wilkins asked in disbelief.

"A cop, or someone otherwise related to law enforcement," Nick said.

"But you just said that you think the murderer was trained in medicine," Mitchell reminded him.

"Which would leave us with someone otherwise related to law enforcement," Nick responded. "The question is this; who is trained extensively in medicine and would have access to these case files?"

Everyone was silent for a moment as they thought about the question. Nick smiled, having already come to the right answer. As he watched the detectives ponder the question, he wondered which one would come up with the right answer first.

"Some of the crime scene guys have extensive medical backgrounds," Wilkins offered.

"Medical examiners," answered the female voice from behind Nick. The detective turned on his heel and faced Anna, her eyes wide but not looking directly in his, as if afraid of being wrong.

"Medical examiners," Nick repeated, smiling.

"Holy shit," Hollings said from beside the far wall. Nick just stared at Anna, astonished that the correct answer had come from a civilian and not from a detective.

"How can you be sure that it's a medical examiner?" Wilkins asked, amazed but still unconvinced.

"Because medical examiners get a badge," Nick said, still watching Anna.

"I don't get it," Hollings said.

"Tracy Scott was a quiet, shy person who never would have just gone home with any guy," Anna said, putting all of the pieces together. "She had to have felt safe enough to take a complete stranger home."

"She finds out that the killer works for law enforcement," Nick added. "He shows her a badge that proves it, and she has no reason not to trust him."

"But there have got to be hundreds of medical examiners in the state," Mitchell said. "How will we know who we're looking for?"

"That much is easy," Nick said, turning back to the detectives slowly. "We have two facts to use to narrow the field. First, these case files were in archives in Hartford. If the killer was able to get a look at the files, he would most likely have worked in Hartford."

"And the other fact?" Hollings asked, smiling.

"The killer knows Alan Camden," Nick said, looking directly at the lieutenant. "The killer knew Alan Camden intimately. He knew things about the old man's past. Once we find out who that could be, then we will be much closer to identifying him."

"Damn," Hollings exclaimed. "The first real leads we've had to follow. What's next?"

"We need to track down Camden's next of kin," Nick said. "We should have had this done by now, but now it's extremely important we find out who the old man knew here. Second, we need to go through the list of all the medical examiners, both past and present without alerting the ME's office. If we tip the killer off, he could go under the radar. Lastly, we need to take this note from the old case to forensics and see if we can get any new prints off of it, and see if we can get a DNA analysis off of the blood. I don't know if they can do it on something this old, but it's worth a try."

Before he was able to say another word, Mitchell grabbed the note off of the board and handed it to Anna, who was already halfway out the door. Hollings had already claimed the assignment of getting a record of all the medical examiners, while Wilkins and Mitchell began talking about how to get a hold of Camden's next of kin.

"I guess that means I better get back to my reading," Nick said to himself. He took one last look at the detectives sitting at the interrogation table, heads close together, whispering about their assignment. For the first time since he started working with the New London Police Department, he felt as though he belonged. As he headed out the door, he wondered if he had possibly found a home.

Chapter 45

Nick sat at his desk, sorting sheets of papers from the old case file by individual murders. He knew he had to read the case file quickly, but after setting all of his detectives to their tasks, he was starting to feel as though he needed to be further along in the case than he was. He made four distinct piles, lining them across the desk from left to right. There were four reports and notes attached to all of them. Nick sighed, feeling even more pressured than before as he realized that he three murders already. He was contemplating reading skipping ahead to the fourth murder report when Hollings knocked on the door frame and walked in.

"That was a good job in there," the lieutenant said. "How did you ever put it together that it was a medical examiner?"

"It seems right," Nick said softly. "Everything seems to fit."

"I've had a friend of mine in administration do some digging," Hollings said. "She's going to send up a list of all of the medical examiners that have been working for Hartford in the past five years. If we need to go back further than that, we are going to have to use official channels."

"Sounds good," Nick said, contemplating the piles on his desk.

"Why don't you seem the least bit excited?" Hollings asked, noticing the detective's mood.

"The old case had four victims," Nick informed her. "We already have three. We're playing catch up and I don't feel like I'm going fast enough."

"Don't worry," Hollings said consoling him. "We'll get this guy. I'll let you get back to playing catch up."

Hollings walked out of the office just as Anna was coming in. Nick sighed and leaned back in his chair, thankful that he had a distraction for a few more minutes. Every time he started reading the old case file, he felt as though he was not fully contributing. He kept having to tell himself that the old case was helping him to confirm his hunches about the killer, but it wasn't enough to make him feel like he was really helping on the case. The detective knew what he really wanted; he wanted to be back on the street. Nick had come to terms with the fact that he was not going to be working with in the Narcotics Unit anymore, but he still had that need to be in the thick of things. Sitting here in this office felt like it was a million miles away from where he wanted to be. Anna came in and stood in front of his desk. He had noticed that everyone was being deferential to him, and he did not particularly like being in a higher position.

"Do you have a minute?" Anna asked.

"Yes I have a minute," Nick said, exasperated. "Anything to keep me from having to dive back into this unorganized shit."

"The forensic lab said they would be able to get some kind of DNA from the blood on the letter from the old case," Anna began, looking up at the ceiling as if reciting what she had heard from memory. "However, they said that without anything to match it to..."

"They won't be able to give me a name," Nick answered, interrupting. "I just want it on file. They are sure they can get some DNA off of it?"

"They said that if they can get DNA from dinosaur bones they can get it off of a sixty year old piece of paper," Anna said, assuring him. "Can I ask you why you wanted me in the meeting this morning?"

"Because you're helpful to me," Nick answered. "I find your insight refreshing. Everyone else here has been a cop for so long that instead of seeing the most obvious answer; they see two or three possibilities. You can see through all of that crap."

"That's it?" she asked, almost expectantly. Nick looked at her for a few seconds, and then turned away.

"Yeah," he answered. "That's it."

Anna thanked him and left the room. Nick sat at his desk, staring at the wall, lost in his own thoughts. He wondered to himself if that truly was the reason that he wanted her to come along with him. He did appreciate her way of thinking, but he was starting to warm to her. He liked having her around; there was something about her personality that meshed well with his. The detective shook his head violently from side to side, as if trying to physically jar the thoughts loose from his mind. He knew that he did not have time for this train of thought, not when there was a killer on the loose searching for victim number four. Having finished with all of the papers pertaining to Virginia Larson's murder, Nick pulled the second stack of papers down in front of him. He inclined the first page a few inches off of the table and began reading about the murder of Stephen McNeil.

Chapter 46

Hartford, Connecticut
April 9, 1943

Detective Terrence Grenier sat at his desk silently staring at everyone who walked past him, stewing in his anger until he had reached the point of a near rage. He had been thinking about the Virginia Larson case, and the more he thought about it, the more upset he became. In nearly two days of investigating, he was no nearer to finding the killer than he had been the day he promised the victim's mother that he would bring them justice. He and Sergeant Michelson had talked to everyone they could think of who might have any insight into the case. They re-interviewed Mrs. Larson, he had a long discussion with her husband and even told them that she was pregnant, hoping that even through their grief and shock they might have an idea of where she might have gone to seek help. The only person Virginia's parents could think of her turning to was the family doctor. They met with Dr. Roger Westcott, the Larson family doctor, who assured the detective that he had no idea that Virginia had been pregnant. Seeing an opportunity to gather some new information, Grenier questioned him about his being at the crime scene that morning, and he just reiterated what the Larsons' had told him. Westcott told the detective that he had been called by Mr. Larson, who informed him that his wife had found the body of their daughter in the yard and Mr. Larson needed him to come over immediately. Westcott seemed very eager to help the detective, reiterating the words he said in the elevator when they collided outside the morgue.

Grenier and Michelson had split up the names of Virginia's other friends that they had been given by Mrs. Larson, and interviewed them all. However, none of them had any information that could give them any new ideas as to who might have wanted to hurt Virginia. When Grenier and Michelson compared the friends' stories, it seemed they were all basically the same. None of them were more than mere acquaintances, and none of them knew any more than the victim's best friend. Every name had been scratched off, every lead had been followed, every hunch and idea thoroughly examined.

"This is bullshit," Terrence said out of nowhere, slamming his fist down on his desk. The noise and his outburst was so unexpected by the people standing and working around him, that it seemed as if the entire police department jumped at the same time. "I can't believe that no one knows anything."

"I suppose we could go back and re-interview Virginia's co-workers at the factory," Michelson suggested. "Someone there might have been lying to us and knew her better than they say she did."

"Someone has to be lying," Grenier stated. "Someone has to know something about her. There has to be something."

"The paper was dusted for prints?" Michelson asked.

"Yes," Grenier said in exasperation. "There were a few partial prints and they are examining them, but it will take forever for them to match their little print sheets to those on the paper; and that's assuming that the killer has actually been fingerprinted before."

"What about the doctor angle?" Michelson asked. Other than questioning Westcott, the sergeant had noticed that Grenier had done nothing to follow up on the suspicion that the killer was a doctor.

"The chief doesn't believe that an educated person could commit cold blooded murder," the frustrated detective explained. "He barely let me talk to the family in the first place. He says there has to be another answer, and until we exhaust all other possibilities, he's not going to let us look into the doctor angle again."

"What other possibilities do we have?" asked Michelson, with a slight sarcastic edge in his voice.

"I know, I know," Grenier answered.

"The fact of the matter is, you're having a hard time believing that a doctor could do this either," Michelson said, picking up on the detective's hesitation.

Grenier jumped up to his feet, and for a moment, Michelson thought that he might try to hit him. However, the detective just stared at the sergeant for a moment, then turned and walked away in the direction of the chief's office. Grenier had thought everything the sergeant was saying. He knew that there was nothing left to do but to follow the doctor lead. However, the chief had become resistant to the idea following some meeting he had been called to a few hours after the letter had been examined. When the chief had returned from his meeting, he seemed flustered and in a bad mood. He called Grenier to his office and told the detective that in no uncertain terms was he to turn his investigation in the direction of a doctor/killer. When Grenier protested, he was given a direct order not to follow any leads that pertained to that particular line of thought until all other leads were exhausted. The fact that he was given a direct, stern order bothered the detective more than anything else. He had known the chief for years, long before he had been given the position of chief in 1941. Their relationship had always been a close one; he was the only person who ever took the time to understand the detective. Even though the chief had been Grenier's superior in one way or another for over five years, the chief had never had to issue the detective an order until today.

Grenier knocked on the chief's door and pushed it open, not waiting for an answer. The chief just sat behind his desk, as if expecting the detective.

"Come in Terry," the chief said. "And close the door for God's sake, I have a feeling you're not going to make this conversation pleasant."

"What's going on around here?" Grenier asked, letting his frustration take control of his emotions. "I've followed every other lead we have and they've led us nowhere, and the only lead that I actually feel good I can't follow."

"I've followed every lead?" the chief repeated, questioning the detective's words. "Don't you mean we've? You and your young partner out there?"

"Now is not the time to be messing with me," Grenier warned. He hated the fact that the chief kept bringing up his decision to have Michelson work with him. "I need you to let me start looking into the doctor angle."

"I can't let you do that," the chief said very matter-of-factly.

"Then I'm going to do it without your permission," the detective announced, trying to establish some kind of dominance over the conversation. However, the chief still did not react emotionally, and the detective knew that if he had any chance of getting at the truth, it was by making the chief so angry that he let something slip.

"Not if you want to stay on this case," the chief answered back.

"Are you going to tell me what's going on or not?" Grenier said, flopping down into a chair in front of the chief's desk. "Because I have to tell you that it is starting to seem like you don't want this case solved."

"You know that I have people to answer to, just like everybody else," the chief said.

"Someone's pressuring you?" Grenier asked, sitting up straight. "Who, the mayor, the commissioners?"

"You've heard of the Board of Commissioners then?" the chief asked.

"Of course I have," the detective answered. "Who hasn't?"

"Then you know that I have to answer to them," the chief said. "You know they pull the political strings of power in the police department and in most of Hartford for that matter."

"So if they tell you to jump off a bridge," the detective said sarcastically, resorting to an old cliché. The chief shrugged, put his hands together and simulated a diving motion. "You've got to be kidding me. Did you tell them that the killer sent a letter stating that the killings would continue?"

"I did," answered the chief. "They did not seem concerned."

"They did not seem concerned?" asked Grenier. "Or was it that they did not seemed surprised?"
The chief smiled at the detective and reclined back slightly in his chair. Suddenly, Grenier understood exactly what was going on. Grenier went silent for a moment, just staring at his superior, an understanding passing between them. The detective crossed his legs and sat back a little in his chair.

"Detective," the chief started his face still wide with a smile from ear to ear. "Let me make sure you understand. I'm ordering that no one from the Robbery/Homicide department waste any time investigating any leads in this doctor-killer scenario."
Grenier smiled back politely, indicating to his superior that he understood.

"Well then," the detective responded. "Let me make sure you understand that I think this is horseshit."

"I'll be sure to note your objections and pass them along to the Commissioners next time we meet," the chief assured him, pleasantly.

"You do that," Grenier said, still smiling. The detective rose from his chair and stood at semi-attention. "Will that be all sir?"

"I'm sure you have more pressing work to do, detective," the chief said, rising and walking around his desk. He reached the door and opened it for the detective. "Please carry on."

Grenier walked out of the room, going over the entire conversation quickly in his head to be sure that he had not missed any hidden signals. The detective approached an anxious Michelson and waved him to walk along with him.

"Well," Michelson pleaded. "What did he say?"

"He said that no one in Robbery/Homicide was aloud to put any time into following any leads that involved a doctor as a killer," Grenier answered, stopping in front of his desk. He could see the disappointment in Michelson's face as he became sullen. Grenier reached down into the large bottom drawer of his desk and pulled out a metal case and laid it down gently on the desktop.

"Wait a minute," Michelson said suddenly. "I don't officially work for..."

"I know," Grenier said, cutting the young man off.

"Then I could..." the sergeant stammered.

"Yes you could," the detective answered, opening the metal case.

"Then I think I will," Michelson said as if coming to a major decision.

"I think you should," Grenier said, looking over to the sergeant with a reassuring smile. As the top of the case was pulled all of the way up, he was able to see what was inside. It was a service revolver, the standard firearm for all Hartford police officers. The detective removed the revolver, removed a small bag of bullets and started loading them into the individual chambers.

"What are you going to do?" Michelson asked, suddenly interested in what the detective was doing.

"While you are doing some digging, I'm going to a meeting with the Board of Commissioners," Grenier answered. "It's time we get the ball rolling."

Chapter 47

Terrence gave Sergeant Michelson instructions as to where he wanted the young officer to start looking, then drove out to city hall, where in the dark back rooms of the building the Board of Commissioners met and was presided over by the mayor. The Board of Commissioners meeting usually met at night and mostly handled certain police appointments, expenditures, and issues of police discipline. Grenier himself had been called to the meetings twice, once to testify about an arrest gone wrong, the second to answer for mistreatment of a suspect in his care. From what the detective had heard, more and more these meetings were held to assign blame. Politicians now ran the Board of Commissioners, and to be called to a meeting could spell the end of an officer's career. Grenier called over to city hall and spoke to a friend who checked and found that the Board of Commissioners met that very morning and were still in session. The detective had a plan, and it was his only plan. He was going to shake things up. The only reason the Board of Commissioners would have to curtail the investigation of a murder was because they knew something they did not want to reveal to the investigating detective. Politicians love positive spotlight, and stopping a killer only receives good press, unless that killer has some connection to the politician. Terrence had a feeling that might be the case here. His round-about conversation with the chief confirmed it.

Terrence parked his car and entered the city hall, headed down the hall and towards the rear of the building, where his contact told him the meeting was taking place. The Board of Commissioners meeting was always held in a different room. If the meeting was held near the front of the building in the larger rooms, the meetings were usually positive. When they were held in the rear of the building, in small dimly lit rooms, the meetings were generally bad. The detective found it amazing that with every cop in the force knowing this little bit of information about these meetings, the facts had not been leaked to the press yet. The media continuously gained more and more power, so much so that reporters from every major newspaper in the state were beginning to be feared and respected by politicians. The power of the pen could sway public opinion. So far Terrence had not had to deal with the media, which he was constantly told was for the best. His chief always told him he was not a very likeable person outside of the police department. The detective thought it was time to put that theory to the test.

Terrence found the room he was looking for and deciding on a grand and hopefully intimidating entrance, busted through the door, making as much noise as was possible. There were twelve people in the room, seven seated around a table, one woman taking notes at a small table off to the side, and four men standing behind the seven seated at the larger table in the center of the room. The woman and the men standing jumped an unexpected intrusion in an otherwise dull and lifeless meeting. However, the seven men at the table were not startled, and just turned their attention to the detective as if he had been expected.

"Well, well, well," Terrence started. "The fearsome Board of Commissioners. For a minute there I thought you all were playing a game of poker."

"Who are you?" asked one of the men seated at the table.

"You can see how I could make this mistake right?" Terrence continued, ignoring the question. "Seven men, sitting around in a tiny, dark room. It hardly seems the place where important decisions regarding the future of the police department are made."

"This is Detective Terrence Grenier," said the eldest of the men seated at the head of the table. Terrence immediately recognized him as the mayor. The mayor reclined in his chair as if he were appraising the detective. "We were just going over the budget, but I'm sure that we could take time to get a report of your progress in the Virginia Larson murder investigation."

Terrence was caught off guard. He had never met the mayor face to face, and certainly had never been introduced to him. Grenier was starting to get the feeling the mayor had known he was coming. Grenier made a quick appraisal of the mayor and realized this was not a man that he was going to shake easily. This was not a man he could intimidate like the worthless criminals he was used to. While the other men sat at the table looking stunned and angry, most of them puffed up men with family money who never worked a day in their lives, Terrence knew immediately that the mayor was not the same sort.

"There is no progress," Terrence said, deciding to put all the information he had on the table. He assumed that if the mayor knew he was coming, he probably knew what progress the police had made in the investigation. Grenier knew that lying about it at this point would only make him look stupid, and he would lose any credibility he might have with the Board. "There isn't any progress because you're stonewalling my investigation."

"Us?" the mayor questioned in an innocent tone. The older man used the same tone every guilty person used when first caught, and Grenier had to check himself to keep from laughing in the mayor's face. "We have no power to initiate or close a murder investigation. Perhaps there is no progress because you are not up to the task."

The stuffed shirts around the table seemed to appreciate that, as they mumbled under their breaths and nodded their bald heads. Terrence smiled; the mayor was a worthy adversary. Without missing a beat the mayor, a true politician, had turned the failure back on Grenier.

"If you have no power, why have a Board of Commissioners at all?" Terrence fired back. This time, the mayor smiled and bowed his head slightly, conceding the point. "No, I think you have power. In fact, I think you have more power than you let people believe. Right now you're using your power to interfere in a police investigation and I want to know why."

"What happens here is none of your concern," the mayor said, authoritatively. "Our job here is to make sure you do your job. And your job is to catch this killer, not to smear the good name of good men by accusing life saving doctors of committing murder."

"I see you are familiar with the facts of the case," Grenier said. "How do you explain what happened to Virginia Larson?"

"Again, that's not our job, it's yours," said one of the stuffed shirts. "You can't really believe that an educated man, sworn to save lives is out there killing people."

Terrence caught the mistake immediately, much sooner than the stuffed shirt did. All eyes at the table turned to him suddenly, as if he had just revealed a secret, and the detective pounced on it.

"People?" Grenier questioned. "As in more than one? I was only aware of one murder so far. What do you all know that I don't?"

"A figure of speech detective," the mayor said as the first of the seven men at the table to regain his composure. "We are simply concerned that you are barking up the wrong tree; to use another figure of speech."

Grenier felt like now was the time to stir the pot, but to do so he would have to put all of his eggs in one basket. He was sure that the Commissioners were using their influence because they were somehow connected with the murderer. If he was right, they would make a move too quickly and make a mistake. If he was wrong, they would laugh him out of there knowing that he had nothing on them. It was now or never.

"Well, you don't have to worry about that," the detective said. "We already know who the doctor is, and we are almost ready to make the arrest. I just thought you should know that before I bring him in and he starts talking, and believe me, he will talk."

There was a little squirming around the table for a moment before everyone was able to compose themselves. Only the mayor remained still, watching the detective's face, sizing him up.

"I don't know what it is you think you know, but if you have something to say, you better tell me now," Terrence warned. Again, eyes shifted back and forth.

"You keep saying him, detective," the mayor said. "Are you going to tell us who this killer doctor is?"

The mayor thought that he would be able to trip the detective up, but Grenier had already prepared himself for this question. His hunch that the Board of Commissioners knew more about this case had been confirmed by their actions. They knew a doctor was killing people, and they might even know who the killer was. They certainly knew more than he did himself.

"I'm sorry, Mr. Mayor," Grenier apologized with a sarcastic smile. "I couldn't compromise your position by revealing confidential information like that until after we make the arrest. I'm sure you understand."

The mayor just smiled knowingly. Terrence turned on his heel and walked out of the meeting, leaving the other six men seated at the table gawking. The detective closed the door behind him as he exited the room and was met at the door by Sergeant Michelson.

"What's going on?" Terrence said. "Were you able to find any information."

"Nothing yet, I was ordered to come get you," Michelson answered. "There has been another murder."

Chapter 48

Arnold Stanich was murdered. Detective Terrence Grenier did not know why this thought continued surfacing in his brain, and yet it seemed to be the most profound thought he could come up with at the time. Grenier found this notion thoroughly ridiculous as he looked down on the victim lying on the floor, covered, soaked through, and nearly floating in a pool of his own blood. The blood had seeped into the carpet in an area of two feet around the entire body. Every step made on the carpet anywhere in the room caused a liquid sucking sound in the fluid flooded carpet around the corpse. The detective examined the only visible wounds, a large open blood stained gash in his neck, running almost ear to ear. Around the throat there seemed to be more deliberate wounds, as if the killer had opened up the victim's throat surgically after incapacitating the victim. Grenier turned his attentions away from the dead body and examined the bedroom where the dead body was found. The room was neat and orderly, everything in its place with the feel of a woman's organizational touch. Grenier made a mental note to look into a possible wife, and then turned his attention back on the body as one of the coroners assistant's called out his name.

"There seems to be another wound here at the back of the skull," the young man pointed out. Terrence walked over to where the victim lay, shuddering every time he heard the squishing sound of the blood soaked carpet. He bent down next to the coroner's assistant and could see an obvious depression right center of the back of the skull.

"Can you tell which came first?" Grenier asked, trying to understand the events of the crime a little better.

"Most likely the blow to the back of the head," the assistant answered. "The blow probably knocked him unconscious, giving the killer time to cut his throat and..."

The assistant stopped suddenly, unsure of how to describe the wound around the neck. Grenier just nodded and held up his hand, stopping the young man.

"Do we know what caused the head wound?" Grenier asked, addressing all of the officers in the room. Everyone started looking around the room for an object with blood on it or something out of place that might draw their attention.

"What about that candlestick?" the assistant asked, pointing up to the dresser from where he was kneeling. Grenier rose and stepped around the body. He approached the dresser, but did not touch anything, looking intently at the candlestick. There was some discoloration at the base of the candlestick. The detective lifted the object gingerly, making sure to leave as little fingerprints as possible. He craned his head to the side and examined the base. Along the back edge, Grenier found a dark stain and a small patch of hair.

"Good eyes," the detective said, commending the coroner's assistant. "This is the weapon he used for the blow to the head. Let's make sure this is dusted for fingerprints."

Two young men in white coats came in with a stretcher, and placed it next to the dead body. The coroner made sure everyone was finished with the body, and then ordered the men to load it on the stretcher and take it to the hospital. Grenier reminded the attendants to take the body to Hartford hospital and to tell Dr. Reynolds to please make this autopsy first priority. Just as the attendants left the room with the body, Sergeant Michelson came in.

"I've canvassed the neighborhood," he informed the detective. "I didn't get much. The only thing we have is the statement of an elderly lady across the street. She says that a black colored car pulled up to the house when she was going to bed around ten last night."

"The victim's daughter is downstairs," Grenier said. "She should be able to tell us whether or not he would have been expecting company."

"Seems a little late at night," Michelson mentioned. "To receive someone other than family at ten at night seems strange."

"Did you find out any other information?" Grenier asked, ignoring the sergeant's comment. Without knowing what kind of man Stanich was, he was not willing to speculate on the hours the man kept.

"Only that Stanich is a widower," Michelson said, flipping through his notes. "Wife died about six months ago. Neighbors said they have not seen much of Stanich since that time."

"Makes sense," Grenier observed. "Man is still grieving; daughter comes by every morning to check in on him. This morning she comes and finds him dead. Notice anything interesting about the victim's wounds?"

"Only that his neck seemed to be flayed open," Michelson answered. "I have to say the wounds on the inside of his throat look like very exacting work."

"Like a surgeon might do?" Grenier asked, whispering. Michelson only nodded. "This guy really is trying to draw attention to that fact. As for this murder, the killer clubbed him on the head with the candlestick, knocking him out cold."

"The killer does not want to deal with the thought of fighting off the victim, so he clocks him on the head to incapacitate him," Michelson said, stating the most obvious possibilities. "Then he's free to cut his throat open."

Why? What did this poor old man do to deserve this kind of death? The question eluded the detective, the answer that could bring all of this madness together. He knew the daughter was downstairs, waiting to give her statement. Terrence looked around the bedroom and could not understand how this case was connected with the murder of Virginia Larson. Detective Grenier exited the room and followed attendants carrying the dead body down the stairs. He would question the victim's daughter, though he held out little hope that she might have any information that would lead him to the killer. The connection would be in the background, something insignificant that a person almost wouldn't notice; but he was sure that there was a connection.

Chapter 49

Grenier found the victim's daughter sitting in an impeccably arranged dining room, sitting at the table staring off into the distance. The woman was pale, her skin so white that he could see the bluish veins underneath. The woman periodically dabbed her eyes with a cloth handkerchief, but never broke her gaze out the window. Terrence stopped behind her, following the path of her gaze with his eyes until he reached the object of her fascination, a birdfeeder. The feeder had been suspended from a low hanging branch on a tree that stood in the middle of the backyard. A fat squirrel was making his way along the branch cautiously, stopping every time the branch dipped and rocked the feeder back and forth. The woman sitting at the dining room table sniffled and dabbed her eyes again, and the detective took the opportunity and stepped out from behind her and cleared his throat.

"Excuse me," the detective began. "I'm Detective Grenier and I will be handling your father's case."

The woman instinctively offered her hand. The detective shook her hand softly and pointed to a chair across the table from her, as if asking her permission. She gave an almost imperceptible nod, and the detective slid into the chair.

"I know Mr. Stanich was your father, but can I get your full name for the record?" the detective asked, trying to break her silence.

"Caroline Stanich," the woman whispered, her voice cracking.

"You found your father this morning, Caroline?" Grenier asked, as if holding her hand through the memory. This time the woman nodded vigorously as her face contorted as though she were going to cry.

"My sisters and I come out every morning, twice a week," Caroline said. "He's been so lonely since my mother died, we were worried about him. We come every morning, clean up for him and cook him enough food for lunch and dinner. It's been...he hasn't been himself."

"How long had your parent's been married for?" Grenier asked, trying to show his empathy.

"Almost sixty years," Caroline answered. "Our mother's death was such a shock to him that for a few months, he did almost nothing. It was everything we could do just to get him to eat and bathe himself."

"Was that the case lately?" Grenier asked. Caroline shook her head back and forth now, dabbing her eyes again.

"There had been a change in him the last couple of months," she said. "He was starting to do things for himself. He even left the house every now and then. He was going to the hospital quite a bit."

"Which hospital?" Terrence asked.

"He went to Hartford hospital," she answered. "Lately, he was always telling us, my sisters and I, that he was sick. Every time we would come out it was a new illness. We thought it was just a reaction to losing my mother so suddenly."

"Was there a specific doctor you father saw at the hospital?" Grenier asked.

"Not that I know of," Caroline answered. "He saw the first doctor to examine him. One of us would have to pick him up from the hospital about once a week. It was hard on us, but it seemed to be harder on the doctors and nurses. They had to tell him quite sternly that there was nothing wrong with him."

"Did your father make any comments about any doctor in particular?" Grenier asked, trying to get all the information he could about Stanich's hospital visits.

"He never wanted to talk to us about his visits," she stated. "He just told us he was sick, demanded to see a doctor, and he would just remain quiet the entire ride home as if nothing had ever happened."

Grenier paused for a moment, collecting his thoughts. He felt that the clue that linked Stanich to the killer, which would help connect the dots in Virginia Larson's murder could be in the medical records at the hospital. There had never been any evidence that led him to believe that Virginia Larson had ever gone to Hartford Hospital, but they had not looked into it either. It was a lead that the detective would have to examine more closely. Suddenly, he realized Caroline was looking at him intently, waiting for him to say something. The detective focused back on the situation at hand.

"Neighbors say that someone came to the house last night around ten in the evening," Grenier informed her. "Did you know if your father was meeting someone last night?"

"He never said anything about meeting anyone," she answered, surprised by the new information. "He did not have any real friends in the area. My mother was his entire life. Is that the person who killed him?"

"I don't know," Grenier admitted. "But you're sure that your father did not intend to meet anyone last night? Is it even a remote possibility?"

349

"No," Caroline assured him. "He had practically become a recluse. He was getting better, but much of that was because of his trips to the hospital. My sisters and I just assumed that he was lonely and needed some attention."

The detective followed up with a few more questions, but he knew that he had heard all the information that would help. He rose, shook Caroline's hand again and ordered a police officer to drive her home. Michelson, who had been silent during the questioning, looked inquisitively at the detective as he approached.

"A pregnant girl and a widower," Grenier stated. "What is the common thread between them?"

"We can check the hospital," Michelson offered. "Larson may have gone there about her pregnancy. She and Stanich may have seen the same doctor."

"I just don't understand how the killer picks his victims," Terence explained. "It's driving me crazy. I can't understand the how or why."

"What if there isn't a how or why?" the sergeant asked. "What if he is killing people indiscriminately?"

The detective shook his head back and forth violently. This was a hypothesis that he refused to believe. There had to be a connection between the victims. There had to be a reason he was doing this;

and there had to be a way to figure out what the connection was.

Chapter 50

New London Police Department
Present Day

Nicholas Grenier set down the last page in the part of the file that pertained to the murder of Arnold Stanich, and then pushed the stack of papers away from him so they lined up with the other stacks. Each pile was an individual murder, and the detective was only through the first two. He sat back, unable to imagine how detectives were able to solve crimes back then, without computers and DNA. Grenier shook his head, thinking of how amazing it was that crimes were solved at all. A thought had been noted openly throughout the file, and that was the fact that the killer did not attempt to hide the fact that he was skilled in medicine and surgery. Nick thought about how that fact pertained to his case. The Nemesis had not attempted to hide the fact that he was medically trained, but Grenier could not imagine that both killers were making such a statement for the same reason. So far, the similarities in the cases came down to the gender of the victim, and the way in which they were killed. Nick started to wonder if reading the old case file wasn't making things more difficult. He wondered if the old case was making him think about lines of thought that did not particularly pertain to the case. After thinking about it for a minute, the detective dismissed the idea. The killer knew about the old case. The killer must have read the old case files; it was the only way to have the detail that was evident in their phone conversation.

There was a knock at the door, and Hollings walked in. She had a solemn look on her face, and Nick knew that she had come to deliver bad news. Nick was almost on his feet when she waved him down, then pulled out a chair in front of his desk and sat in it.

"We've got some things back," she announced. "Forensics was able to run the DNA on the blood on the letter. They're a little unsure of what to do with it since there is no sample to match it to. They also said that the blood came from a male, it had a Y chromosome."

"It thought that would be the case," Grenier stated, unconcerned. "The blood was the killer's, that's why I had them run it."

"You knew it was the killer's, even though your grandfather thought it came from the first victim?" Hollings asked, slightly impressed.

"It was just a hunch," Nick said. "It may prove useful. It can't hurt to have it."

Hollings shrugged her shoulders and went on.

"We tried to find Camden's son, but we haven't had much luck. It seems Camden's wife left him when the son was in an infant. She moved out to California with the boy, remarried and raised him out there. We have information on the boy up until he graduated from high school, after that there is nothing. We tried to contact the mother, but she died about ten years ago from lung cancer and the step father cannot be found. As for the son, there is no trace, it's like he just vanished."

Nick let the chair recline back slightly; digesting the information Hollings had just presented him with. She watched him for a minute before she realized that he had not expected this news.

"I didn't see that coming," Nick said out of the blue. "The divorce thing is understandable, but the fact that his son disappeared, that I wasn't prepared for."

"You think that's interesting, wait until you hear the rest of my news," Hollings said, a sly smiling developing across her face. "It seems that Alan Camden is not Alan Camden."

"Really?" Nick asked, sitting up straight. His interest was now piqued.

"Apparently, Alan Camden changed his name when he was a young man," Hollings explained. "There is no birth certificate on him either. Apparently, a woman brought him to a Catholic orphanage in Rhode Island just a few weeks after he was born. No information was given, just a name and some money. The sisters kept him and had papers drawn up, got him a social security number, and took care of his medical needs. He graduated high school but had no college interests and went straight into the work force. For some reason, he changed his name a few years later and got married. The rest you know."

"Jesus," Nick said, shaking his head. He looked up to the ceiling as he pondered the life of Alan Camden. "You've got to wonder what they're running from."

"What do you mean?" Hollings asked.

"Well, you've got Camden who is dropped off practically at birth at an orphanage," Nick began, putting the information in chronological order. "When he's old enough, he changes his name. Years later his wife leaves him, moves to the other side of the country and then his son disappears at about the same age as Camden was when he changed his name."

"It's crazy," Hollings admitted. "It's one fucked up family."

"Yeah," Nick said, thinking. A thought had come to his mind, and he was concentrating on it so hard he was unable to keep up with the conversation for a moment. "What if the son changed his name?"

Hollings looked at the detective inquisitively for a moment.

"It's possible," she admitted. "Though if he changed his name legally, he would have had to fill out paperwork. There would be a record of it."

"Not if he didn't do it legally," Nick told her.

"He couldn't just decide that he wanted a new name," Hollings said. "He'd have to get a new license, a new social security number, and all sorts of changes would have had to be made."

"What if he changed it back to his father's old last name?" Nick asked. "Alan Camden was born somewhere, gets a birth certificate and probably a social security number. He's dropped off at the orphanage, the sisters don't know what paperwork has been made for him, so they get new paperwork and he's given a new social security number. He changes his name later, and then the second number is changed to match Alan Camden. The son somehow finds out about his father and realizes there is an unused identity, makes some changes and makes it his own."

"There are a lot of ifs in your theory," Hollings pointed out.

"Well," Nick said, reaching out for the telephone on his desk. "It should be relatively easy to find out. What was Camden's last name originally?"

Hollings snapped her fingers together twice, as if trying to spark her memory.

"Westcott," the lieutenant answered. "The sisters recorded his name as Alan Westcott."

Nick dropped the receiver back on the cradle and stared at his lieutenant.

"What?" he asked incredulously.

"His last name was originally Alan Westcott," she answered. Grenier shot out of his seat and started rummaging through the piles of papers on his desk. "What is it?"

"My grandfather," he started sorting through the papers and reports. "My grandfather dealt with some doctor named Westcott. He was the family doctor of the first victim, Virginia Larson."

"A coincidence?" Hollings asked, intrigued.

"No way," Nick responded, finding a note mentioning the last name. He started reading it as he spoke. "No way. Two murder cases almost identically alike, and now a suspect in the old case could be related to a victim in the present case. No way. Look up the old name, Alan Westcott, see if there is any activity related to his SSN. Hell, look up any Westcott's in Connecticut."

"Wait a minute," Hollings said, trying to slow the detective down a notch. "You have the file right there, did Dr. Westcott have anything to do with the old case or not?"

"I don't know," Nick said, looking down at the cluttered mess he had just made. "I haven't gotten that far."

"I think you can..." Hollings began. She was cut off when Anna walked into the room, her face nervous and her voice shaky.

"You have a call," Anna said to Nick. "It's the Nemesis."

Chapter 51

After being informed of the call, Anna went around to all of the detectives on the case and had them meet up in Hollings's office, where special devices had been installed to the phone that would record and trace the call. Nick found himself staring at the phone, trying to decide how to proceed with the call. He was toying with the idea of telling the Nemesis who the detective thought he was, hoping to catch the killer off guard and hopefully have him reveal something. However, the detective's suspicions were just that, suspicions. If he were wrong, it would be clear to the killer that the police had no leads, and if he was right, the killer would know that Grenier was familiar with the old case. Nick did not want to reveal all his cards. Grenier realized that all eyes were on him, expectant looks of immediacy on their faces. Nick just smiled, his sarcastic side wanting them to wait just a minute longer, then pressed the numbered button beside the flashing green light.

"This is Detective Grenier," he answered. There was a pause on the other end of the line, then a sigh. He knew the killer was listening.

"Ah, detective," the Nemesis started. "I don't like being kept waiting. Let's not do that again."

"Is there something you wanted?" Nick asked, not willing to let the killer think that he had control of the situation. In fact, this was the first time the detective had ever heard the killer voice any emotion. In all of their previous conversations, the killer had never seemed upset, demanding, or arrogant.

"You don't sound like yourself," Nick said. "Is there something wrong?"
Grenier was trying to sound caring, attempting to make the killer open up to him.

"I'm bored, detective," the killer admitted.

"I'm sorry to hear that," Nick said. "Don't worry, you'll have plenty to do when we bust you."

"I feel like I am letting you down," the killer answered, ignoring the last comment. He knew it was meant to get a rise out of him, and The Nemesis would not allow himself to take the bait. "This is supposed to be your education. I am supposed to be helping you find yourself."

"And how is killing people helping me?" Nick asked, trying to relate the little knowledge he had about the old case with the killer now.

"I want you to think about something for a moment," the killer said. "What came first, the chicken or the egg?"

The detective sighed inwardly; he was not interested in playing games. However, he knew that the only way to get inside the killer's head was to play along with him. At the same time, he wanted to impress The Nemesis, make him think twice about his adversary.

"The chicken, of course," Nick said. He knew all eyes in the office were still on him; everyone barely breathing with anticipation.

"Very good, detective," The Nemesis said, sincerely impressed. "I have found that a killer is much like that question. Some killers are made, others are born. Killers that are made are made that way out of circumstance; born killers are genetically that way."

"So what was it that made you a killer?" Nick asked, feeling as though he was finally getting somewhere.

"Oh no," the killer answered, a light laugh caught in his voice. "I came from the egg. I was born a killer, just like you."

Grenier looked around the room at the detectives to see the looks on their faces. The Nemesis had made comments like this before, all of his comments eluding that he knew something about Grenier that he himself did not. The Nemesis picked up on the detective's hesitation when he did not respond.

"Do you remember that day at the New London pier?" the killer asked. "I heard what happened, caught between the police and your drug contacts. When you pulled your weapon, you wanted to kill them didn't you?"

"I don't know what you are talking about," Grenier said, denial betraying through his voice.

"I know how you get that detached sensation when you visit a crime scene," The Nemesis began. "I know how that detached sensation leads to visions of the crime. You can see the crime in a way most people can't, and it's because of what you are, cousin. It's about where you come from."

The detective was already experiencing an eerie feeling, having someone tell him how he felt; especially when he had been unable or unwilling to accept it himself. He did not want to have this conversation, and he definitely did not want to have this conversation in front of the other detectives. However, The Nemesis was on the phone, and Nick needed to learn as much about him as he could.

"Oh yeah," Nick asked. "And who am I."

"You're a killer of course," The Nemesis answered. His tone was plain and unwavering, as if he could not believe that Nick did not understand this yet.

"No," Nick answered. "I'm not a killer. I'm the detective who is going to bring you down."

Nick pressed the button on the phone and cut the connection. Everyone in the office was quiet, just looking down at the floor. Nick wanted someone to say something, and yet at the same time he did not want to talk about the end of the conversation. He looked around at everyone, then turned and walked out of the office.

Chapter 52

The Nemesis hung up the phone with a sly smile across his face and a playful laugh in his voice. It had been obvious that he had been right about Grenier. The detective's hesitation was all the reinforcement the killer needed. His assessment of Grenier at crime scenes was right on, and why shouldn't it be; the detective was just like him. Unfortunately, Grenier was not just going to believe him, it would take time for him to understand. He thought about their conversation for a moment. The Nemesis was a killer, and he was born that way. His grandfather and grandmother had been killers too, but they had been made that way by their circumstances; he understood that. His father had been born a killer, but had suppressed it, unable to accept who he truly was. He could not get over what a pathetic waste of life his father had been. It had been easy for the Nemesis to accept who he was, the moment he learned his past was the moment all of the pieces fit together. The enjoyment he received from torturing and killing those poor animals when he was young.

The pleasure he got from scaring other kids, from the mental torture he was able to inflict on the few girlfriends he had been involved with throughout his life. When he became aware of his bloodline, the past that had made him who he was, his future was assured.

These thoughts started a cascade of need, the need to kill again. Thinking about it was like foreplay for him. He thought about how he used to mentally torture his girlfriends. He was always able to find the young women that had been mistreated by their parents; had treated them like they were queens until they trusted only him. Then he would change suddenly, emotionally and verbally breaking them down over and over again. It had been a game to him, like building a house of cards, seeing just how much they could take before they crumbled. However, soon he needed more. After a while he needed that feeling of power he would get at the last minute, when an animal was in the death throws. He could only imagine how much better the sensation would be with a human, and that thought would drive him every waking moment. It got to the point where he could not concentrate on anything else, it had become an obsession. He remembered every second of every murder, how it had started with patients. No one had ever known. As an intern, he would visit his elderly patients late at night and ease their suffering. A small injection of air into their I.V. tube was all it took. He was always careful, making sure that no one saw him, and at first it was enough for him, but that soon changed. He found he did not get the rush from their fear; he never injected his patients while they were conscious. Soon he realized he needed to see their fear just as he needed the look on their faces when they realized that their end had been administered by the person sworn to save their lives.

The timetable was off, and it was his fault. His need to kill was becoming stronger, and his ability to suppress those urges was becoming weaker. There had always been a timetable, the fourth victim being his coup-de-gras. However, he had given into his impulses, and now the schedule was off. He had planned one murder a week, he had planned to ease the detective into it; allowing him to get the full understanding of each murder before the next one would occur. Now his plan for number four would have to be altered to fit the situation; there was no way that he had the patience to wait three weeks. Besides, he feared that Grenier was smarter than the Nemesis had originally given him credit for. He had a feeling that Grenier knew something, that he had been holding something back during their brief conversation. The detective seemed much too understanding, much too calm in the beginning. The Nemesis knew that he would have to play with the detective's emotions. That had been enough, and even though Grenier had never totally lost control, the killer could tell by the tone of the detective's voice that the seed had been planted. He would let Grenier play with that thought for a little while as the killer reconstructed his timetable.

The Nemesis shook his head violently, back and forth. *You have to focus*, he told himself. Bringing

Grenier into the fold was the true objective. All that he was doing, being the Nemesis, was just part of the overall goal of releasing the detective. The Nemesis was certain that Grenier was a killer, just like him, and that together they could be an unstoppable team. Together, no one would be able to stop them. Two killers, born to be what they are, working together. There was no law enforcement agency that had ever dealt with two synchronized killers, and with the background that both Grenier and the Nemesis possessed, they would always be steps ahead. Another thought entered the killer's mind, and he could not help but smile. Once Grenier accepted who he was, the Nemesis would no longer be alone. He would have someone who understood him; he would have someone he could talk to. It wasn't until this moment that the killer understood how truly lonely he was. There had never been anyone he could talk to; there had never been anyone who could understand his feelings. That did not matter now; soon he would accomplish his mission. Soon Grenier would understand the killer inside of him, and in doing so, the Nemesis would surpass his predecessor. *You have to focus*, he repeated to himself, *it's time for number four.*

Chapter 53

Detective Nicholas Grenier headed straight to his office after leaving everyone standing in Hollings's office, staring at the phone. He was furious, and worst of all, he was unsure why. Everything the killer had said rung true. He had wanted to kill on that pier, the urge surged through him like nothing he had ever felt before. Nick had buried the feeling since the incident, trying to rationalize it as a spontaneous emotion that came from being on both sides, from having worked undercover for such a long period of time. After making the excuse, he had kept himself from revisiting the incident in his mind until he was at the Camden murder scene. Though the situation was different, the feeling was oddly the same. It was as though he was awash in emotion, as if a flood had overcome him. Either out of denial or a lack of concern, Nick had not focused on the feelings; attempting instead to focus on the case. Now the Nemesis was making him focus on these feelings, now that he had broadcasted it to everyone in the room. The detective could only imagine the questions going through the minds of the other detectives, of his lieutenant. *How could the Nemesis possibly know what he was feeling?* Grenier kept telling himself that he was not a killer, as if trying to reassure himself.

The door to his office opened, and Hollings walked in. She stood before him for a few seconds, just watching him. There was concern in her eyes, and Nick could not be sure whether or not she was concerned for him or about the information the killer had just announced. Nick just stood there staring back at her, waiting for Hollings to speak.

"He's just trying to get inside your head," she stated after a few minutes. "He's trying to rattle you, see if you'll spill anything."

"Well it's working," Nick assured her. "I shouldn't be the head of this. I've never worked a case like this before."

"No one has," Hollings answered. "You're doing the best you can, better than anyone else I have. You have a natural gift..."

Hollings trailed off and snapped her head back in Nick's direction, a glow to her face indicating she suddenly understood.

"You're letting what he said get to you?" Hollings asked.

"He says I'm just like him," Nick said. Nick walked away towards his desk, unable to meet her gaze. "I don't know where he's getting this crap. Why would he say this shit?"

"Because he's scared," Hollings explained. "He's afraid we're getting too close. He's messing with your head. He'll say anything to try to get you to snap and give up some vital clue that could put him a step ahead."

"A step ahead of what?" Nick yelled, brushing all piles off of his desk in a momentary rage. "I'm no where. I have no idea who or where exactly he is. I have no idea where he is going to strike next. I have no idea of anything except for the fact that he thinks he knows something about me."

Hollings stared across the small room at him, a look on her face very much like the one she had when she had dealt with Anderson. Suddenly, the detective knew that he had done something wrong, though it took him a few minutes to realize what it was. He did not even know what he had said until he replayed it in his mind. Out of the corner of his eye, he saw a hand reach out through the threshold and grasp the doorknob, swinging the door shut. Beyond Hollings, through the window, Nick could see that he had the undivided attention of everyone in the squad bay. Nick looked down at the floor and let out a deep long sigh, bracing himself for the explosion he so deserved. However, Hollings just kept staring at him, breathing slowly and methodically. After a few minutes, when the tension in the room was unbearable, he looked up from the floor into her eyes. Instead of seeing the anger he had expected, her eyes were filled with concern.

"Maybe I should take you off of this case," Hollings said. "When I see the way you handle yourself, it's easy to forget that you've never been a part of a homicide investigation. Put that together with the fact that this is a serial case and... Well, I think I've put too much on your shoulders. You're not ready for this."

"He's laughing at us," Nick said at a whisper.

"What did you expect him to do?" Hollings asked. "Walk in and announce himself? He's playing the game, and according to you, he's playing it the same way the original killer did. You handled that call as well as anyone could have. You didn't give up any information, you listened to him, you weren't condescending, and you didn't give in. No one could have handled it better."

"I didn't get anything out of it either," Nick admitted. "I'm no closer to him than I was before."

"Then keep doing what you're doing," Hollings suggested, pointing to the papers strewn across the floor. "Or quit. I don't care which, but he's going to keep killing; which means someone has got to try and stop him."

Hollings stared at the detective for just a few more seconds, then turned and walked out of the room. Two seconds later, Anna rushed in and knelt down on the floor, saying nothing. She began gathering the pages around her. Nick knelt down beside her and took her hand in his, mouthed the words THANK YOU and I'VE GOT IT. She cocked her head to the side for a second, then nodded and rose. Nick watched her leave the office, and then turned his attention back to sorting the papers.

Chapter 54

Hartford, Connecticut
April 12, 1943

Three days later, Detective Terrence Grenier found himself no where nearer to solving this case, and now he had a third victim. A young hospital orderly had been murdered in the parking area of the Hartford hospital. The body had been found by a young nurse that had just come off of her shift. The body had been dumped faced down on the pavement. When examined by the coroner, the body had been surgically cut up, just like the last two. So far, Grenier had been unable to find any link between this victim and the other two. Michelson had expressed his frustration with the case, and had left Grenier at the police station after coming back from the crime scene. Terrence could understand Michelson's frustration, he shared it. Right now Grenier's frustration stemmed from the fact that he was having to do the routine police work, like question witnesses and do the background work. However, no matter how much more he knew about the new victim, Thomas Fitzgerald, the less he felt he knew about the case.

Fitzgerald was a twenty three year old man who had worked at the hospital in many different departments. *Jack of all trades*, Grenier thought to himself. But there was more than that. Everyone described the young man as handsome and intelligent. However, he found that whenever a woman would show an interest in him, he would have himself reassigned to a different department of the hospital. It turned out that there were some rumors going around that he did not date women. It had never been made clear exactly what his sexual preference was, but it was widely understood that he was not a ladies' man. It seemed that no one had ever gotten close to the young man, which made it difficult for Grenier to get any deep background information about him. Frustrated that he had no clear picture about the case, Terrence pushed his reports aside and pulled out a clean piece of paper. He wrote all three victim's names across the top. Underneath each name, he wrote what he knew about each victim.

Grenier started with Virginia Larson. He knew she was pregnant and considering aborting the baby. She was a young woman who had recently decided to focus her efforts on supporting the war effort at home. Did her killer know that she was pregnant? Did her murder have anything to do with her pregnancy? From what Terrence had been able to discover, Virginia Larson's life seemed to revolve around her work and her boyfriend. The boyfriend seemed to have an alibi, and genuinely seem to care about Virginia. He knew that he could basically exclude her parents, her mother was too obviously grief stricken, and though he had once seen a father kill a child, Mr. Larson did not seem like the type. Frustrated, the detective realized that he knew even less about Arnold Stanich. He was a widower who had suffered a deep depression over the loss of his wife. According to his daughter, Stanich had been plaguing the Hartford hospital staff over non-existent illnesses. Stanich's family thought that their father just needed some attention, and that was why he was making up all of these diseases. Then there was Thomas Fitzgerald. Grenier knew next to nothing about his personal life, save rumors and conjecture by his peers, but the investigation had just started. He knew that there had to be some kind of connection between the three people. They were all killed in the same manner; two of them had an affiliation to the Hartford hospital. Suddenly, Terrence sat up straight in his chair. He had to find out if Virginia Larson had ever been to the Hartford hospital. Just as he was reaching for his phone, Michelson walked in.

"Where the hell have you been?" Grenier asked. "I think I might have found a connection between the victims."

Michelson, smiling, dropped three files down in front of the detective and sat on the edge of Grenier's desk.

"Hartford hospital," Michelson said. "Specifically, the psychology ward at the Hartford hospital."

"How did you know?" Terrence asked, amazed. He picked up the files and flipped through them, realizing instantly that they were medical records. "How did you get these out of there?"

"We've always thought that it could be a doctor," Michelson said. "We weren't getting anywhere with background information, so I decided to think outside of the box a little. After the murder of Fitzgerald, it seemed as though there had to be a connection with the hospital, and I decided to become friendly with one of the assistants in the records department."

"They all had records there," Grenier said.

"Everyone but Larson. She had no records there, but guess which doctor treated the other three?" Michelson added. A smile was spread across his face from ear to ear. Terrence could not help smiling as well seeing the sergeant so pleased with himself.

"Dr. Westcott?" the detective asked. Michelson nodded.

"It seems the good doctor has a lot of privileges at the hospital, as well as his practice," Michelson said. "It seems that Westcott referred each of them to consult with himself at the psychology ward. I can only guess that Larson was picked from seeing her at his office in town."

"Were any of them admitted to the hospital?" Grenier asked.

"No," Michelson answered. "He set them up to consult with him. He would have one meeting with them, each one lasting a little over an hour, and then he would tell them that they did not need any further visits in the psych department. It's all in the notes."

"I don't get it," Terrence said, flipping through the pages until he found the note from the consultation. "What was he doing?"

"He was weeding them out," the sergeant answered. "Each one of them was suicidal. I'll bet Larson was considering suicide over her indecision about whether or not to keep the baby. I can't be certain until I find something from his office, but I bet that she started feeling as though either decision was too much for her to live with. Arnold Stanich wanted to kill himself over his inability to live without his wife. As for Fitzgerald, there were rumors that he was into men. Apparently, his parents had been forcing him to go to church, hoping God would *cure* him. According to the good doctor's notes, the priests did horrible things to him, mentally and physically. Apparently, he couldn't take much more of it."

Terrence scanned the two files quickly, trying to see what the doctor had written down. As the detective read the details, Michelson decided to give him the general overview.

"Westcott would listen to their stories, then dole out some dime store psychology and send them on their way," Michelson explained. "From what I've seen in these notes, these people did not need to be admitted to the ward, but they needed something more than a nice word and a pat on the back."

"I need more information," Terrence said. "How did he know all of the victims?"

"Virginia Larson must have seen him regarding the pregnancy," Michelson said, flipping through the notes. "He had to have lied to us about that by the way. I'll bet she expressed enough concern about her condition to make him suggest a consultation. He met Arnold Stanich during one of his visits to the emergency room for an imaginary illness. He picked up on the real problem right away and suggested that Stanich come in for a consultation. I bet that Stanich jumped at the opportunity to have someone else's attention for an hour. As for Fitzgerald, they met when the young man was working on the ward. People who worked closely with Fitzgerald say that his...preferences were pretty obvious. I think once Westcott heard about Fitzgerald's predicament, he offered a consult."

Grenier sat back in his chair and closed his eyes, taking all of the information in.

"There have to be more," Terrence said aloud. He wasn't exactly talking to Michelson; it was simply a thought that had just occurred to him. "This may help us catch him. There have to be more consultations. If there are, all we have to do is find the ones like the victims, and we might be able to catch him in the act."

"I think we need to learn more about him too," Michelson interjected. "If he's the killer, than I think we need to understand why he is killing people."

"It doesn't matter why he's doing it," Grenier said dismissively. "We just need to catch him before he kills someone else."

Michelson nodded absently, looking down at the floor. Terrence realized immediately that there was something inside the sergeant that needed to understand how the killer became this way.

"Perhaps it would be useful to understand more about him," Grenier said. "Especially if we want to connect him to the three victims we have."

Michelson looked up at the detective appreciatively. The sergeant began to realize that the two men were from different generations of police, each with different ideas of how to handle the case.

"However," Grenier continued. "You have established a friendship with the assistant in the records department. I need you to go back there and search through Westcott's records, but I want you to do it quietly. I don't want to spook Westcott; I want to catch him in the act."

Michelson jumped to his feet suddenly, a serious look in his eye.

"You can't be serious," Michelson said. "We need to collect all the evidence and we need to bring him in. Then we'll lean on him until he breaks."

"He usually takes a two day break between murders," Terrence said. "Now that we have an idea of who the killer is, we can follow him and catch him in the act."

"Then you have no intention of arresting him," Michelson said, suddenly becoming aware of the detective's plan. "You want to kill him."

"He's not going to stop," Grenier said, rising from his chair. "This killer is not going to crack and confess to everything he's done. There is only one way that he is going down, and that is by a bullet."

"Making you no better than him," Michelson fired back as he walked away.

"Where are you going?" Grenier asked the sergeant as he walked away.

"Back to the records department," Michelson answered over his shoulder. "Got to find out who the next victim will be."

Grenier watched Michelson walk away and then turned his attention back to the files on the desk. The detective knew he was right about Westcott; he would never stop killing unless he was dead. He also knew that no matter how much evidence he collected, it would never be enough. There was only one way to stop this killer, and there was only one way that he was going to stop him without risking his job, and that was catching him in the act.

Chapter 55

Michelson drove back to Hartford hospital replaying the conversation with Grenier in his head. The detective was determined to catch the killer in the act, and he was sure that the killer was Westcott. Michelson could not help but feel like Grenier's decision was a bad one; he felt as though they were putting more lives at risk. Grenier did not want to catch him; he wanted to have a reason to kill him. The detective could not understand a person who killed for pleasure. Michelson had to admit to himself that he could not understand it either, but he knew there had to be a better way of bringing Westcott down. There had to be evidence somewhere, no one was so good as to keep from making a mistake. Beyond that, there had to be a reason for killing these people, something had to make him this way. Grenier did not care what made the killer this way; he just wanted the case solved. Michelson could not let the case end that way, something inside of him wanted to apprehend the killer, wanted to see him go to jail. He knew there was only one way to make that happen, and that was to be one step ahead of the killer. He pulled into the parking area and shut off the car. He looked to the other end of the lot to where they had found the body of Thomas Fitzgerald earlier that morning.

As he got out of his car, Michelson could not help but wonder how much confidence it must have taken to dump the dead body in a public place like this. The coroner believed that Fitzgerald had been dead for several hours before he was found, which meant that he had to have been dumped there late the night before or just after midnight that morning. Still, there is always activity around the hospital, and the killer, if it was Westcott, had to be pretty confident that he would not have been seen. Shaking his head, Michelson turned and headed into the hospital. He made his way back to the records area and found the assistant who had helped him earlier was still on duty. Prudence was a nineteen year old young woman who was working her way through nursing school. She seemed shy, but was more than eager to help Michelson out. She was too young to think about questioning Michelson's authority, and if any trouble were to come from letting him poke through people's charts, he would take all the blame to keep her off the hook. Prudence smiled brightly when she saw him approach. He was beginning to think that she might have some infatuation with him.

"Sergeant Michelson," she said, greeting him. "You're back."

"Yes ma'am," he answered, flashing her a grin. "Thanks to your help, I think I'm starting to get somewhere on this case. I was wondering if I could look through you files again and see if there is any other useful information."

"Of course," she answered, opening the door to the records office. "Anything I can do to help. I think it's horrible what happened to poor Thomas."

"Did you know him well?" Michelson asked. He had not thought to ask her this before. After talking to other people who worked closer with him, it seemed as though he did not have many real friends in the hospital.

"No, not really," Prudence admitted. "But every time I ran into him he was very friendly. One of his duties in the morning was to come and pull the charts for patients who had an appointment in whatever part of the hospital he worked in. He would always talk to me, he was always polite..."
Michelson was listening but not looking at her until he heard her trail off. It took him a minute as he replayed her words in his mind, then picked up on where she left off.

"He was always polite, but?" he asked, prodding her along.

"I don't know," she said, looking off to the side as though she were recalling a memory. "He always seemed uncomfortable. As if he didn't know how to act around people. He was always very cautious about what he said, kind of as if he were afraid of revealing a secret. Everyone said it was because he was different."

"How so?" Michelson asked, wondering if this had anything to do with Fitzgerald's sexual preference.

"Everyone said he did not like women," she said. "But he was always nice to me. I don't know where everyone else got that idea."

Michelson realized immediately just how deep the young woman's naivety ran. She could not comprehend the thought of a man not being attracted to a woman. The sergeant could do nothing but smile, knowing that there was a huge world out there that was going to shock the hell out of this poor girl one day.

"Well," Michelson started, changing the subject. "There is some information I need, and I was wondering if you could help me find it."

Prudence's eyes lit up with excitement.

"Just tell me what you need," she answered. "I can get anything for you."

"I need to get a list of the patients who have had psychology consults with any doctor in the past six months," Michelson said slowly, not wanting to overwhelm her. He also held some information back, knowing that he would get a list of more than just Westcott's patients. He was afraid that if he came out and told her who he was interested in that she might say something that would get back to the doctor and tip him off. Since Fitzgerald had worked in the psych ward, he felt he could explain his interest in those patients away easily enough should he raise any suspicions.

"That's a long list," Prudence informed him. "But it's not a problem. Lists of all appointments and visits come through the records office to make sure that all progress notes are filed properly in the charts. It's a kind of double-checking. Any lists beyond last month will be in archives, but I can get those for you."

"Let's start with the lists you have here for the time being," Michelson suggested. "Then we can move to those in archives if it's necessary."

With the energy that any young person has at the age of nineteen, Prudence went to work quickly pulling out lists of names. As she worked, Michelson read through the lists, jotting down the names of only those patients who saw Dr. Westcott. At first, the sergeant thought the search was going to be easy, but as he started to pull the charts, he realized that not all of the patients had been referred for a consult by Westcott. The only commonality he could think to look for would be people who had felt they were suicidal. After reading through the charts earlier, the last two victims had at one time expressed some type of suicidal thoughts. In fact, at the time of their consults, they had gone beyond just thoughts and had expressed a feeling of despair. It occurred to the sergeant only now that in each case, Westcott had indicated that the victims felt as thought there was no way out, and that suicide was the only logical choice. Though not an expert, it seemed to Michelson as if the depression each victim was experiencing stemmed from their situation. They all seemed to have no one to turn to, no one who could understand and help them in their individual situations. If thoughts of suicide were what made each of them a target, then Michelson might have something to work off of.

The sergeant spent hours, reading through each chart of Dr. Westcott's consults, and by the end of the day, he had barely made it through the month of April. After all of the reading he had written down six names of patients that fit the profile of being a possible target, but now after researching the patients, he found that two had been admitted to the psych ward and were still there, and one of the patients had died of natural causes. He was now left with three names that he would have to investigate, one woman and two men. As he closed the last chart, he realized Prudence was staring at him. He looked up and met her gaze.

"I don't mean to interrupt your work," she started anxiously. "But my shift is almost over and the girl who works at night will be really mad if I leave this place a mess."

Michelson looked at his watch only to discover that it was ten minutes to five. He had spent almost five hours straight looking at these charts.

"I'm going to have to clean up these charts before I leave," Prudence said, then stopped and looked from side to side as if to make sure no one was listening. She leaned forward and lowered her voice. "But I tell you what. I'll come in early tomorrow and pull all the charts from Dr. Westcott's consults. That way you can come in and just start reading."

"What makes you think I'm interested in Westcott's patients?" Michelson asked apprehensively. Apparently, he had not been as clever as he thought.

"Oh come now," Prudence said with a smile. "The only charts you read were the patients who met with Dr. Westcott. It's not hard to see that you're interested in his patients. Don't worry, I won't tell anyone."

"You're a very clever girl," Michelson admitted. "But I really need you to keep this secret. You can't say a word about this to anyone."

Prudence held a finger up to her mouth a smiled devilishly. She then collected the charts beside Michelson and turned to file them away. The sergeant smiled and rose from his chair, grabbing the list of names and exited the records office. He headed back out to his car, feeling slightly apprehensive but more pleased with his progress. If Prudence was careful, he could get the information he needed quickly during the day, and hopefully get the information on the potential targets during the evening. Michelson climbed into his car and drove back to the police station, finally filled with some feeling of accomplishment. He felt as though they were finally on the right track, and he thought this could really lead them to catching the killer. He looked down at the list of names on the seat beside him. He knew that he still had a lot of work to do. He hoped that Grenier had found something that might support their theory that Westcott was the killer.

Chapter 56

When Sergeant Michelson returned to the police station, he found Grenier sitting at his desk, surrounded by papers. The detective was talking to someone on the phone, so Michelson went ahead and started getting some preliminary information on the three names he had come back with. He did not get far before Grenier hung up the phone and called the sergeant over. Michelson was afraid that Grenier was going to rehash the argument that they had earlier about the best way to stop Westcott. Beyond the fact that he wanted to understand Westcott's thinking, Michelson found something morally wrong about killing the man. Michelson had been forced to fire his weapon a few times in the line of duty, so he could understand the idea of killing someone in defense of yourself or others, however, he did not believe in playing judge and jury with a suspect. Grenier had already decided that there was only one way to stop Westcott, the detective had already deemed him guilty and beyond redemption. Grenier was sure that the only way to stop Westcott was to kill him, and the only way to do it without going to jail himself, would be to catch the killer in the act. Michelson, however, needed more than that. He could not feel comfortable condemning the man to death before understanding what made him a killer. The thought of letting Grenier have his way made Michelson feel like a killer himself, and that was something that he just could not deal with.

"I've got some information," Grenier said as the sergeant approached. "But first I want to talk to you about our little disagreement."

Michelson sighed, knowing that they needed to get beyond this, but not wanting to have the conversation right now.

"I know that you think I'm wrong in the way I want to handle this," Grenier acknowledged. "But, I've dealt with a lot of homicides in my time. This man is a pure killer, something that I haven't ever dealt with before. All of the killer's that I have dealt with in the past have killed because the victim stood in the way of something they wanted, something tangible. This killer, this Nemesis, kills for no other reason than the satisfaction he derives from it."

"You yourself said this is the first time that you have dealt with this kind of killer," Michelson reminded the detective. "Don't you think it would be helpful to understand more about him, like why he's killing people? Not to mention that we swore to uphold the law, not to consider ourselves above it."

Michelson's speech seemed to take the wind out of the detective's sails. Grenier sat back shaking his head, thinking about how much the sergeant had to learn. The detective could remember a time in which he had been that wide eyed about the world and especially about being a cop. He felt as though the things he had seen during his career as a police officer had given him a different view on the world, but at the same time he could not disagree with Michelson.

"No amount of evidence in the world is going to be enough to get him put in jail," Grenier stated. "He's a well educated doctor, a man who has sworn to protect life. Unless we find him in the act of actually killing someone, I doubt any jury will be able to convict him."

"But that's not our job," Michelson reminded the detective. "Our job is to bring him in."

"Well," Grenier began, pulling himself out of his thoughts. "That's a long way from where we are now. We don't even have enough evidence to consider him as a real suspect. All we have so far is coincidence and some tenuous links between the victims. I can't promise you anything, but if we can stop him by arresting him, we'll do it."

"That's all I ask," Michelson said, not completely convinced of the detective's motives. However, Grenier conceded his point, and for now that was enough. Michelson knew that Grenier was right, and they did not have enough evidence to worry about that yet. "I got through the all of Westcott's April consults, and I have three possible targets."

"I happen to have some information myself," Grenier announced. "Our good Dr. Westcott was never a surgeon, but he did work for the coroner's office for a time. It seems that during the time he was working for the coroner, some strange things started happening to the bodies."

"Like what?" Michelson asked, his interest peaked.

"Apparently," Grenier began. "There were some strange post-mortem mutilations of many bodies that were to be cremated. Since the bodies were already dead, the coroner's office felt no reason to involve the police and initiated their own internal investigation."

"I'm sure that was exhaustive," Michelson remarked, sarcastically. "What did they end up finding?"

"I don't know yet," Grenier said. "I'm still waiting for some kind of final report, but I do know that Westcott left suddenly upon the conclusion of the investigation."

"So he leaves the coroner's office and starts up his own practice, while still maintaining his privileges at the Hartford hospital?" Michelson questioned. "That doesn't sound like much of a punishment."

"I can't be sure, but I think there was something embarrassing that the Board of Commissioners wanted to cover up," Grenier said. "All they wanted to do was get him out of their hair without bringing the situation to the attention of the public."

"So they just released this time bomb on an unsuspecting public," Michelson said. "They knew that he was disturbed. It was only a matter of time before he started killing people."

"Well, it all makes sense now," Grenier observed. "The only group who can run a private investigation is the Board of Commissioners. I'm sure they knew that it was only a matter of time before Westcott started killing, and now that he has they are trying to cover their asses."

"Too late," Michelson said. "So what do we do now?"

"I think our most important priority is to find out who his next target is," Grenier stated. "If he keeps to his schedule, he will kill someone day after tomorrow."

"Well, I'll get busy checking on these names," Michelson said. "I just hope we've got his criteria down. If there is anything I've missed that makes his patients potential targets, I could be looking in the wrong area."

"We have to do what we can," the detective said. "I'm going to have it out the Board of Commissioners, and then we need to do something to keep us aware of all Westcott's movements."

"Like a tail?" Michelson asked, thinking of the difficulty of having a unit follow Westcott at all times without his knowledge. "That's going to be tough."

"That's why we have to be sure of his next target," Grenier said. "We find out who the target is, and then we can set the trap and catch him before he kills again."

Michelson made a face of disapproval, and the detective raised his hands in mock defense.

"I know, I know," Grenier pleaded. "Let's start with what we've got, and then we'll go from there."

Grenier left thirty minutes later with Michelson deep in his paperwork, getting information on the three names he had. He was concerned that the sergeant had spent five hours and only come up with three names of possible targets. It became overwhelmingly clear what a monumental task the detective had ahead of him, and he felt knew that he and Michelson were on their own. No one was going to help them out, not his chief who was afraid of losing his job, and definitely not the Board of Commissioners who were intent on covering up the past.

Chapter 57

Salem, Connecticut
Present Day

Nick finished reading the notes Terrence Grenier had written sixty years ago and placed them down on his coffee table. After the phone call with the Nemesis, Nick had been unable to collect his thoughts and decided to leave the police department and to return to the peace and quiet of his home. There were so many thoughts running through his mind after the call, most of them dealing with the fact that he had so little real information to work from. However, now reading the old case file, he began to feel more optimistic. It seemed the Dr. Westcott in the past had been the killer, or at least so far in his reading, he was heavily suspected. Nick found it interesting that the beginnings of a conspiracy were becoming evident. However, that was not the case now. There was no conspiracy going on, just a killer out for the joy of killing. Nick doubted that he would be able to find a real pattern to the killings and therefore find how the present day Nemesis was targeting his victims. No, Nick knew that stopping this killer would hinge on finding out who the killer is. The more he read of the old case file, the more he felt confident that the Westcott lead was a viable one. Tomorrow, he would go in and focus much of his efforts on finding Camden's son. Something in the back of Nick's mind told him that finding Camden's son was the vital clue.

Nick looked up from his papers to the television. He had the station set to the local NBC station, and he was watching the local six o'clock news with the sound muted. The five day weather forecast flashed up on the screen, and disappointment set in as everyday was filled with cloudy skies and rain. *It is April,* Nick thought to himself, *it always rains in April.* He looked back down to the papers on his coffee table and realized that he was almost finished with the case file. He would have the entire thing read by this evening. Suddenly, Nick saw bright lights play along the far wall of the dining room as the beams of car headlights came in through the windows. The dining room looked out on the front yard of his home, and Nick knew that someone had pulled up the driveway. Inside, he secretly prayed that it wasn't Hollings with news of another murder. He was so far from knowing who the killer was, so far from solving this case. He rose from his seat on the floor and made his way to the front door, just as he heard the rustling of a paper bag on the other side of the door. Nick opened the door and was shocked to see Anna on the other side of it.

"I thought you might need some company tonight," she said, as if he should have expected her. She brushed past him without hesitating, leaving him watching her walk down the hall towards the kitchen. "I brought some Chinese food."

Nick closed the door, wracking his brain to try and remember if he had invited her or if she might have made any mention of coming over. However, he knew he had missed nothing, she had said nothing of stopping by. Nick followed her down the hall, a look of sheer confusion etched into his face.

"What are you doing here?" the detective asked.

"I told you," she answered. "I thought you might need some company. You were not yourself when you left this evening, and I saw you take the case file with you so I knew you were going to work through the night. I thought you could use a fresh pair of eyes."

Anna placed the brown paper bag on the counter and started pulling out pint sized boxes of Chinese food. She opened the boxes, and then looked up at the cabinets, as if waiting for one to open.

"Second one on your right," Nick said, anticipating her next question. "Plates are at the bottom. So you're here to what, help me with the old case file?"

"You seem to be sure there is a connection to the old case," she said. "However, you've been reading that file for days now and haven't come up with anything terribly useful."

"And you're going to read the file and suddenly have the case solved by the end of the night?" Nick asked sarcastically.

Anna stopped what she was doing and turned around.

"You don't have to be a smart ass about it," she said very matter-of-factly. She walked over to the detective, stopping just inches in front of him almost pinning him against the counter behind him. She was too close, and Nick would have backed up if there had been anywhere to go. "I just think you need some company. When is the last time you had anyone to talk to?"

"Too long," Nick answered before he knew it. He suddenly felt embarrassed for letting it slip. Anna put her hand on his arm for just a minute, then turned and walked back over to the plates.

After helping her with the food and pouring some wine he found in the refrigerator, they were sitting on the couch in the living room passing papers back and forth between bites of food. Nick explained where he was in the case file, and gave her a brief run down of the events that had transpired up until now. She listened intently, saving any questions until he was finished. She placed a yellow legal pad in front of her that had been lying on the table and started jotting down notes. Before he knew it, they were deep in a discussion linking the old case to the new one.

"It's more than just picking victims who are the same gender," Nick explained. "The third victim in both cases were homosexual, and the second victim in both cases were both elderly men."

"But?" Anna asked, sensing a question coming.

"But the first victim in the old case was a young pregnant girl," Nick answered. "Other than both being a young woman, I don't see any other connection between them."

"Does there have to be?" Anna asked.

"I suppose not," Nick answered, obviously disappointed. "I just don't understand why the killer would follow so closely to the old case with the second and third victims, and not with the first. Serial killers usually follow a pattern. I just don't see the pattern here."

"Well then," Anna began. "Are you sure there isn't more of a connection between the two? What do we really know about her?"

"Not as much as we probably should," Nick admitted. "I was only brought in after Camden was killed. I guess I did not look at her as closely as I could have."

Anna slid herself off of the couch to the floor and started writing on the legal pad. Nick waited for her to finish.

"I'm making a list of things we need to investigate further," Anna said, sensing his interest. She finished writing and leaned back, her body wedged against his leg.

"While you're writing things to do down there," Nick began, trying to ignore the fact that with each passing moment she was getting closer to him. "Write down Investigate Camden's son."

"What's that all about?" she asked as she jotted the note down on the paper.

"Just a hunch I have," Nick answered. "It appears that the killer in the old case may be related somehow to Camden."

The two continued working late into the night, making notes of anything that linked the old case to the new one. Anna found the list of names that Terrence Grenier wrote years before and started a similar list of the present day victims. Nick knew that they would only get so far tonight, as they lacked much of the background data they could get from the computers at the police department.

"You think Camden is the son of the old Nemesis?" Anna asked.

"I do," Nick answered. "Westcott was the name given to the nuns at the orphanage when the baby was dropped off."

"And you think Camden's son is the killer now?" Anna asked, continuing her line of thought.

"I don't know," Nick admitted. "I definitely think it's possible. However, until we find out what happened to Camden's son, we can't be sure."

"It makes sense though," Anna said. "During the phone call, the Nemesis said he was born to be a killer. If he knows where he comes from, that could explain why he thinks he's born to be this way."

"I thought about that too," Nick answered. "It just might not be easy to find out what happened to Camden's son. From what little information Hollings was able to pull up, it seems he disappeared after graduation from high school."

"Well, it hasn't been easy so far," Anna said with a smile. "Why should it be easy now?"

Nick laughed, knowing she was right. For so long the police had been operating off of very little information. Now that they had a little more information, the case seemed even more insurmountable than before. Nick leaned back on the sofa, thinking about all that they had been able to accomplish this evening. Though they had no new information, he finally felt as though they had a clear picture of where to start investigating.

"So let me ask you a question," Anna started. "How long do I have to keep rubbing up against you here before you kiss me?"

Chapter 58

There was a long silence as Nick absorbed the meaning behind her question. Anna stared at him for a few seconds, and then looked down at the floor as she anticipated his reaction. Nick felt caught between a rock and a hard place, watching her look away from him as he remained quiet. He was attracted to her, but just as she asked him; his first thoughts were of whether or not he could get into trouble with sexual harassment. Nick got up, realizing that after a minute of silence he still had not said anything, and walked into the kitchen. What he did not expect, was for Anna to rise and follow him. They both carried the plates and wine glasses back into the kitchen and as they did, Nick could feel the woman's eyes boring into the back of his head. Finally, Nick turned around and faced her.

"I'm sorry," Nick began. "You caught me off guard with this."

"You're worried about sexual harassment," Anna said.

"Well, yes," Nick admitted. "But mostly, I'm just not used to it being this way."

"Being what way?" Anna prodded.

"I'm not used to," Nick stammered. "It doesn't matter."

"Are you attracted to me?" Anna asked directly.

"Yes," Nick answered. "It's just that I haven't thought of anything romantic in a long time. You just caught me off guard with this."

"Well, let me make it simple for you," Anna said. "I like you, and I've gotten the feeling that you like me. If, in the future, you would like to maybe start something, get together, then I'm all for it."

"Well," Nick said, taking it all in. "That's good to know. And you're right; I do like you, very much."

"Well then," Anna said, looking around the kitchen. "It feels like we got a lot of good work done. I think you were able to clear up what your next step is."

"Yeah, no," Nick stammered. "I really appreciate your help. I wouldn't have gotten this far without you."

"Yeah, it's getting late," Anna said. She walked into the living room and picked up her purse, slinging it over her shoulder. "I should be going."

Nick followed her into the living room, where she grabbed her coat and purse, then followed her down the hall. It was obvious that the jovial mood between the two of them had suddenly changed, and as he followed her, he wondered what he should have said differently. Once they reached the door, Anna opened it just a little, and then turned to face him.

"Some day," she said. "Maybe when this is all over, you can ask me out on a date. Maybe I'll ask you out on a date."

Nick just smiled and looked down at the floor. He didn't know what to say, and felt very embarrassed about the whole thing. He had not picked up on any flirting between the two of them, and was starting to wonder if he should have. Nick was never good at relationships, his work had always come first and that was never acceptable with the women he dated. He looked back up to Anna, as if to say he was sorry, and she smiled slightly, as if to say it was alright. Then she took a step forward and placed a quick kiss on his lips. As she stepped back, Nick stepped forward and kissed her back, this time hard. Before he knew it, they were kissing deeply. Absently, Nick pulled her back into the house, pushing the door closed as he did. Suddenly, it was as if everything else had not happened. They were kissing intensely, and in minutes, it was just the two of them together and everything else, the case, the world, the Nemesis, did not exist.

Chapter 59

Nick woke up the next morning alone in his bed. He propped himself up quickly, looking around the room for evidence that Anna was still there. However, he quickly realized that her clothes were gone and he did not hear anything in the house. For a moment, a brief pang of fear shot through him as he worried whether he had done or said something wrong. His fears were eased as he found a note on the pillow beside him. He opened the note and read it through twice, then relieved, lay back down on the bed. The note had been brief, stating that she was going to have to go back home to shower and change, and did not want to deal with any of the morning after conversations about what they do now. Nick was pleased, also not wanting to ruin the morning thinking about what this meant for their relationship. Besides, after what they had accomplished last night, Nick was energized to get into work and begin with his new look on the investigation. Thinking about all the new work ahead of him, the detective suddenly jumped out of bed and took a quick shower. In less than thirty minutes, he was dressed and driving into the police department. In his mind, he was going over his new plan of attack for the investigation. First, he would assign Wilkins to do a deep background check to find out what happened to Camden's son. He also wanted to find out how many Westcott's there were in the area, whether they were doctors or not. The detective had a feeling the Nemesis was a traditionalist. The very fact that he took the same identity as the killer sixty years before was a hint, coupled with the way he was staying true to form with the victims led Nick to believe that the killer was either related to a Westcott or had the same last name.

When Nick made it into the police department, people were just starting to make their way in, and the activity was beginning to pick up. Nick went into his office and started preparing his assignments when he heard Anna in the outer room. Nick rose from his desk and walked into the outer room. Anna was hanging her jacket up when he walked in. Suddenly, Nick realized that he did not know how to start this conversation.

"Good morning, detective," Anna began with a smile.

"Good morning," Nick began, unsure of himself. "I think we need to talk about something quickly."

"You want to make sure that there isn't going to be any misunderstandings about last night," Anna said, reading his concern. "Look, if this is something we want to continue, then I can transfer to another department so there are no difficulties. It's not that big a deal."

"That won't be necessary," Nick said. "I'm not going to be working here after this case."

"Well," Anna said in a voice that made Nick think she did not believe him. "Whatever happens, we have some time to think about it. In the meantime, this is work and here we keep it professional."

"Sounds good," Nick said, pleased with the outcome. He had been worried that she might say something about being in a relationship and that was not something he could afford to think about right now. Nick set Anna to the task of reading through the end of the old case file, to understand where the case ended up while Nick set up the assignments for the rest of the group. Wilkins, Mitchell, and Hollings came into the interrogation room where they had set up a make shift command center for the investigation ten minutes later, all eager to see what Nick had put together. After everyone sat down, Nick stood and started going through his notes.

"The lieutenant put it together that Alan Camden was an orphan," Nick began. "When he was left there, the name he was given was Westcott. It may just be a coincidence, but the suspect in the old case was a doctor named Westcott. I think we need to find out all we can about anyone named Westcott in this area."

"Why not just find out more about the lineage of the old killer?" asked Mitchell.

"We will," Nick answered. "I believe that Camden was the son of the first killer, Dr. Westcott. According to the lieutenant, Camden's son goes off the radar after he graduates from high school. We need to find him; we need to find out who he became and where he is."

"You think he's the killer?" Hollings asked, trying to follow the detective's train of thought. Nick looked down at the floor, unsure of whether he should actually speak his mind or not. When he looked up again, he realized that they were all hanging on his every word, and his feelings were exactly what they wanted to hear.

"Yes," he heard himself saying. "I do. It seems to fit with the fact that the Nemesis feels he was born to be a killer. If he is Camden's son, and he knows who Westcott is...well, it fits."

"That's *IF* Camden is in fact the child of this old Dr. Westcott," Mitchell pointed out. "Do we have any proof of this?"

"No," Nick answered. "Which is why, while you are finding out what happened to Camden's son, Wilkins will be both finding out about all the Westcott's in the area. From there we will trace any Westcotts we find and dig up their past."

Wilkins looked up, realizing that he had been saddled with a lot of work all of a sudden.

"Sorry," Nick said. "It just seemed to go along with your other assignment."

"No problem," Wilkins said with a sigh, thinking about how he could get it all done quickly.

"Anna is reading the end of the case file," Nick announced. "She should be done with it today, so we should have the final information about the old case soon. There seem to be some similarities between them, mostly the victims. Apparently, both second victims were older men, and both third victims were homosexuals."

"I notice you haven't mentioned the first victims," Mitchell said with a raised eyebrow.

"Yeah," Nick muttered. "Apparently that is the only hang up in my little theory. The first victim in the old case, Virginia Larson, was pregnant when she was murdered. She was considering abortion and apparently all of the victims had been toying with thoughts of suicide. I think we need to investigate the suicide possibility in the present day victims."

"What's the deal with the first victim?" Hollings asked, attempting to get to the point.

"Yeah," Nick started. "There is no clear connection between Virginia Larson and Tracy Scott."

"You mean besides the fact that they were both young women?" Mitchell pointed out.

"Yeah, besides that," Nick answered. He looked over to Hollings questioningly. "I'm going to try to dig into her past and see what I can find out."

Nick looked around the room and everyone was jotting down notes on pads, and he could tell that they were eager to get to busy and Nick found himself feeling as though he needed to say something inspiring.

"Look everyone," the detective began, pulling together his inner strength. "There is a connection between this case and the old one, but stopping this killer is going to happen here, now. This old case has helped us, but now we need to pull together and use what we know to get ahead of this guy and bring him down."

Nick looked around the room, seeing heads nodding up and down and all eyes remaining on him. They were all quiet for about ten seconds, and then all at once, they started laughing in unison.

"What the hell was that?" Hollings asked between gasps for air. "A pep talk?"

"I don't know," Nick answered, feeling very foolish. "I thought you were waiting for something inspiring."

"Yeah, that's what we needed," Mitchell said sarcastically, shaking his head. Just as the two detectives rose from their seats, Anna walked in with a look on her face that demanded Nick's attention.

"What's wrong?" Nick asked, suddenly concerned.

"I just finished the case file," she said. "It ends with a forth victim, and get this, the victim wasn't murdered, the victim was kidnapped."

"Damn," Mitchell commented, suddenly listening to the conversation. "That's something new."

"That's not the real news though," Anna said, a smile spreading across her face. "I think I know where our killer is going to strike next."

Chapter 60

Hartford, Connecticut
April 13, 1943

Terrence Grenier sat in his car in front of the Hartford city hall, summoning up the energy and the courage to face the Board of Commissioners again. The detective was tired, more tired than he had been in a long time. He had spent the entire evening following the Nemesis, watching as Dr. Westcott went about his life, unsuspecting. Westcott did not do anything suspicious, nor did Grenier expect him to do anything that might lead the police to his next victim. Grenier just knew that there was very little for him to do right now, and he needed to size up his enemy. Michelson was busy scouring the pages of medical records, searching for anyone who could possibly be the next victim, and that left Grenier with plenty of time on his hands. The previous night had been boring and predictable. The detective had picked up on Westcott at his office, and followed the doctor to his home. Once there, Westcott remained at home for the rest of the evening. The hours went by very slowly, and Westcott did not reappear until the next morning. Grenier followed him again, and Westcott drove back to the Hartford hospital. If Westcott knew that he was being followed, he showed no sign of it. Grenier knew that the killer would spend the rest of the day following his normal routine, and so decided to break his surveillance. He needed to see the Board of Commissioners and try to get some information from them.

Grenier climbed out of his car and crossed the street in between the cars that made up the morning traffic in the capitol city. Once inside city hall, he bribed a low level clerk to find out where the Commissioners would be meeting. Once the detective received his information, he went to the small back room and waited for the group to arrive. Fortunately for him, he did not have to wait long. The Board of Commissioners, including the mayor, entered the small room apparently oblivious to their surroundings. The men sat down and began to discuss the business of the day, when Grenier cleared his throat. All talking stopped suddenly, as all eyes turned to the detective.

"Ah, detective," the mayor began, beckoning Grenier to the front of the room. "Back again. I hope you have made some progress on this case."

"Oh, we have," Grenier announced. "We have."

"Then you will be making an arrest very soon?" the mayor asked.

"Sooner than you might think," Grenier responded. "However, I have some questions that I think you all can answer. Questions that will help me better understand this killer."

"Anything we can do," the mayor said. Grenier noticed how though all eyes were on him; the only person who dared to speak was the mayor himself.

"I want any information you can give me on an investigation you conducted in the coroner's office," Grenier started. The mayor opened his mouth to protest, but the detective raised a hand to stop him. "I have paperwork here signed by your aide stating an investigation was conducted to ascertain who was mutilating corpses that were scheduled for cremation."

The mayor looked around the table at the other men, who all wore expressions of uncertainty on their faces. All the men were shaking their heads, as if they did not know what the detective was talking about. The mayor turned back to face Grenier.

"I'm afraid I don't know what you're talking about," he stated. Grenier smiled and rose from his seat.

"Yes you do," the detective said. "But I understand if you don't want to admit to it. I'll just take what documentation I do have to the newspapers and see what they can make of it."

Grenier did not hesitate; he just turned on his heel and headed for the door. He could hear the eight men behind him whispering in hushed tones as they tried to figure out whether or not he was bluffing. Just as he reached the threshold, the raised voice of the mayor stopped him.

"Detective," the mayor called out. "Perhaps we can help you with some information."

Grenier turned back and walked over to where the Commissioners were seated. He dropped some papers down on the table and stood before them.

"What were the findings of your investigation?" Grenier asked.

"You have to understand the circumstances," the mayor began. "When we first heard about the mutilations, we suspected someone else entirely. That's why we initiated a secret investigation."

"Who did you think it was?" Grenier asked, confused.

"The mutilations seemed to coincide with..." the mayor looked down at the floor. "With the internship of a certain doctor."

"I'm going to need a little more information than that," Grenier said, prodding him along. "Who was the doctor?"

"We first thought the doctor involved was the son of a politician, and we thought he was mutilating the bodies," the mayor continued, ignoring the detective's question. "We launched the private investigation to try to control the story if it should get out."

"But your aide ended up finding out it was Westcott," the detective said, trying to keep the story going.

"No," the mayor answered. "It was the person we feared. The person guilty of mutilating those dead bodies was the son of a former Board member. You have to understand, the son was very sick. However, there was already too much internal attention to the mutilations. There were others outside of the Board who were aware of the situation, and we knew that something visible had to happen. Someone had to leave, for everyone to feel safe again. Westcott was the newest, youngest member of the department, and he was sacrificed. I don't think he ever knew why. Then, secretly, we removed the Board members son and it looked as though we had dodged the bullet. All other attention to the matter seemed to vanish.

"And it didn't occur to you that you just let a time bomb out on the public?" asked Grenier, unsure of the legality of the mayor's statement.

"What were we supposed to do?" the mayor asked. "We threatened him, told he that if he made a stink about the situation we would make it impossible for him to work anywhere in New England. However, at the same time, we knew that if we didn't offer him anything, he wouldn't have anything to lose by selling his story to the media."

"So you bankrolled him so that he could start his own office," Grenier said, filling in the missing pieces.

"And we didn't interfere with his work in the Hartford hospital," the mayor continued. The story was out there now, he knew there was no reason not to reveal everything to the detective. "Politics can be very tricky, take it from someone who has spent his life in the muck."

"Well it all really worked out well for the Board in the end, didn't it?" Grenier said, shaking his head. "You sacrificed an innocent man for a guilty one, and created a monster in the process. You are no better off now then you would have been then."

Suddenly, there was a lot of discussion going on at the table.

"What exactly do you plan to do?" the mayor asked, suspiciously.

"I plan on catching this monster," the detective answered. Then I'm going to make sure that you never get elected to public office again."

"So you're not going to the media?" asked one of the men around the table.

"There are more important things right now," Grenier answered, very non-committal.

Grenier walked out of the room, satisfied with the answers he got. He was not sure whether or not the Board of Commissioners were telling him the full truth, especially now that one of their decisions might have led to a mass murderer. However, he got the real information he was after. The Commissioners confirmed that there had been a cover up, and the detective was now sure that he was on the right track. The killer had to be Westcott, and now they just needed to figure out who the next victim was. Grenier knew that Michelson was working as hard as possible to narrow the field, and the best thing for him to do was to continue his surveillance of Westcott, just in case Michelson could not find out who the next victim was in time.

Chapter 61

Prudence had kept true to her word, finding the charts of the three patients that Michelson had asked for the night before. He sat down at the same chair and desk that he had occupied the day before and slipped the first chart off of the top of the pile, opened it and began reading. The notes, which started off clear and concise, began to trail off and become incoherent as they continued down the page. The words themselves were still neatly written, but the detail to which Dr. Westcott had clung to in the beginning of the interview seemed to diminish towards the end of the first visit. Flipping to the next page, indicating a new visit, Michelson found that the notes were barely notes at all. It seemed to the sergeant that Dr. Westcott had become bored with this patient, as he read seemingly unconnected words that the doctor jotted down, as if just attempting to appear interested in the patient's story. Michelson closed the file and pushed it forward. The sergeant could not believe that this man was to be The Nemesis's next victim. He did not think that Westcott considered the patient worthy of his attention; however, the sergeant knew that he could discount nothing. This patient still seemed to garner more attention from Westcott than other patients, and that was why Michelson had added the patient's name to the list.

Michelson took the next file off of the stack, heaving it up and letting it drop in front of him. This file was nearly three times as thick as the previous chart, which the sergeant noted with some interest immediately. He opened the chart, reading the name Gertrude Rainer in big letters. Underneath her name was an address, presumably her home address. Michelson remembered from the information Prudence had provided him, that Gertrude Rainer had seen Dr. Westcott more times that anyone else. He had been interested to understand why, and now the sergeant had his chance. He pushed the top papers aside until he reached the note of the first consult Rainer had with Dr. Westcott. From that moment on, Michelson was enthralled. The notes Westcott had taken on Rainer were epic. As Michelson read down the page, he found side notes in the margins, describing Westcott's personal thoughts pertaining to Rainer. The doctor had formed some sort of emotional connection to Rainer; something that was obviously one sided. As he continued reading, Westcott described the young woman as a head strong, strong willed personality who had found that she was getting no where in what she termed as "a man's world". According to the notes, Rainer felt that the only way to move forward in the world was to be what everyone wanted her to be, a more subdued, quiet woman; however, Rainer felt unable to do that. Arrows drawn off to the margins would lead to Westcott's personal thoughts, many pertaining to the young woman's beauty. The more Michelson read, the more uneasy he felt. There was an unusual amount of attention being paid to Gertrude Rainer; so much so that Michelson wondered if Westcott had not developed an obsession for his patient. After three hours of reading and re-reading, of jotting down notes of his own, Michelson closed the file and stared at it. Rainer's case was clearly different from the last patient. Michelson was certain that Westcott was obsessed with her, wanting to "break her spirit" as he noted so many times in the chart. Suddenly, Michelson was wracked with indecision. He felt as though it were obvious that Rainer was to be his next victim, however, he would have been remiss in his role as a police officer not to investigate the last file. Michelson just was not sure of how much time he had left.

"How's it going?" asked a female voice from behind him. Michelson turned in his chair to see Prudence smiling at him. "Finding everything you need?"

"And then some," Michelson answered. "You did a very good job."

The young woman seemed to smile wider at the compliment, her cheeks becoming flush.

"If you need anything else, don't hesitate to ask me," she said, not wanting to leave.

"Actually," Michelson said, thinking of something. "You could tell me if Dr. Westcott is working today."

At first, Michelson wondered if he had made a mistake by openly announcing his interest in Westcott, then thought better of it, remembering that she had put the clues together the evening before.

"Oh, he picked up his charts first thing this morning," Prudence answered, thinking back. "He had a good stack, so I assume he will be here until at least after lunch."

"I don't suppose there is a way for you to find out when his last appointment is?" Michelson asked, proddingly.

"I think there is a way I could find out without seeming too interested," Prudence said, that devilish smile returning. "But it's going to cost you."

"I bet," Michelson answered. "See what you can find out, I have to read this last chart."

The sergeant heard the young woman walk away as he turned back around to face the desk. Looking back down at Gertrude Rainer's chart, he knew that her case did not belong in the same stack as the previous chart. Pushing it aside, he grabbed the last file and began reading through it. Reading the first few pages, Michelson became concerned that he possibly had two potential victims. Westcott kept several pages of detailed notes. However, as the patient continued to see Westcott, the doctor seemed to lose his interest again. Like the first file he read, the notes began to become less and less clear. It was obvious that Westcott was losing his interest in this patient as well. In these two cases, the patients seemed to have a need to please Westcott, and so every suggestion he made seemed to be met with extreme enthusiasm. This was completely different than what Michelson had read in Rainer's chart. She was very head strong, feeling as though she needed to please no one but herself. When Westcott would make suggestions, they would be blocked by her extreme stubbornness. Westcott seemed to thrive on this struggle he had with her. Michelson began to understand the attraction Westcott had with Rainer. Patients that were so eager to please held no interest to Westcott, but a patient who fought his advice and expertise was a challenge that the doctor just could not pass up. Closing the chart, Michelson felt more confident than ever that he had found the next victim. Just then, Prudence burst into view.

"I'm so sorry," she stammered. "I made a mistake."

"What is it?" asked Michelson, jumping up from his chair.

"Usually Dr. Westcott is here until late afternoon or early evening," the young woman explained. "However, his nurse told me that he cut out early today. He's already gone."

"Oh shit," Michelson exclaimed, grabbing his jacket and Rainer's chart at the same time. He flipped the chart open, searching for any personal information about where the young woman lived and worked.

"I'm so sorry," Prudence added, seeing the sergeant flip frantically through the pages.

"It's not your fault," Michelson said, quickly jotting down any pertinent information. "You did a great job, and I owe you big time. Don't think I'm going to forget that."

He turned to the young woman and looked in her eyes. He could tell that she felt as though she had let him down. He smiled at her, and brushed a single tear from her cheek. He mouthed the words THANK YOU and then brushed past her, leaving her alone in the records room. As he left the hospital, he wished he could have done more to assuage her fears, to make her understand how much he appreciated her work, but he simply did not have the time. The Nemesis was out there somewhere, and like a predator, he was stalking his next victim.

Using the information he gained from her chart, Michelson first tried to find Gertrude Rainer at her home. Upon his arrival, he found no one there, and decided to check her work. He had remembered her talking about her work with Westcott during their sessions, and though she never revealed the address, the sergeant knew the name of her work well enough to know where it was. He arrived at Rainer's work fairly quickly, but it took some time for him to find someone who could help him. He spent ten minutes waiting in the administration office while the clerk tried to find out who Rainer was. Becoming frustrated, he walked out of the administration office down to the actual clerical floor where Rainer worked. She worked in the billing department, and once Michelson found that out he was able to find someone who knew her. Unfortunately for the sergeant, the shift change had just occurred and according to the floor supervisor, Rainer had left for the day. Frustration setting in, Michelson knew that time was running out; he had to find Rainer soon.

Michelson first found a phone and called in to the station. He was immediately transferred to the chief, who demanded an update on the case. Michelson informed the chief that he had found a potential victim, and was in the process of physically tracking her down. He made his concerns about Westcott known, and asked the status of Detective Grenier. The chief informed him that after a meeting with the Board of Commissioners, Grenier went out and had failed to report in. Michelson knew immediately that Grenier was trailing Westcott. After hanging up the phone, Michelson felt some relief as he knew that even if he was unable to warn Rainer today, Grenier was on Westcott. Michelson then headed back to Rainer's home, unsure of what he was going to do if he should find no one home again. As he thought about it, he realized that he did not know what he was going to do if he actually was able to talk to Rainer. *What was he to say? I'm sorry to inform you that you are the target of a multiple murderer.* He had no idea of how she would react to this news. There would also be some uncomfortable minutes as Michelson would be forced to explain how he came to this conclusion. *I was reading through your psych notes during your sessions with Dr. Westcott.* That was sure to not go over well. Trying to imagine how he was going to handle the situation, he saw Rainer crossing the walk of her home to her car. Before Michelson could stop his car and signal her, she was inside and pulling out onto the street. Michelson decided to follow her and approach her when she reached her destination.

Finally, Rainer steered her car into the parking lot of a local high school. Following behind her, Michelson watched as she drove down toward the gymnasium, where crowds of young men and women were standing around outside. Michelson realized immediately that there was some sort of dance/social going on. He had hoped to confront Rainer in a less social setting, but watched as she parked her car and hopped out, waving to some young ladies standing on the sidewalk. Michelson parked his car across from hers and got out. Having lost sight of Rainer for just a moment, he found her again walking and laughing with her group of friends just as they entered the double doors of the gymnasium. The sergeant sighed and crossed the parking lot, then stepped up onto the sidewalk and headed towards the door. It was just then that he saw Grenier leaning against the wall of the gymnasium, his eyes fixed on a man that was also heading towards the door. Michelson knew immediately that the man was Westcott, and that this was the time and the place that he would strike again.

Chapter 62

Grenier watched as Westcott handed something to the young woman standing at the door to the gymnasium, then passed through the threshold. There was something very wrong about his being here, around all of these young men and women who were clearly ten years his junior. The social had been organized as a place where young people could meet, and it was especially geared towards young service men who had returned home from the war and needed to get back amongst people their own age again. Watching the doctor walk inside, Grenier felt very uneasy about the entire situation. The detective was convinced that Westcott was The Nemesis, but he could not understand why he would come here, in such a public place. If he was going to move against his next victim, Grenier would need more of a police presence to stop him. However, to call for any sort of back up, he would have to find a phone and that would mean leaving the scene for at least five to ten minutes. Grenier knew that anything could happen in that amount of time, and knew that he could not risk leaving the killer unsupervised for that long. Grenier realized that he was alone and that if anything happened, he was going to have to stop Westcott himself.

Grenier pushed himself from the wall and walked towards the door to the gymnasium. At the front door, two young women stood at a small table, greeting people as they entered. One of the women asked the detective if he had a ticket, and once informed that he did not, she told him that he could buy one at the door. Grenier knew that if he flashed his badge she would have no choice but to step aside and let him in. However, he had lost sight of Westcott, and he wanted to maintain a low profile for the time being. He did not want to lose the element of surprise and so paid for the ticket and stepped inside. Only half of the overhead lights of the gymnasium had been switched on, making it harder for the detective to see the faces of all of the men and women inside. Thin, hardwood paneling had been placed over the basketball court, and a small square area had been roped off for the dance floor. There was some music playing as three couples danced slowly. Most of the young men and women were standing around the sides of the floor, huddled into small groups. This made it harder for the detective, as he had to get closer and stare at each individual as he searched for his killer. The detective was becoming frustrated as he was having difficulty finding Westcott and he knew that more and more people were coming inside every minute.

Grenier tried to act nonchalant as he walked around the gymnasium, scanning the young faces.

He knew that he would draw some attention, as he was clearly older than the crowd the social had been geared to. Many of the young men were in their service uniforms, and he nodded to them as he passed by. As the time passed and the music played on, more and more people began mingling and filing out onto the dance floor. It was going to be impossible to maintain a low profile if he had to go out onto the dance floor alone. All of a sudden, his eyes passed over a familiar face, and quickly, he jerked his head back to find the face again. That was when he saw Westcott, walking alone on the other side of the gymnasium, eyeing a group of young women. Grenier felt his senses sharpen as he focused on the killer. The detective began making his way around the dance floor towards the other side of the gymnasium to where Westcott was standing. Grenier tried to formulate a plan in his mind, trying to assess the safest way to apprehend Westcott should something happen. As he crossed, he watched as Westcott approached the group of young women, talking to one in particular. The young woman seemed surprised, then a little embarrassed as he greeted her. Though he could not hear their conversation, it seemed as though the young woman was introducing Westcott to the other women in the group, and then stepped aside to talk to the doctor in private. Grenier paused for a moment and waited, watching as the doctor spoke to the young woman. It was obvious that Westcott was trying to explain himself, trying to ease the young woman's apprehension. The detective could tell from the look on her face that she was not buying his excuse, but somehow, Westcott had convinced her to dance with him. Grenier watched as the two stepped out onto the dance floor and Westcott took the young woman into his arms.

This is bad, thought Grenier to himself. The detective had a feeling that this was the next victim of The Nemesis, and right now he had her right where he wanted her. Of course, Westcott would not kill her right here in front of all these people, but he was now alone with the woman. The only thing Grenier could do was wait and follow them if they left together. Any hopes of catching Westcott before he killed again were fading fast. Grenier looked around the gymnasium, knowing that he was going to have to find a place where he could observe without drawing any attention to himself. As he looked around, his eyes passed over the dance floor, and his eyes met with Westcott's. There was an immediate look of recognition, and Grenier knew that all of his quick planning, all of his attempts to keep a low profile were for not. Westcott jerked back suddenly, twisting the young woman around and grabbing her by the throat. The woman cried out suddenly, and the couples closest to them stepped back quickly, blocking Grenier's line of sight. The detective vaulted himself over a table that bordered the dance floor and whipped out his side arm, pointing it directly in front of him. Immediately, women all around him started screaming and backing away, and suddenly Grenier was face to face with The Nemesis, who was pointing a gun back at him.

"Don't you dare come any closer," Westcott screamed, jerking the gun back and slamming it against the young woman's head. "I swear I'll blow her head off."

"You do and I'll put a bullet right between your eyes," Grenier warned, taking careful aim. The detective knew that it was a hopeless situation for him. Westcott had a hostage, and Grenier did not have a clear shot. There was no way this was going to end well. Three uniformed men stepped forward, ready to pounce on Westcott.

"Get back," Grenier ordered. "I'm a police detective. If you move he will kill her."

The three men backed away a little, though still ready to jump into action. The young woman was sobbing now as Westcott started slowly pulling her backwards.

"How the hell did you find me?" Westcott asked, shouting above the noise of the crowd.

"It wasn't hard," Grenier answered back. "We've been on to you for days now."

Westcott cocked his head to the side and smiled a sadistic grin.

"You're lying," the doctor said. "If you knew about me, you would have stopped me long before now."

"This ends here, tonight," Grenier shouted. "There is nowhere you can go."

"You're wrong," Westcott said, pressing the muzzle of his gun harder against the young woman's flesh. "She is my ticket out of here. You know that I won't hesitate to kill her, and I know that you don't want her death on your conscious."

Grenier realized that Westcott was steadily backing away, and with every step forward the detective made, the killer took two steps back with his hostage. There had to be a back door that Westcott was aware of. That had to be his plan of escape; however, alone the detective did not know what he could do to stop him. They were now off of the dance floor, backing towards the far wall. Grenier knew he had to stop this before they reached the back door.

"She dies, you die," the detective stated. "It's that simple."

"She's not the only one who can die here tonight," Westcott pointed out. "I don't think I have to be too good a shot to hit anyone of these people."

Westcott began waving his gun around at the crowd, which caused a panic and suddenly a sea of young bodies started making a mad dash for the door. Momentarily, Grenier's view was blocked as people ran between him and the killer. That was all the time The Nemesis needed to make his move for the back door. Yanking hard on the woman's throat, he pulled her along behind him as he reached the back wall. Just then the door burst open and a tall man with a gun jumped in. Unfortunately, the man did not have time to register what he saw and react. Westcott pumped two bullets into the young man and watched him fall, then ran through the back door with the young woman in tow. Finally, seeing Grenier bolting after him, he fired three more shots through the door, causing the detective to dive for cover and was gone. By the time Grenier was back on his feet, he had lost sight of Westcott. The detective ran for the door and jumped through, ignoring the wounded man on the floor. Westcott was nowhere to be found. Grenier turned back, cursing and then saw the body on the ground. Michelson lay on his back, his hands clutching his abdomen as thick, blood poured out from around his fingers.

"Oh shit," the detective exclaimed as he dropped to his knees. "Hang on buddy; I'll get you to the hospital."

Grenier yelled for help as he saw men and women running around the gymnasium. The detective looked back down at the floor, jerked Michelson up against him and screamed for help again. Grenier put his hands over the wound, trying to stop the blood. It gushed over his hands and he watched in despair as the light faded out of his partner's eyes.

Chapter 63

New London Police Department
Present Day

When Anna was finished relaying the information she had read from the end of the old case file, Detective Grenier pushed his chair back from the table in the middle of the interrogation room that the officers had been using as their command center, and walked over to the mirrored glass. He stood there silently for several moments, staring at his reflection. The room was utterly quiet; no one dared to speak. Detectives Wilkins and Mitchell were still seated at the table, contemplating this new information, while Anna and Lt. Hollings stared at Nick, waiting for his response. Nick's mind was racing with the possibilities. He knew that this new information threw everything out of wack. The Nemesis had gone out of his way to recreate the old case, making sure that the murders and victims were all the same. Nick knew that there was no reason to believe that he would not attempt to carry out the next step in the same fashion, by kidnapping a woman from some social event. Nick turned away from the mirrored window and studied the faces of the detectives around him. Both Mitchell and Wilkins were still looking down at the top of the table, as if in deep thought. He knew what they were thinking; how were the police going to find the right social gathering and stop The Nemesis from striking again. If the killer was successful this time, it would put even more stress on the police to catch him, and this time he would have a living victim.

"I have to admit," Nick began, getting the attention of everyone in the room. "I did not see this coming."

"I don't see how we can stop him," Mitchell said, the pressure beginning to wear on his emotions. "We don't know where or when he is going to strike. This could quite possibly be the worst case scenario."

"No," Wilkins interjected. "The worst case scenario would be that he actually pulls this off. If he kidnaps a woman and the press finds out about it, we will have a very short amount of time before he kills her and we're blamed for it."

"Let's not get ahead of ourselves," Nick said, trying to find something positive. He turned to Anna to ask her a question, and saw her staring at him with a big grin on her face. "What are you smiling at?"

"Like I said earlier," Anna remarked. "I think I already know where he is going to strike."

Suddenly, all eyes were on her. It was as if a ray of sunshine had pierced the clouds of depression that had closed in around the detectives. Everyone turned to her with baited breath, eagerly anticipating what was to come.

"Well," Hollings prodded.

"I did some research," Anna began. "This dance/social was an event to get young people to meet each other, like a planned dating event. It was especially geared towards soldiers who were coming back from the war. It was a way to ease them back into normal life, especially when it came to the opposite sex. So I was trying to think of something that would be today's version of that event."

"And?" Nick asked, unable to contain his impatience.

"Over the last couple of weeks, a local radio station has been advertising a speed dating event it's promoting," Anna continued. "WTXI is promoting this event where you go and sit down at a table with a member of the opposite sex, and you have five minutes to talk and get acquainted. After the five minutes, you get up and go to the next table, and so on and so on."

"I've heard about this," Mitchell said, his eyes lighting up. "The women sit at the table, and the men have to go from table to table. It's to make it possible for everyone to meet as many people as possible."

"This just might be it," Nick said aloud. "How big is this thing? How heavily has it been promoted?"

"The event is being held at Insomnia," Anna said. "The very nightclub where Tracy Scott was picked up."

"That's it," Nick said, filled with certainty. "That's where he's going to strike. This is the perfect opportunity to catch him."

"How?" Hollings asked. "If you stop the event, then he will..."
She stopped short, her mind only one step ahead. Suddenly, she realized what Nick had in mind. The detective had no intention of canceling the event. In fact, he needed it to happen now more than ever. Nick planned on capturing The Nemesis at the nightclub, he planned on using everyone there as bait.

"Do you know what you're suggesting?" Hollings asked, the consequences running through her mind at lightning speed.

"I haven't suggested anything yet," Nick reminded her.

"If this thing goes wrong in any way," Hollings started. "All of our careers will be over. The press will crucify us for using innocent civilians as bait to lure in a killer."

"They won't all be innocent civilians," Nick said, trying to reassure the lieutenant. "This is a perfect opportunity to catch this killer and stop this once and for all."

"I suppose you have a plan," Hollings said, unsure of all of this.

"I do," Nick answered. "First, I want Wilkins and Mitchell to carry on with the assignments that we set up earlier. Wilkins, find all of the Westcott's in the area, especially doctors and do a background on them. Mitchell, track down Camden's son, one way or the other. Find out what happened to him. You guys have got twelve hours."

"Why only twelve hours?" Mitchell asked, confused.

"Because first thing tomorrow morning we will be setting up the sting operation to catch The Nemesis," Nick answered, already planning the details in his mind.

"I had to ask," Mitchell grunted under his breath. Nick followed the two detectives out of the interrogation room and made his way back to his office, oblivious to the fact that Anna and Lt. Hollings were following him, waiting to learn more about what he had planned. Nick sat down behind his desk and pulled out a yellow legal pad and started making notes, unaware that the two had followed him right into the office and were staring at him. After a moment, Hollings cleared her throat to get the detective's attention. Nick looked up into the awaiting eyes of the two women.

"And what about us?" Hollings asked. "You don't have anything for us to do?"

"Actually," Nick answered. "I do. First, we are going to need to wrangle up about twenty single male officers by tomorrow morning, and we are going to have to be quiet about it."

"Why only men?" Anna asked, ready to pounce if there was even a hint of sexism.

"Because," Nick began, without looking up. "The victim is going to be a female. The Nemesis knows that this particular female is going to be there, and if we try to interlace female officers into the sting and we happen to pull out the killer's intended target, he will be suspicious and the jig will be up."

"But if we interlace male officers in with the men," Hollings interrupted, understanding the detective's logic. "Then we will have officers on the inside and we will be able to keep from tipping the killer off."

"Exactly," Nick said. "Anna and I will be busy setting this thing up with the radio station. What did you say it was again?"

"WTXI," she answered. "They broadcast here out of New London."

"We'll convince them to give us their support," Nick said.

"Is that it?" Hollings asked, only now realizing the enormous amount of work her detectives had to complete in such a limited amount of time.

"No," Nick answered. "I actually need you to do one more thing. I need you to call the governor; I need you to tell him that I'm calling in my favor."

Chapter 64

Nick stood facing the window in the upstairs office of the nightclub Insomnia, looking out over the dance floor that was quickly being transformed into a lounging area for the night's events. All in all, the detective was very pleased by how everything was going so far, and astonished by the amount of work so many had accomplished in so little time. Convincing the radio station to work with the police department had taken surprisingly little coercion. Nick had been prepared to play hardball with the station owner, but once he mentioned the free publicity that would come from working with the police, the station owner was only too willing to play ball. Then, there was the FBI. Nick needed the help of the FBI's technical unit, but he was afraid that by just contacting the FBI's field office in New Haven, Connecticut he was going to get some gung-ho agent that wanted to take over the investigation. However, that could not have been further from the truth. Hollings had contacted Governor Haisley, who was most interested in keeping the case local as that would maximize his exposure to the media, and had him prepare for a fight with the Special Agent in Charge. Agent Howell, however, had no desire to take over the case, as he was overloaded with his own investigations. Howell was willing to lend his technical crew to the case for the evening, and was promised by the governor himself that he would get special recognition. By noon, everything seemed to be falling into place, and Nick began to think that this would all be much easier than he had expected.

However, there were problems. The first problem being that Detectives Wilkins and Mitchell had not returned yet from doing their research. In fact, the two detectives had yet to check in. Nick needed whatever information they had been able to dig up, and the fact that they had not returned made the detective question whether or not he was on the right track. Hollings, on the other hand, was concerned that something had happened to her officers. She had tried them on their cell phones every half hour for the last four hours and there had been no response. Now it was six in the evening and in two hours the speed dating event would begin. Nick needed to know who he was looking for before the killer arrived. It was the only way that Nick could maintain the upper hand. A lot of people were expecting this sting operation to end up successfully, and Nick knew that it was all going to fall on him if it didn't. The entire operation had been his idea.

"Where the hell could those two numbskulls be?" Hollings said from her place behind the detective.

"You told them that they had only twelve hours to get their information. They should be back by now."

"They are probably following up on something," Nick said, not turning around. He meant for his tone to be reassuring, however, he too was beginning to get worried.

"Nevertheless," Hollings rebutted. "They should have at least checked in by now."

Hollings walked over to the window and stood beside the detective. He was looking down on the floor that was now entirely covered with paneled hardwood. A few men were carrying in a rolled up column of carpeting, making their way to the edge of the new flooring to lay it down.

"Is everything going according to plan?" she asked, looking back over to the detective.

"For the most part," Nick answered. "We had some problem with the security people the station had hired for the event. However, we have now replaced them with some of our own cops, the biggest body builders we could find. Hopefully, they will look like bouncers and not arouse the killer's suspicions."

"So tell me how this thing is going to work again," Hollings said. Nick had gone over the plan with her at least four times now, and he was sure that she knew everything by heart. However, if talking it through one more time would calm her nerves a little, then he would appease her.

"All of the perspective daters, both male and female will come in through the front doors where they will be patted down by the bouncer," Nick began, pointing off down the dark hall at the far end of the open room. "Then they will give their name and personal information, including address, to the woman at the podium. They will have a name card made up quickly and then continue on to the bar. All the women daters will be civilians, however, we will intersperse an undercover police officer with every other male dater.

At eight on the dot, Angela MacKenzie will come out and greet everyone from the stage, then get the event rolling. While we start, the FBI's Identification Team will be using digital images taken throughout the hallway to identify every person here. Once they find Westcott, we will have eyes on him at all times. MacKenzie plans on walking through during the event, greeting people individually, just as the station had planned originally. We don't want to do anything to make the killer suspicious. In case we don't make an identification, we will be watching all the males at all times for anything unusual. The killer is going to try to make this the same as the old case, so my guess is his victim is going to be surprised when she runs into him."

"So you don't intend on taking him here?" Hollings asked. She had asked the same question the last three times he went over the plans, and Nick could not help but sigh aloud.

"Not unless he does something we can nail him on," Nick answered, his frustration getting the better of him. "You've got to remember, we have no hard proof yet. Everything we have is circumstantial, or based on a case that is sixty years old."

"Especially seeing that we don't even know what our killer looks like," Hollings interjected. Nick just nodded; no matter how far the police thought they had come, they still had further to go. Nick stared down at one of the nightclub staff, an attractive young woman, provocatively dressed, standing in front of the podium where the daters personal information would be taken. "Are you sure this was such a good idea, putting a civilian so close to the killer?"

"No choice," Nick answered. "The killer has been here before, hell he found his first victim here. He may know who the staff members are. If we put an undercover down there, someone he doesn't recognize, he might smell a trap and bolt."

"You realize," Hollings began. "You are using all of these people as bait. This is a very dangerous game you a playing."

"And a very worth while one if everything turns out right," Nick answered.

"You have no problem with putting civilians at risk?" Hollings asked, eyeing the detective suspiciously.

"If he's out on the street," Nick began. "Civilians are at risk anyway. If we can stop this tonight, all of this will be worth it."

"I hope so," Hollings answered. "I hope so."

They were quiet for a while, both turning their attention back to the floor which had now been covered in the carpeting. Systematically, the lights around the room were being lowered to set the mood. Nick was checking off each process in his mind like a list, anticipating the next move of the staff and undercover officers down below. However, he began to focus on what Hollings had just said to him, the fact that she thought it strange that he had no problem using innocent civilians as bait. He could not understand why he had no emotions about this. *What if Anna was down there*, he asked himself. Though he was not in love with her, he cared about her, and he knew that he would never have wanted her to be involved in this. However, in his heart, he saw all of these staff members, and the other guests as nothing more than a means to an end. The thought of the killer possibly killing one or two of them did not really concern the detective if he was able to capture the killer tonight. He shook his head for a moment, as if to clear his thoughts. He could not believe that he was so intent on catching this killer. *Why? What is it about this guy that has me so wrapped up?* He could not help but wonder if he would be this way on every case if he decided to become a homicide detective. It was not the way to live, and he knew that.

As the last of the lights dimmed, he saw the small lights at each of the tables light up, and the iridescent glow from the black lights all around the nightclub. The club would be much brighter than it would usually be so that everyone could see and make their way around, but the real reason was so the police could keep an eye on the killer once they identified him. Nick saw the lights around the bar come on, the blue lighting from behind the bar making the water from the fountain seem brighter. He heard some commotion and watched as people started to file in from down the hall that led to the entrance of the nightclub. He knew everything was starting; the event would be beginning soon.

It's showtime.

Chapter 65

Nick watched as everyone got into position, moving to their perspective places, all knowing what their job was tonight. The detective did not dare show his face down on the floor. Whoever The Nemesis was, whether it was Westcott or someone else, the killer knew what Nick looked like, and if he saw the detective he would know it was a trap. Nick knew that it was best if he stay up in the main office overlooking the floor. The office was recessed, overlooking what was usually the dance floor, its tinted glass making it impossible for the people below to see in, but just perfect to watch the people below. There were three sets of binoculars for getting better views of individual daters. Each officer down below had an earpiece in, supplied by the FBI Technical Unit, so that Nick could remain in contact with any one of them at any time without drawing attention.

So far, the detective was pleased with what he saw. A steady line of people were making their way from the long hallway where the digital cameras were snapping pictures of them, to the I.D. station.

The hostess there was getting everyone's personal information, and apparently was not getting any hassle from the guests. Nick had originally been concerned that the guests or at least a few of them would question giving that information. However, the hostess simply told them that it was so they could give information to any of the daters that showed an interest in another guest. Each guest was given a number, and was told that if another guest showed an interest they could get the information they needed based on the number they supplied the hostess. It all seemed so obvious, so matter-of-fact that Nick began to feel as if it would be almost impossible for the killer to suspect a trap. The security at the entrance, who the detective had switched out with his own officers, would be patting down everyone as they entered the nightclub. They would say it was a routine matter, as the bouncers usually patted down any males coming to Insomnia on any regular night. However, Nick wanted to make sure that the risk to any civilians inside was minimized. The last thing he needed was The Nemesis actually being able to carry out a hostage at gun point, or worse yet, killing someone. Nick knew how this scene had gone down sixty years ago, and was determined not to let that happen here tonight. A sudden knock on the door jarred the detective from his thoughts.

"It's almost time for us to start," said a female voice from behind him. Nick turned to see Angela MacKenzie, the DJ from the station's morning show and organizer and promoter of tonight's event. "I'll have to go down there in a few minutes."

"Are you comfortable with everything?" Nick asked, concerned. "Do you have any questions or concerns?"

"Oh no," MacKenzie answered, waving a hand at him. "This is simple. I'm just going to run the event the way I had originally planned. I don't even know who all of your people are, so it's not going to bother me. I plan on making my speech, then coming up here as things get started. Later on, I will make my way back down to the floor and mingle with the guests."

"Sounds good," Nick replied. "Just don't stare too hard at any of my people. Just act normally."

"Like I said," she began. "I don't even know who most of them are. Things will be fine, you'll see."

With that, the morning show hostess left the office just as Hollings and some other officers came in and set up computer laptops. Two of the men were from the FBI, though none of the officers either in the office or on the floor wore anything to identify them with. Nodding to himself, Nick smiled and was pleased with the way everything had worked out. He watched from above as MacKenzie made her way through a curtain and out onto the stage. The crowd of guests turned their attention to her and made their way over to the stage. Nick picked up a radio unit and called out to the officers at the nightclub entrance.

"How many more are left to come in?" Nick asked. There was a crackle and some static.

"Just a few more," the male voice answered. "It's really starting to thin out here."

"Good," Nick answered. "When the last of them are in, close the doors and don't let any other people come in."

Below them, MacKenzie was making some small talk with the guests that were gathered around the stage, joking and laughing. Nick realized as he looked down, that there were many more participants than he had originally expected. As he watched the last of the guests approach the hostess at the I.D. stand, he knew that somewhere in the crowd of guests below, The Nemesis was looking for his mark. The detective was finding it hard to maintain his excitement.

Finally getting the signal that everyone was accounted for and processed, MacKenzie took the microphone off of its stand and got the attention of the crowd.

"Good evening, everyone," she began. "I'm Angie MacKenzie, from MacKenzie in the morning, and I am pleased that you could all be a part of our first annual Speed Dating Event. We have a lot of very beautiful people here tonight, so there's no reason for anyone to go home alone."

Everyone in the crowd began laughing and cheering.

"But really," she continued. "I know how difficult it can be to find someone these days, and I really hope that this event will help you all find someone. However, even if it doesn't, the drinks are free and there is going to be some great entertainment, so I expect everyone to have a good time."

Again, the crowd erupted into applause and cheers.

"Now for the ground rules," MacKenzie continued. "Everyone here has been given cards with a number on them. The women will be stationed at a particular cocktail table. This will cut down on the chances of anyone having the same date more than once. Each date will last seven minutes, at which point, a buzzer will sound and the men will get up and go to the next table. Feel free to give your cards to whoever you want, and as many people as you want. The hostess who checked you in has everyone's information, and all you have to do is take the card you were given to her and she will give you the corresponding name and phone number. That's it; the rest of it is up to you. Now let's get this party started."

With that, everyone started clapping and cheering and another voice came on the speaker system, getting the attention of the crowd and making them turn towards it. MacKenzie stepped down off of the stage and shook hands with a few people, then made her way back to the stairs that led up to the office.

The woman on the microphone was getting everyone set in their places, the women making their way to their assigned cocktail tables, the men joking with each other. It seemed to the detective as if everyone below him already had a drink in their hands and was having a good time. MacKenzie pushed the door open and walked over to the detective.

"How was my speech?" she asked.

"Right on the money," Nick answered. "Everyone seems excited; everything is going according to plan."

"See your boy yet," MacKenzie asked.

"Speaking of which," Nick said, picking up the radio and calling down to the hostess at the podium. "Any names on there matching our killer?"

"Nothing," a male's voice answered back. "No name recognition so far. We're still working on it though."

Nick was not worried about this though. He knew that the killer would not use his real name, whether he suspected that Nick knew the name Westcott or not. The killer was very careful, and Nick knew that he was not going to leave any clues to his identity. The detective watched as the first date got started and then turned to the FBI specialists staring at the laptop screens behind him.

"Got anything yet?" Nick asked. Neither man looked up, just shook their heads and continued staring at their screens.

"This is going to take some time," the agent answered. "We got good digital shots in the hallway, but now we need to process them with the Facial Recognition Software. That's going to be slow going."

"What about the names given to the hostess below?" Nick asked, making sure all of his bases were covered.

"We are running those names now," the other agent answered. "Matching the information they gave us with our information."

"You do realize that there is a good possibility that some of these people will not have a match at all," the first agent interjected.

"What do you mean?" Nick asked, suddenly concerned.

"All of our software, both the Facial Recognition and the I.D. software run through names fed into it through almost every government agency," the agent explained. "We are running off of photos and data from every DMV in New England, the Department of Corrections, the FBI, and any other information that has gone into a government database such as passport information, etc., etc."

"Yeah so," Nick said. "That should pretty much cover all of our bases, right?"

"It should," the agent agreed. "But there is always the chance that there are one or two people that are trying to stay under the radar, and they might not be in our system. In my experience, it's usually the person you're looking for that doesn't match any data we have."

"Not to mention our digital shots did not get any frontal shots," the other agent added. "The Facial Recognition Software will be taking the image it receives and will make an approximation of what the face looks like. Nine times out of ten it's a 90% match, but there's always that one time."

"You guys aren't making me feel any better about this," Nick said, suddenly concerned about the success of his operation. He looked over to the lieutenant, who seemed equally concerned.

"Hey, we're just giving you the facts," the first agent stated. "I don't want you to get your hopes up and then have the dashed because you didn't get the results you expected."

"Well, let's just see what we do get," Nick said, reminding himself to take one thing at a time.

The buzzer rang out and everyone rose from their seats, many people shaking hands and hugging, many handing each other cards with numbers on them. Nick walked back over to the window and tried to watch the reactions of all of the women as the men moved to the next table. Waitresses came along and took more orders and a few minutes later, the buzzer went off and the second dates began. Nick sighed, not seeing anything out of the ordinary.

"There are a lot of dates left," Hollings reminded him, walking up beside him. "If he's here, we'll find him."

The detective continued watching through the next couple of dates, making comments every now and then. Everything seemed to be going smoothly, all the guests seemed to be having a good time, and as the fifth date began, Nick started to get worried that he may have had this event all wrong. He started thinking about the old case, trying to think of something that would be a present day equivalent to the dance/social event sixty years ago. He had been so certain that Anna was right, that this would be where The Nemesis made his next move. The killer was obviously familiar with the nightclub, having picked up his first victim here. However, perhaps the killer was too smart for that, and was not going to go back to a place he had already been, for fear of being recognized. Either way, the night was not looking good for the police; and it was not looking good for Nick.

"Oh my God," MacKenzie said, suddenly excited. "That's my doctor there."

"Where," Nick said, spinning around to the DJ. The woman pointed out the window to a group of tables off to the left side of the floor. "There, that's the doctor that I see. I had no idea he was going to be here."

"What's your doctor's name," Hollings asked, walking over to the woman. Nick picked up all three pairs of binoculars just as she passed. Suddenly, everyone's attention was on MacKenzie.

"Dr. Westcott," the woman answered, suddenly confused. Nick handed her a pair of binoculars and she put them up to her eyes. "Number thirty one there at table eight."

Just then the buzzer sounded and everyone rose again. Nick looked through his binoculars, searching the area for the man with the number thirty one tag on.

"There is no Westcott on the list," the second agent stated, scanning the list of names.

"What's going on here?" MacKenzie asked, becoming very concerned.

"What's the name given on the list for number thirty one," Nick asked the agent, not taking his eyes off of the man who he now suspected to be The Nemesis.

"The name is Camden," the agent answered. "Jack Camden."

"That's it," Nick said, under his breath. "I've got you now."

"That can't be right," MacKenzie stated, not understanding what was going on. "There has to be some kind of mistake. That's Dr. Jack Westcott. He's a family practice doctor in Westerly, Rhode Island. He's my doctor."

"You're sure," Hollings said, pushing the binoculars up to MacKenzie's face again. "You're sure that is your doctor."

"Of course I'm sure," MacKenzie answered. "He's been my doctor for years."

Hollings looked over at Nick who already had the radio in his hand. Nick smiled, though for a moment mentally, he was a wreck. He had set up this operation on the assumption that one of the female daters would be the killer's target. Nick had never suspected that it could be someone else, much less the promoter of the event. However, the more he thought about it, the more sense it made. There were too many coincidences for the detective to ignore. This was his killer, this was The Nemesis. This was his nemesis.

"All eyes on number thirty one," Nick said into the radio. "Number thirty one is the suspect, I want eyes on him at all times."

Nick replaced the radio on the small table and retrieved the binoculars from next to it. He watched the man with the number thirty one label as Hollings escorted Angela MacKenzie to the next room. Nick could not hear anything she said though. He was lost in his own thoughts. After barking some orders to the agents at the computers, he turned his attention back out the windows. *I've got you,* he said to himself. *I've got you now.*

Chapter 66

The Nemesis watched Angela MacKenzie give her opening speech, smiled when everyone else smiled, laughed and applauded when the crowd applauded. He may have only been here for her, but he knew that he was going to have to keep up appearances for a while. He had not known what to expect when he arrived here, and the pat down from the security guards was definitely not what he expected. When he reached the hostess's podium, he then had to give his personal information, something else he was not prepared for. Thinking quickly, he gave the only name and address that came to him. He did not expect to be handing out any cards with his number on them tonight. He was only here for one person, and he knew that he would leave with her, one way or another. When the speech was over, everyone applauded, and The Nemesis watched his target intently. However, instead of coming out and greeting everyone in the crowd, after shaking a couple of hands, she headed back to the back of the stage and through a curtain. Though it threw off his plans a little bit, it did not bother the killer. He knew that she would be in and out of this event all night, and he knew that he would get his chance with her alone. Suddenly, The Nemesis heard a loud buzzer that caught almost everyone in the audience off guard. Immediately, a woman with a microphone was ushering everyone to their places, having the women sit at their assigned tables and giving the men a pack of cards especially arranged. The Nemesis groaned to himself, looked at the number on the top of the stack of cards, and made his way over to that table.

The seven minute dates seemed to last forever. In fact, he felt his time there was excruciating. The woman, whose name he forgot the moment they were introduced, seemed to just chatter on and on. For some reason he had told her that he was a doctor, not being able to think up a lie fast enough. The young woman responded just the way he knew that she would, becoming all excited and jittery at the thought that she might start dating a doctor. It took everything to keep from reaching right across the little table and strangling the woman. Inside, the killer laughed at the thought. *All of these years of patient dedication and discipline lost because I could not stand listening to this idiot's chatter*, he thought to himself. *Now that would be ironic.* However, The Nemesis knew his mission, and he was not going to risk it for anything. At the end of the seven minutes, he and the woman exchanged cards, and he made his way over to the next table to which he was assigned, nervously watching out all over the club for MacKenzie.

All of the dates seemed to be the same. None of the women there wanted to hear anything from the men except what they did for a living. All of the women after had the same response as the first. The Nemesis just shook it off, keeping his patience, knowing that it would all be worth it in the end. The killer wondered how these women would react when men who did not make as much money told them what they did for a living. The date would probably go south immediately. However, The Nemesis did not care to put much thought into this, as he was busy with other things. He kept an eye out for MacKenzie, of which he saw nothing. By the fifth date, he was beginning to get concerned. He had planned to have at least made contact with her by now. In his mind, he had gone over every possible scenario that could develop between them based on her reaction when they met. He was her doctor, and he was sure that she would be slightly uncomfortable when she ran into him. He had been prepared for this. Ever since she started coming to his office, ever since he had performed his first examination of her, he had been entranced. There was something about this woman that he could not get out of his head. He knew that outside of being her doctor, she did not even know that he existed. That really did not matter to him, he knew that he was never going to have a relationship with this woman, and a relationship was not really what he was looking for. He was looking for the perfect last victim, and once he reminded himself of that, he knew that MacKenzie was the one. After her first visit, he began listening to her morning show religiously. That was how he found out about this event. In fact, he made sure never to mention her work during her visits, always seeming uninterested, so when they "ran into" each other, she wouldn't think that he was stalking her. He had planned the night out so carefully, and now the more he waited for her, the more anxious he became.

The Nemesis looked down at the next number on the stack of cards, wondering how many more of these dreadful women he was going to have to deal with before he got the opportunity to approach MacKenzie. He took a look at the number, found the table on the other side of the floor, and started to make his way over. Just as he did that, he could not help but suspect that he was being followed. As he looked around, he noticed a lot of people looking at him. Even those that were not looking at him directly seemed to be interested in him to some degree. He felt as though everyone had noticed something embarrassing about him, like toilet paper stuck to his shoe. They kept looking at him, or around him, focusing on every little move that he made. Suddenly he noticed the man standing behind the hostess at the podium put his hand up to his right ear, and The Nemesis knew immediately what was happening. This was a trap. The knowledge from this thought almost stopped him cold. A quick pang of panic shot through his system, and then focusing, he turned slightly and made his way over to the bar. The bar was in a centralized location, he would be able to view the entire room from there. There were always about five to seven minutes interval between each date, and at the most, only two had elapsed so far. There were some men who were still talking to the women from the last date. That meant he had five minutes, five minutes to come up with an escape plan. He was not going down like this; he was not going down tonight. He was The Nemesis, he was born to be who he was, and he was going to finish his mission one way or another.

Looking back over the room, he noticed that the majority of the eyes were on him. Many of the men that the killer had thought were part of the crowd must have been undercover police officers. They spread out around the room, as if trying to box him in. Out of nowhere, a waitress walked up to the bar and placed an order. Suddenly, everyone stopped. The Nemesis knew what they were thinking. They were terrified that, if he knew that he was cornered, he was going to take her hostage. He looked out at one of the men coming closer to him and smiled a knowing smile. He then looked over to the waitress.

"I bet you can't wait for this night to be over," The Nemesis commented.

"You have no idea," she answered back. "At least its overtime."

The bartender placed her order on her tray, and the woman turned and walked away. The Nemesis let her go. He had no intention of taking her hostage; she was not even the person that he had been interested in. He was here for MacKenzie, and though his original plan may be useless now, he was not done yet. The Nemesis quickly sized up the situation. The men around him had stopped making their way forward, and the killer knew that whoever was in charge realized that it was too dangerous to take The Nemesis down with so many civilians at risk. However, The Nemesis also knew that he could not try to take one of these people hostage to get out. The cops would shoot him dead without hesitating. There was very few options left open to him, and knowing that, the killer began to become enraged. Though he did not see Grenier, the killer knew that the detective was behind this. Somehow he had known about the original case, and somehow he had put together the similarities and had known where The Nemesis would strike. Deep down, the killer knew that this just strengthened his beliefs, but for the meantime, the killer had to find a way out of here. He had to get away without being followed.

"Sorry about the wait," the bartender said, tossing a dishrag over his shoulder. "What'll you have?"

"A shot of tequila," the killer answered. The bartender poured the shot and placed the salt rimmed glass directly in front of the killer, along with a lemon. The killer downed the shot quickly, grimaced at the strong, foul taste, and turned to the bartender. "You call that tequila? Let me see that bottle."

The bartender, unsuspecting, pulled the bottle down off of the shelf, looked at the label and placed the bottle down on the counter. He did not see The Nemesis reaching into his pocket, or if he did, he thought nothing of it. With lightning reflexes, the killer grabbed the bottle off of the counter and put the mouth of the bottle against his lips, allowing the liquid to fill his mouth. Just then, reacting on their training as police officer's, the men around him moved forward instinctively. The killer deftly flipped open a Zippo lighter and lit the fuse, then just as the men were upon him, spit the liquid out in a fine spray, catching on the flame from the lighter and becoming a fireball that exploded three feet out in front of him. Everyone instinctively dropped to the floor. The killer flicked the lighter again, again spitting fire out everywhere. This was not getting the desired effect, and he realized why. The officers were getting back up on their feet and The Nemesis knew that he had precious little time, so he launched himself up on a barstool, then on the counter, and lit a fireball one last time. That was all he needed. Suddenly, the sprinkler system erupted, spraying a fine mist of water everywhere. Again, people were dropping to the floor as they were pelted with the stinging water. The Nemesis knew that the system would be spraying water everywhere and that this was his only chance. The killer jumped down from the counter and ran around the bar towards the back. He had memorized the layout of this nightclub from the very beginning, from when he knew he would find his first victim here. There was a back door, mandated by the fire code, and he headed in that direction. He heard voices and hid for a moment, just in time as two men ran by heading to the main floor of the club. The

Nemesis smiled after they passed, knowing that he had not been seen and slipped out the back door and was gone.

Chapter 67

Detective Grenier watched the events below him unfold with increasing frustration. He left standing orders for the officers on the floor to monitor the suspect, not to approach or engage him. However, to his dismay, a group of seven male undercover officers were now spreading out across the floor below, caging the man in. Confusion was starting to set in amongst the other members of the evening's event, as attention was drawn away from the dating area, and diverted to the men breaking away from the crowd. *What the hell are they doing*, Nick thought to himself as he watched. He shouted into his radio, repeating his order to stand down. Now other members of the dating crowd, civilians, were starting to pull away from the area designated for meeting and make their way towards the other men. This was exactly what Nick had hoped to avoid, innocent civilians drawn into a dangerous situation because officers on the floor drew attention away from the crowd. Apparently, the officers below also saw what was starting to happen, and backed off. The man Angela MacKenzie had identified as Dr. Westcott had stepped over to the bar and was waiting there. Nick had the bad feeling that the cover of his officers had been blown, and as he watched the man below looking back and forth at the men who had now caged him in like an animal, he was suddenly certain of it. Whoever Westcott was, he now knew that he was the subject of this attention.

"We have the facial composite now," the first FBI technician announced. Nick looked over his shoulder momentarily.

"Call Lt. Hollings back in," he answered. "Have her bring Ms. MacKenzie in to confirm it."

Nick turned his attention back down to the floor, where it seemed as though the entire event had stopped. Unsure of what to do, and why so many of the male guests had stepped away from the dating area, the head of the event decided not to ring the buzzer allowing guests to mingle amongst themselves. Many of the women were pointing over to the area where the others had gathered. Nick could imagine the atmosphere on the floor had become very intense, and wondered to himself how long this standoff between his men and the suspect could continue. If this man was the killer, he would surely try to escape; or worse, take a hostage in an attempt to escape. However, the man had to know that was futile; the officers below would kill him as soon as an opportunity presented itself. Nick watched as an attentive waitress made her way over to the bar, slipping past the undercover officers before they were able to realize what was going on. She stepped over to the bar and placed her tray on the counter. *Oh shit*, Nick thought to himself, as a wily smile spread across the face of the suspect below. In that instant, he knew beyond any doubt that this man was the killer that Nick had been looking for. However, now the detective was faced with a new problem. He waited with the radio perched up in front of his mouth, just waiting to call the officers stationed at the back door to come in and take the killer down.

"That's him," he heard MacKenzie say from behind him. Hollings had led her out to look at the picture conjured up by the computer.

"Is there anything we should alter?" the technician asked. "Any distinguishing features we should add?"

"What do you mean?" asked MacKenzie, not understanding.

"This is a computer composite," the technician explained quickly. "Every face is basically symmetrical. We took the pictures we had, matched it with an old driver's license photo from Rhode Island, but I need you to tell me if there is anything we need to add to that picture."

"No," MacKenzie answered frankly. "It's a spot on match. You wouldn't be able to tell it's from a computer."

Hollings smiled at MacKenzie and pointed back to the room at the far end of the office, then made her way over to the detective. She noticed the anxious look on his face, and felt that she should get an update on the situation.

"What's going on?" she asked, unable to mask her concern.

"He's our killer," Nick answered, sure of himself. "However, I think we might have ourselves a situation."

Hollings looked down below and noticed the young woman at the bar, talking to the killer.

"Oh shit," Hollings exclaimed. "How did those idiots let this happen?"

"I don't think they knew what she was doing until it was too late," Nick answered, defending the officers. "If he tries anything, we'll have the two officers at the rear door in here before he can blink an eye."

"If he tries anything," Hollings began. "They'll shoot him dead before he can blink an eye."

"I know," Nick said, concerned. "We need to capture this guy alive. There are a lot of questions that we need answered."

There was a sigh of relief between them as the waitress smiled to both the bartender and the man standing at the counter, picked up her tray and walked away. It seemed as though everyone in the nightclub breathed easier all at once, a collective sigh of relief that though inaudible, could be felt amongst all of the police officers in the building.

"That was too close," Hollings stated. "There's still the bartender. If Westcott has a gun on him…"

"He doesn't," the detective assured her. "He was patted down at the door. Besides, he feels a gun is beneath him. I bet he knows what will happen if he tries to take someone hostage. If he knows that he's been trapped, then he knows that we know history too, and will be expecting that move. No, right now he's wracking his brain, trying to think of a way out of here."

"What way is there?" Hollings asked, unsure of what everyone was waiting for. "There is nowhere for him to go. He knows he's caught, why prolong it any further. I say that we go down there and slap some cuffs on him."

"With what evidence?" Grenier repeated. "The best we can do is hold him on suspicion of murder."

"Then we'll get a warrant and tear his life apart," Hollings answered. "We'll find more than enough to hang him on."

Nick was listening to his lieutenant, but something caught his attention down below. There was a look in the killer's eyes, a look that told the detective that he was not through yet. The killer knew that he was backed up against a wall, between a rock and a hard place; however, the detective could not help but feel that The Nemesis was about to start something devious. Nick quickly ran through all of the possibilities of escape in his mind, trying to anticipate any move the killer could possibly conceive of.

He has no gun. He can't shoot anyone.

He's cornered and outnumbered. He can't get away.

The bartender is larger than him and he most likely can't hurt him.

He's ordering a drink from the bar. He's pulling something out of his pocket.

The detective seemed to be the only person that picked up on this last point. He watched the confused and amused faces of the police officers surrounding him as he ordered a drink from the bartender, none of them suspecting anything malicious. Even Hollings muttered something, but Nick was already out the door, heading towards the steps. He did not know what the killer had in mind, but he knew that The Nemesis had no intention of being defeated tonight, and that if Nick did not move quickly he was going to try to get away. Nick flew down the stairs, taking two at a time and jumped through the curtain on the stage, startling some ladies standing around the edge just as the killer pushed himself up upon the bar, spitting fire at the officers hurtling themselves toward him. A moment later, stinging water pelted down from the ceiling as an alarm shrieked and the sprinkler system discharged water all around the room. The guests screamed and ran in all directions, several times careening with the detective as he attempted to make his way to the back door. At this point, there was no question in which direction the killer was headed, the back door was the only option even remotely possible, and covering his eyes from the stinging water, he passed the bar and many confused officers milling around. As Nick passed the bar, he ran into the two officers who were supposed to be posing as security at the back door. They stopped him physically before recognizing who he was. They then continued past him, trying to find out what was going on, leaving the detective standing in a large puddle of water, watching the back door close, knowing that his killer had slipped through his fingers again.

Chapter 68

Governor Haisley and Special Agent Howell came into view of the media and their cameras just as they stepped up to the stage where a podium had been set up for the press conference. Both men were smiling, laughing with each other as if they shared some inside joke known only to them. Haisley stepped aside, offering the FBI agent the opportunity to step onto the stage and talk first, though he already knew the agent would decline. This act had been set up well in advance, both men playing their parts perfectly for the cameras. The agent, of course declined and the governor ascended the stairs of the stage and took his place in front of the podium. His face was repeatedly illuminated by the flash bulbs of press's cameras that were taking pictures at a feverish rate. Governor Haisley spread his papers out in front of him, placing them in order while giving his staff enough time to distribute a packet of information to each member of the press. Everyone was getting ready; this press conference was going to be held live, interrupting almost all evening television on the major networks.

All three major networks were present, as well as a few local radio news stations and most of the major newspapers in Connecticut. Haisley watched as his aid finished handing out the packets, stepped aside and gave him the thumbs-up signal that all was ready. Then looking out into the cameras, watching them all suddenly click over from a red light on top to a green light, indicating that they were live and ready to go, he spoke.

"Ladies and gentleman, my fellow Connecticut citizens," the governor began. "The New London police department, with a great deal of help from our own local FBI branch, has had a successful sting operation in Mystic this evening, and the man who calls himself The Nemesis, who has killed three victims so far, will soon be in police custody."

Hands immediately shot up into the air, anticipating a pause in the governor's speech, however, he motioned for everyone to remain calm and the hands began to slowly sink back down.

"The suspect has been identified as Dr. John Westcott, a Rhode Island primary care physician," Haisley continued. "As you will see in your packets, you have all been provided with a picture of the suspect, as well as his vital information. This information has been distributed because Dr. Westcott has eluded custody up until this point, and we believe that he is armed and dangerous. Though we know he will be in custody soon, we want to minimize the risk he presents to the public."

"You keep saying he will be in custody soon," a reporter interrupted, unable to keep quiet any longer. "Do you plan on arresting Dr. Westcott? Are you saying that he is The Nemesis?"

"We will be making an arrest," the governor answered frankly. "As for your second question, the facts do seem to support the evidence that Dr. Westcott is in fact The Nemesis."

"You said that the police carried out a successful sting operation," another reporter chimed in. "How can you call it a success if your suspect was able to elude the police?"

"We believe that it was the intention of Dr. Westcott to abduct and torture a woman from the dating event held at the Insomnia nightclub," the governor answered with a smile. "Though working on an extremely short timetable, the police were able to infiltrate the event and keep Westcott from accomplishing that. I call saving a life a definite success."

"What information led the police to the fact that The Nemesis would strike at the nightclub?" asked a female reporter.

"If you knew the killer would be going to the nightclub, you must know who the intended victim was," another reporter screamed out. "What can you tell us about the intended victim?"

At this point, Nick reached forward and pressed the power button on the bottom right hand corner of the television, watching the image twist sharply and then disappear. The detective sighed and sat back down on the edge of the desk in the upstairs office of the nightclub. His clothes were still wet, which caused him to have to lean up against objects instead of sitting in a chair. He had given Anna a set of his home keys so that she could run back and gather up a dry set of clothes. While he waited, he supervised the debriefing of all of the officers who had been down on the floor below involved in the operation. The debriefing had been pretty quick; most of the officers did not know much about the operation outside of what to be on the look out for. Each story had been almost exactly the same, and when it was all over, the detective let the officers go home. All of the guests had been questioned as well, especially the few number of women who had the seven minute dates with Dr. Westcott. All of them described him as handsome, confident, emotionally and physically strong, intelligent, and distracted. Each woman said that it seemed as though he did not want to be a part of the dates, as if he were waiting for the buzzer to sound so that he could move on.

Once all of the interviews and debriefings were finished, Lt. Hollings and Grenier got together to compare notes. As they talked over their findings, Nick could not help but feel as though he almost botched the entire operation. Nick had been so sure that it was a guest that was to be the next victim that he had not even considered the fact that it could have been any of the women who had worked behind the scenes. The detective kept thinking about what could have happened had MacKenzie not identified Westcott. *What would have happened had she gone back down on the floor like she had planned? Would The Nemesis now have his forth victim?*

"Stop beating yourself up," Hollings said, watching the detective ease himself back into a leaning position against the desk. "We had very little time to get as far as we did. We are now sure who the killer is, and we will have him caught in no time."

"Yeah by flooding the media with his picture and information," Nick said, disapprovingly. "We are giving out too much. This is all going to play right into his lawyer's hands when it comes time for trial."

"That's not our problem," Hollings stated. "It's our job to catch the killer; it's the DA's job to convict him. We stopped him from abducting a woman tonight. If he was planning on following the old case to the letter, then we've also stopped him from raping her too."

"What?" asked a shocked female voice from behind them. It was just at that moment that the lieutenant and the detective realized that Angela MacKenzie had entered the main room of the office and could overhear their conversation. She went pale immediately and looked as though she were going to lose consciousness. Hollings moved quickly, grabbing the woman's left arm and guiding her into a chair.

"So I was the intended target?" Angela asked, a panicked look of fear filling her face.

"We can't be sure," Hollings said. "We are going to assign you police protection until he is caught just in case though."

"I can't believe..." began the shocked young woman. "I never thought I would be..."

"It's best not to think about it," Hollings said, attempting to calm the woman down. The lieutenant could tell that the young woman was beginning to fall deeper and deeper into shock the more she thought about how close she had come to being a victim.

"You said he was going to rape me," MacKenzie said, looking up at the detective.

"The lieutenant is right," Nick started. "We don't know anything for sure yet. Is there nothing that he said or did when you were his patient that made you suspect something was out of the ordinary with him?"

"No," MacKenzie answered, shaking her head violently. "He was always very polite, caring, attentive and compassionate. He seemed like the perfect doctor."

"Had you told him you were hosting this event?" Nick asked, trying to understand the killer a little better.

"No," she answered again. "He never seemed overly interested in my work. He probably heard that I was hosting the event from our spots on the radio. We hyped this thing up pretty heavily."

"You used the words polite, caring, and attentive," Nick began. "Did he seem at all overly attentive to your medical condition?"

"No," the woman answered, her frustration mounting. "He never did anything that made me feel uncomfortable. He never did anything at all that would make me suspect that he was anything other than a good doctor."

Nick sighed under his breath, but smiled at the young woman and thanked her for her help. The detective turned away and walked back over to the windows overlooking the nightclub. The floor below was now bustling with uniformed police officers, crime scene investigators and technical agents from the FBI. Nick's thoughts drifted back to the comment made by the reporter on the television, and he was right, The Nemesis was still out there. However, the killer was no longer in control. Westcott's picture would be plastered everywhere in a matter of hours, and though Hollings seemed to feel as though this would bring a quick resolution to the case, Nick could not help but feel as though the events this evening had just made things worse. The Nemesis did not seem to Nick to be someone who was going to let himself be arrested, nor did he seem like a person who was going to give up. Just because he had been thwarted this evening, Nick still believed that this killer planned on finding his forth victim. Unfortunately, now with the attention on the killer, Nick was afraid of how far this cornered animal would go. The more Nick thought about this, the more concerned he became. Just then, Anna walked in with a duffel bag in her right hand and placed it down on a desk, then held up a cell phone in the other.

"I brought a couple of different things," she said. "I thought I'd let you decide. And an officer outside just said that she has a call from Wilkins and Mitchell."

"Well it's about fucking time," Hollings said, rising from her kneeling position beside Angela MacKenzie.

"They say they have been following Westcott since he left here," Anna continued. "They say he's heading for the casino and they want to know if they should stop him before he gets on tribal land."

"No," Nick answered, grabbing the duffel bag. "Tell them to keep watching him, and not to let him out of their sight. Tell them I'm on my way."

"What are you thinking?" Hollings asked, unsure of the detective.

"He's starting to make mistakes," Nick answered. "The casino has more high tech surveillance than anywhere else in the state. We'll watch him while he's in there, and then take him as he leaves."

"I don't know if we can make an arrest on tribal lands," Hollings said.

"Then we'll get him the moment he drives over the border," Nick said, filled with confidence. "Either way, we'll have him before he has a chance to try again."

Chapter 69

The Nemesis tore out of the parking lot of the nightclub, watching carefully for any cars that might be following behind. Anger, frustration, confusion all flooded his mind, merging together and threatening to boil over. As he crossed over lanes of traffic in an amateurish attempt to keep any police cars from following him, he had to also concentrate on his emotions, realizing that now was not the time to unleash them. He needed to concentrate on getting away, as his eyes slipped back and forth between the rearview mirror and the front windshield of the car. So far, he had not seen any cars that looked as though they might be following him; however, it was late in the evening and all he could see were headlights. He could not even be sure that he would have known what to look for if he could clearly see the cars around him. This frustration was not helping him keep his emotions in check. Paranoia was rampant as he stared at every car that he approached or passed, scanning every driver in an attempt to ascertain whether or not they might be a threat. Merging with the far right lane, The Nemesis could see the on ramp to the interstate, and flipped his right turn signal on and in an instant disappeared into the speeding traffic of Interstate-95.

To the killer, it seemed as though he had been driving forever. He tried to watch for any cars following, but the further he got away from Mystic, the safer he began to feel. If he were being followed, surely the police would have pulled him over by now. He knew that he had slipped away, but only by the skin of his teeth, and if he knew Grenier, he knew the detective would pick up the scent again soon. The Nemesis allowed himself to relax though, knowing that this state of anxiety would only lead to rash decisions, which would only lead to him getting captured and arrested by the police. He flipped the switch on the rearview mirror down, causing the blindingly bright lights of a car behind him to be muted, and quieted his mind. Pushing away thoughts of impending doom, the killer focused on his breathing, inhaling deeply through his nose and exhaling thoroughly through his mouth. As relaxation sunk in, he found himself becoming tired. His eyelids were heavy and he was having trouble keeping them open. He finally pulled over into a rest-stop on the side of the interstate and got out of the car. He entered the rest-stop and purchased a large bottle of soda and a few candy bars. He then exited, ripping into one of the chocolate bars and consuming it quickly. He returned to his car and, looking down at the pavement, could hold back the flood tide of his anxious thoughts no longer.

What the fuck happened? Grenier had been there, the nightclub event was a trap. The Nemesis could not believe that he had let himself nearly be caught by the police. He had planned for months, scoping out the nightclub, memorizing all of its exits and entrances. He had investigated and learned everything there was to know about Insomnia and the Speed Dating Event. He had listened to Angie MacKenzie's show every morning, picking up on even the most subtle clues when she advertised the event. The killer could not believe that the event had been a trap all along, and thinking about it further, he knew that it could not have been. The police had not known about The Nemesis for months, as he had only killed Tracy Scott two weeks ago. *So the real question is, how long have they known about you*? The Nemesis thought about this for a few minutes, realizing that it could only have been a few days at the most. Nicholas Grenier, nor the entire police department, would let an innocent person get killed if they knew who the killer was. Somehow, they just figured out about the old case, and luckily put two and two together and figured out where he would strike next. However, they knew now; they knew who he was; they knew about the old case, they might know everything. The Nemesis had been so sure that Grenier would not figure it out, that it would be The Nemesis himself who would help the detective along the path, that he had let himself become complacent, and had nearly been caught.

Fuck! The Nemesis kicked the front driver side tire, smashing his toe against the inside of his shoe, sending searing pain up his leg. The thought of not being in control was horrifying to him; however, the thought of all of those months of careful planning being upset by a day or two of quick police planning was worse. He found himself tensing as the rage spread through his body. The killer climbed back into the car and got back on the interstate, deciding to turn around and head back towards Rhode Island. After turning around at the next exit, he headed north, trying to think of the next steps in his plan. He knew that he could not go home again. Even though he had used his birth name, Jack Camden, he knew that it would not take Grenier long to put all the clues together; that's if he had not already done so. The police would be swarming all over his house in a matter of hours, and though it was something that The Nemesis had always prepared for, he had not expected the police to be on to him this soon.

The car was another problem. The killer had rented it under the name of Dr. John Westcott, as he was known now. There had been no choice in the matter, his current driver's license and insurance information was all under that name. As soon as they knew who he was and where he lived, it was not going to take them long to find out that he rented a car. He was going to have to dump the rental and steal a different car. There were easy ways to get away with that, especially if you only needed the car for a short period of time. All he had to do was to find a place with a large parking lot; a large parking garage would be even better. The Nemesis had not gone into this without having plenty of back-up strategies.

Now, he was going to have to use them. Now, he was going to have to use them all to keep from getting caught by the police before he was able to complete his mission.

The rearview mirror caught the glare of a car's headlights again, causing him to wince. The new halogen headlights that were installed on all new car models may illuminate the road better, but they gave him a terrible headache. The killer pulled out of the slow lane, merging into the fast lane so as to move ahead of the car with the irritating headlights. However, the car crossed over the lane too, causing him to have to reach up to flip the switch on the rearview mirror again. Just as his thumb touched the switch, the killer noticed something about the car. Actually, it was the license plate that caught his eye. When coming out of the rest-stop, he had noticed the plate. Though they were not vanity plates, the three letters caught his attention because they spelled out the initials of the name he was given at birth. The same car was now following him, remaining directly behind him. At first, the killer told himself not to panic, thinking that there could be hundreds of explanations, the most logical being they both left the rest-stop at the same time. However, The Nemesis quickly remembered that he had turned around at the next exit so as to get back into the north bound traffic. He knew the chances of this car having to turn around too, not to mention at the same exit, was very remote. He could not be sure if it was the same car as when he noticed the headlights the first time, before stopping at the rest-stop, but he was beginning to think he was being followed.

The killer, without switching on his right hand turn signal, slid into the slow lane, merging closely between a semi trailer and an SUV. He glanced back into the driver's side mirror, waiting to see what the car behind him would do. The other car accelerated just enough to be in his blind spot, making it impossible for the killer to pull back into the fast lane. Then, the killer realized that the SUV behind him was dropping back, and sure enough the other car slid in right behind him. That was all the proof the killer needed. He was being followed, and the only possibility was that he had been followed from the nightclub. This night had already been a disaster, and now he was being followed, surely to be pulled over and arrested. It had come down to this. No forth victim, no revealing to Nicholas Grenier who he was meant to be, and no glory. All of this would end and nobody would ever understand why The Nemesis did any of this, he would be nothing but a footnote on the evening news. A thought came to him suddenly, *Run. If they try to pull you over, make a run for it.* While this was certainly a possibility, there seemed something final about it. It seemed desperate and foolish, like the last act of a guilty man. He did not want to go out like that; he did not want to be a joke.

It was when he was thinking about going on the run that he passed a sign for Interstate-395. The interstate would branch off in less than a mile and I-395 would head north whereas I-95 would continue east through Rhode Island before turning north to Providence. It was at that moment that an idea sparked in the killer's mind; an idea that, though not fully formed, might save him from his plight. Instead of going out either in the next few minutes or the next few hours, there could possibly be a way for him to get away from the police who were tailing him, a way to get away clean. Get away so that he could continue on with his plans. The sign directly overhead showed that the interstate would split in the next few feet, and the killer was still in the far right lane. Glancing quickly over his shoulder, The Nemesis jerked hard on the steering wheel, sending the car into the middle lane, and then the far left lane. He did not have the time to check on the car that was tailing him, as cars around him were slamming on their breaks to accommodate this insane actions. From the far left lane, he was able to merge onto the ramp that became I-395. A few cars flashed their high beams at him, showing their irritation at his reckless maneuver. He just brushed it off, accelerating his car away from the pack until he felt he was far enough away. He continued to glance back into the rearview mirror, looking for the car that had been following him. After less than a minute, he found that he had not been able to slip his tail after all, seeing the car pull up behind him. Oddly enough, neither the driver nor the passenger made any attempt to signal him to pull over. He could not understand why they would not attempt to go ahead and arrest him now. It did not matter to him though; he still had plans forming in his mind.

He still needed to lose the police and get rid of this rental car. He needed to find a place with a lot of people, and a place where he could steal a car and not have the police find out about it for awhile. The idea for the perfect place popped into his head immediately, realizing that it would still be difficult. He was going to a place that had the strictest security and the most advanced surveillance outside of a government agency. He was going to a place where there were video cameras everywhere, monitoring every move a person made. He was going to a place that had more people crammed into one place on this Friday night than anywhere else he could think of. He was going to the casino.

Chapter 70

There were two tribal casinos in Connecticut, and as Nick had learned after leaving the nightclub, Dr. Jack Westcott had been followed to the newer of the two. The Mohegan Sun casino lay just outside of Norwich, Connecticut, and in the daytime looked like a huge tower made out of mirrors. The sunlight was reflected off of the huge building, the largest in the area. Times like now, in the darkness, the building could only be distinguished by the lights from the tower windows. Though muted, they still showed through the tinted windows. There had always been something strange about looking out over relatively flat land of one and two story buildings to see this monstrous geometric tower rise high into the sky. Taking the back roads, Nick finally pulled into the parking area outside of the casino twenty minutes later and was directed to the third level of the parking garage by the casino security. Nick drove slowly up the concrete parking structure until he reached an area where local and state police were stationed. The police had parked themselves directly in front of

Westcott's rental car, making sure there was no way he could get back to it to escape. Nick spoke with the officers on the scene, who were planning to have the car searched by the crime scene unit, then towed away after Westcott was apprehended. He was then informed that detectives Wilkins and Mitchell were inside the casino, at the surveillance center.

Stepping inside the casino was like entering a different world, like stepping from one dimension to another. It was as though Nick had left the world of reality, the world of suburbs and schools, shopping malls and fast food restaurants; and had entered the world of glitz and glamour, entertainment and fancy shopping, excitement and desperation. The casino was a world that never stopped. Even at this extremely late hour, the building remained packed, a mob of people slowly making their way around the outer concourse. Inside the ringed concourse, people placed money down on tables and slipped coins into slot machines hoping for that huge payout. It was a world the detective could not really understand. He had never had the desire to gamble, never thought that he was going to strike it rich on that one lucky hand in blackjack, or that one lucky pull at the slot machines. The world inside the casino intrigued him in the way that it seemed time stood still. Inside this building that never seemed to end, the hour always seemed the same; there were no windows or clocks, nothing to indicate the passage of time. It was a world onto itself, with hundreds of restaurants and stores, a spa, and a hotel. If a person had the money or inclination, they would never have to leave. After watching the people around him for a few minutes, the detective was reminded of the real reason he had come here, and quickly found an employee to take him to the security center.

After slipping through a keypad locked door marked EMPLOYEES ONLY, Nick was guided down a maze of hallways to the security center. Once inside, Nick stood in awe. The security center was a huge room with flat panel television screens and computer monitors everywhere. Every surface seemed to contain keyboards and other devices for controlling the surveillance equipment that covered the casino. Nick found detectives Mitchell and Wilkins receiving a lesson from one of the security personnel on how the casino monitored its patrons. Nick made his way down the steps and over to them.

"Give me an update," Nick said, getting the two detective's attention. "Where is Westcott now?"

"He's making his way to the mall," Mitchell answered, pointing to one of the monitors directly in front of them. The image was looking down on Westcott and others walking around him as he made his way into the area where all of the stores were located.

"There are a lot of people down there," Nick observed. "I don't want to lose him amongst the crowd."

"I wouldn't be worried about losing him in the mall," the technician answered. "That area has literally thousands of surveillance cameras and is well lit. Not only are there cameras all throughout every individual store, but there are cameras covering every angle of the walkways. I'd be more concerned about the concourse. It's a smaller area with much heavier traffic and is very poorly lit."

"Why is that?" Mitchell asked, confused. The detective assumed that a casino would always want to keep areas well lit to observe its patrons.

"The concourse is one big circle," the technician explained. "It leads to every gaming pit, most of which are on the inside of the concourse. The gaming pits are always darker, something about the way the light affects people, especially when they are gambling."

"No shit," Wilkins muttered, shaking his head.

"Let's just keep our eyes on Westcott," Nick suggested. He watched as his suspect walked slowly amongst the crowd, always making sure to stay around large groups of people. The man seemed to be oblivious to the fact that he was being watched by the cameras; however, the detective knew that Westcott had to know he was under surveillance.

"I just don't get it," Mitchell said, watching the same monitor. "How does he expect to get away from us here? He has to know that there are cameras everywhere. There is no way he can get out of here without being seen."

"This is the desperate act of a desperate man," Wilkins said with little concern. "He knows he's caught. He knows it's over and his back is against the wall. He obviously made us while we were following him. He knows he is about to be arrested and he thinks the best way to go now is to go down in public."

"Or he wants to take a hostage," Mitchell suggested. "Maybe he's trying to make sure that he can't be arrested. Maybe he wants to create a situation in which we have no choice but to kill him."

"Suicide by cop," Nick said, nodding. He had heard about it many times, desperate criminals who either knew they would never survive in prison or wanted to go out in a blaze of glory would create a situation where the police would have no choice but to kill them in order to protect other lives.

However, as he listened to the possibilities being offered by his fellow detectives, he just could not believe any of them. There was a purpose to The Nemesis's mission, at least in the mind of the killer. Nick had picked up on the focus and determination from the first time he talked with the killer over the telephone that night in his home. Now, weeks later, Nick knew that there was more to the killer's move here than met the eye. Nick felt that if it came down to it, The Nemesis would make the detective kill him;

however, the killer was going to do everything he could to complete his mission. Nick could not help but ask himself the question that everyone else was thinking. *What the hell is he up to*? Unfortunately, no answers were forthcoming.

"What exits are down there where he is?" asked Nick.

"None that aren't well guarded now," the technician assured him. "None of those doors marked exits take you directly outside. All of them lead through hallways to the outer concourse, which leads you to either the Summer or Winter entrances, where the garages are. At this point, there is nowhere he can go that we won't see him."

Nick sighed, as if unsatisfied with the answer. The Nemesis had to be following a plan, no matter how ill conceived or incomplete it may be. There had never been a point in this case when the killer had not had a plan. Even in the nightclub, the killer knew that setting off the sprinkler system would help to cause enough confusion and distraction as to help him get away. Now he seemed to be wandering around down around the strip of stores, but the detective knew this was just an act. The killer was either working out a plan just recently conceived, or fine tuning one previously devised. Either way, Nick needed to move on him now. Though the detective could not conceive of a way in which the killer could escape, he needed to make the arrest now before The Nemesis found a way to elude them again.

"What's the deal with arresting someone on tribal land?" Nick asked aloud, the question geared towards anyone of the security personnel or police in the room.

"Lt. Hollings made some inquiries," Mitchell answered. "Apparently there is no problem whatsoever. The state police are called down here all the time to take people into custody who have been shoplifting or trying to steal from the dealers. It's no problem."

"Alright then," Nick said. "We're going to move on him now. I want you two to stay together and keep your weapons holstered. I don't want to start a panic. I'll be with a member of security, and the moment he's not in with a group of people, I mean the very second, we move in and make the arrest. I don't care who does it, we just need to get him quickly in case he does try to take someone hostage."

"Take these," the technician offered. He handed each of the detectives a single earpiece connected to a small microphone that came halfway down their jawline. The pieces slipped over the ear and looked a lot like the hands-free devices Nick had seen for cell phones. "I will watch him from here and be able to direct you. You can talk into the mouthpieces. It should cut down on any confusion."

The detective acknowledged the technician's contribution, motioned to one of the security officers and they all exited the security center. The detectives each tested their communication devices as they were led down a corridor that put them right into the mall. Mitchell and Wilkins exited at the point where the mall merged with the concourse, as Nick was led by the security officer to the far end of the mall so they all could meet in the middle, Nick hoping that they could capture the killer before he made his move. However, the detective could not help the feeling of dread and apprehension that was creeping up in the back of his mind.

Chapter 71

The moment Nick exited the maze of passageways and was on the ground level of the mall, he realized immediately the benefits of being in contact with the technician in the security center. The walkway was crowded with groups of people, slowly moving from one store to the next, window shopping or browsing at different displays. There was a general flow to the foot traffic, heading away from the concourse on the right, and back towards it on the left. However, as people gazed back and forth, finding shops or restaurants that interested them, they would cross over each side, interrupting the flow and making it nearly impossible for the detective to keep his concentration focused on finding his suspect. Remarkably, he knew that it must be like this all of the time. Moving between the two currents of foot traffic, Nick stopped and looked around, trying to get a fix on where exactly he was so he could relate his position to the technician in the security center. Tourists of every nationality swarmed around him, and knowing Westcott from his picture, the detective focused on any Caucasian males.

"He's on your right side," the voice of the technician chimed in his ear piece suddenly. "He's about midway through the mall at this point. You probably can't see him yet."

"Which store is he near?" Nick asked, realizing that with this many people, the only way that he would be able to fix his position was by using the actual stores as a reference.

"He just stopped. He's directly in front of the waterfall," the technician answered. "He almost looks as if he's going to order a drink."

"Keep your eyes on him," Nick said. He could only assume that this must all be part of the killer's plan to elude the police. Nick knew that he could not let that happen. The detective picked up his pace as he made his way towards the manmade waterfall in the middle of the casino mall. He knew that there was a bar right in front of the waterfall, and knew that was where the killer was waiting.

"You are the closest to him," the technician informed him. "You will be on him in less than a minute. He's wearing a black long sleeve shirt and gray slacks. Do you see him?"

The detective did not see his suspect. He knew what Westcott had been wearing from the event at

Insomnia, and now the only changes seemed to be the removal of his sport jacket. Nick could see the bar now, but he still could not see Westcott. He looked over to the security officer who was accompanying him, but the man just shook his head.

"Can you see me?" Nick asked the technician.

"Yes, you are coming into view now," he answered. "Now you are both in view. Wait, your suspect has circled around and is now moving away from the bar. He's heading towards the other detectives."

Nick swore under his breath and quickened his pace even faster to catch up with Westcott. Now the detective could hear a conversation between Mitchell, Wilkins, and the technician. They were being guided to a certain point, and Nick was using the information to close the gap. Nick saw Mitchell come into view on the other side of the walkway, about one hundred feet ahead of him. Nick looked on the other side of the walkway, searching for both The Nemesis and Wilkins when he spotted his suspect. Westcott was trying to make his way around a large party of tourists, trying to blend in while moving around to the far side. The tourists began pointing to a particular store, and the entire group suddenly moved to the right, making their way inside. Just as they did, Nick saw Detective Wilkins walking towards the group. They had the killer trapped now, and now Nick just needed to know whether or not Westcott knew it.

As the group all headed into the store, Nick watched Westcott moving in with them, as if trying to make it appear as though he were part of the group. Wilkins made a motion with his hands, questioning whether or not to follow, and Nick immediately shook his head. They would wait for Westcott outside to ensure the safety of the shoppers inside. This game was starting to take its toll on the detective's nerves; he just wanted to make the arrest and get out of here. Nick was beginning to see the killer's reasons for coming to the casino. It was large, it was populated, and it was becoming difficult to track one person. Detective Mitchell passed behind Nick, cutting off the store opening to the right.

"Go on inside and keep him in sight," Nick told Wilkins as he approached. "Do not try to arrest him; just know where he is at all times."

"What about the cameras in the store?" Wilkins asked. "Why not depend on them. If I go in there you will only have two people on the entrance when he makes his way out."

"We'll get some more security down here," Nick assured the detective. "I would just feel better if we actually were watching him; you know the police."

Wilkins frowned for a moment, but then nodded his head in agreement. Nick knew that the other detective understood where he was coming from. Nick did not want the killer to be able to elude them again, and especially now when they had the perfect chance to capture him. Nick watched as the other detective entered the store, weaving himself in between browsing tourists. From where he stood outside the store, Nick could see Wilkins feigning interest in a shirt on a rack as Westcott picked up a sweatshirt and a hat. Wilkins turned back quickly, looking questioningly at Nick. Grenier nodded and pointed back towards Westcott. Wilkins then followed him throughout the store until the killer made his way back towards the dressing room. Nick now knew what was going on. Westcott was going to change clothes and hopefully slip in with some tourists in an amateurish attempt to evade the police. Nick could tell that Wilkins also knew what Westcott was up to, and waited at the entrance of the hallway to the changing rooms. Becoming frustrated with the waiting period, Nick entered the store, leaving only Mitchell outside to watch the entire entrance. Nick walked up to Wilkins who was obviously upset about the wait as well.

"You think he's going to try to wait us out?" Nick asked, trying to peer down the hall. Unfortunately, from their vantage point neither detective could see the changing rooms, or which one of them Westcott had gone into.

"I don't know, but he's been in there an awful long time," Wilkins said. "This is getting ridiculous."

"He's still in there, right?" Nick asked, suddenly realizing how easy it would have been for Westcott to get out of the store had he been able to slip past Detective Wilkins.

"An employee said this is the only way in or out," Wilkins assured Nick. "And he hasn't come back this way."

"Do you have any cameras in the changing area?" Nick asked into his microphone.

"No," the technician answered. "That's the only place we don't have any surveillance. However, there should be an employee down there who gives a key to each customer. He or she should be able to tell you whether or not he's come out."

"There's no other way out of there, right?" Wilkins asked again for reassurance.

"Nope," the tech answered. "That's the only way out."

"This is bullshit," Nick said. "I'm not waiting anymore."

Nick walked down the hallway, followed by Wilkins. When they arrived at the changing area, the small desk where the employee should have been sitting was empty. Above the desk were a series of hooks, each corresponding to a particular room, each with a key on the hook except for one.

"Number three," Nick said, pointing at the hook. Both men had already removed their sidearms from their holsters and were pointing them out in front of them. "Dr. John Westcott, open the door and exit the changing room walking backwards with your hands behind your head."

There was no answer from inside the changing room, which really had not surprised Nick as he assumed Westcott would be desperately thinking of a way to get out. Nick yelled the man's name again and repeated his orders. Nick noticed that he heard nothing from inside the room, no movement, no breathing, no nothing. Wilkins held up a hand, waving Nick over, and kicked the thin wooden door in with his foot. Inside, lying on the floor were the clothes that Westcott had been wearing when he entered the store, a black shirt and grey slacks.

"Fuck," Nick exclaimed, realizing he had been had. He yanked at his microphone. "Mitchell, can you hear me?"

"Yeah," Mitchell said. "He hasn't come out yet."

"He might have," Nick said. "He's changed clothes."

"What is he wearing?" asked Mitchell desperately.

"What the fuck did he bring in here?" Nick asked Wilkins.

"A grey Mohegan Sun sweatshirt and a pink ball cap," Wilkins said with a shrug. "He must have had some pants too."

"Did you catch that?" Nick asked Mitchell.

"Shit," Mitchell said. "There was just a group of them who left the store about two minutes ago."

"Damn it," Nick yelled. "He slipped in with them."

Wilkins had already bolted back down the hallway in Mitchell's direction. Over the headphones Nick heard the technician giving the detectives directions as he identified the group and its location. Nick walked back down the hall, knowing that all of the casino security as well as the detectives were going to be on the group in seconds. He heard the voice of young woman as she walked down the hall, swearing.

"That asshole almost ran me down," she said, pointing back in the direction Wilkins had just gone. Nick smiled at the store employee for a moment, about to give her a quick explanation. Then something came to his mind.

"Where is the employee who hands out the keys?" the detective asked, pointing back to the hooks on the wall.

"Oh," the girl shrugged. "He must be on break."

"But he didn't come back this way, I've been watching the entire time," Nick lied.

"There's an employee entrance at the back of the changing rooms," the girl said. "It leads to the storeroom and break room."

"Are there hallways that lead out of the building back there?" Nick asked.

"Yeah," the woman answered. "They lead to the loading docks and you can exit that way."

Nick immediately showed the woman his badge and asked her to take him back to the break room and introduce him to the employee who should have been there. When they arrived at the break room, it was empty except for the store manager, who assured the detective that he was the only person scheduled to be on break at that time. Nick swore and began running to the very back of the storeroom and into the hallway that led to the loading dock. The detective's mind was racing with the possibilities of what might have just happened. His worst fear was that he had kidnapped the boy and was being led out of the building. Nick immediately called the security office and had them start scouring the cameras in the back hallways for anything out of the ordinary. In the meantime, he could overhear that Mitchell and Wilkins had caught up with the group of shoppers and was now detaining them. Nick continued running down the hallway, praying that he was going in the right direction and that he would come upon Westcott before he was able to exit the building. The detective finally reached the end of the hallway where the loading docks began and stopped running, cursing to himself.

"Hey Nick," Wilkins voice came in over the headphones. "Can you hear me?"

"I'm here," Nick answered. "Please tell me you've got him."

"No, he's not here," Wilkins said. "But I've got someone here who doesn't fit, and I think I know how Westcott got past us.

Chapter 72

Hours later, with the sun rising over the eastern horizon and life beginning emerge in New London, Connecticut on a beautiful morning, Detective Grenier sat at the desk in his office feeling miserable. He continuously rubbed his hands over his face, feeling the sandpaper-like growth of his beard. He felt dirty and exhausted, wishing that he had taken the time to stop by his home to shower and change before coming back into work. However, after leading a detailed search of the entire casino and finding nothing of Westcott, Nick decided to return to the police department and find out what Wilkins and Mitchell had come up with. When they had located the group of senior tourists in the casino, the detectives did not find Westcott among them; however, they did find a young man trying not to be seen. As Nick used the casino security to search for his suspect, Wilkins and Mitchell took the young man back to the police department for questioning. Once Nick returned, the detectives relayed the young man's story; explaining how he was involved with

Westcott's get-away. The young man had been the employee at the store in the casino responsible for giving out the keys to the changing rooms. Westcott had apparently offered the young man two thousand dollars to change into the outfit that he had picked up and let Westcott use the boy's employee shirt for half an hour. The boy, having been told by Westcott that he was playing a joke on a friend, thought it would be an easy way to make some money.

After Westcott and the young man exchanged shirts, the young man exited the changing rooms and fell in with the senior citizens group. Nick surmised that Westcott put on the employee's shirt and walked through the back and into the hallway that led towards the loading docks. Whether Westcott knew where he was going or not, Nick could not be sure; however, wearing the employee's shirt kept him from calling attention to himself. Even the technicians in the security office did not think anything about it, watching a man in a store uniform shirt walking back through the employee hallways on their monitors. Nick felt as though this had been a major failure, even though everyone around him was congratulating him on finally putting a face and name to The Nemesis. To Nick, the entire night had been a disaster. He had not anticipated the killer's moves correctly, and because of that he felt as though he had given Westcott the perfect opportunity to escape from both the nightclub and the casino.

"Stop beating yourself up," Hollings said as she walked through his door. "You've had a very good night."

"Oh, really?" Nick asked, sarcastically. "I had the killer cornered twice, and he got away both times."

"You confirmed the identity of the killer," Hollings reminded him. "Now his name and face are being broadcast all over New England. You stopped him before there could be a forth victim, and you've got him scared."

"You would have had the identity within hours anyway," Nick answered, waving her off. "Wilkins and Mitchell had pretty much found him through a basic background check."

"Maybe," Hollings responded. "But we wouldn't have had anything to arrest him on. We could have brought him in for questioning, but as you've said, we have no solid evidence linking him to the crimes. He would have lawyered up in a heartbeat."

"Still," Nick observed. "Twice we had him cornered and he gets away both times."

"He hasn't gotten away from anyone," Hollings said. "The casino security is still conducting its search. They are going to find Westcott hiding in a janitor's closet somewhere in there. Remember, he left his car in the garage, and it's still there."

"No," Nick said, having already anticipated the killer's moves. "He's long gone by now. He's probably already stolen another car from one of the garages or parking lots and is having a good laugh over breakfast at this point."

"It doesn't matter," Hollings stated. "His mug is still all over television and in the papers; and even if he did get away, which I don't believe, someone's going to notice him and call it in. Then we'll charge him on the crimes committed in the nightclub."

"None of which are connected to the murders," Nick reminded her. "What about the kid?"

Nick was referring to the terrified young man who had made the deal with Westcott only to find himself in police custody hours later.

"He swears that he had never seen Westcott before," Hollings answered. "I believe him, he's just a dumb kid who made a big mistake. It turns out the money Westcott gave him was a hundred dollar bill wrapped around a wad of singles."

Nick laughed under his breath, rose and walked around his desk to the window looking out over the squad room.

"So instead of two thousand dollars, he gets one hundred and nineteen dollars and a lot of trouble," Nick states. "I hope it was worth it. Even if the district attorney does not press charges, the kid is still probably going to lose his job."

There was a period of silence while Nick was staring out the window, trying to anticipate the repercussions of the killer still being on the loose. Nick had not been able to predict that he would go after the radio host, Angela MacKenzie; and now that he was back on the street somewhere, the detective was suddenly aware that her safety might be in jeopardy. It was at that moment, when he was about to ask his lieutenant about MacKenzie, he realized that she had been staring at him the entire time.

"I don't mind telling you," Hollings said finally. "You look like shit."

"Thanks," Nick answered. "It's been a long night. What are we going to do about MacKenzie?"

"I was wondering how long it would take your mind to pick up on that," Hollings said. "Don't worry, she's fine. The FBI has offered to provide her with personal protection for the time being. I have to say, I'm impressed. You realized that she was still in danger faster than most detectives would have."

"Yeah well, I don't relish telling her that I let the man who is trying to kill her slip through our fingers," Nick said, imagining the woman's response.

"Shit happens," Hollings said, shrugging her shoulders. "Things aren't going to go your way all of the time. Just remind her that she is safe with the FBI agents, and that we are going to have Westcott in custody soon, very soon. There are going to be a lot of times when you have to give bad news to a victim or a victim's family. You need to get used to it."

"No I don't," Nick answered. "I'm out of here after this case."

"Yeah, yeah," Hollings said, unconvinced. "So you keep reminding me."

Just then, Anna knocked on the open door to alert the two officers to her presence and then stepped into the office.

"We got a call from the casino security," she started. "Apparently there has been a report of a stolen car from the employee parking lot."

"Ten points for me," Nick said, flashing a winning smile at his lieutenant.

"And," Anna continued, looking over at Nick. "You got a call from a retired Hartford police chief who said that he needs you to stop by his house right away. He says he has pertinent information for you regarding The Nemesis case."

"Who's the chief?" Hollings asked, interested.

"Get this," Anna said, making sure she had their attention. "His name is Chief Michelson."

"Michelson," Nick said in disbelief. "As in Sergeant Michelson of the old case?"

"The same," Anna answered, nodding.

"I never put that together," Nick admitted, realizing that he had heard of the former chief many times over his career. "He's still alive?"

"Apparently," Anna responded. "And he wants to see you as soon as possible. In fact, it sounded pretty urgent. He said he had information for you."

"Sounds like you better get going," Hollings said. "Take Wilkins and Mitchell with you. They might be helpful."

Nick collected the other detectives and they all headed out to the directions that had been provided by the former chief. Nick could not believe that he had not thought about the fact that there could have been someone still alive from the old case. He had just assumed that since his grandfather was dead and there did not seem to be anyone else involved as heavily with the case, that the only information he would be able to get would come from the old case file itself. However, here was a living witness to the case; someone he could have called upon before now. Nick was also interested in learning more about his grandfather. Nick only had memories, sometimes just partial memories of his grandfather. To him, it was just like pictures in a photo album. The old man had died when Nick was still young, and most of the memories he did have were stories relayed to him by his grandmother. She used to tell him how much he looked like his grandfather, and how they would have gotten along very well together. She always said they would have been like "peas in a pod". Nick could not help but smile as he thought about this.

The detectives arrived just over a half an hour after receiving the message and walked up to the door. Nick rang the doorbell and heard the click of the lock. They watched as the door opened and an elderly man stepped forth. The old man stared at Nick for a moment, and then reached out with a thin, weak hand as a tear formed in his eye.

"Terrence," the man said with barely an audible whisper. Then the man's hand went limp and his whole body seemed to sway for a moment before he started to collapse. Nick instinctively took a step forward and grabbed man before he hit the floor. Detectives Wilkins and Mitchell surrounded him in a flash and they carried the old man into the house.

Chapter 73

The three detectives carried the former police chief into the house where they were met by a woman who helped guide them to a chair in the living room where they could deposit the old man's limp body. Nick watched while the woman administered oxygen and fetched the old man some water. It took several minutes before he was able to breath normally again, and several minutes after that before he was able to focus his attention on anything other than his own health. Nick asked repeatedly if there was anything that he or his detectives could do, but the woman replied in the negative each time. Uncomfortably, the three detectives were left with nothing to do but look on helplessly. Nick watched as the woman checked the man's pulse and respiration, before making an exasperated plea for him to restrict his movements. The old man said nothing but waved her away with his free hand as held a plastic mask over his nose and mouth with the other. The woman stood and walked towards the hallway, meeting Nick halfway.

"Are you his nurse?" Nick asked. The detective was feeling uneasy about trying to get the old man to recall information about the old case in such a delicate medical condition.

"No, I'm his daughter," the woman answered, obviously irritated by the detective's assumption. "I'm also a doctor."

"I'm sorry doctor," Nick said, checking himself. "I meant no disrespect. Is he alright?"

"He's just fine," called the old man from the chair. "I'd appreciate it if you would include me in your conversation if you are going to talk about me."

Nick turned back to the former police chief and smiled.

"I'm sorry sir," Nick said. "I received a message that you had some information regarding my case. I was concerned about bringing up such a difficult case in your condition."

"My condition," Michelson laughed as he rose from his chair. Immediately, his daughter was at his side, again pleading with him but he just waved her away. "My condition is, I'm dying. We are all dying, I just happen to be way ahead of the curve."

The old man motioned for the detectives to follow him as he led them down the hall of his home to his study. There the old man offered them all seats and sat down himself in a wooden desk chair directly in front of an enormous desk that neatly showed pictures of the old man and what Nick could only assume as his family.

"I'm sorry if I startled you," Michelson said. "It's just that you look so much like your grandfather."

"You knew him well?" Nick asked, forgetting the case for a moment.

"Terrence?" Michelson asked. "I was probably the only person who did, aside from your grandmother. He was a very good man, a great man. He taught me everything I know about being a detective, about being a police officer, about being a man. He loved your grandmother very much, and she him. I know he would be very proud of you."

"Thank you sir," Nick responded, not knowing what else to say. He pointed to one of the pictures on the Michelson's desk. "Is that your wife?"

"Yes," answered Michelson as he lifted the frame in his frail hands and smiled. "That was taken many years ago. She left us eight years ago."

"I'm so sorry," Nick said, realizing that the conversation was headed down a depressing track. The detective knew that he needed to get the old man back on course; he was losing time.

"I've been waiting for this moment," Michelson said, ignoring the detective's response. "I have been waiting for you to come so that I could give you the information you needed; so that I could join her. It's odd, this damned case has given us all so much, and yet it's taken so much too."

"I don't understand," Nick said.

"The case gave me my wife," Michelson said. "It introduced your grandparents; it gave us all the wonderful families that we have. And yet, it took away your grandfather's desire to be a cop, it caused your grandmother so much pain; it opened a door of death that you are forced to close. It's so unfair that you should have to fix the mistakes of our past."

"I'm not following," Nick admitted. "What did this case have to do with my grandmother? What mistakes are you talking about?"

"Just because your grandfather was able to stop The Nemesis then doesn't mean the case died, as you can plainly see," Michelson said. "Your grandmother and I have been planning for this day for decades, waiting and watching in case our worst fears, her worst fears should come true. She never could have involved Terrence; she loved him too much, and was too afraid of what he would do if he knew the truth."

Nick sat in his seat, listening as the man continued on. Sitting there, he was trying to make sense of the puzzle that was laid in front of him. He could not understand how his grandmother, who to his knowledge had not met his grandfather yet, could have known and involved herself in this case.

"She thought she was safe for a long time," Michelson continued. "When Camden's wife left him and moved out to California, she and I thought that the chain may have been broken for good. But it wasn't, and somehow the boy must have found out about his heritage. When he went off the radar after his high school graduation, Gertrude was sure that the cycle would start again."

"What the hell are you talking about?" Nick asked finally, unable to contain his frustration at his inability to understand the story Michelson was relaying.

"Your grandmother, Gertrude," Michelson said slowly, as if prodding the detective along. "Gertrude Rainer, the forth and final victim in our case."

Nick rose from his chair, stepping back a little involuntarily as he tried to comprehend the information he was being supplied. He nodded, wanting Michelson to continue. However, a feeling of dread was creeping up inside him as he started to realize that he did not want to hear anymore.

"Damn," whispered Wilkins under his breath.

"What a horrible life to lead knowing that you have two grandchildren, one good and one bad," Michelson stated, shaking his head. "One grandson a police officer, one grandson a killer; cosmic fate can be very cruel."

Michelson stopped the moment Nick fell over. He slowly lifted himself from his chair, looking confused at the detective. It was at that moment that he realized that all of the officers were on their feet. Mitchell ran over to Nick's side, trying to help him up as Wilkins approached the former chief, taking him by his arm.

"What the hell are you saying?" Wilkins asked, unable to comprehend the truth. "Nick and Westcott are related? How can that be?"

Michelson looked between Wilkins and the detective lying on the floor several times before he understood what was happening. Suddenly, he rushed to Nick's side, getting down on the floor beside him as quickly as his body would carry him. He put his hand against the younger man's face.

"Oh my God," he said. "Oh my God, I'm so sorry; your grandmother never told you. You didn't know, did you? I assumed that was why you were on the case, why you had come back from your leave of absence at just this precise moment. I'm so sorry, I'm so sorry. No one should find out this way."

Mitchell helped the detective up as Wilkins brought the former chief back to his feet. Nick felt as though the room were spinning. His head was hot, almost feverish, and waves of nausea were washing over him as he was trying to comprehend the meaning of Michelson's words. He sat in the chair, hunched over his legs with his head in his hands.

"If Gertrude Rainer was his last victim, I take it you and Terrence Grenier were able to stop him before Westcott killed her?" Wilkins asked, trying to get Michelson to explain the case in chronological order.

"No," Michelson answered, watching Nick to make sure that the detective was all right. "I had been shot. Terrence continued on without me. As for Westcott, he knew that he was caught; he knew that his killing spree was coming to an end. When he kidnapped Gertrude, I think he changed his plan. He had no intention of killing her."

"His intention was to make sure that one day his progeny would continue what he started," Nick said, without looking over. "That's what you're saying, right?"

Michelson nodded at Nick, a look of utter sorrow spreading across his face. Something unspoken passed between the two men, and suddenly they both knew what had happened to Nick's grandmother.

"What the hell are you saying?" Wilkins asked in frustration. He could see from the expression on their faces that the two men knew something they were not sharing. "Why wasn't any of this in the case file?"

"Terrence and I took the final reports out of the file to protect Gertrude," Michelson answered. "I told Terrence that I burned them, but I never did. Later on, when your grandmother came to me with the truth, we hid the documents away just in case history repeated itself."

"I'm still missing something," Mitchell stated. "Why would you have to protect Rainer? You just said that she was the victim."

"Because Westcott raped her," Nick stated bluntly, finally understanding the horrifying truth. "Westcott knew that he was going to be caught sooner or later and had a terrible plan for the future. They wanted to keep the information from getting out."

"No Nicholas," Michelson answered, looking into the detectives eyes. It was at that moment that the former chief realized how little the detective truly understood the case, and himself. He reached into his desk and retracted an old leather satchel and handed it to the detective. "We were protecting her, but not because of the rape. I didn't know about that until years later, and your grandfather never knew. Your grandfather was protecting what happened from coming to light. Your grandfather was protecting HER."

Chapter 74

Hartford, Connecticut
April 15, 1943

Detective Terrence Grenier rode with Michelson in the ambulance to the Hartford Hospital, praying for the first time that he could ever remember. His mind was calling out to anyone who might be able to hear his thoughts; any consciousness that existed beyond the scope of humanity to deliver whatever aid that could be rendered. Grenier was not a religious man, he did not attend church, he did not pray; though he had been raised a catholic by his parents. However, a lifetime of witnessing the hypocrisy of those that claimed to be moved by the hand of the Almighty, the physical abuse of an alcoholic father, the mental abuse of a mother so desperate to escape her imprisonment, and years of dead bodies had taken away his desire to look towards the sky and speak to the consciousness he had been told existed beyond the clouds. Now, understanding the hypocrisy in himself, he begged for the life of the man who had quickly become his friend. Though his mind was screaming out for God's help, his eyes were fixed on the blood streaming out of the wound in Michelson's abdomen. The medic was yelling at Grenier, waving his hand in front of the detective's face, trying to get his attention. Finally, snapping out of his stupefied gaze, he focused on the directions the medic was giving him and placed his hands and all the pressure he could muster on the gunshot wound.

It seemed to Grenier as though it took forever for the ambulance to arrive at the hospital, but when it did, everything seemed to move rapidly and orderly. Someone had radioed ahead and a group of nurses and doctors were waiting for the ambulance to arrive. Grenier followed the group as they quickly rolled the gurney out of the ambulance and into the hospital. He tried to follow the group into the elevator car, but was stopped by a large nurse and informed that he could not come any further. Quickly asking which floor they were taking Michelson to, he watched as the group disappeared behind the elevator door. Grenier rushed up the steps to the surgical unit and found upon arrival that the group had already exited the elevator and wheeled Michelson into surgery. Being told by a nurse that there was nothing for him to do now, he immediately called into the police station to inform the chief of what had occurred. The detective was not surprised to learn that his boss had already heard all about the events at the dance and that he was already gathering a group of police officers to go to Dr. Westcott's home. Terrence did not believe that the doctor would return to his home, knowing that the police would look for him there, and his chief agreed with him. However, no one had followed Westcott after shooting his way out of the dance with his hostage, and the chief knew that at this point there were no clues as to where the killer might be going.

The detective spent the next few hours pacing back and forth up and down the hall, intercepting any doctor or nurse who he thought might have some new information. Two hours after Michelson had gone into surgery, Grenier noticed a young woman sitting in the hall watching his every move. The detective really took no more notice of her than that until he realized that she listened in on the conversation every time he would talk to a doctor or nurse. He watched her without seeming like he was watching her, trying to figure out where she might fit in Michelson's life. Telephone calls came back and forth as Grenier updated the chief on Michelson's condition and the chief updated Grenier on what they had found. So far, the police had found no trace of Westcott and his hostage. The chief was supervising the search of Westcott's house, but so far they had not been able to find any clues of where Westcott might have gone with the young woman. When the conversation ended Grenier hung up the phone and sat down in a chair across from where the young woman was sitting, obviously waiting anxiously for news. At this point, the detective was no longer interested in who the young woman was as his mind was now filled with doubts surrounding his actions and the events of just hours ago.

Scrutinizing everything he had done in the last few days, the detective realized that he had not spoken to Michelson since the morning. As memories meshed together and time seemed to spread, he was unsure when the last time he had spoken to the junior man, but was sure that Michelson had gone to the hospital to review the medical records of Westcott's patients. Something had made Michelson sure that this young woman was going to be his next target. Grenier had been following Westcott after dealing with the Board of Commissioners. There had been no communication between the two officers, no way of knowing the other was going to be there at the social event. When Grenier had made his move on Westcott, it was because he assessed a danger to the young woman. The detective could not think of anything else he could have done. Westcott had acted too quickly, and there were too many innocent civilians who could have possibly been hurt. Even had Michelson not been there, there was no way that Grenier could have stopped Westcott from taking the young woman out of there. He just did not have the opportunity to get a shot off at Westcott without hitting and most likely killing the young woman.

"Detective Grenier," a voice called out from behind him. Grenier turned around a faced an older man. The older man offered his hand. "I am Dr. Lambert; I operated on your partner."

"How is he?" Grenier asked, noticing the young woman on the other side of the hall rise and make her way over. "Is he going to be alright?"

"We were able to remove the bullet," the doctor informed him. "It did tear open a part of his lower intestine, but we were able to repair the damage."

"Will he live?" asked the detective, his insistence coming out in his voice.

"We are pumping his system full of antibiotics," the doctor tried to explain. "If we are able to keep him from getting any infections, then he should come out of this just fine."

"Thank you," Grenier said, allowing the emotion to flow over him for the first time since coming to the hospital. The detective shook the doctor's hand vigorously.

"We're not out of the woods yet," the doctor warned, not wanting to get the detective's hopes up. "He is going to be here for many days, we need to watch him very carefully."

The doctor continued to make his explanations, worried that the detective did not fully understand the dangers that still loomed for the wounded officer. Grenier promised that he did in fact understand, and shortly after the doctor left, called the station to leave a message for the chief that the surgery had been a success. The switchboard operator took the note and then informed the detective that the chief wanted him to come down to Westcott's home as soon as possible. The police had been searching the home, though scouring would have been a better word for it, looking for anything that would give them either evidence for the case, or a clue to the direction in which Westcott had taken his victim. Grenier hung up the phone, unsure of what he should do. He did not feel as though he could leave Michelson, even though the sergeant was out of immediate danger. The detective had known from the start that he was not going to stay at the hospital forever, but leaving now seemed awfully careless. Grenier looked over at the young woman who was sitting by herself.

"Do you know Sergeant Michelson?" Grenier asked as he approached the young woman.

"We met only recently," the woman answered, looking up but making sure not to make eye contact. She seemed a little hesitant, as if unsure of what to say. "I work down in the records department. I was helping him with a case he was working on. When I heard he had been shot, I came up to see that he was alright."

"But you've been waiting here for hours," Grenier remarked as he sat down beside her.

"I know," Prudence answered. "It just seemed like the right thing to do. I...he has been very kind to me."

Grenier looked down at the floor and let her words sink in. He knew that he needed to go, and knew that he needed to ask this girl to stay with his friend; however, he was unsure of how to go about asking so that she would understand and be able to relay the information to Michelson when he woke up.

"The man who hurt him is still out there," Grenier started.

"You mean Dr. Westcott," Prudence said, immediately realizing that she had said too much. Grenier snapped his face up from the floor and looked into her eyes.

"How did you know that we were investigating Westcott?" the detective asked, staring at the girl.

"It was the charts that the sergeant was requesting," Prudence answered. "I didn't tell anyone. I was helping him, pulling the charts he was looking for. All of the patients had that in common; they had all seen Dr. Westcott."

"He has a hostage," Grenier said, seeing now no reason why he should not give this woman all of the information. Apparently, Michelson had felt as though he could trust her and that was good enough for Grenier.

"Will you catch him?" the young woman asked.

"Yes, that I promise," answered Grenier. There was no doubt in the detective's voice and Prudence knew that there was nothing this detective would not do to make good on his promise. "But I can't do it from here. I need to be out there, searching for him."

"I'll stay here," Prudence offered immediately. "I will stay here and watch him. If he wakes up before you get back I will explain what happened."

"I would appreciate that," Grenier said, smiling at the young woman for the first time. "There may be some other police officer's that stop by in the meantime, but I would appreciate it if you would stay and tell him why I've gone."

"I'm sure he'll understand," Prudence answered. Grenier gave her some further information, leaving the station phone number so that she could call in and update him if there were any changes in Michelson's condition. When he left the hospital, he did not feel guilty and knew that he had not abandoned his friend. He could tell just by looking into the young woman's eyes that she cared deeply for him and that Michelson was in good hands.

Chapter 75

Sergeant Jeffrey Michelson opened his eyes and was greeted by a calming white light. The light seemed to encompass his entire field of view, and the police officer's first instinct was to blink several times in an attempt to clear his vision. Michelson knew that he was lying down, but could not remember where he was or how he got there. He tried to run through his most recent memories, but was drawing a blank. Nothing was coming back to him, and as he lay there in a mentally disconnected state that he could only compare with dreaming, he was not even sure if he was moving his head and blinking his eyes. He stopped for a moment and tried to focus. *I am Jeffrey Michelson*, he thought. At least he knew who he was. *I am a police officer.* This thought shocked the young man, as he realized that he had not been thinking about his occupation; this thought just seemed to come out of no where. However, he knew his name and occupation, and that had to be a good place to begin. The white light that had covered his field of vision had, while still calming, begun to change. It was as if he were looking through a telescope and trying to focus the image. He now understood that the light was really blurriness, and that his eyes were now beginning to focus. He could make out objects from the white haze, though he could not yet make out what those objects were.

Michelson decided to focus his concentration, while waiting for his eye sight to return to normal. He had a feeling that this thought about his occupation was significant. *Does being a police officer have something to do with my being here*? He tried to recall the last thing he could remember. It took some time before he could even see himself as a police officer in his mind. Suddenly, he remembered some crime scenes, murder scenes. Between these horrific memories was an image of young people dancing. There was a strange light in a large dark space, and for some reason, Michelson was looking on at these young people. He was watching them, but Michelson could not understand why. This was how his memory came back to him over the course of the next thirty minutes, in flashes. Some of these flashes he would recognize immediately, some would take him a while before he knew what they were or when they happened. What was more frustrating was the fact that they did not seem to return to him in chronological order. He felt as though he had just shuffled a deck of cards and was now trying to put the cards back in numeric order one by one. As he continued to allow these memories to float back, trying to arrange them in proper order, he found that his vision had almost totally improved. He looked around now and could distinguish objects around him. He was inside a white room, his bed close to the windows that were allowing the sunlight to shine through Venetian blinds. He was tucked into white sheets, and as he looked overhead, he found two glass jars hanging upside down over his bed, little clear tubes running down from them.

"Good morning," said a soft female voice beside him. Michelson turned to the left and was greeted by the warm smile of a young woman sitting in a chair beside the bed. There was something familiar about this woman, and though he could not yet remember who she was, he felt comfortable with her. "You've been out for two days. I was wondering when you would wake up."

"Where am I?" Michelson asked, forgoing the first question on his mind. He did not want to hurt her feelings by making it clear that he did not remember who she was.

"You're in Hartford Hospital," the young woman answered. "You were shot. They brought you here for surgery."

"I was shot," Michelson stated, new images flashing in his mind. He now saw the young people dancing and talking to each other, and he remembered being fixated on one individual, and man who was older than those around him and did not seem to fit into the crowd. There was something malicious about Michelson's feelings toward this man. "I was following a suspect. Westcott, Westcott was his name!"

There was some sense of accomplishment for Michelson as he began to remember these recent events. He still did not know why he had been following this man, or why he felt so much malevolence towards him. He could see the events that had transpired in his mind. He watched as the suspect, Westcott, talked to a young woman. Then he remembered a panic, young people running around. Westcott had a gun, and was holding it against a woman's head. There was a standoff; a police officer was pointing his gun at Westcott, trying to talk him down. The killer and his hostage were making their way in Michelson's direction. Michelson remembered letting the door close a little, getting ready to take Westcott by surprise. Unfortunately, he misjudged and pushed through the door too soon, and Westcott fired.

"Son of a bitch shot me," Michelson said aloud, his memories now flowing in chronological order.

"You are going to be alright though," the young woman informed him. "The doctors who performed the surgery said they removed both bullets and there was no major internal damage."

Michelson turned back to the young woman sitting to his left and recognized her immediately.

"Prudence," he said softly.

"You remember me now?" she asked, smiling at the police sergeant.

"What are you doing here?" he asked, surprised and yet comforted and pleased by the fact that she was sitting here beside him. He could not imagine what kind of panic he would have gone through should he have been alone when he came to.

"I was getting off of my shift when they brought you in," she explained. "I, I did not want you to be alone when you woke up."

"You've been here all this time?" Michelson asked, remembering her comment about how long he had been unconscious.

"Your partner, Grenier was here with you for a long time," Prudence answered, attempting to deflect the question. "But he had to go; some information came in about the man who shot you."

"That's not what I asked," Michelson started, not letting the point drop. "Have you been here the entire time?"

"I wanted to make sure that you were alright," she explained, bashfully looking away from the police officer. "You're the first person to treat me like an adult, like a real woman."

Michelson smiled at the young woman, reaching out for her hand. At first, she was about to protest, concerned about his moving a muscle so soon after surgery. However, with what little strength he could muster, he grasped her hand in his and looked into her eyes.

"Thank you," he said. She smiled, turning away again, and then looking back over at him when he did not release her hand immediately.

"It was nothing," Prudence replied, reiterating her claim. "I just wanted to make sure that you were alright."

"I am now," Michelson answered, overwhelmed by an emotion that he had never felt before. Something inside told him that she would have been here everyday if he had been unconscious for an entire week. Something told him that she cared about him, that she loved him in a way that only a young person can. In that moment he knew that she would love him for the rest of his life, and that he would love her for the rest of her life. It was as if he could see the future, though there were no pictures in his mind; only feelings. Warm feelings, feelings of love flowed through him, and unable to maintain his composure any longer, tears began to flow down his cheeks. Immediately, Prudence jumped up from her chair and ran to him. At first she did not understand, thinking that he must be in severe pain or overcome by the thought of what had occurred days before. However, when she reached his bed, he put his hand around her arm and pulled her near.

"I'm going to marry you Prudence," he whispered in her ear. She pulled back suddenly; shocked by his words, uncertain that she had even heard him correctly. Her eyes were now greeted by his smile as he mouthed the words again. "I'm going to marry you."

Chapter 76

When Terrence Grenier arrived at the address given to him by the switchboard operator at the station, he could not help but gape in amazement. If it had not been for the huge number of police cars that lined the street, the detective would have been certain that he had taken down the address incorrectly. The house was a charming colonial New England style home, freshly painted within the last year with a well tended yard. Grenier's first instinct was that the home had the feel of a woman's touch. The grass was unusually green for such an early point in the spring, and there were already some flowers starting to poke their way out of the soil of the well maintained flower beds. To Grenier, it almost seemed as if the home did not belong on this street, or anywhere in this neighborhood. It was as if it had been transplanted from somewhere else, somewhere that was warmer and more pleasant. Grenier got out of his car, crossed the street and made his way up the sidewalk path to the front door. A uniformed officer stood guard at the door, and knowing the detective by site, moved out of the way immediately without bothering to look at the detective's police badge. Before stepping across the threshold, Grenier turned and took a last look at the exterior of the home. He could not help but wonder how a man who could so coldly and brutally kill other's in such a gruesome manner could also maintain something so beautiful. Grenier found it impossible to understand how these two distinct opposites could exist within the body of one person.

Stepping through the threshold, Grenier was met by a stench that stopped him and almost made him turn back. The horrible stench of rotting garbage, sewage, and other scents that he could not identify overwhelmed his senses and he could not help but gag. Taking a moment to control himself, the detective tried to take short, shallow breaths of air through his mouth to try to keep from becoming overwhelmed again. Looking around the interior of the home, Grenier found himself shocked by what he saw, especially after coming in from such a beautiful scene. The front door led the detective straight into the living room, not that there was any way to distinguish one space from another. Piles of yellowed newspapers lined the walls of the living room and went down the hall as far as Grenier could see. The home seemed dark and dingy inside, as if the owner had painted the walls a light dull brownish color. However, after running a finger over the wall, the detective soon realized that the color had come from years of neglect. The walls and floors were covered in dirt and dust; huge cobwebs obviously visibly from the corners of the ceiling. Forgetting to breathe through his mouth, the stench of the place was starting to overwhelm the detective again, and he had to stop and bend down. It took all the discipline he had to keep from vomiting all over the floor. Grenier knew that if he heard one person gag or vomit, there would be no stopping him from doing the same. When Grenier righted himself again, he saw his chief come out from around a corner with a handkerchief pressed up against his nose and mouth.

"This place is disgusting," Grenier said aloud. "How could Westcott stand to live in a place like this?"

"I don't know," the chief answered. "But apparently he did. How's Michelson?"

"He's out of surgery," the detective answered. "If he doesn't get an infection, he should be fine. Where is all of the furniture?"

"Follow me," the chief said, leading the detective up the stairs to the second floor. "It seems that the only place Westcott actually kept up was his bedroom."

The detective stepped into the bedroom and it was as though he had stepped out of a world of black and white and into a world of color. Many years later, watching the progression of television from monotone to technicolor, the detective would always associate the change with that moment. The air inside the room was not as strong and the detective found himself able to take deeper breaths. The room itself was the definition of neat and orderly. Everything in the room had a place, everything was kept neat and clean. The detective's eyes scanned over the furniture looking for anything out of the ordinary, but found nothing. There was a bed in the far corner, a large cushioned chair beside a large wooden radio, and a roll-top desk with the cover pulled down and a wooden desk chair beneath it. The room was laid out perfectly, as if straight out of a newspaper advertisement. This room was the only connection the detective could find to the beautiful gardening he found outside. However, none of it connected to the rotting waste that was the rest of the house.

"What have you been able to find so far?" Grenier asked, looking back to his chief.

"Nothing so far," the chief answered. "Nothing that tells us where he is going. However, we did find a large book that Westcott was using as a journal. It tells in detail what he did to the other victims and why."

"Well," Grenier said impatiently. "It must tell us something about what he plans to do with this victim."

"Her name is Rainer, Gertrude Rainer," the chief stated, ignoring his subordinate's breach of etiquette. "He apparently met her at the hospital and he seems to have a sort of obsession with her. It talks of torture and mutilation."

"But the journal doesn't give you any clue as to where he might have taken her?" Grenier asked incredulously. The chief just shook his head with a disappointing look on his face. "What about the desk? Did you find anything in there?"

"We haven't gotten in there yet," the chief answered. "It's locked."

Grenier glanced over at his superior, flashing a look of disbelief. He then approached the desk, and pulling his service revolver from its holster, smashed the handle against the thin wood of the cover several times until the small metal lock came loose from the wood and the detective was able to roll up the cover. Inside, the desk was kept orderly, just like the rest of the room. Fresh sheets of paper were piled neatly in the far back of the desk, cubby holes containing papers were all perfectly aligned, and an expensive pen was kept in a box with pencils kept neatly beside it. With no regard to the time and painstaking detail with which the killer kept his desk, Grenier started pulling papers out of the cubby holes, reading over them and them dropping them on the floor out of his way. Grenier glanced at one and turned back to his chief, holding the paper up for him to see.

"The address and starting time of the social event last night," Grenier said, putting the paper back down on the desk. He then rummaged through more files, finding receipts, notes, and property deeds all filling the remaining cubby holes. His frustration getting the best of him, Grenier swept the pile of papers onto the floor on top of the others and pulled out the desk chair and sat down. "There has to be something here that will lead us in the right direction."

Grenier asked for the journal and a young officer brought over a huge leather bound book and placed it in the detective's lap. Grenier opened the first page and started scanning the information, knowing that he did not have time to read in depth the sick thoughts that swam through the mind of this killer. However, no matter how cursory the glance, the detective could not help but read some of the perverse and terrible ideas and desires that Westcott dreamed of. Some pages were of his nightmarishly murderous fantasies, others were detailed descriptions of the crimes starting with Virginia Larson. Grenier wondered now if three lives would be safe now had he any clue who the killer was. He could remember the first day he met Westcott, coming out of the Larson home, telling the detective how he was concerned for the mother's nerves. An anger unlike any he had experienced before filled the detective as he sat there. It was guilt that was causing these feelings, and Grenier knew it. He felt guilty for not being more opened minded about the possibility of an educated man being a killer. He felt guilty for the way in which he had handled the case, and though he handled it the same as any other; he knew this was not like any other case. Most of all, he felt guilty for what happened to Michelson. As the detective sat there, he began to zone out, looking more through the book than at it. His blurry field of vision fell upon the papers he had callously dropped on the floor, and one word burned into his mind, bringing him back to reality.

"What the hell?" Grenier asked, placing the book on the desk and bending over to pick up the papers. He sat back up straight and started reading the fine print on one of the pieces of paper marked DEED. Grenier smiled suddenly as he began to understand what he was reading. Then a thought entered his head and the detective realized that he was holding the one clue that he was looking for. Grenier jumped up from the chair and ran out of the room.

"Where the hell are you going?" the chief asked, following him down the steps.

"I know where the son of a bitch has taken her," Grenier said, running down the stairs and out of the house. The detective jumped into the car and started it up, giving the chief only seconds to jump into the back seat. A few officers, unsure of what was going on, decided to follow Grenier in their squad cars and soon there was a convoy of police cars headed south from Hartford.

"Are you going to tell me what this is all about?" the chief asked, attempting to brace himself as Grenier took a hard right.

"There was a deed in his desk," Grenier answered. "It's to an abandoned mill in Norwich. One of the fabric mills along the river. That's where he's going. It's the only place that's safe for him right now."

"What's the rush?" the chief asked. "Surely he's killed her by now."

"Maybe," Grenier answered. "Maybe not. We know that he likes to torture his victims as long as possible. She might still be alive."

Terrence realized in that moment that his guilt was causing him to act in this rash behavior. The chief was probably right, Rainer was most likely dead. However, that was not Grenier's prime concern at this moment. His concern was stopping Westcott, stopping him from getting away again. If Westcott got away, it might be years before he started killing again, but there was no doubt in the detective's mind that he would kill again. Grenier could not let that happen, and he knew it was his responsibility now to make sure that Westcott was stopped; stopped by any means necessary. Forty minutes later, with three police cruisers following in close pursuit, Grenier and the chief crossed over the Norwich town line. Grenier was not familiar with the town, but he knew roughly where the river was and drove in that direction, finally approaching the mills five minutes later. The commotion of the police convoy had piqued the attention of the Norwich police and now a line of their police cars had arrived with the Hartford police outside the mill address Grenier read off of the deed.

While the chief went to explain the situation to the Norwich police, Grenier and the uniformed officers wasted no time in storming the building.

Grenier gave quick directions to the other officers and they all slowly made their way through the abandoned mill, searching for Westcott. Grenier had his service revolver pointed straight out in front of him, knowing that he would fire the moment Westcott came into view. The detective had no plans to arresting this killer, had no plans to let him walk out of the building alive. Westcott was a killer, he was The Nemesis he claimed to be, and Grenier was going to be the only one standing when this was over. Grenier reached the end of the warehouse and took the stairs to the second floor. There he found the second floor more densely packed as machines lay scattered around and great roles that once held fabrics were littered across the ground. The detective made his way through the obstacles as carefully as possible, desperately trying not to make a sound. Out of the corner of his eye, he saw two uniformed officers coming up the stairs from the far end of the mill, and the detective gestured for them to keep quiet. Both officers nodded in understanding and continued their search. Suddenly, while passing one of the offices on that floor, an officer stopped and motioned for the detective to come over. As Grenier approached he heard the soft sound of a woman crying coming from the other side of the door. Grenier knelt down and crept to the window, trying to get a good look inside. However, the furniture inside the office was blocking his view. Grenier knew this was the moment he had been waiting for, and remembering his resolve, he stood and slowly opened the office door.

The detective could feel the tension exuding from the two other officers as they entered the office behind him. The inner office was dark, and Grenier silently made his way towards the sound of the crying, his weapon ready to fire the kill shot in an instant. A soft, golden light streamed through a door on the far right of the inner office and as the detective approached, he motioned for the other officers to wait. Grenier placed his hand on the knob of the door and listened for just a moment, and then waiting no longer, threw the door open and stormed into the room. The scene he was greeted to with was far from what he had imagined. The young woman he knew to be Gertrude Rainer sat trembling in a corner holding a letter opener, both herself and the opener covered in blood. On the floor in front of her was the body of Dr. Westcott, a shocked look on his face, his clothes covered in blood. The young woman held the knife out in front of her, ready to protect herself again if necessary.

"It's alright," Grenier said, holstering his weapon and offering an empty hand. "I'm with the police. I'm here to help you."

The girl stared at him for a moment, as if trying to ascertain whether or not he was telling the truth. Her eyes darted back and forth between Grenier and the two officers behind him. She pushed herself up to a standing position, keeping the letter opener out before her. The young woman was shaking violently in fear; Grenier raised both hands to try to sooth her.

"Do you recognize me?" he asked. "I was at the social last night. I tried to stop Westcott."

"Last night," the woman said, barely whispering. "That was only last night?"

Losing her strength in the confusion of time, the young woman let the letter opener slip out of her hands and fall to the floor. In that instant Grenier rushed her, taking her into his arms before she fell to the floor. He looked down at her, attempting to be as soft and understanding as he knew how.

"It's over now," the detective assured her. "You're safe now. But I need you to do something for me. I need you to tell me what happened."

Chapter 77

When Gertrude Rainer opened her eyes, the first thing she was aware of was the sharp, throbbing pain stabbing through the back of her head. She almost moaned as she tried to move, but was acutely aware that she was moving, and that she was not alone. It took her a moment to focus her mental clarity, for her memory to develop a clear picture of what had happened. She had been at the social, she had originally been on the planning committee with her friends, and they had talked her into going. Suddenly, a face flashed before her mind's eye and she was filled with dread. Her doctor, Dr. Westcott had arrived at the dance. She had been caught off guard by this, was even slightly confused. He had never mentioned any interest in this event, though Rainer remembered mentioning it many times during her sessions with the doctor. The social had been a source of frustration and despair with the young woman, feeling the pressures of trying to put on a perfect event for service men who had just recently returned home, while also dealing with the fact that there was no one special in her own life. All of these thoughts had made life very difficult for the young woman in the last six months, and she had even considered taking her own life.

After a fanciful line in her diary was read by Rainer's mother, the young woman was forced to get out with her friends more and to see someone at the hospital. Rainer's mother was a nurse and knew a little about the field of psychiatry and referred her daughter to a doctor there. That was how Rainer began seeing Dr. Westcott, first twice a month, but then the doctor insisted on seeing her more and more, until it started to make the young woman uncomfortable. Rainer felt that she had never been serious about taking her own life, certainly not serious enough to warrant this much attention from the doctor. Then her uneasiness about the doctor himself began to concern her, the way he looked at her, the sly or coy comments that he made, the way he smiled at her. She could feel his eyes probing her, like cold, slimy hands caressing her body, and the more she noticed his behavior, the more uncomfortable she became. Her memories of the incident at the dance started to come back to her like a haunting nightmare in reverse. She remembered the man jumping through the door with a gun, the two loud claps of thunder and the pungent, burning aroma that she could only assume was gunpowder after the two shots. She remembered being dragged across the dance floor by her hair, another gunshot and people screaming. She could remember looking down the barrel of a gun, knowing another gun was pressed hard against her head. Though she could not recall the words, she remembered a heated exchange between Westcott and another man she took to be a police officer. She remembered the apprehension and disgust as Westcott presented himself to her and asked her for a dance. She remembered his hands; how they felt exactly the way she felt when he looked at her.

With all the memories flooding back and arranging themselves in her mind, Rainer immediately expected to be terrified for her life. However, something else burned inside her; the will to live. She almost laughed out loud suddenly, realizing the irony of the emotion. Her light depression had put her in touch with a man who now wanted to kill her or worse, and the thought of getting away from this sick demon was spurring her desire to live more than the months of counseling ever had. She turned her head upwards and found herself looking up at the back of Westcott's head. The pain in the back of her head made it impossible for her to move any further, so she relaxed her neck and slipped back into the position she had awakened in. She was in a car, laying face down in the back seat. Unfortunately, from her position, she could not make out where they were or where Westcott was headed. She could tell that the night was closing in, but the remaining sunlight had given her enough illumination to make out her surroundings in the car. She could hear the doctor in the front seat, cursing away, occasionally slamming his hands down on the steering wheel. Obviously he had not expected to be interrupted by the police. She found it interesting and terrifying at the same time as she listened to his words. The doctor was talking to himself, asking questions and answering them at the same time. It was as though there were two people in the front seat. Focusing back to the matter at hand, Rainer decided in her head that it was better for her not to draw attention to the fact that she was conscious. Though she had no memory of it, she could only guess that Westcott had tossed her roughly into the back seat. She had only moved her head and neck since waking up; her body was still in the same position. Slowly moving her right arm which was draped over the edge of the seat, she felt around the floor with her hands for anything that she could use as a weapon. Unfortunately, she came up with nothing, not even a scrap of dirt existed on the floor or underneath the seats. Then, to her horror, she felt the car come to a complete stop and heard Westcott shut off the ignition.

Rainer was terrified and unsure of what she should do next. Possibilities ran through her mind like a picture show. The only element of surprise she had was in the fact that Westcott did not know she was conscious. However, he was bigger and stronger than her, and would most likely be able to overcome any physical assault she attempted, especially from the position she was in. The only chance she had was a swift kick to the groin, or a well placed kick to the face. With either move, she would still have to get up quick enough and get past him, something she was not sure that she could do in her condition. However, as she heard the click of the door handle, she knew it was too late to come up with anything and tried to let her body goes as limp as possible. The door opened and she could sense Westcott leaning inside the car. Suddenly, she smelled something strong underneath her nose, causing her to pull away instinctively.

"Good evening, Gertrude," Westcott said, pulling her roughly out of the back door of the car. "We're here. I think you've been sleeping long enough."

"Where are we?" Rainer asked, looking around the area in a daze. It was a grim scene, and from where she stood, she could barely tell it was the beginning of spring. The building before her was old and abandoned, and though the brick gave it a crimson color, the waning evening light along with the emptiness gave it a grim eerie feel. There were no leaves or even buds on the trees surrounding the building. It was as though any vibrancy of life, any hope for something new had been drained out of the old mill and everything around it.

"Don't worry about where we are going," Westcott retorted with a nasty snarl. "We are somewhere where the police will never find us. You and I are going to have some fun together. Now walk!"

"What do you mean fun together?" she asked in a terrified tone.

"I said walk, dammit," Westcott said, shoving her further. Rainer found it difficult to walk, her equilibrium already being out of balance by the blow to the head she received in the parking lot, and now walking over these loose, uneven stones. Westcott kept his hands on her, pushing and pulling her this way and that until they reached the door to the abandoned building. The doctor fished out a large, old key and slipped it into the lock on the door, then pushed the door open and roughly forced the young woman through.

Inside, Rainer could see nothing. Her footsteps echoed and sounded like an army marching through in a parade. Noises bounced off of the walls and seemed as though they were coming from all around the already disoriented young woman. She jerked her head back and forth in a vain attempt to discern anything that might tell her where she was. She could hear something in the darkness, something constant in the background; she heard water, running water. She knew that she had to be near a river or stream, and remembered that there were many old mills in Connecticut that were built on the banks of rivers. She knew that she had not been unconscious for very long, and that Westcott could not have taken her very far. She focused on these thoughts as Westcott guided her from behind, making sure that she did not run into anything as she made her way through the warehouse. All of a sudden, Rainer found herself walking on a something much different. The floor did not feel the same as it had, there was a different noise to it and the floor seemed to sway almost imperceptibly. Then the young woman felt a movement and realized that she was on an elevator. She could not sense any walls around her, and assumed she was on a large freight elevator. Her ride was very short, and before she knew it, Westcott was pushing her out again.

Again, she found herself being guided by Westcott along an unseen path. She never hit anything, but was continuously tripping over her own feet, much to the frustration of her captor. Twice he yelled at her, slapping her once on the neck and another time on the back of the head. A shooting pain radiated around her head and little bolts of white lightning filled her mind as she squeezed her eyes shut in anguish. This time, however, he stopped her and pushed her roughly into a wall. Again, she heard the jingle of keys and then the peel of an unused door opening for the first time in years. Westcott grabbed her and forced her inside.

"Welcome home," he said, pushing the door shut behind him.

Rainer fumbled around as she attempted to get her bearings in the new room. She heard Westcott mumbling on the other side of the room and turned in his direction to try and gauge the distance between them through the sound of his voice. Suddenly, a light was switched on, causing the young woman to turn away sharply, blinking heavily until her vision cleared. She turned back towards Westcott, squinting her eyes to make him out. The man she had known as her doctor was barely the man who stood before her now. There was rage and desperation in his eyes and face. For the first time, he looked as though he were not in control of his situation; an image of him Rainer had never seen before now. She could make out a gun in his left hand, the barrel tracing a line across an old, unused desk where on the other side of the room. Westcott was off in his own little world again, replaying the scene in the gymnasium, unaware that Rainer was staring at him. He easily dropped the gun on the top of the desk and started beating his fists against his head as he talked to himself. He started to step away, lost in thought. The young woman looked over at the door, then back towards the gun and her captor.

She knew that the door to the office was further away than the gun, and even if she did get away and out of the building she was still in the middle of nowhere. The problem with trying to get the gun was it's proximity to Westcott. If he heard or sensed her coming, he could whip around and shoot her. *What's the difference*, Rainer thought to herself, *he's going to kill me anyway.* All of a sudden, this was the plan. To go for the gun while he had slipped into his insane little world and kill him if he tried to stop her. An idea that she once thought herself incapable of now seemed utterly plausible as she gauged her distance to her captor. The young woman slipped her feet out of her shoes and softly made her way across the room towards the desk, and the gun. Westcott's voice seemed to get louder, and Rainer was unable to gauge whether it was because he was raising his voice or because she was closer to him. However, she watched Westcott's every move the way prey watches a sleeping predator as it makes its escape. She was ten feet away from the gun, then eight feet, then five. She reached out with her hands, ready to fire it the moment she had it in her sweaty palms. She was three feet now; she paused watching Westcott momentarily, and then took another step forward. She was just a foot away now; if she reached her hand out a little further she could just grab it. In that moment, Westcott whipped around, grabbing both of her wrists in his big hand. He slapped the gun off of the desk with his free hand and yanked Rainer further, pulling her closer to him.

"Can I help you?" he asked, a purely evil grin spreading across his face. "Did you want to be close to me?"

"Let me go," she shouted, pulling hard against his iron grip.

"Let you go," he said mockingly. "Let you go. I have no intention of letting you go. This is your new home, this is our new home. And we are going to make the most out of it."

Westcott pushed himself against her and suddenly she knew what his intentions were. Summoning all of the strength she had left, she kicked and clawed at him, she tried to knee him and bite him; anything she could do to get away from this monster, her monster. However, her efforts were useless, it was as though she were trying to claw her way through a brick wall; Westcott was just too strong. Grabbing the young woman's shoulder with one hand, he twisted her around so that her back was to him. She screamed, tried to kick out from behind, tried to grab for his groin; anything to incapacitate him for just a moment so that she could get away. Westcott slammed her down hard on the desk, causing the air to be knocked out of her lungs. Instinctively, she tried to push herself up, gasping for air. Westcott grabbed the Rainer by her hair and slammed her head into the desk, hard. Suddenly, her vision began to cloud, her stomach turned to mush, and the familiar darkness took over.

When Gertrude Rainer awoke again, she found herself in the same position as before. She was laying face down, her body twisted at a strange and painful angle, and the voice of Westcott in the background, conversing with himself. For a moment, Rainer hoped that everything she had remembered happening before had been a bad dream. However, as pain wracked her entire body, she knew that it was no dream. A single tear slipped from her eye and rolled down her cheek, and though she had no memory of what happened, she knew. Her entire body hurt, her muscles in her arms, legs, abdomen, all felt as though she had spent an entire week exercising. However, the muscle pain was barely noticeable to her; it was the pain from between her legs. Her world, her consciousness closed in around her as she was about to accept death, as she was about to pray that she die quickly. Just before she resigned herself to her fate, another thought flashed into her mind, the thought of her captor dead. This thought was the spark that brought her back, the spark that re-ignited her will to live. Rainer looked around the room quickly, trying to see where Westcott was, but could not see him. She thought quickly to herself, trying to reason whether or not killing this monster was possible. As she thought about it for a moment, she suddenly realized that she did not care whether or not it was possible, she was going to kill him. He had killed her, stolen and smothered the one thing that she had, the one thing that was hers. In all of the doe-eyed romantic fantasies that she and her friends had shared in secret, this one thing was hers; and he had taken it from her.

She sat up slowly, not wanting to arouse Westcott's attention. She looked around the room for the gun, peering around the corner where she had been flung like trash when Westcott was finished with her, looking for the gun that she had remembered him knocking onto the floor. She did not see it, but she did see something else. The drawers to the desk had been pulled out and thrown on the floor, as if Westcott had been looking for something, could not find it, and in frustration started throwing things around the room. On the floor, approximately a foot from the overturned drawer and three feet from the desk was a shiny, metal letter opener. She could tell from where she sat that the tip was dull, but it was still a point and would what she needed it to. Though Rainer could not remember telling her body to move, she could see herself moving on all fours across the room, slowly making her way towards the letter opener. She grasped the handle and slowly got on her feet, having to right herself several times as she regained her equilibrium. As she stood, she could see Westcott facing the windows as the morning sun was coming into view, talking to himself. Her hands were shaking; she took the letter opener in both hands and raised it over her head.

Suddenly, and without realizing it, she was moving towards him. She knew that her mouth was open, though she could not be sure if she was screaming or crying or both. Westcott turned around just as she brought the letter opener down. The weapon penetrated the man's skin just to the left of his sternum and lodged against his rib. For an instant, Rainer stood there, supported by the weapon and Westcott. She yanked hard, trying to free the weapon and as she did, the surprised captor began stepping away with the weapon still embedded in him. As he turned, she yanked the letter opener free and struck again, this time missing his chest entirely and entering his abdomen. This time, Westcott fell to the floor and was gasping, flailing out to stop the attack. However, Rainer was not herself anymore, she was a killer; a killer with a purpose. As if there were no consciousness, no mind, just the body she struck over and over again until she had no more strength, until she could not lift the weapon again. Westcott flailed out with his arms, reaching out in the emptiness as though seeing something in a dream. Suddenly, he was not the evil captor who had abducted her at gunpoint; he was not the sinister doctor who molested her with his eye. He was just a pathetic dying man, dying, dying, dead. There was no relief when his limbs went limp and stopped moving, there was no victory in his death, and she certainly did not feel as though she had won back what he had stolen. There was nothing, she was alone.

Gertrude Rainer finished her story and looked up at the detective, who just stared at her in wonder. He seemed to be in shock, unable to talk, unable to find any words of comfort. All he could do was reach forward and brush a lock of hair out of her face. They were alone in the office now, the other uniformed officers having been ordered to stand by the door. The detective looked down at the doctor's dead body and pulled out his service revolver. Grenier stood and aimed at the dead body carefully, and fired five times. The uniformed officers stormed the room in a panic, though ready for action. Grenier looked at officers for a moment, and then holstered his weapon.

"When we entered the office, Westcott had the knife and was about to stab Ms. Rainer here," Grenier said, as if his words could alter the past. "He turned in surprise and I shot him. Any questions?"

"But detective..." one of the uniformed officers began.

"But what?" Grenier demanded. The officer fell silent and nodded, then looked at his partner who was also nodding. They knew what was happening here, and they knew their place was to back up the story of the detective. Grenier then turned his face down to the young woman sitting in the corner. "Any questions?"

Gertrude shook her head and then started crying. Grenier wanted to reach down and console her, knowing that there was probably far more to the story that she had told him. He felt that she had left something out just before she mentioned being knocked unconscious a second time, but he knew that this poor young woman had been through an ordeal he would never understand, and whatever she chose to keep to herself was her business. The detective saw his chief and other officers running towards the office, and walked away from the crying woman, to tell them his story.

Chapter 78

When Jack parked his car on a pleasant September evening on the side of the road across the street from the Norwich Free Academy, he did not know what he expected to get out of this unannounced visit. Ever since that day he came home and overheard his mother and his step-father fighting, ever since learning that the man he had been made to believe was his real father made it clear that there was no bond between them, ever since he watched the man walk out of his life forever, Jack had been changed. The transformation had been almost instant, changing him from a naïve boy to a focused young man. Even his mother noticed a difference, and in the first few months she even encouraged it, hoping that it would take his mind off of the changes in his family life. However, there was something frightening to her in his change in attitude. There was a change in character as well. For the first month the boy would ask her questions as to who his real father was, and fearing that what he would find would be a disappointment too much for him to bear, she never answered him.

571

Finally, she had enough, and told him that there was nothing for him in the past and that he should let it go. However, he could not let it go. His desire to know where he really came from burned inside of him, and his mother's evasive answers and pleadings only stoked his curiosity. Finally, he felt that he must know the truth. There had to be a reason for his mother to keep the information a secret, and he felt as though he had a right to know.

Unfortunately, the young man had no idea where to start looking. Jack had no idea that he had been whisked away by his mother from the other side of the country and brought to California to start a new life. All of his memories were from California, and so when he learned that he had been born in Connecticut, he almost laughed out loud and told the woman in charge of the archives in Sacramento that she was a liar. Wanting to find out who his real father was and having no idea how to go about it, the young man decided that he had to try to find all he could about his birth. When asked to provide his social security number, the archivist noted that the first three numbers did not correspond to California and went out of her way to find out that they corresponded with numbers issued in Connecticut the same year that Jack was born. The young man rushed home in rage, demanding that his mother tell him everything about his birth, his father, and any other family he might have on the east coast. In that instant, he realized what was driving this desire to know more about his past. The need for family, the need to find someone who would love him and not cast him away was what was fueling his need for information. The thought, the hope, that there was someone in Connecticut who he was related to, who would take him in and make him part of their family was too strong a driving force to be blocked by his mother's feeble evasive maneuvers. He knew that the emotional hole inside him came from the subconscious knowledge that the man his mother was married to was not his real father and that finding his real family would fill him in a way that he could not understand.

Through the rest of his senior year in high school he searched, calling the state of Connecticut for information, finally laying his hands on his birth certificate. He told his mother nothing about the fruits of his investigation, especially after she made it clear that she did not want to hear another word about it. The name Alan Camden was like finding a hidden treasure to the young man who had labored so long and was now starting to see results. Knowing his mother the way he did, he was certain that she must have been married to this man. There was no way that she would have just had a child with a man and not have been married. His mother had been a strong willed woman through all of his young life, a characteristic that only seemed to change after his step-father left them. He was able to get his hands on a divorce decree, and finally Jack was beginning to feel whole. There was a man out there who was his father, and though he did not know the circumstances surrounding his parents divorce, there was someone one there who could not toss aside their bond so lightly. Wanting to know more, Jack dug deeper in an attempt to find out more about his father. However, every time he searched for information regarding Alan Camden he got no where. Other than where Camden went to school and where he worked, Jack kept drawing a blank. He found it impossible to dig up a birth certificate on Camden, and just when he was about to give up his search, he found out that his father was an orphan. Though that explained a lot about the missing records, it did not tell him anything more about his father's past. There was only one word that the administrator of the orphanage could provide the young man with and that was a name, Westcott.

However, with just that one word to go off of, Jack felt as though he could go no further. Using microfiche, Jack did a cursory search through the local newspapers in the years around which he assumed his father was born and was shocked when he came across the name. The young man was crest-fallen and horrified as he read how a young doctor in Connecticut had killed three people and kidnapped a forth before being gunned down by police. However, something about the case intrigued the young man. He could not be sure whether or not this Westcott was any relation, and even if his mother did know, she would not be of any help. He read the stories over and over again, finally writing down what he read word for word. He searched through articles in all of the local papers, looking for any differences in the stories. He spent many nights staring up at the ceiling, wondering where the name of Westcott fit in with his father and the orphanage. Westcott had been killed almost a year before Camden had been born, and yet whoever left the baby at the orphanage must have given it that last name. It did not take the bright young man long to put the clues together. Obviously, the mother left the baby at the orphanage, giving that name to the nuns when she dropped him off. The mother could not have been Westcott's lover; had she been she would have most likely either kept the child or given it away with her own name. No, Jack was certain that the only way in which a woman would give up a child that she carried but with the father's name was if the child was a horrible reminder to her of Westcott, of her experience with him.

Getting up in the middle of the night, Jack poured over all of his notes searching for the answer as to whom Camden's mother might be. Two men and one woman were murdered; a woman was kidnapped but was saved by the police. The media had somehow gotten word that the first victim, Virginia Larson, was pregnant; however, she was not far enough along to save the baby had there even been the chance. That left only the one woman Westcott had kidnapped. If she had been raped, then Jack could understand why she would leave the child at an orphanage, and especially with her rapist's last name. Jack could not imagine how difficult it must have been for the young woman to watch the life grow inside of her for nine months, the life that was born from evil. He wondered time and again why the young woman did not abort the pregnancy. To these questions, Jack had no answers. However, the young man was reasonably certain that he knew where he came from, and he had a plan. Jack was a very intelligent young man, and a very good student. It was not difficult for him to get accepted to many colleges all over the country, but paying for them was another issue. Their was very little money between Jack and his mother, especially since his step-father left. Though he had been accepted to two schools in New England, there just simply was no money for him to go. Jack resigned himself to get his bachelor degree at the state college, and then continue his education on the east coast. Jack changed his name to Westcott shortly after starting his first year in college and through a few little lies was issued a new social security number. Jack wanted to leave everything from his childhood behind and start new when he got to New England. Finally, when he was accepted to Brown medical school, it seemed as though he would get his chance.

That was how Jack Westcott found himself standing in front of the Norwich Free Academy, looking around at the many buildings that made up the high school campus. He was impressed, and had he been younger would have been slightly intimidated by everything around him. The school had the look of a private learning institution, with grand old buildings, some dating back to the mid-1800's. As Jack crossed the street and walked onto the campus grounds, he approached a sign informing readers that the school first opened in 1854. He heard the screaming of fans and the large lights beaming down behind the buildings and, filled with curiosity, he followed the voices. Jack had not dropped his investigation after learning who his grandfather was.

Though it disturbed him to know that he was related to a killer, to a psychopath, it also was a relief in many ways. He had always been afraid of the sense of pleasure he received from hurting animals as a child. Now, he understood that this might be genetic, and that he needed to find outlets for his anger and pain so as to be able to function as a normal member of society. Now that he was going to medical school on a full scholarship, he felt that he was on his way to achieving something that he could call his own. He had researched Gertrude Rainer quite a bit though in his four years of college in California. He learned that four years after the incident involving Westcott, she married the lead detective on the case and they had lived a quiet life in Connecticut. Though he had no plans to interrupt their lives, and he certainly did not want to dredge up the past, there was still an overwhelming desire just to see her. She was, after all, his grandmother. He knew that he did not need to talk to her; he just wanted to see her.

That was why he was here, tonight, overlooking a football game on this early September evening. Just as he had arrived at the Grenier house in Salem, the old man and the woman were getting into their car and driving away. Some strange urge caused Jack to follow them, and this is where they led him. The old man and the woman met another couple in the stands and sat down and cheered. Jack could not understand, obviously there was a family member on the team, but there was something inside of him that started to burn. He watched this family, laughing, clapping, and oblivious to the fact that he was watching them. They pointed out to the field and Jack followed their fingers out to where the team was getting set on the field. He watched the play, memories of his own short career in pee-wee football coming back to him. He could see the team's defense lining up in front of the visiting team's offense. The ball was snapped and the two lines slammed into each other with a sickening crunch. He watched in awe as a defensive back deftly penetrated the line of large bodies pushing and pulling at each other and dove forth, grabbing onto the quarterback and wrenching him off of his feet. The crowd erupted in cheer, everyone was on their feet and Jack found himself clapping along with the crowd not realizing it. However, in the back of his mind, all he could hear was his father yelling at him from the sideline, telling him how useless he was. Jack realized all of a sudden that he was shaking; the thoughts of his step-father caused an anger that he had assumed was gone, to start boiling up inside of him. Jack shoved his hands into his pockets, clenching his fists tight.

The two teams lined up on the ball again, and Jack found himself staring, mesmerized by the game. Again the ball was snapped, and again both lines slammed into each other with shocking force. The quarterback skipped backwards, looking from side to side to find an open receiver. Finding his man, the quarterback stopped his shuffle and pumped his feet forward, then released the ball in a perfect spiral. A hush fell over the crowd and even Jack held his breath as he watched the action. It was obvious who the ball was intended for and this perfect pass seemed as though it were about to become the perfect play when another player in red and white seemed to materialize out of nowhere, snatching the ball out of the air as if it had always been intended for him. Again, the crowd erupted in cheers, people jumping up and down screaming for the player to run. Suddenly, Jack realized that the ball had been intercepted and the same player who had wrestled the quarterback to the ground in the last play was now running in the opposite direction with the ball. Finally, the defensive back was brought down but not before making it half-way across the field. Then he heard the name over the loudspeaker; Grenier, the last name of the detective who had caught and killed his grandfather. Jack watched as the young man removed his helmet and made his way over to the sideline. His teammates were slapping him on the back and even the coach slapped his hand in congratulations. When he reached the bench, Jack could make out the old man rustling the boy's hair and the old woman giving him a grandmotherly kiss on the cheek. Suddenly, Jack wanted to scream.

Jack turned and walked away from the field, his entire body shaking with anger and hatred. He made his way back to the car, but it was as though he was not watching where he was going. His attention was on the images that were filling his mind. He remembered how his step-father had treated him, pushing him around and telling him he would never amount to anything. He remembered the pain and anguish that he had learned to deal with as he grew up, even though he had no idea where it came from or why he was afflicted with this utter loneliness and despair as everyone around him seemed to be so carefree. Here, looking on as this family loved one another and cheered for one another, he could only feel like a cast-off once again. Until now, it had not bothered Jack that Rainer had given his father away so many years ago. He had tried to understand what she had gone through, and knowing that there was no way he ever could, he tried to sympathize with her. Now, watching her with her family, a family that obviously was unaware of her past, he realized that he was just as alone here as he had been in California. No one here loved him, no one there loved him. No one here would ever care for him; no one there had ever cared for anything but themselves. But through all of the pain and anguish he found hope. In his mind, he could see a way in which he would be understood here; a way that he could keep from being alone. He knew that the truth would save him from his loneliness and despair because the truth was the only weapon he had, it was the only thing he had, the only thing that was his.

When Jack Westcott opened his eyes, he was no longer seeing the past; he was The Nemesis, and this was his time. He knew that he could not let the events of last night stop him from his ultimate goal. He shook his head from side to side in wonder, unable to believe that it had only been twenty four hours ago when he had almost been caught by the police in the nightclub, and even earlier than that when he barely eluded the police at the casino. This was it, he had to finish what he started. Unfortunately, he knew that Nicholas still did not understand why, though The Nemesis was fairly certain that the detective knew that he could not stop. Before this was all over, Nicholas Grenier would come to understand the true meaning behind everything The Nemesis had done, and when he did, he would no longer be The Nemesis, he would be Jack Westcott, and he would no longer be alone.

Chapter 79

Anna Meaders arrived back at Nick's house in Salem, Connecticut just as the skies above began to darken, submitting to the night. She was quickly becoming unable to control her excitement as she imagined the night she had planned. It was to be nothing special, nothing terribly romantic, just a night to share with him. Anna could not remember the last time she felt this way for a man. She did not kid herself into thinking that she was already in love with him, she was not that naïve. However, there was something about him that attracted her from the start. A confidence and understanding, not just of crime and police procedure, but of the entire world in which he existed. It was something that she could not explain, but she was drawn to him. When he asked her to accompany him when he questioned Tracy Scott's friend she had been honored, nobody but Lt. Hollings had ever treated her as anything more than a secretary. Every time she watched him, she wanted to know what he was thinking, she wanted to help him and he had given her that chance. She was so grateful for the opportunity to go through the old case file, and when she was able to report her findings, he gave her the floor, letting her present what she had found. In short, she had never met someone like him, someone so secure with themselves they did not feel as though they had anything to prove. That was what she saw in Nicholas Grenier.

She climbed out of the car and retrieved the bag of groceries she had purchased from the back seat. She could not wait to see him when he came home; she knew that it had been a tough two days and that the poor man had not even been given a chance to sleep. She planned to make him dinner, then relax and spend the rest of the night together. In her mind, the case was almost over. In fact, it seemed as though everyone felt that way. The police were now certain who their suspect was, pictures of him had been on television and in the paper, and every cop in Connecticut and Rhode Island were on the look out. She had heard nothing since Nick had left for the casino, but she could not believe that the killer could get past the police again. She wondered what he would do when the case was over, whether or not he would join the New London police department. Nick kept saying that he would not; in fact, he had made some comments that led Anna to believe that he was thinking seriously about quitting the police force all together. However, she did not think that he could actually bring himself to quit. She had never met anyone who was so obviously born to be a cop, someone with so much police intuition as he possessed. She hoped that he would not quit, she hoped that he would decide to stay in the area. She hoped that their relationship together was not just a one night affair; she hoped.

Anna let herself into the house with the keys that Nick had given her early that morning when he needed her to pick up some clothes. She closed the door behind her and headed for the kitchen, switching on the lights as she went. In the kitchen, she placed the bag of groceries down on the kitchen counter and began sorting through them, searching for the ingredients to start her work. All of a sudden a thought popped into her mind. What if he did not want her here when he got home? Suddenly, she was unsure of a lot of things. She knew that he had experienced a rough two days, and she had no intentions whatsoever, but she could not believe that he would not at least appreciate a home cooked meal. She cleared her mind of the thought, and began working on the salad. However, some doubt remained and she began trying to figure out what the detective's intentions were towards her. He had always been open and receptive towards her. When she came over three nights ago, he had been shocked by her straight forward manner, but he was not put off by it. In fact, they had experienced a great night together, and she did not take him to be a person who had one night stands with women. Even though it had been just sex, there was still the emotional connection between them. *Stop it*, she told herself. *You always do this. Just take it one step at a time and enjoy yourself.* She laughed awkwardly at herself and was thankful that no one else could hear her thoughts or else she might be thought of as crazy.

Once Anna was finished preparing the salad, she put the bowl in the refrigerator and went out into the dining room and set the table for two. As she set the table she could tell that Nick did not spend much time making formal meals. It would not have surprised her that any meals he did eat at home were consumed in front of the television. Once she was finished with the table, she began setting out the ingredients for the entrée that she was going to prepare. She searched through the cabinets for the necessary pots and pans, hoping that he had some of the little ingredients that she had assumed would be here. Once satisfied she had everything necessary to make the meal, she began heating the oven and opening some of the grocery packaging. To her surprise, she heard the jiggle of the front door and was suddenly filled with excitement and a little bit of apprehension. She walked into the hallway and reached for the doorknob.

"I didn't expect you to be home yet," she said as she began to answer the door. She was met by the cold eyes of a face that she had come to know quite well in the last twenty four hours, and yet as she stared there for a minute, she could not understand what was happening.

Anna stared blank faced into the eyes of the man she knew to be Jack Westcott, unable to comprehend what was happening. Then he smiled a sick, demonic smile that seemed to reshape his entire face. Suddenly, she knew what was happening. The Nemesis was here for his next victim. Nick had been right all along. The Nemesis would not let the setback that was last night's fiasco stop him from his ultimate goal, whatever that was. Anna slammed the door back as hard as she could, knowing that the killer was too far through the threshold to push him out entirely, but hoping to gain a few seconds to get away. The Nemesis just batted the oncoming door away as if it were paper and laughed. Anna twisted her body violently and began running back down the hallway. She felt the slight tug against her blouse as the killer tried to grab her but did not get enough of a grip. Her first thought was to run into the kitchen, hoping that she could possibly get one of the kitchen knives to use as a weapon. However, with her mind racing, she quickly ruled the kitchen out as she noted that there was only one entrance and that even if she got a hold of a knife, she would still be trapped. She was shocked that, even though terrified for her life, she was still thinking rationally. Anna ran into the living room, desperately looking for anything that she could use as a weapon. She was quickly followed by the killer. She moved to the right, but he countered her. She then moved to the left, only to be blocked again.

"How long are we going to play this game?" The Nemesis asked, the evil smiled still spread across his face. "Back and forth, back and forth. There's only so long we can keep doing this.

"How far do you think you are going to get with me?" Anna asked, trying to put on a courageous front. "Better yet, how far do you think you are going to get alone? The police know who you are Westcott, Camden, The Nemesis. Your picture is everywhere, the police are everywhere."

"Yes, yes, I know," the killer acknowledged. "And yet here I am for my forth victim. Trust me; this is the last place the police would think to look for me."

"You're pathetic," Anna spat, grabbing an empty tapered vase off of the entertainment center and holding like a club. "You could not get your first victim, Angela MacKenzie so you've come after me."

"I'm pathetic?" the killer mocked. "You're the one holding a flower vase as a weapon. As for the nightclub, you're right. Your boyfriend is more intelligent and cunning than I gave him credit for."

"Even if you do get me," Anna began, trying to widen the gap between them by moving to the sofa. Unfortunately, The Nemesis guessed her move and headed in that direction, cutting her off. "He'll find you before you can kill me. Your best move now is to run and hope you don't get caught before you cross into Mexico."

The Nemesis laughed out loud, listening to her words. In his mind, however, he was trying to get the advantage and capture Anna. She was quick, and though he mocked her, he could tell the vase was heavy and if she hit him in the head he would be out like a light. He knew what he needed was a diversion, and looking down at the coffee table that separated them, he started to form a plan.

"Thanks for the advise," the killer said. "But it was never my intention to kill you or MacKenzie. If you think it was, then obviously you and Nicholas don't know as much as you think you do."

With that, he pushed the coffee table forward with his foot, trying to divert her attention so he could move around swiftly and grab her. However, with surprising speed and agility, she jumped the table as he moved towards her and brought the vase down towards his head with astonishing speed. He twisted away just in time as the vase collided with his shoulder and shattered. He closed his eyes, instinctively, to keep the ceramic glass from getting into his eyes, and that was all the time she needed to get passed him and head towards the stairs. Anna bounded up the stairs, taking them two at a time, while at the same time trying to remember the layout of the house well enough to plan her escape. However, as she reached the top of the stairs, she knew that there was no way out. The only plan of escape that she could possibly try was to jump out of one of the windows, and she knew that she would most likely injure herself in the fall. If The Nemesis followed her outside, which she was certain that he would, he would have no problem catching her. Suddenly, as the desperation started to wash over her, she knew that the only hope for her lay with Nick. She had to let him know she had been abducted as soon as possible. Hearing the killer stomp up the stairs, she rushed into the master bedroom and grabbed the phone. She punched in the numbers for 911 and turned just in time to see the killer's fist swing into her face. Then there was nothing.

Chapter 80

Nicholas Grenier could sense that someone had walked into the office, the room that was no larger than a walk in closet was not big enough for him not to. Hollings stood in the doorway, watching as he roughly piled his belongings into a cardboard box he had salvaged from the trash. She appraised him carefully, something had happened at Chief Michelson's house, something that had yet to be explained to her. As she watched him, she found herself overcome with the desire to embrace him. The misery seemed to exude from him, so much so as to make her hurt just to look at him. He was no longer a man, at least not the man she had recruited. He was broken; four hours had taken a man certain of himself and transformed him into this. When he first arrived, he had the look of death upon his face. She tried to stop him then, tried to get some answers, but he just walked passed her as if she did not exist. After watching him walk into his office, she turned to get an explanation from the other two detectives, but was met with only silence. Whatever they had all found, it was something that had stopped them all dead in their tracks, it had sucked the desire right out of them. A word came to mind, one word alone. Zombie. She watched as he pulled his sidearm out of it's holster, removed the clip and secured the safety mechanism, then placed it on the desk. He pulled his shield off of his belt and looked at it for a moment, sliding his thumb across the grooves.

"What happened?" she asked, unable to watch any more. He did not look up at her, just continued to caress the golden badge. For a moment, she was certain that he was going to cry.

"I am not a police officer," he answered. She did not know how this answer pertained to his question, but she was not going to interrupt him. "He was right. He was right all along."

"Who was right?" she asked, almost whispering.

"My cousin," Nick answered, knowing that she would not understand. "I am a killer."

"No," Hollings answered. "You're a police officer."

"I wanted to kill them," Nick said, staring at the badge. The shield had meant so much to him, ever since the day he became a cop. There were so many symbols that he had attributed to the piece of metal. He had always thought of it as a line in the sand, the symbol of justice. Now he knew what it really was, it was the line that divided him from the criminals. It was the only thing that had kept him from being one of them. "That afternoon on the dock. The police were there, the dealers were there. Everyone was packing, suddenly everyone was pointing their pieces at everyone else. I heard it then. I didn't tell anyone, but I heard it clearly."

"What did it say?" Hollings asked, staring at the detective.

"It said, 'Kill them'," Nick whispered. He then looked up at her with eyes that she had never seen before. "Kill them all."

It startled her for a moment, seeing his face distorted in such a way. Then she realized that she had seen that look before. She had seen it on The Nemesis's face just before he escaped from the nightclub. In fact, she realized that the two faces looked eerily similar. It took a moment for her to remember that he was not the killer.

"I heard it clearly," Nick said finally looking back down at the badge. "And for a moment, I considered it."

Hollings turned her head and stared at the floor, allowing his words to sink in. There was such a sense of despair in the room that she almost felt as if it was going to smother her. She allowed the words to form shapes in her mind, she allowed herself to be in his position there on the dock, faced with what he faced. In that moment, she knew what had to be done. Hollings pulled her sidearm out of her holster and pointed it directly at Nick. The action was so unexpected that he turned his attention towards her, and then saw the look on her face. There, standing in front of him, was a true police officer.

"I have been a homicide detective longer than you have been a cop," she said, her poise unflinching, her face betraying no emotion. There was only the focused determination of a police officer. "I have seen deaths so gruesome, atrocities so heinous, that they defy any kind of rational understanding. Understanding the mind of a killer, does not make you one. I didn't ask you to join this case because the killer wanted you on it, I asked you to join because I saw something in you, as a cop. I know what happened on the dock that night. I read all of the reports, and now I've heard your own version. I can be your friend, I can even be your confessor..."

Hollings trailed off for a moment, the placed her forefinger tight against the trigger and pulled it back ever so slightly, pulling it back so far as only one who had fired a gun many times would know to pull.

"But if I ever hear you say that again," his lieutenant continued. "Then it will be over between you and me. I will become your nemesis, and I will be far more persistent than Westcott ever was. Now you need to decide whose side your on, and you need to decide right now because I've got a killer out there and I need to know who's with me and who's not."

Nick looked down at his desk, then at the badge that still lingered in his hands. He traced the outline of it briefly, then clipped the shield back onto his belt. Nick was not certain whether or not Hollings was right about him, and he was definitely not certain about himself as of yet but he was certain that he was not ready to walk down that path willingly, the path of the killer. He looked up at Hollings and smiled.

"What was that supposed to be?" he asked mockingly. "A pep talk?"

Hollings laughed out loud and holstered her weapon quickly. She looked into her detective's eyes, and deep smile spread across her face.

"I don't know," she admitted. "I just thought you needed to hear something inspirational."

Suddenly they heard a noise from the far doorway and looked up to see the lieutenant's secretary standing there.

"If you're not going to kill him," she said sarcastically. "Then there is something I think you both should know. We got a call in from the Colchester police. There was a 911 call placed from your house, detective. There was no message, but the phone is still off the hook. The police have secured the scene, they say it looks like a burglary. They say the house was tossed."

Hollings turned her attention back to Nick.

"It can't be a coincidence," Hollings stated. "What do you think it means?"

Nick allowed himself to retreat to that part of his mind where he felt his deep understanding ran. He allowed himself to go there willingly, for the first time calling upon it personally without it being thrust upon him. He opened his eyes and stared back at his lieutenant.

"It means he's calling me out," Nick said, lifting the sidearm and the clip out of the box and fitting them back together. "It means he's ready to end it."

Chapter 81

When Nick arrived at his house, the quiet woods in all directions had been lit up by the multitude of police squad car that were parked in the driveway, the grass, and along the street. As Nick climbed out of the passenger seat, he realized that this was the most attention the old house had received in many years. It seemed as though everyone actually on the grounds and inside the house were part of the New London police department, while the Colchester police stood beside their cars on the edge of the road. Nick and Hollings were given a brief rundown of what had happened, and then were allowed to enter. There were a few crime scene technicians inside, but they weren't actively working, as Nick and his lieutenant seemed certain who had broken into his house. Nick walked inside and felt bad immediately. The house was a mess, but as he quickly took inventory in his mind, he could not think of anything that was missing. Nick made sure to make a note of every piece of furniture, every piece of art on the walls, and every piece of electronics. However, he was certain that nothing was missing. Many of the smaller furniture items would have to be replaced, but nothing was missing. Nick was certain that this was the work of The Nemesis.

Lt. Hollings and her detective followed a uniformed officer up the stairs to the second floor. The officer showed them which phone had been used, and informed them that nothing had been touched or moved from it's original position. The crime scene techs dusted the phone and got two different sets of prints. Hollings seemed to think that was another break for the police. She kept saying that if his prints were on the phone, they would have him on B&E as well. Nick was not particularly interested in that, though. Nick continued on throughout the house, searching for a clue that might help him understand why the killer came here in the first place. Nick knew that Westcott was still playing him deadly game. Westcott still believed that he could make Nick into a killer like him, there was no reason for him to think anything had changed. Nick thought that the clue would come from something that was missing, however, he had not been able to discover any items had been removed from the house. Nick went back downstairs, leaving Hollings with the uniformed officer to take the rest of the tour through the house. Meanwhile, Nick scoured the downstairs, searching. Finally, he was met by Hollings who had a curious look on her face as she watched him.

"There's nothing here," Nick said.

"What nothing?" Hollings asked.

"I expected him to leave me a clue as to why he did this," Nick answered. "A clue to explain where he plans to go next."

"This is a child's tantrum," Hollings stated. "He's pissed that he was almost caught twice now and he wants to intimidate you."

"No," Nick answered, shaking his head. "This means much more than that. There is a message here, and we need to find out where it is and what it means. You have to remember what you're dealing with, a highly educated man who wants everyone to believe that he is superior. Tossing a house would be beneath him, a child's tantrum just as you said. He would consider that beneath him. I promise you, there is a clue here."

Hollings and Nick stood there, planted in the living room for a moment, just looking blankly at their surroundings. The lieutenant felt as though they were looking for a needle in a haystack, but Nick seemed certain that he knew what he was talking about, and he also seemed energized. She did not want to derail him now.

"How much time would he have spent here?" Hollings asked.

"I don't know," Nick admitted. "If he felt safe, if he thought he knew where I was and how long it would take me to get home, then he might have spent hours here."

Nick started over towards the hallway just as his feet brushed up against some broken pieces on the floor. Nick stopped and bent down, lifting the pieces into his hand. He then stood and looked to the other side of the room.

"What's the matter?" Hollings asked.

"This vase belongs over there," Nick said, looking in the other direction. "Yet it's smashed over here."

"So?" Hollings asked. "He took it and threw it on the ground."

Nick shook his head but said nothing. Something was wrong with that thinking. The house may have been disarranged, furniture turned over and a general mess all around, but this was the first object that he had found broken. Something just did not seem right to the detective, the answer seemed to be right in front of him, he just could not see it.

"Do you have anything to drink in this place?" Hollings asked, watching Nick try to put the clues together in his mind. Nick was shaken from his thoughts for a moment and put the pieces back down on the floor.

"Yeah," he answered. "Follow me."

They made their way to the kitchen, which was just the way Nick had left it. Apparently, Westcott had not bothered with the kitchen. Nick opened the refrigerator and retrieved a can of soda off of the top shelf, and just as he went to close the refrigerator door, he stopped. Nick opened the door wide again and stared inside. Something had caught his eye, something that had not been there before. Nick pulled the large salad bowl out of the refrigerator and let the door close.

"What is it?" Hollings asked.

Nick did not answer her, just placed the bowl down on the counter and stared at it for a few moments. He was certain that he did not make the salad, but was unsure where it had come from. He turned and looked around the kitchen, searching for any other clues. That was when he saw two bags on the small kitchen table. He walked over to the bags and rummaged through them, searching for a receipt. Just then, his cell phone rang, causing him to jump. He pulled the phone out of his pocket and stared at the screen, which read UNKNOWN. Nick pressed the answer button and held the phone up to his ear.

"Hello, detective," the male voice answered back. "I hope you found your home just as I left it."

"I did," Nick answered. "However, I must confess that I am not getting the message."

"That's too bad," The Nemesis said. "I thought you would be able to see through this in a matter of seconds. Just because we've had some near misses doesn't mean that I am ready to quit yet."

There was something in the killer's voice that spurred Nick's mind on to start making the connection. Neither the detective nor the killer spoke for a few moments, The Nemesis waiting for Nick to realize what must have happened. It did not take long. The bags of groceries on the counter, the knives and the cutting board in the sink, the salad in the refrigerator. Nick had not used these things, he had not cooked in a very long time. Anna had been here, she must have wanted to surprise him, and The Nemesis had surprised her. Nick had underestimated the killer all along.

"If you touch her..." Nick began.

"Well, I'm afraid I've already done that," the killer answered. "But don't worry, I haven't gotten as far as my grandfather did."

"You do and I'll kill you," Nick stated.

"I know," the killer answered. "Making you just like me. You see Nick, I told you what you were, told you I was here to help you. Now do you understand?"

"I hope you have your affairs in order," Nick said and pressed a button that ended the call. He turned and exited the kitchen, heading for the front door.

"What did he say?" Hollings asked. "Who does he have?"

Nick ignored her, walking out into the brisk night air and pulling out the keys to his car. Mitchell knew better than to try and stop Nick, so he just climbed into the passenger seat. He had a feeling that there was not enough time for talk.

"Nick!" Hollings shouted. The detective stopped just as he was opening the car door and turned back to her.

"Anna," Nick said. "He has Anna, and he wants me to put an end to this."

"How do you know where he is?" Hollings asked.

"If he's stayed true to form, then we know exactly where he is," Nick answered. "He wants to end this where his grandfather ended it."

Nick then climbed inside and started up the engine, peeling out of the driveway and off into the distance. Hollings stood there watching the taillights flicker and fade off and knew there was only one thing to do, follow him.

Chapter 82

Nick shut off the car's headlights as he turned off of the main road and onto the gravel path that led up to the abandoned warehouse. He then shut off the engine and the two detectives sat there, staring out of the windshield, thinking about what lay inside for them. Mitchell had said nothing during the fifteen minute drive, just watched Nick and watched the passing cars. Nick could not tell what the other detective was thinking, whether he believed Nick or not. All Nick cared about was Mitchell was here to help. Mitchell turned away from the view out the window and looked at Nick.

"Hollings won't be far behind," Mitchell said. Nick just nodded without looking back at the other detective. "Are you sure that he's got her in here?"

"As sure as I can be," Nick said. All of the windows had been boarded up a long time ago, so the detectives could not tell whether someone was inside. "We've stopped him every other time. He still wants to prove to me that I am a killer, and he thinks my killing him is the only way to do that now."

"You know," Mitchell started. "You can't kill him. Not this guy, not like this. You'll never know why you did it; if it was out of revenge or because you had not choice. Let me go in, let me take him."

"No," Nick said, calmly. "We go in separately. You find Anna and get her out of the building. I'll go after Westcott."

"Nick," Mitchell said, using the detective's first name for the first time. Nick just held up his hand and cut him off.

"If I don't face him," the detective began. "Then I'll never know whether or not I could have overcome this."

"This is dangerous," Mitchell said. "I hope you know what you're doing."

For the first time, Nick turned and looked at the other detective.

"Anna is in there," he said. "We have got to get her out before this wacko rapes her. He wants to keep everything true to the old case, this is the only thing he has left to do."

Mitchell nodded, silently. He did not want anything to happen to Anna, but at the same time, he believed that if she were going to be raped, the killer would have done it already. It had already been two hours since the 911 call was placed from Nick's home. If they used that as a timeline, she could be dead already.

"I know what you're thinking," Nick said, watching as the detective worked through the facts in his head. "Whatever's happened, I don't believe she's dead. Not yet."

With that, the two detective's exited the car and as quietly as possible, made their way into the warehouse. This particular warehouse was the not the same one that the first Nemesis had been shot and killed in. That particular warehouse had been demolished many years ago, just as many of the warehouses in this part of Norwich, Connecticut had been. There were not many left standing, and this particular building was the oldest and the largest left in the city. Nick could not help but believe that this is where Westcott would have taken Anna, and it did not take him long before he was proven right. When the two men entered, they found it very difficult to make their way around. The entire ground floor was dark, the only illumination coming from the light of the old street lamps streaming though the opening. However, as the detectives made their way back towards the back of the building, they found light coming down from the second floor. They headed in the direction of the light, trying to come up with a solid plan.

They found that the second floor of the warehouse was just one large open bay. Huge machines that Nick could not imagine a purpose for stood in formation, two rows of six machines, and they all reached high up into the warehouse. Above the machines were metal gangways and platforms, and at the very far side of the building was a row of small offices. Both men agreed that was where they should look for Anna, and as they crept along the floor, trying to stay as concealed as possible, Nick started to hear some noises from the gangway above. He looked up and saw a man far above, pacing back and forth on the metal platforms. Nick told Mitchell to go and find Anna, and though he protested, he finally went under order. Nick watched the detective go off towards the offices and then turned and made his way back in the opposite direction. Nick climbed the metal stairs as quickly and quietly as possible until he was on the same level as Westcott. He then made his way across the platform, though without a plan. He knew the killer had to be armed, though at this point he was not sure what weapon The Nemesis would use. Nick looked at the gun in his holster, and for a minute was afraid to draw it. He was suddenly afraid that because of all he had found out in the last two weeks, and especially the shocking information that had come to light in the last twenty four hours, that he might not be able to keep himself from killing this monster. Nick pulled the weapon out of the holster and let it rest in his hand, thinking about the weight of it. He knew that so much rode on the decision of the next few moments, a decision that would tell Nick, Hollings, the entire police force what kind of man he really was. However, there was one thought that Nick could not escape. The killer was here, and he had to be stopped tonight.

It was that thought which gave Nick the energy and confidence to stand up and come out of the shadows, his gun raised and ready to fire. As he stepped into the light, he realized he had a perfect shot at Westcott, who was turned away from him, talking to himself. However, Nick felt as though there had to be closure, and he could not let himself walk down a path that led to his killing Westcott. As he watched the older man talk to himself, he realized that he was no longer looking at The Nemesis, he was just looking at a man. Nick knew then that the time was now.

"Jack Westcott," Nick called out. The other man whipped around to find himself staring down the barrel of the detective's gun. "Place your hands behind your head and walk backwards slowly towards me."

"Hello Nick," Westcott said, ignoring the detective's orders. "I knew that you would come. You and I are so much alike."

"You and I are nothing alike," Nick said. "Now do as I said, I don't want to have to kill you."

"But that's why you are here," Westcott said. "It's what we were born to do, to kill."

"You're so pathetic," Nick said, taking a step forward. He began to understand in that moment, how much he had feared this man and what this man represented. "You are totally unable to make a life of your own. So lonely that you need something to latch onto, and the only thing you could find was the past."

"What do you know about loneliness?" the killer spat back. "What do you know about being pathetic? You who could not embrace the change that was coming in his life, so desperate to cling onto the life as an undercover police officer that you drove yourself into a depression and almost thought about quitting the police force entirely. No, Detective Grenier, you and I are very much alike, very much looking for something."

"Turn around," Nick ordered. "You're under arrest."

"I'm not going in," Westcott answered back. "You are just going to have to kill me."

"That can be arranged," Nick said. "But it won't make me a killer. You failed, and all you'll be remembered as is a deranged doctor who killed three people."

"You better be sure," Westcott answered, and then moved his wrist back so fast that it took Nick a moment to register what was happening.

Westcott lunged at the detective, Nick finally realizing that there was a thin bladed knife in his hand, probably the murder weapon in the three other murders. Nick stumbled back, trying to dodge the blade that was aimed for his face. Moving on instinct, he was unaware of his positioning on the platform and fell back and rolled, just as the killer launched himself on top of the detective. Westcott hit the metal gangway heavily, and groaned as he tried to get up. Nick jumped to his feet and reached out to keep Westcott down on the platform, but the killer was too quick and lashed out at the detective with his legs, tripping Nick and sending down on his back. Westcott rolled and leapt on top of Nick, this time landing right on him, trying to bring his knife blade down alongside the detective's throat. Nick grabbed the killer's arms and rolled, pinning them on the bottom and using his legs to exert enough pressure to keep the killer down. Nick then twisted the blade out of the killer's grip and pointed the blade down at the killer's face.

"Do it," Westcott said. "It's very easy, much easier than you think. When it's over, you'll feel so relieved."

Nick stared at the other man, considering his position. The blade felt so light in his hand that when he thought about it, he realized that the killer was right. It was probably very easy to cut through someone's flesh, cut through their organs, watch the life drain from their eyes. He could see himself doing it in his mind, he could see himself stabbing this man over and over again. Then Nick smiled. He took the killer's wrists in his hand and slammed them hard against the metal platform.

"Do it, Nick!" Westcott shouted. Nick brought the sharp edge right down to the killer's eye and then rose. Westcott looked back and forth, trying to understand what was going on. Nick through the knife on the platform and took a few steps back. Westcott glared at the detective, anger and confusion twisting his facial features. He watched as Nick retrieved his gun from where it had fallen. "What the hell are you doing?"

Westcott tried to jump to his feet, but found himself restrained. He looked over at the rail that lined the platform and to his amazement, found that the detective had deftly secured his right hand by cuffing it to the metal railing. He looked up at the detective in disgust, finally understanding that his attempt to make Nick like him had failed.

"You are under arrest," Nick said, pointing his weapon at the killer. "You have the right to remain silent. Anything you say can and will be used against you in a court of law. You have the right to have an attorney present while you are being questioned, and if you cannot afford an attorney one will be provided to you at no cost by the state of Connecticut."

"You fuck!" Westcott shouted, pulling against the cuffs in the futile attempt to get free. "Damn you. This isn't over. It can't end like this."

"I've made my choice," Nick said. "I am a police officer, that was what I was born to be. You are a criminal, and that's all you'll ever be."

Nick turned and walked away from what was left of The Nemesis, and man cursing and spitting as his terrible dream had come to an end.

"This isn't over," the killer shouted. "You forget why we're here. You forget about Anna. We had some fun, she and I."

That was when Nick stopped his tracks. He turned back, not realizing that his gun was in his hand. His mind became clouded, there was only one thought and reason did not enter into it.

"If you did anything to her," he started, but the killer just laughed.

"Oh my dear detective," Westcott started. "History will repeat itself. And you know what, I think that she kind of liked it."

That was all it took, it was all it would have taken for Nick to pull the trigger. He raised the gun to eye level and pointed it at the killer. Westcott did not even flinch, in fact, it seemed as though he were welcoming what was to come. He did not notice until it was too late, the two people standing behind him, or the female foot that was aimed for his crotch, colliding at a devastating speed. Both Nick and Mitchell, who stood beside Anna behind the killer flinched as though they could feel the pain themselves. Westcott screamed and collapsed on the floor.

"You wish," Anna said, bending over the killer as he writhed in pain. She then proceeded to kick him twice in the stomach before Nick pulled her off.

"Are you alright?" Nick asked. She smiled and nodded.

"I knew you would come," she said, softly. "He didn't...he didn't get a chance to."

Nick put his finger up to her mouth and stopped her, not needing her to go any further. Mitchell stepped around the killer and pushed the other two forward. Nick suddenly realized that Mitchell had something against heights and wanted to get down as soon as possible. Nick turned to Westcott who was pulling himself back up to his feet.

"You're going to make a lot of friends in prison," Nick said and smiled. Westcott lunged forward, but this time he was not stopped by the handcuffs. Nick realized only too late that the old bar attached to the railing snapped under the force of Westcott launching all two hundred plus pounds at them. Nick knew there wasn't time to react, and positioned himself in front of Anna knowing that was all he could do. Just as it seemed like Westcott was going to collide with them, Nick heard a shot and then another. Each bullet slammed into Westcott and pushed him back further. There was a final shot and Westcott went down. Nick turned and looked back to see Mitchell standing there with his gun drawn. Anna rushed behind Mitchell and Nick took two steps forward, and bent down over Westcott's dying body.

"I just didn't want to be alone," Westcott sputtered. "Can you understand that. One way or another, I was tired of being alone."

"You won't be now," Nick said, and watched as Westcott's body went limp and the light of life faded from his eyes. Nick stared at the body for several seconds, then placed his hand over Westcott's eyes and closed the lids. He turned back and looked at the other two.

"Can we please get down from the gangway, please," Mitchell said, then turned and led Anna back downstairs. Nick stayed, however, stayed with what was left of Dr. Jack Westcott until the police arrived to take him away.

Chapter 83

The next few days seemed like a blur, more like a collection of images in a photo album. The police worked hard for the next few days tying up loose ends, linking Westcott to each and every victim, to each and every crime. As it turned out, he was linked in one way or another. It turned out that Westcott had been Kim Harris's doctor, and after hearing her talking about her night life, Westcott followed her and found Tracy Scott, the perfect first victim. Westcott found out about David Martinez through a drug representative that called on Westcott's office. It turned out that Martinez had dated the drug rep several times, and the he had relayed the true nature of The Range to Westcott during a meeting. As for Alan Camden, the connection to Westcott had been clear. Nick had called to notify Westcott's mother personally of the situation, but she had refused to come, even had refused to claim the body. In the end, Nick paid for the burial expenses.

"I can't say that I understand it," Hollings said as she watched the coffin being lowered into the ground.

"He was family," Nick said. "He didn't have anyone who cared about him in life, the least I can do is show a little compassion to him in death."

"You're a bigger man than I," Hollings mentioned, then turned and walked back to the car.

Once the case was closed, the police handed the file off to the district attorney for review, and then the Investigations Unit in New London, Connecticut began to get back to normal. Since the case had been officially closed, Hollings had not seen nor heard anything from Nick. She had not been too concerned at first, but as the first few days became a week, then two, she began to get more and more concerned. She noticed that Anna was also concerned, as it turned out she had not heard from the detective either. Though Hollings wanted to find out where Nick was and if he was coming back, she was also afraid of what his answer might be, and had delayed calling him as long as possible. Finally, after two full weeks had passed, Nick came in.

"I was wondering if I could speak with you," Nick said after knocking on her door.

"I was wondering if you were ever going to come back to work," Hollings answered.

"That's what I'm here about," Nick said, walking into the office and standing directly in front of her desk. "I would like to permanently transfer here, if there is a space for me."

"There is," Hollings answered. "There has been a lead detective opening for a couple months. I think we could use you here."

"You don't think it would cause too much of a problem?" Nick asked. "I mean with the other detectives."

"They'll get over it," Hollings answered. "However, I don't think there will be any problems."

"There is one thing," Nick said. "I still have one more week of leave. I'd like to take it. I know what side I'm on, I just need to come to terms with some things."

Hollings nodded. She could not imagine what the last case had done to him, changing his perspective of his and his family's past the way it did.

"That's fine," Hollings answered. "But I think you better see Anna on your way out."

Nick left the office not understanding why Hollings would have brought Anna up. When he asked her, Hollings just shook her head and pointed out the door. Nick made his way across the squad bay, feeling all eyes on him. When he entered the small outer office, he saw a box on Anna's desk and her belongings inside.

"What's going on?" Nick asked, watching her pull some personal items out of her desk drawers.

"I'm leaving the police department," Anna answered. "I was just working here until I got my criminal degree. However, I stayed long past that. I need to get on with my life. You showed me that I am more than just someone's secretary."

"Where will you go?" Nick asked.

"I applied to the FBI," Anna answered. "I got my acceptance letter last week."

"I'm sorry," Nick said, looking down at the floor. "I've been wrapped up in the case, in what happened. Congratulations, I'm happy for you."

Anna just looked at him and smiled. She placed some items back down on the desk and walked around it to stand directly in front of the detective.

"I won't be working here anymore," she said. "But that doesn't mean that we can't see each other. I figure, this will actually be safer than worrying about rules and regulations about inter-department romances."

Nick smiled and looked back down at the ground, trying to find the words.

"But you don't want to keep dating," Anna said, reading his face like a book.

"It's not that I don't want to," Nick said. "It's that I can't stop thinking about what danger I put you in. Just because Westcott didn't rape you, doesn't mean that he wasn't going to. He picked you because of me. I can't live thinking that anything I do might put you at risk. I'm a police detective, I've come to terms with that. There isn't time for anything else right now."

He waited for it, for her to scream or hit him or just get angry. However, she did not. She just nodded, a single tear streaming down her face. He started to pull away from her and felt her pull him back, then kiss him and pull away. Nick looked at her for a moment, his mind racing through the decision he had made, then turned and walked out of the office heading for the exit of the squad room. Every detective and officer he passed nodded in sign of respect and just as he reached the doors to the squad bay he heard Hollings's voice.

"There has been a shooting down by the hospital," she announced. "Who's up?"

There was some mumbling around the bay and Nick hesitated for just a moment. He was a detective, he had come to terms with that, but it did not mean that he had to take every case that came through the office. He hung there for just a moment.

"Shit," he mumbled under his breath. He turned back and walked right up to Hollings who was smiling maliciously at him. He took the piece of paper out of her hand containing the names and addresses, then pointed at Wilkins and Mitchell and walked out of the squad bay with the two detectives in tow, heading towards his next case.

Printed in the United States
202099BV00001B/1-9/A